ALL

Audrey Wills
in Scotland, L
in Leicestersh
her way arou
to see even mc   More recently,
she has taught cookery and studied English
Social History.

By the same author

A CANDLE IN THE WIND
INHERIT THE EARTH
THE SAVAGE TIDE

AUDREY WILLSHER

All Shadows Fly Away

HarperCollins*Publishers*

HarperCollins*Publishers*
77–85 Fulham Palace Road,
Hammersmith, London w6 8jb

A Paperback Original 1996

1 3 5 7 9 8 6 4 2

Copyright © Audrey Willsher 1996

The Author asserts the moral right to
be identified as the author of this work

A catalogue record for this book is
available from the British Library

ISBN 0 00 649307 6

Set in Palatino by
Rowland Phototypesetting Ltd,
Bury St Edmunds, Suffolk

Printed in Great Britain by
Caledonian International Book Manufacturing Ltd, Glasgow

This book is dedicated to the memory of my grandfather,
THOMAS MILLIKEN,
killed Carron Ironworks, Falkirk

Acknowledgements

With special thanks to Joyce and Charlie Goodman for their memories of the 'Battle of Cable Street' on 4 October 1936. For background to the BUF, Robert Skidelsky's book *Oswald Mosley* also proved very useful.

1

'And about time too, my girl. We're all here working our fingers to the bone while you're upstairs titivating.' Edna Henderson's tone was sharp, but she couldn't quite disguise her maternal pride as she gazed at her lovely daughter. Kitty was so like Tom in looks, while Frances – she glanced across at her younger daughter – poor child, favoured her.

'How do I look, anyway?' Blithely ignoring her mother, Kitty did a twirl round the small kitchen, her primrose-coloured dress with its gored skirt swinging out to reveal slim legs in art silk stockings.

Frances, who never had the least difficulty in hiding her admiration for her seventeen-year-old sister, applied herself with even more diligence to the task of spreading margarine on to slices of bread and pretended not to hear the question. But Kitty came and posed in front of her like a mannequin, right hand resting on her waist, left shoulder thrust forward and head tilted slightly back.

'Well?' she enquired, determined to provoke Frances into some sort of response.

Unable to hide her resentment, Frances glowered at her sister but refused to answer. As if she don't know, vain thing. But she still craved, with a longing that hurt, for hair that was blonde like Kitty's. Even to be able to afford a marcel wave instead of having to make do with Dad's pipe cleaners would have helped. And if only her eyes were dark blue and not a rather muddy brown, her breasts rounded like Kitty's and oh, all sorts of other things . . .

No one could censor thought, but her mother was giving her a warning look, daring her to say anything unpleasant.

1

'You look all right ... I s'pose,' Frances grudgingly admitted. Then, having said what was required of her, she went back to preparing the sandwiches, slicing cucumber, opening a tin of salmon and mashing it up with an angry energy. Why's Kitty asking, anyway, when she's bin preening in front of the blinkin' mirror all morning, Frances wondered and gave the pepper pot an extra vigorous shake. A pity too some bloke had to go and tell her she was the spittin' image of Ginger Rogers and almost as nifty on the dance floor. Talk about giving 'erself airs. It had bin bad enough before, now there was no holding her. It wasn't that she was ugly or anything, just that beside Kitty she felt dull somehow, diminished by her bright light. And it had been like that as far back in childhood as Frances could remember. 'Oh isn't she angelic!' complete strangers would exclaim, patting Kitty's golden curls, and her sister had come to expect the limelight as a natural birthright. It was Kitty, too, who always seemed to have the new dress, she, as the younger sister, the hand-me-down.

But it was a waste of time complaining to Mum. Edna Henderson wasn't a woman to pander to imagined injustices, she had neither the time nor the patience. 'The world's an unfair place, and the sooner you realize that and count your blessings, the happier you'll be, my girl. And remember, you can trap more flies with honey than vinegar, so try and smile sometimes.'

Tiring of her task, and seeing Kitty had carefully avoided finding herself anything to do, Frances pushed the pile of sliced bread towards her.

'Here, I've bin at this job for ages and you 'eard what Mum said. So make yerself useful and finish these off. There's still heaps to do and I ain't changed yet.'

'Don't say ain't, it's common.'

'Oh is it now, miss 'igh and mighty,' Frances answered in a mincing tone.

'You'd better watch out, or else ...' Kitty threatened.

2

'Or else what?'

'Or else I'll give you one . . .'

Edna Henderson finished filling a large black kettle, banged it down on the gas stove then turned to her two daughters with an angry glint in her eyes. 'You're like a pair of alley-cats. Will you stop it or I'll box both your ears. And don't think you're too big, either,' she added warningly, when Kitty gave a small snigger. 'Now get on with doing those sandwiches, Kitty, an' see you cut them into four.'

Kitty wrinkled her nose. 'Ugh, salmon. It'll make my hands smell and what if I get grease on my dress? It'll be ruined.'

'No it won't, not if you wear this.' Wasting no more time in argument, Edna Henderson removed her apron, slid it over her daughter's head and tied it firmly round her waist. 'The party starts at three, everyone else is giving a hand and so can you, young lady. Dad's gone to see about the beer, your Aunt Gloria's outside helping set the tables, and young Roy's just fetching yer Nan and Uncle Donald.'

Kitty pulled a face. 'They're not coming are they?'

Edna, who wasn't blind to her daughter's faults, rested her hands on her waist and enquired coldly, 'Don't you think they should be included in the fun, then?'

Frances didn't bother to wait to hear how her sister would wriggle out of that particular corner. Leaving them to their discussion, she went upstairs. With Aunt Gloria's single bed pushed against the wall and the huge iron one she shared with Kitty next to it, Frances had to squeeze round the door. In the bedroom there was hardly room to swing a cat, but her new dress hanging on the picture rail lifted her spirits immediately. When she'd first seen it in Wickham's shop window, she'd never imagined she'd be able to afford it, but then her lovely generous Auntie Gloria had slipped her ten bob on the q.t. Flopping on to the bed, she cupped her chin in her hands and gazed at it with a sort of reverence.

3

She'd never had a dress this expensive in her life before and Frances could still hardly believe it was hers. With its scattering of poppies and daisies, sweetheart neck, fashionable cape sleeves and pleats inset with material the same bright red as the poppies, it would transform her. 'My, you look quite the young lady,' Gloria had said the first time she tried it on. And she had to admit, wearing it she no longer felt like a gawky fifteen-year-old. Frances rolled over on her back and stared at the ceiling. She saw herself walking down the street, head held high, hips swaying provocatively, and young men turning to gape not once but twice, maybe even three times.

Buoyed by this vision of herself, Frances slipped off the bed and went to the small mirror nailed above the chest of drawers. Perhaps today, just this once, she could outshine Kitty. Her features were boringly familiar to her but, trying to imagine what sort of impression they would make on a stranger, she explored her face with her fingers. Eyes brown, but not squinty like Joyce Flynn's next door, lashes quite long, nose snub, mouth – Frances pouted and moved closer to the mirror – passable. But were they kissable lips? Never having been kissed, she wasn't sure. Taking the dress from its hanger she held it in front of her. Frances sighed. If only she had bosoms. Her fragile self-confidence threatened to plummet again, but she held on to it by remembering what her stars had said in Dad's paper that morning. What was it? 'A momentous day lies ahead for Librans, which will have repercussions down the years.' Her dress now an imaginary partner, Frances closed her eyes and, crooning softly, swayed around the room. Dare she? Dare she hope that today she was going to meet HIM, the one and only?

Kitty's voice intruded on her small daydream and, not feeling up to one of her sister's sarky remarks, Frances draped the frock over the bed-rail and went and quickly lifted the window. Her elbows resting on the sooty sill,

4

she regarded Tudor Street with a tingle of expectation and excitement. Overnight it had been transformed, its shabbiness disguised by yards of miniature Union Jacks looped between houses and multicoloured balloons bobbing above lamp-posts that were wound round with paper-chains left over from Christmas. Trestle tables covered in red, white and blue crepe paper stretched half the length of the street, while strung across it was a banner declaring: GEORGE AND MARY 1910–1935. LONG MAY THEY REIGN.

The English weather wasn't inclined to be obliging, particularly in early May, and rain would have put paid to any street parties. So like the whole of the country, Frances had been studying the forecast and scanning the skies anxiously for the past week. Sunday had been dry and warm, but no one had dared hope it would hold until Monday. Amazingly, the sky had been cloudless when the mayor presented the schoolchildren with their Jubilee mugs and it stayed that way, right through to the War Veterans' church parade Dad had refused point blank to take part in. 'I've seen enough of war, death and destruction and I don't need reminding of it,' he'd declared firmly to his disappointed wife, after she'd gone to the trouble of polishing his medals.

With the sun now scorching her pale cheeks, Frances guessed the day was set to stay fine. It was so hot in fact, doors and windows stood open to catch the air, and in the Mitchell house almost opposite someone switched on a wireless. It was obviously in need of a new accumulator for it crackled badly. But the dial was twiddled, then loud and clear Frances heard the posh voice of a BBC announcer describing the scenes around the West End: the decorations, the beautiful floral displays and the high jinks of the crowds who'd been to cheer the royal procession on its way to St Paul's. Although later, like everyone else, she would probably raise her glass in a toast to the King and Queen, Frances considered them to be a rather dull couple. (The King collected postage stamps and what could be more boring than

5

that?) But along with most other young English girls she had a soft spot for the handsome, slightly rakish, bachelor Prince of Wales, and the two little princesses, Elizabeth and Margaret Rose, she thought really sweet. The refined tones of the announcer faded, the crackling started up again, then the much coarser voice of old man Mitchell bellowed, 'Billy! For Christ's sake turn that bleedin' din off.'

It might be Stepney but, like everyone else, Frances accepted without question that living in Tudor Street put you a cut above the residents of neighbouring streets. Didn't they have bay windows and running water? And here there was no stepping straight from the house on to the pavement, here they had small front gardens enclosed by a low brick wall. But most important, the family finances weren't run on tick – nothing was bought that couldn't be paid for – and they prided themselves on paying their rent on the dot. Apart from the odd one or two, like the work-shy Charlie Flynn next door, men were in regular jobs and so families were a notch up from dire poverty. Even so, every adult was aware of the uncertainty of their situation, knew they were holding on by the skin of their teeth and the long, shuffling lines of defeated men at the Labour Exchange haunted their dreams. The fear of unemployment, the shame of public assistance and the means test, that knot of unease was always there in their bellies so they clung on to their respectability, guarding it fiercely and wanting something better for their own kids.

For one day, though, they'd put life's uncertainties behind them and as women emerged from houses balancing plates of sandwiches, jam tarts, chocolate swiss roll and battenberg cake, Frances eyed them hungrily. She also had a tempting glimpse of dishes of pink blancmange and red jelly being borne to the tables. But it was the tinned pineapple chunks, sliced peaches and evaporated milk that made her mouth water, because these were luxuries only affordable on high days and holidays in the Henderson household.

6

In a burst of patriotic fervour, a mother cleverer with the needle than some had decked her young daughter out in a striped red white and blue frock and as she twirled proudly she was subjected to the intense and envious scrutiny of her small friends. Boys with better things to do ran riot and got under everyone's feet and Frances saw small, purloining fingers reach out from under a table. But they were swiftly rapped, then a woman bent and pulled a youngster out by his ear. 'That's enough of that, you little varmint,' she scolded, cuffed him one and sent him on his way howling indignantly.

But the really serious business was being conducted at the end of the street where men were piling up crates of beer for later in the evening. It was then that Dad would get out his accordion and the dancing would begin. He'd been on at her all week to sing a few popular melodies with him, but she couldn't, she knew she'd just die of embarrassment standing there in front of a crowd.

Seeing Aunt Gloria dodge across the street and up the short path, Frances leaned precariously over the ledge. With a bird's eye view of the top of her aunt's head she saw the giveaway black line in her parting where the peroxide was growing out. And there she was always trying to make out she was a natural blonde. Frances smothered a giggle at her aunt's small deceit and called out, 'Oo, hoo.'

Her aunt looked up and waved. 'I'll be up in half a mo.'

'Will you do me hair?'

'If I've time, sweetheart.'

Frances was about to withdraw her head when she saw Roy some way along the street, expertly dribbling an empty tin can. His shirt was hanging out, his socks were round his ankles and he whistled tunelessly through his teeth. At his heels and gazing up at him with canine devotion was Tinker, short-legged, rough-haired and of dubious parentage. About ten paces behind came Nan Atkins. Even further behind her was the shambling figure of Uncle Donald,

7

who'd gone off to the Great War a brave, gay young blade and come back a ghost.

With Nan there was no nonsense about concessions to the hot weather: as usual, she was dressed in heavy black wool and so firmly hooked and laced into her whalebone corset, she put Frances in mind of a stag beetle. As the space between her and Roy lengthened, she stopped, leaned on her stick and shouted after her grandson, 'Wait for me, you holy terror, or I'll get your pa to tan yer backside.'

Frances laughed out loud. She was wasting her breath. Dad would do no such thing. He'd never laid a finger on any of them in his life.

Leaving the window open, she dusted the grit from her elbows, went to the washstand and poured water from a rose-patterned pitcher into a matching bowl. She'd made her weekly visit to the public baths on Saturday so she wasn't really dirty, but even so she made sure she gave herself a thorough wash and even remembered to do between her toes. When she was finished she unwound the pipe cleaners from her head and turned just as Gloria edged her way round the door.

Her aunt paused and without thinking said, 'My, you look just like Shirley Temple,' whereupon Frances burst into tears.

Alarmed, Gloria rushed and put her arms around her niece and sat her down on the bed. 'Hey, what's up?'

'I look awful. I always do.'

'Rubbish. How can you say that with your lovely complexion.' To wipe away some of the tears, Gloria stroked the peach-bloom skin with the back of her hand. Why did the young never appreciate what they had, she thought with a sigh. When you were coming up to thirty and lines were beginning to appear round the eyes, and maybe the first few grey hairs, keeping up appearances was more of a struggle. She understood Frances's insecurities, though, knew how overshadowed by Kitty she felt. The natural

rivalry between sisters was exacerbated by Kitty's outstanding looks and her ability to steal the limelight wherever she
went. And Frances was so easily pulled down by circumstances so, aware of the fragility of her self-confidence,
Gloria tended to fuss her younger niece more.

'Me hair's a mess and my chest is flat,' Frances wailed.

'Your breasts will develop, don't worry. Just give 'em
time.'

'But no one thinks I'm a day over fourteen.' Frances gave
another heartrending sob.

'You might not think so now, but in years to come you'll
be really glad you don't look your age.'

Finding this hard to believe, Frances tugged dejectedly at
the corkscrew curls. 'What am I gonna do about these?'

'All they need is a bit of water. When I'm done with you
you won't recognize yerself. Now stop crying or you'll end
up with red eyes and a shiny nose, then you'll look a proper
sight.'

The tears subsided to an occasional hiccup and Gloria
went over to the jug, dipped a flannel into the water, then
laid it over the rampaging curls. Frances could feel the water
dribbling wet and cold down her neck, but she endured it
without complaint. Relaxing, she closed her eyes and let her
aunt's fingers work their magic, because if anyone could
perform a miracle it was Gloria. She had the touch and
should have been a hairdresser, not a waitress, everyone
said so.

After a minute or so Gloria tossed aside the flannel and
gave the hair a quick rub with a towel. Taking up a brush,
she pulled it with firm strokes through the curls. With great
patience she continued brushing, then after a while she
began to fiddle, tweaking at the hair and pausing every
now and then to study her niece with a critical eye. Finally
satisfied with her creation, she pulled Frances to her feet
and picked up the dress. 'Come on, let's get this on you.'

Frances stepped into the dress, was buttoned up, then

given a gentle shove by Gloria towards the mirror. 'Go and take a good look at yerself.'

With a wary expression, Frances moved forward. For a moment she didn't recognize the girl staring back at her, then her face cleared. Gloria had done the impossible. The tight curls had gone, the crown of her head was a smooth cap then the hair billowed out round her face in a flattering cloud of soft brown curls.

Floating on a small bubble of optimism, doubts became a thing of the past. Looking like this, and with a new dress and everything, something special had to happen today, it just *had* to. Closing her eyes, Frances clenched her fists. It must, it must, it must she intoned under her breath, willing it with all the power of her being.

'Well, whatdya think?' she heard Gloria say.

Frances allowed herself a final look then turned to face her aunt with a radiant, grateful smile. 'I don't know 'ow you do it.'

'Just let's say I've got talent, kid,' Gloria answered in a fair imitation of an American film star. 'But out of the way now, I've got to see to meself and that might take a bit longer.'

While she rolled a new pair of stockings up her legs, followed by garters to keep them in place, Frances watched Gloria apply what Dad called her 'war paint', a ritual of unending fascination. Today, as always, her aunt started by dabbing blobs of Pond's Vanishing Cream over her nose, cheeks and neck, advising as she smoothed and patted, 'Never pull at the skin, sweetheart, it'll do it no good at all.' When her face shone with grease, she dipped a swansdown puff into a box of peach-coloured powder and applied it so lavishly the air was filled with chalky particles that caught in Frances's throat and made her cough.

Gloria laughed. 'Sorry, love, but you know what they say; a little bit o' powder, a little bit o' paint, makes a girl's complexion look like what it ain't. Now where's m' rouge?'

'There it is.' Frances pointed to a small dark blue box amid a clutter of bottles and jars.

'Ah.' Gloria opened the box, took out a pad and angling her head, smoothed rouge over each cheekbone. Leaning closer to the mirror she outlined her mouth with a vermilion lipstick after which matching nail polish was carefully stroked on to her long nails. She waited a minute or two, waving her fingers in the air until the polish was dry, then stepped into an apple green chiffon dress with a frill round the bottom. By way of a finishing touch she removed the stopper from a bottle of Evening in Paris and dabbed it on her wrists then behind her knees.

Realizing nature probably couldn't be improved upon any further, Gloria linked arms with her niece and studied their reflections with a dispassionate eye. 'Couple of nice-looking tarts, ain't we?'

'I might be if I wasn't flat as two pennies up top,' Frances retorted, coming over all glum again.

Gloria pondered briefly on her niece's lack of normal female assets, then her face expanded into a smile. 'Hold on a tick, yer aunt's had a brainwave.' Bending, she rummaged around in her drawer and pulled out a pair of stockings. 'If you want bosoms, duckie, you shall have 'em,' she said, stuffed the stockings down inside Frances's petticoat, then stood back and surveyed her handiwork with a sense of pride. 'Well? How does that feel?' she asked.

Prodding the unfamiliar protuberances, Frances had a second of doubt, swiftly stilled when she saw how nicely they filled out the front of the dress. 'Perfect,' she smiled and hugged her aunt in gratitude.

'Let's get goin' then.'

'Is Harry coming?' Frances asked, following her aunt out of the bedroom.

Harry was a delicate subject and Gloria shrugged, feigning indifference. 'Don't ask, love, don't ask. You know Harry, you can never pin 'im down. But I've no intention of letting it spoil my day. Who knows, I might even find meself another chap. 'Cos I don't know about you, but I'm game for anything right now.'

2

Frances dabbed at some cake crumbs on the tablecloth, sucked them off the end of her finger, then leaned against her mother with a sigh of contentment. 'If I eat another mouthful, I'll go pop.'

'And you won't be the only one,' observed her mother, glancing up and down the tables at the litter of empty lemonade bottles, paper hats and streamers. 'There'll be a few crusts for the sparrers, if they're lucky, and that's about it. And just look at those Flynn girls licking them jelly and blancmange dishes clean. Whatever next!' Edna Henderson tut-tutted disapprovingly at the behaviour of her next door neighbours' kids. She'd been in service, had worked for the gentry, knew about manners and standards of behaviour, and had instilled them into her children. 'But then, how can the poor woman hope to control ... how many is it now?' Edna knew, of course, but it served to remind her what a good man she had herself and to count her blessings.

'Not counting those who died, nine, all girls,' her husband Tom provided on cue. 'And unless she's eaten a bit too well today, by the looks of her I'd say there'll be another along to make ten before long.'

'My sainted aunt,' exclaimed Edna. 'When is that man going to stop?'

'Charlie don't rate daughters very highly, so 'e won't give up until Ivy provides a son, you know that,' chimed in Minnie Hogg, their other neighbour.

'Well let's hope she obliges this time, or he'll kill the poor creature soon. She looks at about the end of her tether.'

'Aye, then where will he be, with all them bairns to look

13

after,' Tom Henderson pondered. 'But I don't hold out much hope. So far it's been a wee girl, regular as clockwork, every year.'

'What wiv Dora and Joyce not quite right in the 'ead, and poor Peggy wiv 'er club foot, the poor cow is probably just hoping it'll be normal. By God she's got more'n her fair share of troubles with that Charlie.' Minnie shook her head sadly. 'I reckon there's tainted blood somewhere.'

'Or it's bin weakened with all that booze Charlie pours down his throat,' added Edna. 'But the way he knocks her about, I'm surprised any of the kids survived.'

It would be hard to find anyone in the street with a good word to say about Charlie, and Minnie and Edna gazed sympathetically at his exhausted-looking wife with her swelling belly and silently commiserated with her. When it came to *certain matters*, the two women both had considerate husbands and they pitied poor Mrs Flynn for having been landed with the feckless, violent Charlie.

Frances's somewhat patchy grasp of the mysteries of pro-creation and birth had been picked up listening to talk such as this, and she'd heard some incredible stories while crouched, quiet as a dormouse, under the kitchen table. Now she sat, the sun warm on her back, eyes half closed, but alert to every word. But then, just as it was getting interesting, Minnie Hogg stood up.

'Looks as if it's time to make the tea, Edna.' She indicated some of the other women now moving towards their houses.

Frances felt a slight twinge of guilt at not offering to help, but she had grown indolent from too much food. Ten minutes later her mother came struggling back with a heavy enamel teapot and her dad jumped up to assist her.

'Here let me take that from you, hen.'

'Thanks, love.' Edna gave her husband a grateful smile and sank down on the bench.

Tom Henderson turned to Frances. 'Mum's been run off her feet all day: you pour the tea, there's a good lassie.'

Frances scowled at her sister sitting a little way along from her. 'Why can't Kitty do it?'

'Because I asked you to, that's why.'

The tone, quiet but firm, was one Frances knew better than to argue with. For although, unlike many fathers, he never raised either his fist or his voice to his children, he had carried with him from Scotland some of the sternness of his own Presbyterian upbringing and they defied him at their peril. There was no messing, punishment was swift, often taking the form of a loss of privileges that could hurt almost as much as any blow. Knowing that even today he was perfectly capable of ordering her to bed, Frances picked up the teapot and started to pour.

'Roy, you 'aving tea?' she asked, but with ill grace.

'No.'

'No what?' said his mother automatically.

'No thanks. Mum . . .' Roy went on in a wheedling voice, looping an arm round her shoulder. 'Can I go an' play?'

'That boy's got buttons on 'is bottom,' observed Nan in her carping way. Her opinion was the only thing she was generous with and it was the first time she'd spoken. Not being one for light-hearted tittle-tattle, she'd munched her way stolidly through the food, offering nothing to the conversation. 'He can't sit still for a minute.'

'You might not have noticed, Mum, but he's bin as good as gold these past two hours.' Defiantly, Edna Henderson patted her son's cheek. 'Off you go, but don't forget there's games soon and prizes.'

Before anyone could change their minds, Roy sped off, with Tinker bouncing excitedly at his heels. The small dog's stomach bulged with illicit titbits, but his tail was waving like a flag and his brown eyes were bright in anticipation of adventure.

'He can always soft soap you, can't 'e?' Nan's tone was

resentful, for it was her considered opinion that her grand-children were over-indulged. 'Meself, I never believed in spoilin' kids.'

'I remember,' Edna Henderson muttered under her breath.

'What was that?' Nan paused in the process of opening a tin of snuff and taking a pinch.

'Nothin', Mum.' Not feeling up to an inventory today of all her shortcomings as a mother, Edna stood up and took the teapot from Frances. 'I'll finish this off now.'

'But what about Dad?' Frances cast a glance in the direction of her father, who was now trying out a mixture of dance tunes and Scottish melodies on his accordion. She watched him, thinking to herself, He's easiest the most handsome man in the street. His hair was still thick and fair and he carried himself ramrod straight, like the ex-soldier he was. Dad always reckoned he was a throwback to some marauding Viking, but his parents had been Gaelic-speaking crofters, driven from their unproductive piece of land by starvation. Frances knew the story well. How they'd wrung the last chicken's neck and eaten it, sold their few sticks of furniture, then taken to the road, sleeping under hedges until they came to Falkirk where the mountains were slag heaps, it rained soot, and when the sky glowed red it wasn't from the setting sun but the blast furnaces. Here grandfather had found work at the ironworks. It was back-breaking, filthy work but there was a wage packet at the end of the week and they had a roof over their heads. Life seemed set on an even keel and they even talked of buying their own small house. Until the terrible accident. Grandad was inside cleaning one of the boilers when someone turned on the steam. His burns were terrible and he died in agony twenty-four hours later. Grandmother struggled on for two more years, but when Tom was fourteen she died. Alone in the world, he'd joined the army. It was these childhood experiences which made him so protective of his own family. He could be stern, but there was no questioning his deep love for them all.

'I'll soon sort your dad out,' Frances heard her mother say. 'Now drink that and go and enjoy yerself.' She poured a cup of tea and Frances, taking her advice, gulped it down then went and sat by Gloria.

'No Harry yet.'

Gloria, who never knew when the unreliable Harry would turn up, smiled, putting a brave face on it. 'No, but I'm expectin' him any minute.'

'Well, all I can say is that once that work-shy fly-by-night sits down at this table, I get up from it.' Displeasure oozed from every pore of Maud Atkins and her face was brick-red with the heat. But she sat straight-backed, her spine as rigid and unbending as her mind.

Fighting to control her anger, Gloria stood up. 'To spare you I'll go then, Mum.' She pulled Frances to her feet. 'Come on, duckie, let's promenade.'

'What you wants to remember is that if you lie wiv dogs you get fleas. And he'll never marry you, you know,' Nan shouted after them.

Although it was generally, but secretly, agreed amongst the family that Gloria had missed the boat as far as marriage was concerned, Frances was still stunned by her grandmother's spitefulness. How could she be like that and to her own daughter? She glanced up at her aunt. Her face was pale under her make-up and there was the merest trembling of her bottom lip.

Barely managing to restrain herself until they were out of earshot, Frances took her aunt's hand, gave it a sympathetic squeeze then spat out, 'Old devil!'

Gloria straightened her shoulders and tried to smile. 'She's got a tongue rough as emery paper, my mum.'

'What makes her like that?'

'Heaven only knows. We've all puzzled over that question. What I do know, though, is that she can't bear to see

17

other people happy. Mum won't feel she's achieved anything until she's put a damper on today. Mind you, she's
always had it in for me, right from before I was even born.
She told me 'erself she swallowed every sort of concoction
she could think of to get rid o' me, but I was a stubborn
little bugger and wouldn't budge.'

'Mum ses we should make allowances for her,' Frances
said, although remembering her own reluctant visits to her
nan's as a child, the silent teas and the vile seed cake she'd
been forced to swallow, she failed to see why.

'I've made plenty in my time. And it's all right for yer
ma to talk, she didn't 'ave to put up with her as long as I
did. Edna was lucky, she went into service at fourteen, met
yer dad when he was convalescing during the war, fell for
his Scottish accent and married 'im at twenty. It was my
bad luck to get stuck at 'ome after yer grandpa died, until
I couldn't stand it no longer. By the time I came to live wiv
yer ma and pa, I was just about ready for the loony bin. Alf
and Bert had the right idea, taking themselves off to Canada.
I sometimes wish I'd gone too, there's opportunities out
there.'

Frances only had dim memories of her two uncles, who
were sandwiched in age between her mother and Gloria.
At Christmas, the obligatory parcel and letter with a photograph of their growing families would arrive from Canada
for Nan, but otherwise they heard nothing of them.

'God knows, Harry's got 'is faults,' Gloria went on, 'but
at least he makes me laugh. And he enjoys life, which is
more than can be said for me mother.'

'She couldn't 'ave always bin a misery, though.'

'Don't you believe it. Mind you she 'ad it hard wiv your
grandpa. He was a real boozer and led her a merry dance
wiv other women. And the more she nagged the worse 'e
behaved. A vicious circle, really. I thought things might get
better when 'e died, but they didn't, she was too much into
the habit by then.'

Listening to Gloria, a constantly niggling fear resurfaced in Frances's mind. 'You don't think I'm like 'er, do you?'

'Of course not. Whoever put that idea into yer head? Kitty?'

Frances nodded.

Gloria tutted. 'I thought as much.'

'I do get a bit down in the dumps sometimes, though, don't I?'

'You're growing into womanhood that's all. It's a difficult time and yer body's at sixes and sevens. That probably makes you edgy, but you'll be fine soon. Just you wait and see, in no time everything'll be coming up roses. And you're not the least bit like your nan, so don't fret about it. If anything I'd say you favoured yer dad, with that lovely voice of yours and you bein' musical like.'

Frances felt a great wave of affection for her aunt. She could set her mind at rest in so many ways. Although she loved her mum deeply, she felt closer to Gloria. Because Gloria always had time to sit down and discuss things and listen. Mum thought problems were the result of idle hands and an idle mind. She felt her aunt understood her more, and with her determinedly optimistic view of life, she could scare away the black dogs when they came snapping. Reassured by her words, Frances found herself able to view her grandmother in a slightly more tolerant light. 'And Nan's got 'er good points. She looks after Donald.'

'She's got no choice, 'as she? And she can whine away at 'im to her heart's content.' Gloria was quiet for a moment. 'What a waste. He was such a lovely lad. I can remember 'im just before he went off to France, so 'andsome and proud in his uniform, then next time we saw him 'e was done for.'

'Mind yer backs, ladies.' Several of the men were now dismantling the trestle tables, and as Frances and Gloria dodged out of their way, a couple of them stopped for a breather and Frances was very conscious of their interested glances.

Gloria gave her a nudge. 'Here, do you notice how blokes keep giving us the glad eye?'

'It's you they're lookin' at, not me.'

Gloria giggled. 'No, it's you as well. It's yer titties that 'ave done the trick.'

Frances stared down at her protuberances. Although she was quite pleased with them, she'd still waited nervously for snide comments from the rest of the family. But when no one said a word, they quickly became part of her and she forgot about them.

They'd reached the end of the street and were about to turn back when Frances gripped Gloria's arm. 'Hey look, there's Harry.'

Gloria's face lit up. 'Where?'

'Coming this way. He's got a chap wiv him, too.'

'Make out you haven't seen 'em.' Quickly Gloria started to walk back up the street, moving at such a speed Frances had a job keeping up with her.

'What you doin'?'

'I'm not falling into his arms.'

Behind them Frances heard Harry calling Gloria's name. But she didn't slow down for him and when Harry did manage to overtake them, he was mopping his forehead with a hankie.

'Phew, you were goin' at a fair old lick then. What's yer hurry, love? Why didn't you wait when I called you? This ain't no weather for rushin' about in.'

Dad, who could be depended on to find a nickname for anyone, called Harry 'foxy face' behind his back. And with his thin face, narrow nose and deep-set but alert eyes that didn't miss a trick, it was a pretty accurate description. He was also a natty dresser and while he talked he studied his reflection in a window. And he obviously found much to admire, for he patted his hair, which shone black and smooth as patent leather, with a self-satisfied air.

'I didn't 'ear you. Did you, duckie?' Gloria gave her niece a conspiratorial wink.

'No.' Frances liked Harry; he was easy-going and when he had money in his pocket he was very free with it. But he also hurt Gloria a lot with his neglect and since that was where her loyalties lay, she felt no compunction about lying to him.

'That's all right then. Anyway I've brought someone I want yer to meet.' Harry adjusted the knot in his tie, brushed a speck of dust from his shoulders then turned and beckoned to the young man, who'd hung back while this exchange had been going on. 'You're never gonna believe this,' Harry continued, 'but I was in the Cat and Fiddle drinking the royal couple's 'ealth, when I meets this geezer 'ere . . .'

'Andrew Seymour's the name,' the young man corrected with a quick glance at Frances.

'Sorry, mate. As I was saying . . . I gets into conversation wiv Andy 'ere and d'you know what? He ses 'e don't hold wiv royalty and thinks they ought to be done away wiv. Can you imagine it? I was tickled pink, I can tell you. Anyway in spite of everyfink 'e didn't 'ave to be asked twice to come along for the knees-up.'

'Well do you think it's right, all this money being squandered today when we've three million unemployed?' asked Andrew, speaking up for himself at last.

'Ooh, he's really on 'is soap box, ain't 'e?' Harry mocked.

Andrew coloured slightly. 'Sorry.'

'What you've gotta do is just treat it as a bit o' fun, old chap, 'cos in these depressing times we certainly need somethin' ter cheer us up. But speaking for meself, I could certainly find a way to spend the lolly, if anyone offered it to me. I'd take my beautiful lady 'ere on a Mediterranean cruise for a start.' Harry put an arm round Gloria's waist and squeezed her and she gave him an indulgent smile in return.

'I could find a much better use for it,' answered Andrew severely, obviously not caring for Harry's flippant manner. 'For a start there's the school where I teach. It's damp and dark, hasn't got proper lavatories and in the winter the children get bronchitis. It needs pulling down and a new one built, with big windows that let in the light.'

Gloria, happy now that she was with her Harry, gave Andrew an encouraging smile. 'Yer quite right love, it's a crying shame.' Then linking her arm through Harry's, she sauntered off with him.

Never in a month of Sundays would it have occurred to Frances to contribute to the debate, so while Andrew was airing his opinions in the same cultured tones as the BBC announcer's, she studied him covertly. And she was very taken with what she saw: the curly brown hair worn romantically long, the luminous grey eyes. Flannel trousers and a snow-white shirt, unbuttoned at a strong neck, all added to his attractiveness.

Young men never usually showed any wish to linger in her company, so Frances expected Andrew to walk away. Instead she became aware of his grey eyes appraising her and this made her feel so self-conscious she could do nothing but stare at her shoes. Let him go too . . . please, she silently prayed, then heard him say, 'We don't seem to have been properly introduced. You know my name, but I'm afraid I don't know yours.'

'Frances.' Forced to look up, she saw that Andrew was smiling at her in an open, friendly way.

'Are you going to show me where the dancing is then, Frances?' he asked, trying to put her at her ease.

Her heart was beating erratically and her tongue felt as if it was glued to the roof of her mouth but she did manage to blurt out, 'It's just a bit further along.' She pointed to where sand had been sprinkled in the road. As she spoke, she heard her father start to play a waltz tune and bravely ventured a few more words. 'That's me dad playing the accordion.'

'Is it now? Perhaps you'd like to take a turn on the floor with me?' Aware of her desperate shyness and without waiting for a reply, Andrew took her hand and drew her towards the area where several couples were already dancing.

In preparation for this evening, Gloria, who was an excellent dancer, had spent hours teaching Frances the basic steps of the quickstep, waltz and foxtrot. Whenever her parents went out the carpet was rolled back, the gramophone was wound up, a new needle put in the head and then the sounds of Jack Hylton and his Band would fill the room. Frances knew she'd never move with the fluidity of Kitty, but normally she wasn't bad. To be asked to dance, and by someone as good-looking as Andrew, was the fulfilment of all her dreams. But his sheer maleness, the pressure of his hand on the small of her back, caused such a confusion of emotions, that instead of relaxing to the tempo of the music, Frances held herself rigid as a plank of wood.

After an eternity the dance came to an end, everyone clapped politely then before Frances could move away, her father started to play an old-fashioned waltz. Without saying anything, Andrew held out his arms in invitation and as she went to him, she heard one woman say to another, 'Isn't that the young Ferguson girl? My I hardly recognized her, she looks so grown-up today.'

The words acted like a salve to her doubts and as they whirled in a dizzy spiral round the floor, and faces became a blur, Frances heard her own unforced laughter, and felt her whole body tingle with pleasure. She was like a bird escaped from its cage and flying free, its wings almost touching the heavens.

She wanted to go on dancing for ever, but as all things must, the waltz finished and with it the magic. Gasping, they both collapsed on to a bench and grinned at each other with a sort of complicity.

'I enjoyed that, didn't you?' said Andrew.

Tongue-tied again, Frances nodded and waited for him

to make some excuse and move off. Instead she heard him say, 'Shall I try and get us a drink?'

Frances was about to give another nod then silently berated herself. Say something for gawd's sake or he'll think you're a half-wit. 'Yes, I'll 'ave a lemonade, please,' she managed, then watched with a sense of unreality as he fought his way through to the drinks table.

Her senses heightened by happiness, Frances was aware of the world around her in a way that she'd never been before; the dusk falling, candles flickering in jam jars, the rise and fall of conversation and occasional bursts of laughter. At last life was opening up its mysteries to her. Tonight anything could happen.

Andrew returned and was handing Frances her glass of lemonade, when Harry and Gloria went foxtrotting by. 'Well, whatdya think to it then, my old son? Enjoying yerself?' Harry called out.

'I certainly am, Harry. Thank you for inviting me to come. I've got a marvellous dancing partner, too.'

Unused to compliments, Frances flushed scarlet, took a gulp of lemonade, then said the first thing that came into her head. 'I don't dance as well as Kitty.'

'Who's Kitty?' asked Andrew.

'My sister. She's bin told she dances like Ginger Rogers.'

'Is that so?'

Hearing his tone of amused disbelief, Frances added unwisely, 'Ask her yerself, here she comes.'

But Kitty was miles away and might have passed by if Frances hadn't put out a hand to detain her.

'Hey, where you goin'?'

Since her sister was about the last person on earth Kitty wished to talk to, she decided to ignore such a stupid question and walk on. But then she saw that Frances had a young man sitting next to her. Kitty, who had a quick eye for such things, saw immediately that he was a cut above the leering, pimply youths who hung around street corners. He was

24

also rather good-looking. Intrigued enough to want to know more, she stopped.

Frances, unusually bouncy and confident, gave Kitty a happy smile. 'I'm havin' a marvellous time, ain't you?'

'Yes, thanks,' Kitty lied, irritated that a silly mouse like her sister, who couldn't even speak the King's English, should be enjoying herself, and with a presentable young man, when she wasn't. But Kitty ached to be in more refined company, and she thought with longing of all the dances going on in posh hotels up West. That's where I should be, she decided. Realistically, though, she knew the best she could hope for tonight was to be held in the sweating grip of some inarticulate local lad who breathed beery fumes in her face. She was wasted here, her looks and intelligence unappreciated. In fact she was so fed up with it all, that a moment ago she'd decided to give up and go home. However – she gave Andrew a quick look – it wasn't too late to have second thoughts. How he'd strayed into this part of the world, heaven only knew, but it was her bet he'd be glad to be rid of Frances. Bestowing on her sister a smile that ought to have immediately put her on her guard, Kitty said sweetly, 'Aren't you going to introduce me to your friend, then?'

'Oh . . . ah . . . yeah, this is Andrew.' Frances made the introduction in her usual awkward way, but Andrew didn't appear to notice, probably because he was staring at Kitty.

He stood up and, extending her hand, Kitty treated him to the full battery of her charm – large blue eyes that held his grey ones and a dazzling, dimpled smile. 'Pleased to meet you, Andrew.' She spoke carefully, pitching her voice low and enjoyed watching his reaction. It was always so easy, too easy.

Too late Frances saw the way the wind was blowing, the meaningful glances, Andrew's reluctance to let go of Kitty's hand. Desperate to regain his attention, she said rather feebly, 'Andrew's a friend of Harry's.'

'Not a friend, just an acquaintance. We've only just met,' answered Andrew, not taking his eyes off Kitty.

'Do I 'ear my name bein' taken in vain?' asked Harry, as he and Gloria twirled past them again. He let go of Gloria and pulled Frances to her feet. 'Come on gel, let's you an' me trip the light fantastic. You don't mind do you, Andy old son?'

But Andrew didn't hear and as Harry pulled Frances away, leaving the two of them alone together, he said quite innocently, 'Quite a toff ain't 'e? Just up our Kitty's street I would say.'

Frances, too choked up to answer, watched them over his shoulder, Kitty giving her all, Andrew falling willingly into the trap. They moved on to the dance space, their bodies moulded together and Frances felt such a leaping jealousy her head swam and her eyes misted over. Until a couple of minutes ago she and Andrew had been getting on so well she had forgotten her shyness. Then, just like that, Kitty had snatched her happiness away. She was like a greedy kid in a sweet shop, what she saw she had to have; and like a sweet paper, Andrew could just as easily be discarded. At that moment the hatred Frances felt for her sister at her casual theft was so powerful, she began to shake.

Feeling her trembling body, Harry held her at arm's length. 'Hey, what's up?'

'Nuthin'.' Frances heard her voice cracking.

'Don't give us that. 'Course there is.'

'Leave me alone, can't you?' Wrenching herself away, Frances went and stood at the edge of the floor.

Harry shrugged in annoyance. Women and their blinkin' emotions. As if 'e didn't 'ave enough of it from Gloria. Then, seeing he was getting the come hither look from a lovely young thing on the other side of the floor, he forgot about Frances and went and asked her to dance.

Teeth and fists clenched, Frances closed her eyes and wished with all her heart that a bolt of lightning would flash down from the heavens and shrivel Kitty into a cinder at Andrew's feet. But her sister's tinkling, rather affected laughter told her she remained robustly alive. Then Frances heard her father call, 'Right, the next dance is an excuse me waltz, ladies and gentlemen,' and she knew she had her chance. With a courage born out of desperation she moved on to the floor. Andrew was hers, she'd found him first and she'd get him back. Patting Kitty on the shoulder, she smiled a sugar sweet smile. 'Excuse me.'

Kitty turned with eyes that were as glacial as an arctic winter. But as she continued to stare, she fixed her gaze on Frances's breasts and a smile of triumph slowly spread across her features. 'Whatever is that?' she said and giggled behind her hand.

Uncertainly Frances glanced from Kitty to Andrew, caught a look of pure embarrassment on his face and steeled herself to look down. Creeping over the neckline of her dress was one lisle stocking.

'Oh no!' Frances went chalk white then the red spread slowly up from her neck until her face was suffused. Mortified, totally humiliated, she gave a wild sob, then turned and stumbled off down the street, pinning her hands against her ears to block out the sound of mocking laughter she was convinced she could hear following her.

3

Halfway down Tudor Street, Frances stopped, pulled the hateful stockings from her dress and hurled them into the gutter. 'Cow! Bitch! God how I hate 'er.' Cursing her sister, she ground viciously at the stockings with the heel of her shoe and indulged herself by imagining it was Kitty's pretty face she was reducing to pulp.

Because of Kitty she'd never be able to look Andrew in the face again, because of Kitty her life was in ruins and she might as well be dead. Briefly, Frances considered some final dramatic gesture, the railway line maybe, and visualized grieving faces around her coffin. A young life cut short, they would say and turn accusing eyes on Kitty – the scene was so vivid, tears of pity for her dead self rolled down Frances's cheeks.

She eased her bottom on to a low wall, breathed deeply and in an effort to control her tears, stared up at the starry vastness of the heavens and tried to concentrate on identifying the various constellations her father had told her the names of. But her thoughts always returned to Kitty and the way she'd deliberately set out to pile humiliation upon humiliation. But that was her sister all over, she didn't give a toss for other people's feelings, probably wasn't even aware they had any. She had it coming to her, though. One of these days, the tables would be turned and she'd know what it felt like to be belittled, stripped of your dignity and hurting so much you felt minus a skin.

Away in the distance she could hear the gaiety and laughter that her sister had excluded her from. A man, obviously drunk enough to think he sounded like Richard Tauber, was singing 'Girls were made to love and kiss'. Not me, no one will ever want to kiss me, thought Frances, and saw herself walking through life solitary and unloved. In the thrall of her own misery, she didn't hear the door closing, the footsteps, the creaking gate.

'Hey oop, what's wrong 'ere, then?'

Startled, Frances looked up and found herself being scrutinized by a total stranger. All too aware of what a sight she must look with her red, puffy eyes, she hung her head again. 'Nuthin',' she mumbled, wishing he'd just clear off.

The young man shrugged. 'Well I've 'eard some strange stories in me time, but cryin' about noothin', that takes the biscuit. Still if you don't want to tell me that's your business.' He drew a packet of Gold Flake from his pocket and held it out to her. 'Here, 'ave a gasper, that'll perk you oop a bit.'

Unwilling to admit that she didn't smoke and glad to have something to occupy her, Frances took a cigarette. She tapped it on the back of her hand like she'd seen Jean Harlow do, and placed it between her lips. The young man struck a match, cupped his hands and leaned towards her. As the cigarette ignited, Frances inhaled, felt the bitter taste of nicotine in her throat and started to cough violently.

'Ain't you ever smoked a fag before?' The young man sounded slightly incredulous.

'No,' Frances managed to gasp.

'Don't worry, you'll soon get the 'ang of it. The first few drags is the worst, after that it's a dawdle.' To demonstrate his own skill, he inhaled deeply, closing one eye against the smoke.

Frances watched him then tried another puff, with a little more success, and felt the nicotine seeping through her bloodstream, relaxing her and steadying her nerves. She wiped her eyes, blew her nose, smoothed her dress and began to feel better.

Her new-found companion removed a thread of tobacco

from his tongue, studied his index finger intently, then asked in a casual tone, 'It'll be ten soon, I wa' just goin' to see 'em light the bonfire. You coomin'?'

He began to walk on, seeming not to care whether she followed or not. But Frances sensed that, in his way, the young man felt as ill at ease with himself as she did, only he made a better job of hiding it. Remembering her earlier excited anticipation of the day, Frances sat and watched him. There wasn't a remnant of that left now, but it didn't mean she had to sit back and allow that sister of hers to cheat her out of every pleasure in life, did it? She slid down off the wall, took one final drag of the cigarette, flicked it into the gutter, then calling, 'Hey, wait for me,' hurried after him.

'You're not from around 'ere, are you?' Frances asked when she caught up with him.

'How'dya know?'

'Well 'cos you speak peculiar.'

'I like that, it's you lot down 'ere who speak foonny, not me. Anyway if you wanna know I'm from a bit further north, a place called Leicester.'

But he didn't really sound offended, so Frances, who was now growing more curious about him, ventured a further question. 'What you doin' at Mrs Goodbody's, then? You a relative or somethin?'

'I'm lodgin' wi' her. I've just got meself a job down 'ere at a wine importers. Me name's Norman, Norman Hall. What's yours?'

'Frances Henderson. Don't your parents mind, you movin' down here?'

'I ain't got any. There was just me and Mam and when she died they put me in a home.'

'That must be awful, not having any family.' Frances tried hard to imagine what it was like and failed.

Norman shrugged. 'I've got used to it.'

Since it was obvious he didn't want to be drawn further

on the subject, they walked on in a slightly awkward silence until they reached the piece of waste ground where a huge bonfire had been built. There was a great crush of people and in the lamplight features were blurred.

Frances stood on tiptoe and looked about her, searching for Andrew and Kitty, wanting them to see she hadn't ended up on her own, that she had a bloke too. She glanced sideways at Norman. Not that he was much to write home about. A bit on the thin side and a couple more inches on his height wouldn't have hurt. Still beggars couldn't be choosers and maybe he felt the same way about her.

'Can we have some quiet, please,' a voice called and an expectant hush fell as the crowd waited for the church clock to strike ten. In Hyde Park, at that exact moment, the King would press an electric switch and set light to a beacon. Simultaneously, up and down and across the United Kingdom, a chain of beacons, two thousand in all, would be lit by his loyal subjects.

The bonfire stood high as a house and as the first chime struck, a match was put to a paraffin rag and shoved into the base. The dry wood caught and flared and a great cheer went up. The intense heat scorched Frances's cheeks and standing slightly back from the crowd it struck her that there was something strange ... primitive, that was the word she was looking for, about the dark silhouettes set against a glowing, orange ball of fire. They reminded her of people at the beginning of time, clad in animal skins and crowded together round the fire for warmth and safety.

'I don't know where you get your weird imagination from,' her mother would say accusingly, when Frances went off on one of her flights of fancy. 'It must be your dad's side, the Sottish bit o' you, it's certainly not me. More probably it's that sister of mine. She's always stuffing your head with tripe, encouraging to read those trashy novels, taking you to the cinema, poring over horoscopes. It's enough to give you brain fever.'

It was true, Gloria did help feed her romantic imagination, but Frances had always preferred the imaginary world, it was kinder than the harsh, uncaring real one. And she loved the cinema, the dark, scented interior, the warmth, music, glamour and all-pervading happiness. That was where she spent her time and pocket money. She also collected photographs of all her favourite film stars which she stuck in an album. After seeing *It Happened One Night* she'd fallen desperately in love with Clark Gable and had bravely written to him. When some months later an autographed photograph of him smiling his slightly sardonic smile had arrived all the way from Hollywood, to her mother's intense irritation, Frances had walked around in a dream for a week.

As the bonfire died down and the last of the children were hauled off to bed, a group of women, a trifle on the merry side, formed themselves into a circle, grabbed their skirts and kicking out their legs with rumbustious energy, started to belt out 'Knees Up Mother Brown'. A man standing nearby nudged his mate and, egging the women on, shouted, 'Come on, give us a real treat, gels, lift yer pins a bit more and show us yer bloomers.'

With shrieks of raucous laughter the women obliged, flinging their legs high into the air and providing the men with a more than adequate glimpse of hefty thighs and pink, elasticated knicker-legs.

Frances felt her skin prickle with embarrassment and she didn't dare look at Norman. What must he think, grown-ups behaving like that? But she knew it would get worse before the night was over. The noise, coarse jokes, broad language and uninhibited behaviour would grow in direct proportion to the intake of beer and stout. And from the way pretty Connie Phipps was behaving it didn't look like it would be long before the feathers started to fly there. Only a few months wed, she was flirting with all the men and Dennis, her husband, possessive at the best of times, was watching with a face like thunder. Frances saw his fists clench and unclench as Connie wiggled provocatively up to an old boyfriend, Stan Hughes, and waved a cigarette at him.

'Feel like lightin' me up, Stan?' she invited boldly.

'Not 'alf I don't,' grinned Stan. Very deliberately he took the cigarette from between her fingers, flung it away then grabbing hold of her he bent her back and kissed her. It was a real film-star clinch, which went on and on and the crowd whooped and whistled its appreciation.

Dennis strode over, grabbed Stan by the scruff of the neck and pulled him away from Connie. 'Home, you slut!' he bellowed at his wife, pointing with an outstretched arm to their house.

But Connie, who'd had more gin than was good for her, just tossed her curls and looked defiant. 'Sod off. You ain't tellin' me what ter do, Dennis Phipps. You could do wiv takin' a few lessons from Stan anyway. Bloody 'opeless in the sack, you are.'

'Why you . . .' Apoplectic with rage at this public airing of his sexual prowess, Dennis made a lunge at his wife. Seeing what was coming, Stan, who still fancied Connie like mad, bravely but unwisely, put himself between them.

'Leave 'er can't . . .' He didn't finish. Dennis aimed a blow at his solar plexus and with a grunt of pain, Stan doubled up.

'I'll teach you to mess wiv my wife, you bugger,' ranted the wronged husband, hammering on Stan's skull with his bare fists.

'Stop it, you'll kill 'im!' Connie screamed, and like a cat with its claws unsheathed, she leapt on to Dennis's back.

'Gerrorf.' Dennis swung round and round trying to shake her off, but Connie clung on, giving Stan a chance to scramble to his feet and out of harm's way.

The crowd was now beginning to take sides and Dot Mitchell from over the road put her hands to her mouth and shouted, 'Take 'er 'ome and knock some sense into 'er, Den – it's what she needs.'

'If I got 'er 'ome I'd knock somethin' into 'er and it wouldn't be sense,' her old man leered.

Mrs Mitchell gave him a withering look. 'Mucky sod. She ain't fussy, Connie, but even she wouldn't look twice at a fat slob like you.'

'Belt up woman, yer mouth's too big,' her husband retorted and pushed her hard on the shoulder.

Dot Mitchell, who was a strong, heavy woman, gave him a vigorous retaliatory shove. 'It ain't as big as yours, arse'ole.'

'Come on, pack it up you lot, before someone gets hurt. It's all gone far enough,' a voice ordered and Frances saw her dad push his way towards the warring couple. 'It's been a good day, we don't want it to end in tears or with the narks here, do we?' His tone was jocular but he spoke with the authority of one used to intervening and arbitrating in the street's domestic disputes.

'No, we don't,' agreed several voices. Without another word Connie slid down off Dennis's back and smoothed her dress, which had ridden up round her thighs. Both she and Dennis, sobered by their altercation, were looking a bit sheepish and when Dennis turned and walked off to their house, Connie watched him for a couple of seconds then, calling his name, followed him on slightly unsteady legs.

Everyone waited to see what would happen. A few words were exchanged, then arms were slipped round each other's waist and joined hip to hip they went indoors. After a minute, curtains were drawn in the bedroom, a light went on then quickly off again, accompanied by cheers and ribald remarks from the crowd.

The drama was over, Dad struck up 'Love is the Sweetest Thing', on the accordion, a group of young men went to serenade the Phippses under their window and Stan quickly found consolation in the arms of another young woman. They were all mates again, and even the Mitchells seemed inclined to make it up. Glass chinked against glass and bets

34

were placed on there being a happy event in the Phipps household in nine months' time.

'When the drink's in the wit's out,' observed Norman, turning to Frances.

'Eh?' Frances, who was watching her dad and feeling proud of the way he'd settled matters, looked at him vaguely, for it was so long since he'd spoken she'd almost forgotten he was there.

'Do you see any point in life?' Norman went on.

'That's a peculiar thing to ask anyone.'

'No it in't. They're disgustin' that lot, wi' their booze and carrying on. If they weren't on this earth do you think it would matter one jot?'

'They've got as much right to be 'ere as you have,' Frances retorted, stoutly jumping to the defence of the neighbours whose behaviour she'd been silently criticizing a moment before. 'They got a bit carried away, that was all.' But still she felt she'd had enough; enough of the party and enough of Norman. Without bothering to say goodnight she turned and walked away. However, when she pulled the key attached to a piece of string from the letterbox and opened the front door, she found him standing behind her.

'Fancy coomin' to the flicks Friday?'

Frances was on the point of saying she'd be washing her hair when she heard Kitty's affected laugh and saw her and Andrew coming up the street hand in hand and looking as thick as two thieves. She felt a pain in her chest. Kitty was doing this deliberately to flaunt Andrew in front of her, but she'd show 'em she didn't give a toss. She waited until they drew level with the house, then treated a surprised Norman to her sweetest smile and said, loud enough for them to hear, 'Go to the pictures with you? I'd love to Norman, thanks.'

'Anythin' particular you fancy seein'?'

'Ginger Rogers and Fred Astaire are on at the Empire. Can we go there?'

'Sure.' Norman gave a quick salute. 'See you outside, seven-thirty.'

By now, Andrew and Kitty had walked on past, and amazed at what she had done, Frances stumbled over the threshold. She had a date. With a man. The first one in her life.

4

The measured clop of Buttercup's hooves, the clatter of milk bottles and the Woodbiney coughs of men on their way to work were as accurate a measure of time as any clock and Kitty, waking to these sounds, allowed herself one stretch and a yawn before sliding out of bed.

In one of the many books she plundered in search of advice and enlightenment, Kitty had read that it was unlikely that a late riser would ever make much of a mark in the world. Since then she'd disciplined herself to wake early. Gathering up clothes scattered round the bedroom, she glanced at her aunt and sister, saw that they were burrowed under the blankets like hibernating dormice, and silently rebuked them for their idleness.

But then what were either of them going to do with their lives? It beat her what Gloria saw in Harry, but she seemed to have only one ambition and that was to get him to the altar. 'Next year we'll get spliced, love,' Harry would promise with monotonous regularity. But he was as slippery as an eel and he always managed to wriggle his way out of his obligation. It had been a bit of a joke in the family at first, but as time rolled by they began to feel sorry for Gloria, then embarrassed, particularly when she took to saying, a bit desperately, 'Harry's got the wedding ring, you know, I've seen it.'

But then if she had any sense, Gloria would have ditched Harry years ago. Frances wasn't much different. She'd probably marry the first bloke who asked her, have a kid within the year and never move more than two streets from where she was born. Two of a kind, really. Thank heaven I'm not like them, Kitty thought complacently. When I see an opportunity I grab it.

Still, them being asleep gave her time to herself, which was a luxury in this house. Kitty retrieved her shoes from under the bed then, checking she had everything, she tiptoed from the bedroom. Downstairs Tinker thumped his tail lazily in greeting, but didn't move from his basket. On the table there were the remains of a hastily eaten breakfast, half a mug of cold tea, a slice of toast. By the looks of it Mum and Dad had overslept after last night's shenanigans and had had to scramble to get out of the house by six, she to her office cleaning job, he to the Post Office sorting office.

Feeling hungry, as she passed Kitty picked up a piece of cold toast, chewed it briefly, then with an expression of disgust at its leathery texture, flung it back down on the oilcloth. And that was another of the many things she disliked about the way they lived – oilcloth covering. 'Why can't we have a tablecloth and serviettes,' she'd recently and unwisely complained to her mother.

'They're called napkins, for your information, my girl,' snapped Edna Henderson, who'd been in service long enough to know her way round a formally set dining-room table.

Kitty, who didn't care to be caught out in matters of etiquette, looked sulky. 'Well napkins, then.'

'Who'll buy them and, more important, who's going to launder them? If past experience is anything to go by, certainly not you, young lady.'

Kitty bristled. Her mother could be so unreasonable. 'I would if I had time,' she pouted.

'Well yes, there we are then, that means never. So except for Sunday afternoon tea, the oilcloth stays.'

In the scullery Kitty lit the gas, put the kettle on and, when the water was sufficiently hot, poured it into an enamel bowl standing in the stone sink. Reaching up for the bar of Palmolive soap she kept hidden on the top shelf, Kitty removed her nightdress and, as she did every morning without fail, washed every part of her from top to toe.

Soaping her arms and breasts, Kitty left behind the dull view from the window and the struggling flowers in Dad's patch of garden. Her imagination soared over the Stepney roofs and chimney pots to a nice new semi somewhere in leafy Woodford. As she replenished the hot water she went from room to room in this imaginary house, furnishing each one in her mind's eye. Chintz coverings and cream walls in the lounge, a limed oak bedroom suite. The nursery would have to be white, of course, set off with a Kate Greenaway frieze. And one child only, but to make sure she'd go and get advice at one of those clinic places.

Of course, there was the small matter of finding a husband, and a suitable one, but she had plenty of time to look around and she knew she'd be a credit to any man. She also had definite views about what she wanted and she'd no intention of settling for any old Tom, Dick or Harry. It would be a barter: her looks and intelligence for security and status, with love, if it happened, a bonus.

Quite early on, Kitty had decided that she wasn't going to drift along with the tide like so many of the girls from her background did. She needed a shape to her life. So she started to map out for herself a sort of seven-year plan of self-improvement and she became a compulsive maker of lists, writing down in a small notebook the titles of books she should read, plays she ought to see. On another page in capital letters she printed GOALS TO BE ACHIEVED and under it wrote: Secretary at twenty, marriage at twenty-three, child at twenty-five, then as a sensible precaution added a question mark. For even with the best laid plans, Kitty knew life could sometimes trip you up.

Kitty finished washing, dressed, and was pouring herself a cup of tea when she heard movement from upstairs. Gulping it down, she cleaned her teeth and grabbed her handbag. She must get out of the house before Frances put in an appearance, she just couldn't stand her mournful, accusing face, not this morning. It wasn't as if she'd really nabbed Andrew off Frances; how she could imagine that Andrew, with a father who worked in a bank, would look twice at a gawky kid like her, was a mystery. He was very keen on equality, though, had even confessed to being a member of the Communist Party. But perhaps some things were best overlooked, because Andrew, Kitty decided, was definitely going down in her notebook under the heading HUS-BAND as potentially very suitable.

'Miss Henderson.'

Immediately the supervisor spoke, Kitty looked up from her typewriter with an alert expression. 'Yes, Miss Yeo?'

'Mr Robert Travis wants you to take some letters. Will you leave what you are doing and go up straight away, please.'

'Yes, Miss Yeo.' Kitty picked up several well-sharpened pencils and her pad and hurried up to the first floor, stopping to check that her stocking seams were straight and her blouse tucked in before tapping on a glass-panelled door. She waited until a voice called 'Come in', and as she entered Robert Travis looked up and smiled.

'Good morning, Miss Henderson.'

'Good morning, Mr Travis.'

Kitty sat down. Those dark eyes, which she thought held a hint of melancholy in them, didn't linger on her face and breasts greedily like most men's did. Instead he concentrated on sorting through a large pile of papers. 'Sorry to keep you, I seem to have mislaid a letter.'

'That's all right, Mr Travis.' Kitty crossed her legs, twitched up her skirt just a fraction, rested her pad on her knee and waited with pencil poised. From experience she knew that as soon as Robert Travis found what he was searching for, he would start dictating at breakneck speed. But in the meantime she was in no hurry and it was a pleasure just to lean back and admire the handsome features; the dark hair which sprang back from a pronounced widow's peak and the mouth that would be nice to kiss. In fact she liked everything about him. His natural courtesy and the way he always rose to open the door when she left his office. In particular she loved the faint smell of expensive soap as she brushed past him, which lingered pleasantly in her nostrils for the rest of the day. Just her type of man. A pity then about the signet ring on the second to last finger of his left hand. That definitely put him out of bounds. She knew of girls who'd got themselves involved with married men and it lead nowhere except misery. Thank heavens she had more sense.

Kitty's first job had been as an office junior with a firm of solicitors, and she never recalled the place without a small shudder. The offices, in a tall, narrow building off Chancery Lane, were so gloomy the hissing gas had to stay on even in summer. A century's dust covered everything and old men sat on high stools, poring over crackling parchment documents the same colour as their own skin. It had taken Kitty less than a day to decide nothing on earth would induce her to stay.

So without telling her parents, who considered the job a good opportunity, she bought the evening paper and scanned the Situations Vacant columns until she saw what she wanted. As soon as she walked through the doors of the Pennywise Assurance Company, saw the chrome and glass main hall and the uniformed porter with his peaked cap and gold braid, Kitty swore to herself that if she got the job she would work hard towards becoming indispensable to the company. A woman might never rise higher than a secretary, but she'd be the best one they had.

Although Robert Travis joined Pennywise after Kitty, he did have family connections with the firm, so when he started requesting her personally for dictation, she'd been immensely flattered. But then she was good at her job, she knew that, even if she was still stuck in the typing pool after two years. Secretarial jobs were few and far between and when a vacancy came up, it naturally went to an older, more experienced girl. But Kitty planned to change this and she devised ways to get herself noticed, making sure she was the first typist at her desk in the morning and the last to leave at night. She'd also kept on with her shorthand classes, setting for herself a goal of a hundred and forty words a minute.

And Robert Travis was just the opportunity she'd been waiting for. As he climbed the company ladder she intended to be just one rung behind.

If Kitty ever wanted information about anyone in the firm she never had to ask much further than her friend Rose Mumford. It usually took Rose no more than a week to have the complete history of any new employee, so while they were sitting in an ABC café one evening shortly after Robert Travis's arrival, she had discreetly quizzed her friend about him.

'He's not among the top league of Travises,' Rose informed Kitty and popped a piece of iced bun into her mouth. She finished chewing, swallowed, took a sip of tea and went on, 'More second division, a cousin twice removed or something.'

'How'd you find all this out?'

Rose looked mysterious. 'I have my sources.'

'Was it Percy?'

'Yeah, since you ask.'

Percy, who was chauffeur to Sir Sidney Travis, absolute head of the company, also stepped out with Rose from time to time, so her information could be counted on as pretty reliable. But it still astounded Kitty how much Rose managed to wheedle out of people.

Only a second cousin – that had come as a bit of a blow. But then, Kitty reasoned, a name like Travis must carry some weight. Anyway, he had success written all over him and it must be only a question of time before he was promoted.

'Ah, here it is,' said Robert Travis, breaking into her pleasant meanderings. He pulled a letter out from the pile of papers with an expression of triumph then without pausing started to dictate. 'Dear Sir, thank you for your letter of the . . .'

Keeping up with him easily, Kitty's pencil flew over her pad, making the neat shorthand symbols. When she returned to the typing pool at dinnertime she had fifteen letters to type and her neck and fingers ached.

Frances, following Kitty out of the house about a half an hour later, saw that Tudor Street had a forlorn, morning-after look. Burst balloons and bunting hung limp and dejected, empty beer bottles stood on doorsteps like lonely sentinels.

This street looks just like I feel, thought Frances, and she yawned widely. But then it was no wonder she felt tired when she'd lain until the small hours, staring up at the revellers' ghostly contortions on the ceiling, her thoughts swinging between her terrible humiliation in front of Andrew and alarm at the idea of going to the pictures with Norman. She'd have to make conversation with him, but what would she talk about?

She'd feigned sleep when Kitty crawled in beside her, but she was still wide awake when, much later, Gloria stumbled in, more than a little the worse for drink, too, judging by the thumps and muffled curses.

So what with one thing and another, she'd overslept. However Frances had managed to make a decision. The first chance she had she would tell Norman she couldn't go to the pictures with him. After all, why should she make do with second best? She'd got it off pat, what she would say – how she'd forgotten she was visiting an elderly relative with her parents on Friday evening – and with luck she

43

might catch him on his way to work. Frances reached Mrs Goodbody's and was slowing her pace when the church clock at the end of the street began its ponderous chiming.

Lord, eight o'clock, I'll be be late for work. Panicking, Frances forgot all about Norman and sprinted up Tudor Street into the main thoroughfare. Taking her life in her hands, she darted between clanking trams and cursing draymen. She took short cuts through alleyways and somewhere along the way a mangy dog attached itself to her and yapped at her heels until she reached Cannon Street Road. Here, having had enough of the animal, Frances turned and screamed, 'Clear off!' which, to her astonishment, it did, turning and making off after a bread van.

Nursing a stitch in her side and trying to suck air into her lungs, Frances hobbled down the street. The shop was on the corner of Cannon Street Road and Cable Street, and as she approached, Mr Jacobs came out and started taking down the shutters from the window above which was painted Jacobs & Son, Tea, Coffee and Provisions Merchant.

She'd made it! By the skin of her teeth. 'Sorry, Mr Jacobs, but I overslept,' she gasped, deciding that honesty was the best policy.

Her employer's sight was poor and he wore thick pebble glasses, but his eyes twinkled benignly behind them. 'Today I vill make allowance. After all, yesterday vas special vas it not? Our King and Queen on the throne twenty-five years.' He shook his head in wonderment. Although he'd left his native Poland a long time ago, Mr Jacobs had never really got to grips with the English language and he still spoke it with a strong accent. However there was no doubting his loyalty and gratitude towards his adopted country. 'You are lucky, Frances, to be English,' he would often tell her. 'Here people do not live in fear of a knock on the door at midnight. You have freedom of speech, democracy, tolerance.' Then wagging a finger at her he would go on, 'But remember, they are rights hard to come by, easy to lose, so never take them for granted.'

'No, Mr Jacobs,' Frances would answer obediently, only half understanding what he was getting at.

Limping badly from his rheumatism, he went back into the shop and following him, Frances smelt the familiar aroma of hot salt beef, coffee and the strong-tasting sausage that hung in the window and which Mr Jacobs's customers bought in huge quantities.

For working from eight to six with an hour for dinner, from Monday to Friday plus Sunday mornings, Frances was paid nine shillings a week. Two shillings was hers to do what she liked with, the rest she handed over to her mother. As a little extra, often on a Friday evening, Mr Jacobs would cut her a few slices of salt beef or give her a jar of rollmop herrings to take home for supper.

Frances slipped a white overall over her dress and asked as she did every morning, 'Tea, Mr Jacobs?'

'If you please, my dear,' Mr Jacobs answered and went to serve his first customer, because the shop was now open for business.

The flat over the shop was stuffed with heavy furniture and smelt of age and bird droppings. On a faded yellow velvet button-back chair sat Mr Jacobs's mother. Mudder, as he called her, was very old and very tiny, her white hair was crowned by a lace cap and she had a green parrot perched on her shoulder.

'And how are you this morning, Mrs Jacobs?' Frances asked, without expecting an answer. If she'd ever spoken any English, Mrs Jacobs had long since forgotten it and her reply was a toothless smile. However the parrot was always ready to answer on her behalf. A loquacious bilingual bird with twenty years' naval service, Porteous's vocabulary had a salty vigour. He stared at Frances with beady, malevolent eyes then squawked, 'Bugger off.'

'Bugger off yerself,' Frances laughed and went to make

the tea. This was her regular morning task, and she knew exactly how Mr Jacobs and his mother liked it – in a glass with a slice of lemon. Waiting for the kettle to boil she sliced bread, buttered it and removed the crusts.

The tea made, Frances took it into the old lady, along with the plate of bread and butter. 'There you are, Mrs Jacobs.'

'*Dziękusę*,' she replied, which Frances knew to be 'thank you'.

'You're very welcome.'

'You're very welcome,' the parrot mimicked, then gave an ear-piercing screech.

'Belt up, Porteous,' Frances answered back and watched with exasperation as Mrs Jacobs fed the parrot the paper-thin slices of bread she'd so carefully prepared. After all my trouble she gives it to that moth-eaten specimen, she muttered. Frances poured herself some tea, drank it quickly then, leaving the old lady chatting away fondly to her feathered friend, hurried back down to the shop.

'Don't let it get cold, Mr Jacobs,' Frances said as she put the glass of tea down on the counter beside him. Then she saw the line of housewives winding out through the door and realized there was little chance of her advice being be taken this morning.

'Right, who's next?' Frances called out briskly, and moved further along the counter.

'Me,' said a stout woman, elbowing her way forward.

'What can I get you, Mrs Paton?' asked Frances with a professional smile.

Mrs Paton plonked her shopping basket down on the counter and leaning on the handle said, 'Somethin' cheap, tasty and nourishin' which will stretch to a family o' seven.'

What do you think I am, a bleedin' magician? Frances wanted to say. Instead she smiled again and guided the woman to the cold meats. It was going to be one of those mornings, she just knew it.

*   *   *

By six, Frances was glad to see the back of the last customer. She was dog tired and had had enough of weighing sugar, slicing meat, and being asked if she'd enjoyed the Jubilee party and having to lie that she did.

'Here you are,' said Mr Jacobs, as she was about to go. Slapping a bar of chocolate in her hand he closed her fingers over it. 'That is for being a goot girl and vorking hard.' He patted her cheek playfully. 'Now go and say goodnight to Mudder.'

Obediently, Frances climbed the stairs to the flat. She found Mrs Jacobs asleep, but Porteous stretched a green wing and squawked something in Polish, which, knowing the parrot, Frances guessed was obscene.

It was a warm evening and she took her time walking home, nibbling at the bar of chocolate and comforted by its melting sweetness in her mouth. Passing Mrs Goodbody's she glanced up at the bedroom window, but there was no sign of Norman.

Never mind, thought Frances, Friday was still a long way off so she had plenty of time.

Indoors she found that her mother had already gone off to her evening cleaning job and Dad wasn't home from work, so the house was empty except for Roy and Tinker.

As she walked into the kitchen Roy lifted his head from the comic he was reading. 'Where's me tea?'

'You've gotta pair of hands, see to it yerself,' Frances snapped, and stomped off upstairs. Finding Gloria's latest copy of *My Secrets* on top of the chest of drawers, she flopped down on the bed and was soon so gripped by the weekly serial, she didn't hear her aunt's tired footsteps on the stairs.

'What a day,' Gloria groaned, coming into the room. Easing off her lace-up shoes she collapsed on to the bed beside Frances, lit a cigarette and inhaled deeply, drawing the smoke into her lungs with obvious pleasure. 'That's better.

I've bin run off me feet all day. The customers 'ave bin real buggers and me nerves are all shot to pieces.'

Frances tossed the magazine aside and rolled over to face her aunt. 'Can I 'ave one of yer fags?' she asked feeling she ought to get in some practice.

'Certainly not, you're far too young.'

'A puff, then,' Frances cajoled, and prising the cigarette from between her aunt's fingers she took several inexpert drags.

'Hey, leave off or yer pa will skin me alive.' Gloria snatched the cigarette back.

'Spoil sport,' Frances mocked. 'Well what about treating me to the flicks t'night, then?'

'Sorry, love. I think the customers were all skint after the holiday. I hardly got any tips today. Anyway I'm meeting Harry in about an hour. We're off to the dogs at Clapton Stadium. You could come if you like, I don't suppose he'd mind.'

'Dad wouldn't let me go. You know what he thinks of greyhound racin'. Reckons it's all fixed and anyone who backs 'em is just throwing good money after bad.'

'That's yer dad for you. He's never bin, so how can he know? I think it's good fun. Harry's mate Arthur will be there and you have a laugh, a drink an' a joke. Got to keep yerself cheerful, y'know.' Pointing her toes like a ballerina, Gloria lifted one leg in the air, then the other and subjected them both to a careful scrutiny. 'How much longer d'you reckon these pins of mine are gonna hold out?'

'They've got a few years of wear left in 'em yet, I'd say.'

'Well I've had enough of blinkin' waitressing, I want out before I get fallen arches and varicose veins. But what I need first is a bloke ter keep me in a manner I'm not accustomed to. I don't suppose you know one.' Gloria turned her head on the pillow and grinned at Frances.

'Only Mr Jacobs. He's probably got a fair bit stashed away. You'd be marrying his ma as well, of course.'

'Yeah, and the bloody parrot,' laughed Gloria. 'Anyway I've decided, I'm tellin' Harry tonight; either 'e makes an honest woman of me or I look elsewhere.'

'And about time, too.'

'You're quite right, love. I've been patient long enough and a girl's got to think of her future. I'm not getting any younger.' Hoping the mirror might tell her otherwise, Gloria swung her legs off the bed and went and peered at her reflection. 'God, what a hag I look,' she groaned, then in a businesslike manner set about putting it to rights.

'That's nice,' said Frances, as her aunt finished dressing and pinned a glittery leaf-shaped brooch to her dress.

'Yeah, Harry gave it to me last night. But he can't buy me off. I'm definitely having it out with him.' Gloria smoothed her dress over her hips with a slightly nervous movement. 'Wish me luck.'

'Good luck,' Frances repeated obediently, and thought: God, I hope I never get that desperate. She waited until her aunt had gone out, then went downstairs and started laying the supper, putting bread, cheese and pickled onions on the table and filling the kettle. Dad would have stopped off at the British Legion for a drink, but he'd want something to eat when he got back and Mum would be in soon, tired out and dying for a cuppa.

After she'd finished her chores Frances wandered through to the front parlour, ready to rush and light the gas under the kettle the minute she got her first glimpse of her ma. At the end of the street some older boys were having a game of pitch and toss and keeping their eyes peeled for a bobby, then four of the Flynn girls came out with a piece of washing line. Peggy, who couldn't skip because of her crippled leg, held one end, soft Dora the other, while the two younger ones took turns skipping, their long plaits swinging up and down as they chanted, 'One, two, three O'Leary, I saw Kate Macleary, sitting on a dromedary, eating chocolate biscuits.'

Roy, wearing motor-cycle goggles, hurtled past in a

crudely made go-cart, steering while Billy Mitchell pushed. But Frances knew her aeroplane-mad brother wasn't really crouched in an orange box on wheels. No, in his imagination Roy was one of the world's great aviators, looping the loop in his Sopwith Camel, thousands of feet above the streets of London.

And about to come a cropper. Frances tensed herself and then it came, the sound of splintering wood, followed by a yell of pain. She pushed up the window and leaned out. Her brother was lying in the gutter. 'You all right, Roy?' she called, but without any great sense of anxiety, because accidents were a common occurrence in her brother's life.

Roy stood up, brushed himself down and examined a graze on his knee. 'Forced landing,' he explained and got back into the badly buckled cart.

'You'd better not disappear, Ma'll be home in a minute,' Frances warned. But Roy and Billy were gone, this time ruthlessly machine-gunning down any enemy aircraft that unwisely got in their path.

Frances was about to close the window when she noticed Norman sauntering up the road. Now was her chance to tell him. But as he reached the house, her courage failed her and she stepped back behind the curtains until he'd gone by. Idiot, Frances berated herself, slammed the window down hard, went over to the piano, sat down and lifted the lid. She tinkled around with the keys, picked out a tune, then to cheer herself up, started to sing, one of Al Bowlly's songs, 'Guilty of Loving You'.

Giving her all, Frances threw back her head and banged away on the keys. Her voice was full-throated and strong – too strong for one of her teachers at school, who'd complained she was drowning out the rest of the class. 'I don't know where a small girl gets such powerful lungs from,' Miss Downer had fretted, and this remark had inhibited Frances for years. But although she often wondered herself where the power came from, she did enjoy singing. Settling down, Frances decided to see how many popular songs she knew by heart.

She was so engrossed, she didn't hear the first anguished scream. But the second one, accompanied by the wails of terror-struck children, cut through her consciousness and Frances leapt to her feet. Rushing outside she saw that Charlie was pursuing his terrified wife down the street. Angered by this familiar scene, she tore after him, but by the time she caught up with them, Charlie had grabbed his fleeing wife by the hair and thrown her to the ground. 'I'll teach you to argue wiv me, you cow,' he ranted and sitting astride her he repeatedly struck her across the face, while a sobbing Peggy pleaded, 'Leave 'er alone, Dad, leave 'er alone,' and lashed him with the skipping rope.

'Stop it!' Frances ordered, grabbed at his collar and tried to pull him off, but he took aim at her with his foot. Fortunately by now other neighbours were coming to Ivy's aid. Without a word, Mr Mitchell strode out of his gate and, lifting Charlie bodily, aimed his huge fist straight at his nose, while everyone cheered their approval. It was rough justice but it appealed to their sense of fair play.

Staggering from the impact, Charlie snivelled, 'Now look what you've done,' and stared at the blood dripping on to his open hand.

'Good,' answered Joe Mitchell. 'I hope it hurt good an' proper. It's about time someone taught you a lesson, you soddin' bully. Why don't you pick on someone yer own size instead of yer wife and kids, eh?' Mr Mitchell thrust his thick neck forward in a threatening manner and wisely, Charlie backed away.

'Are you all right, Mrs Flynn?' asked Frances, bending to help Ivy to her feet.

'A bit of a headache, but that's all.'

'Look Ivy, do you want me to go an' get the police? See this bugger put away for a bit?' asked Joe Mitchell.

'Oh no,' Ivy answered in a frightened voice. 'I don't want

no coppers round 'ere, prying into our business.' With shaking fingers she tried to push her lank grey hair back into its old-fashioned bun. 'I just want to go back indoors if you don't mind. Peggy will look after me, won't you love?'

'Of course I will, Mum.' Supporting Ivy, and with the smaller children clinging to their mother's skirts, Peggy limped back into the house. Just before she closed the door, she turned and with an attempt at a smile, called to the neighbours, 'Thanks for your help.'

Meanwhile Charlie, his nose swollen and bleeding, slunk off down the street to look for the nearest boozer.

5

'Good evening, Miss Henderson.'

Kitty looked up from her book and, flustered at finding Robert Travis standing over her, hastily banged *How to Improve Your Word Power* shut and shoved it into her handbag. 'Oh . . . oh, good evening, Mr Travis.'

He smiled. 'Would it be imposing if I joined you?'

'N . . . no, of course not.' Kitty whipped up her gloves and shuffled along the park bench to make room for him.

'Phew, a scorcher, isn't it?' Sitting down beside her, Robert Travis eased out his legs and began fanning himself with a folded evening paper.

In the company of men Kitty was usually the one in control, but Robert Travis had caught her completely unawares and she felt so conscious of him next to her that she couldn't bring herself to look at him directly. Instead, sitting bolt upright, she watched from the corner of her eye as he flung his bowler hat down on the bench and unbuttoned his waistcoat. As a further gesture to the heatwave, he loosened his tie then, with a grimace, ran his index finger round the inside of his starched collar.

'Instruments of torture, stiff collars and city clothes. How I hate the dratted things, particularly in this weather. Women dress so much more sensibly than men, don't you agree?'

Taut with nerves, Kitty nodded mutely, convinced that if she opened her mouth out would pour a load of inconsequential nonsense.

He twisted round on the seat and studied her for a moment. 'I must say you look deliciously cool, Miss Henderson.'

'Thank you.' His compliment had to be acknowledged but, knowing her face had turned pink under the scrutiny of his brown eyes, Kitty felt a rush of conflicting emotions. One part of her wanted him to go, the other longed for him to stay.

If Robert Travis was aware of the effect he was having on her it didn't show. With a relaxed air he spread his arms along the back of the bench and gazed upwards through the trees. Kitty didn't quite have the courage, but she knew she only had to lean back a fraction and her bare skin would make contact with his fingers, a thought that sent small spurts of fire darting down her spine.

'I felt I needed to unwind before going home and this seemed like the ideal spot on such a pleasant evening. An oasis for tired workers. Is that why you've come, Miss Henderson, to enjoy a little quietude before facing the Underground and home-going hordes?'

Kitty struggled to collect her wits and answer him. 'No, I'm killing time really. I've got an evening class but it doesn't start until seven.'

'So what is this class for?'

'Shorthand.'

He straightened up in surprise. 'But your shorthand is already excellent, Miss Henderson.'

Kitty didn't need telling she was good, but it was still nice hearing it from Robert Travis's lips and some of her old poise returned. 'You should always try and and improve your skills,' she informed him with an earnest expression, quoting from one of her many books. 'I want to get my speed up to a hundred and forty words a minute.'

'My word, that's some speed.'

'I know, but I need it if I want a better job. There's a lot of competition around these days.'

'You're not thinking of leaving us, are you?' Robert Travis looked genuinely alarmed. 'Why you're one of the best typists we have.'

Kitty felt a small frisson of excitement. Here was an opportunity almost being handed to her on a plate. Back in her stride, she said in a serious voice, 'Oh, I don't want to leave, Mr Travis, but I don't want to spend my working life in a typing pool either. So if a better job came along, maybe as a secretary, well . . .' She shrugged meaningfully.

Robert gazed at her with a thoughtful expression. 'Mmm, well we mustn't let that happen, must we? It would be a crying shame to lose a valuable member of our staff like you.' He pulled back his cuff and looked at his wristwatch. 'It's such a lovely evening and so pleasant here, I'd like to linger a little longer, but I suppose I'd better be on my way.' With some reluctance, he buttoned himself back into his pinstripe suit, tapped his bowler back on to his head, and stood up. 'Into the fray. I will no doubt see you tomorrow, Miss Henderson. Goodnight.'

'Goodnight, Mr Travis.' Kitty flashed him a smile that no man, unless he had a heart of stone, could resist.

He tipped the brim of his hat in a final farewell, then strode off with the confident, long-legged ease of the well-to-do and swinging a furled umbrella, although there hadn't been rain for days.

Kitty tried to return to her book after he'd gone, but there was a such a curdling excitement in her stomach, a sense that things were about to happen, and so many plans buzzed around in her head she found it impossible to concentrate. She mustn't hope for too much, not immediately anyway, but Robert Travis, she knew, was a man who honoured his word and every time he saw her he'd be reminded of that vague pledge and eventually he'd have to do something for her. Kitty stretched her arms above her head and gave a small, pleasurable sigh. Her plans were working out very, very nicely.

A gentle breeze blew through the trees, sending the last of the almond blossom scuttering away along the path. Kitty didn't often allow herself to relax and do nothing, but she found it pleasant to sit, indolently enjoying the warm sweet smell of wallflowers and watching the world go by. An elderly man was tempting a squirrel with a bag of monkey-nuts; a well-dressed lady walking her poodle watched fondly while it did its business right in the middle of the path; a couple lay face to face on the grass, staring into each other's eyes with the total absorption of the newly in love. The woman with the dog, Kitty saw, had now left the gardens and was letting herself into one of the three-storey houses that surrounded the square. Many of them were let out in rooms, and it gave Kitty an idea. Perhaps I could rent one when I'm promoted, she thought. Be independent, a true business girl. There'd be a stink at home, of course, but she'd be eighteen in January so Mum and Dad couldn't really stop her. And to get away from Tudor Street . . . just imagine . . .

Kitty sat for so long she arrived at the evening institute hot and late. Then to cap it all she found herself making a complete mess of her speed test. Because however much she tried, instead of the shorthand symbols on her pad, all she could see that evening were Robert Travis's handsome features.

The heat going home on the Tube was unbearable and Robert gazed at the greasy, pallid faces of fellow city workers with a sense of distaste. Forced into intimacy people avoided eye contact and expressions were blank. Strap-hanging, he felt himself being crushed against the bodies of total strangers, smelt unwashed armpits and remembered Kitty's dewy youthfulness and the fresh eau-de-cologne scent of her. He knew without in any way being vain that young Miss Henderson found him attractive. After all he was a normal man and the signals hadn't been hard to pick up; the skirt twitched a trifle higher than was necessary when she sat down, her eagerness to please, the pert smile. But feeling years older, these small wiles had only amused him; he'd never allow himself to be attracted to a mere typist. But coming across her unexpectedly like that in the square, the neat head with its blond cap of hair bent over that ridiculous book, had awakened a response in him and she'd no longer seemed such a child. He'd even found her naked ambition endearing. But he knew he had to curb such thoughts. As a married man it was a dangerous path to travel, and he had no desire to add further complications to an already difficult situation.

Resolutely putting Kitty out of his mind, Robert managed to find a seat at the next stop and he read his evening paper with determined concentration until he got off at Holland Park. On the way home, he stopped at a tobacconist for cigarettes and allowed the chatty shopkeeper to delay him far longer than was necessary.

Hobart Mansions, solid and Edwardian, with lots of highly polished brass, declared its respectability to the world. Robert paused with his right foot on the bottom step and looked up at the third floor. Occasionally Imogen would be standing at the window waiting for his return and if she waved that was a good sign. But she wasn't there tonight. Dragging his reluctant feet up the steps and into the hall, Robert rang the bell for the lift. As he heard it clanking down, the dead weight of hopelessness settled on his shoulders and he thought: If it was a normal marriage I wouldn't be bothering with the lift, but sprinting up those stairs two at a time to my young wife. Instead here he was, married barely eighteen months and already dreading the evening ahead.

To herself – and only to herself because she'd never be that disloyal – Gloria reckoned greyhound racing was a bit like having sex with Harry; thirty seconds and it was all over.

But in spite of his failings, she still loved 'im, bless 'is heart. With a fond look in her eyes, Gloria watched Harry as he studied his racecard, conferred with his mate Arthur, then made a cross against a dog. If only the bugger would name the day, though. But mention the word marriage and he'd have some excuse ready, like how times were hard and how he couldn't afford to just yet, and after five years of waiting that was no laughing matter. But if Harry'd put his mind to it and not squandered what he earned on gambling, they could have married a long time ago. After all, him and Arthur had a nice little dodge going, moving around London, renting an empty shop here and there for the day and selling off damaged or bankrupt stock by what they called Dutch auction. They'd lure a few people in, give them some spiel, then start reducing the over-priced goods so rapidly, the more gullible customers were conned into believing they were walking away with a real bargain.

Tom, who hadn't got much time for Harry, called them a pair of cheapjacks and reckoned most of the stuff had fallen off the back of a lorry. But Harry swore blind it was all legal and above board.

Gloria watched him pull a roll of pound notes from his pocket and peel off several. That whole lot could be gone by the end of the evening, then it would be Shanks's pony home tonight, and it was a long way after a day on her feet. On the other hand he could double it, which would mean a fish and chip supper and home in style in a taxi. But even if he left the track with every pocket stuffed with notes, knowing Harry, he'd have lost it all on the gee-gees by next week. Because if it had legs and moved, Harry would bet on it.

'You puttin' anyfink on the first race, love?' Harry called to her.

'Yeah, a bob to win on the same dog as you.' Harry and Arthur studied form, so Gloria found it easier to rely on their expertise.

'Matelot it is, then.'

Gloria handed him a shilling. She was no gambler, but it was boring unless you had a bet. Although she made out to Frances she enjoyed it, Gloria knew she wouldn't care if she never set eyes on a greyhound again in her life. She only came because of Harry.

They'd made a point of getting to the track early, but for the past half-hour punters had been pouring into the stadium, and there was some not too gentle pushing and shoving. But no one was going to elbow her out of the way, Gloria decided, and gave as good as she got. On the whole, though, the atmosphere was one of noisy geniality and optimism – you had to be an optimist to be a true gambler – and the attitude was, if you lost a few bob, what the hell did it matter.

The boys went off to find a bookie, but when after a good ten minutes they still hadn't returned, Gloria began to look round anxiously. Why don't they get a move on? she muttered and grimaced as she felt her ribs being crushed against the fence and a heavy boot on her toes. Craning her neck, she peered over the heads of the crowd and caught sight of them only a couple of yards away, talking to two men. Among the sea of flat caps, mufflers and Woodbines the men stood out, for they wore expensive-looking coats in a pale, soft material, rings flashed in the evening sun and large cigars were clamped between their teeth. Her job had taught her the difference between expensive and cheap cigars and as the smoke drifted across to her, Gloria sniffed and thought: Havana.

But she also felt a ripple of unease, because although she only knew of the men by reputation, their olive complexions marked them out. The Mantoni brothers, Giorgio and Rikki, she was sure of it, and a right pair of villains too. Notorious for being into every known racket in the area – prostitution, dope, gambling, extortion – they still managed to evade the law, and consequently were feared and admired in about equal measure by the locals. What could they be wanting with Harry and Arthur? Disturbed, Gloria strained her ears, hoping to catch a word or two, but it was impossible with the din.

The heads of the four men leaned closer together in what struck her as a secretive manner, their expressions grew attentive and her unease deepened. They remained in a huddle until the dogs were led out, then as the greyhounds were paraded up and down by the kennel lads, she noticed Rikki slip a cigar into Arthur and Harry's top pockets. Some jovial backslapping followed, then the two of them came swaggering back, looking pretty pleased with life.

'What was all that about?' she asked, gazing suspiciously from one to the other.

'Uhmm . . .' said Harry.

'They were givin' us some red 'ot tips,' Arthur interrupted, his fleshy, sensuous face a picture of innocence. 'There ain't nuthin' Giorgio don't know about dogs. When they comes out the trap 'e knows exactly where they'll be.' Arthur had a quick look at his racecard. 'Lively Lad in the next race is a dead cert, 'e ses.'

'Oh yeah?' Gloria's tone was heavy with sarcasm. But the dogs were being put in the starting traps and now wasn't the best time for confrontation. Instead she gave Harry a look that said, I'll get the truth out of you later, and in return got a sheepish grin.

The frantic yelps of the imprisoned greyhounds and a disembodied voice on the Tannoy announcing, 'The hare is on the move!' gave Harry the excuse to turn away. The noise had now given way to an expectant hush and a moment later the doors sprung open and six sleek, highly strung dogs shot out like arrows from a bow, accompanied by a roar that could be heard to Essex on that warm, still evening.

A few, those who had a great deal at stake, were tense and watchful, but it was impossible not to get caught up in the excitement. Leaping up and down, Gloria screamed, 'Come on, Matelot, come on!' with the best of them. The dog was number one and against the rails, but his red jacket helped to mark him out. Their speed was truly amazing – in a blink of an eye they were on the other side of the track, and dogs and colours became an anonymous tangle. There was a collective moment of held breath then, a beautiful sight, Matelot streaked round the bend of the sandy track, teeth bared, his lissom brindled body at an acute angle and neck and neck with another dog. Gloria, Harry, Arthur, every punter who'd put money on him, was screaming now. The gallant-hearted animal managed one final spurt of energy on their behalf and hurled himself first across the winning line, in pursuit of quarry he was destined never to catch. Elated and loving him, the crowd went wild and showed their appreciation by tossing their caps in the air.

'Phew,' said Harry when things had calmed down, 'that was a close one.' Matelot had been a favourite, so the odds were small and Gloria hadn't won much. However Harry, who'd put a fiver on the dog, looked pleased as punch. 'I reckon we're on a winning streak tonight, kiddo,' he said, gave her a quick kiss, plucked the betting slip from her fingers, and hurried off to collect their winnings.

But Harry was wrong. Matelot was their only win that evening and Lively Lad lagged all the way to come in last.

'So much for your dead cert,' Gloria couldn't resist saying.

'Yeah, I reckon the bugger stopped for a pee on the way,' grumbled Arthur and tore up his slip in disgust. There were a few near misses after this, but by the time they left the stadium at the end of the meeting, Gloria could guess from their glum expressions that she'd be buying the drinks.

But then it was come day, go day, with Harry and Arthur anyway. Neither of them had any financial commitments and being skint didn't bother them. Arthur, like Harry, was unmarried and had what Gloria thought of as an ugly, attractive face. The skin was pitted through adolescent acne, the nose was a bit large, his mouth too generous, but he had a nice way with him that women found attractive. However he was even more unlikely to tie the knot than Harry, for he made it quite clear to his lady friends that he'd never leave his mum Queenie, to whom he was absolutely devoted.

'You don't mind buying the first round, do you love?' Harry wheedled when they reached the White Horse. 'I'm cleaned out, look.' He turned his trouser pockets inside out and gave a helpless shrug.

'I've no choice have I? You daft pair haven't the faintest notion of how to hold on to money. But it's one drink and that's yer lot.'

'Thanks, love.' Harry slapped her behind playfully. 'My usual tipple, a Guinness.' He moved nearer and nibbled her ear. 'And I'll reward you later on.'

'Get away with you.' Gloria pretended to cuff him one, but she was laughing as she walked to the bar.

When she came back with the drinks the two of them were talking dogs: dogs they'd bet on, races they should have won.

She endured it for about ten minutes then her patience ran out. 'Can you change the subject, please? The meeting's over and you both lost – forget it.'

Stumped for conversation now, Arthur took a swig of Guinness, wiped the froth from his lips and gave a gaseous belch.

'Manners!' Gloria reprimanded him.

'Beg your parsnips,' Arthur apologized good-naturedly and, whistling through his teeth, he swung back on the legs of his chair and stared at an advert for Nut Brown tobacco. Then Gloria could see that Arthur was having what passed for an idea, because his expression brightened and the chair-legs thumped down on to the sawdust floor. 'You know what, Harry, you an' me ought ter be thinkin' about buyin' a dog and having it trained.'

'You're right there, old son,' replied Harry. 'Another Mick The Miller.' He leaned back looking dreamy-eyed. 'Boy, we'd make our fortunes.'

Gloria's heart sank to her boots. Chances of marriage were slim enough – a greyhound and they would vanish into thin air. 'No you wouldn't,' she interrupted. 'It'd just cost you a fortune having it kennelled and trained.'

"Course it wouldn't. We'd keep it at 'ome and train it ourselves.'

This was a load of rubbish, of course. She doubted if Queenie would want the responsibility of some highly strung greyhound, not with her shaky legs, and Harry lived in one very small furnished room.

But Arthur's enthusiasm for the idea was growing by the minute. 'Tell you what, Harry, why don't you an' me go down Aldridge's Sunday and see if we can't find ourselves a pup?'

'What a good idea,' said Harry and Gloria felt so despondent she had to have a second gin and orange. She'd paid for it and was on her way back to the table when the pub door swung open and the Mantoni boys sauntered in, coats slung casually over their shoulders, their eyes shadowed by the brims of their trilbies. In deference the other customers turned to watch them and the almost tangible malevolence they brought with them silenced the bar. They earned their respect through fear; many an ear had been slashed off or face disfigured by the razors they carried in their breast pockets. And the brothers, who were extremely close, wallowed in the terror they saw in people's eyes, for fear equalled power. As they stood there now, preening themselves, Gloria was reminded of cockerels on top of a dung heap. This was their manor and nobody was going to argue about it, not if they valued their looks or their lives. They'd seen off the Veasey mob and the Pope mob – recently human remains had been found buried on Hackney Marshes, last year a torso had been washed up on the Thames Estuary – but nothing could be pinned on them, and their power was absolute. In fact they got away with so much, it was taken for granted that the rozzers were in their pay.

Rikki glanced around him in a lordly manner, saw Harry and Arthur and raised a hand in greeting. 'What's your poison, lads?'

'A pint of mild and bitter will do me nicely, Rikki,' Harry called back, all obsequious but puffing out his thirty-eight-inch chest as all eyes turned to regard him, and basking in his new-found status of being associated with the hard men.

'Guinness for me, Rikki,' echoed Arthur.

'And the broad?' asked Rikki, lapsing into the slang of American gangster movies.

'If you mean me, my name's Gloria.'

'Sorry, Gloria.' Rikki returned her icy stare with a wolfish smile which revealed several gold teeth. His lower lip was wet and sluglike and Gloria shuddered instinctively. If she spent a moment longer in their company she would feel tainted.

'Nothing for me,' she answered shortly. Downing her gin and orange in one go, she slammed the glass on the table and said in a tight voice, 'If you don't mind, Harry, I'd like to go home.'

'Hold on, gel, the boys 'ave just bought a round. Let me drink it at least.'

'You do that then.' Gloria leaned closer and lowered her voice. 'But I hope the time never comes, Harry, when you wish you'd walked out of here with me tonight. Tangle with those two and you'll soon find yourself in deep water, floating face down, most likely.' She picked up her handbag and gloves. 'One last chance, Harry.'

For a second he looked uncertain then Rikki called, or rather ordered, 'Come and give us a 'and, sport,' and Harry leapt obligingly to his feet.

'Don't try and get in touch with me,' she hissed and slammed out of the pub.

As she left, Gloria heard Rikki say, 'What's wrong wiv your polone, Harry? Keepin' 'er short, are you?' This remark was followed by Giorgio's high-pitched almost girlish giggle, then Harry's ingratiating snigger. That hurt a lot. 'Traitor!' she spat out, but at the same time she was filled with a sense of foreboding on his behalf. 'Oh Harry, you fool, you stupid bloody fool, what are you getting into?'

Still angry at the way the evening had ended, Gloria lay in bed listening to trams clanking emptily along to the depot. For the first time she dared to ask herself if she and Harry had a future together. She loved him like anything, but she was no spring chicken and looking at it realistically, time wasn't on her side. She was determined, though, not to be one of that great army of women doomed to go to the grave a spinster. For there was an alternative. Walter. Walter with his brown boots, hair parted in the middle and old ways. Walter who came in every single day to the restaurant and always left her a tip. Walter who would need very little encouragement and who had made a point of telling her he was a widower with his own house. He might be on the dull side, but unlike Harry he had reliability stamped all over him and she couldn't see him consorting with criminal types.

Gloria had almost drifted off to sleep when something metal clattered into the gutter and she was instantly awake again.

'I'll bloody get you, Joe Mitchell.' Charlie Flynn's voice boomed out in the empty street and the dustbin lid was kicked again. A stream of obscenities followed, then a brief silence and Gloria thought contemptuously, He'll be pissing his wages away against a wall, I suppose. She pulled the blankets over her ears to try and blot out the noise, but she heard him stumble through the gate, try and fail to get in through his front door. This set him off again and the threats came thick and fast. 'Let me in, you bitches, before I murder you all,' he yelled, and hammered with his fist against the door.

Having had enough and ready to give Charlie a mouthful,

65

Gloria slipped out of bed and padded to the window. Leaning out she saw the door open a crack and Peggy's frightened face appear round it. 'Hush, Dad,' she murmured, but he was still ranting as he forced the door wide open and stumbled over the threshold.

What a life that poor woman has, Gloria thought, when the door crashed closed behind him. Turning away from the window and wondering why the commotion hadn't woken the whole street, she climbed back into bed. Chilled, she snuggled under the bedclothes and made a decision. Harry could go to the devil. Her life wasn't going to be like Ivy's. With a bit of luck she'd be moving out of here soon, to a much posher area with refined neighbours who didn't roll home drunk seven nights a week. Calmed and reassured by these thoughts, Gloria turned over on to her side and quickly fell asleep.

6

Frances heard about Ivy's miscarriage from her mother while they were sitting around the table having supper the following evening. 'I don't want to say too much,' Edna nodded in the direction of Roy, who was all ears, 'but it was terrible. Thank God she's in hospital now and in capable hands. Mark my words, that swine of a husband will send her to an early grave if he goes on like he's doing.' Her mouth was set in a a grim, straight line. 'I get so angry I often feel like giving him a dose of his own medicine.'

'There are a few more in the street feel the same, Mum, but nothing's gonna change Charlie,' Frances answered, and wondered what had possessed Ivy to marry him in the first place. And all those kids! She felt sorry for Ivy, of course she did, but secretly she thought that maybe losing this last baby was a blessing in disguise. 'Anyway, what's gonna happen to the little uns while she's in hospital? They'll starve if it's left to their dad.'

'That's bin sorted out. Minnie and me will keep an eye on them and Father O'Brien says he'll come round every day.'

'Well, at least in hospital the poor woman will get a few days' rest,' observed Tom.

'And some decent food, I hope. She's anaemic and under-nourished. But what's the betting she's in the family way again within the month?'

Tom shook his head in dismay and as he cut himself a hunk of cheese and speared a pickled onion, Tinker leapt from his basket and started to tear round the room, barking excitedly.

'Someone's at the door,' shouted Roy unnecessarily.

'Shut up, Tinker!' Edna scolded, then to Frances, 'Go and see who it is, love, and if it's Peggy or one of the other girls bring them through. But if it's someone wantin' advice, your dad's not in.'

'Don't worry, I'll sort them out,' answered Frances, pushing back her chair. Like her mother, she was tired of having mealtimes interrupted by neighbours who, regardless of the time, felt they were entitled to call on her dad. Owning, as he did, bound copies of *Everyman's Home Lawyer* and *Everyman's Home Doctor*, her father was considered to be something of an expert on these subjects and people were for ever at the door wanting ailments diagnosed or seeking advice on some legal matter. Tom would listen patiently while they explained their particular problem, then he'd consult one of the large books and they'd go away satisfied and doubly pleased at not having to cough up money for a quack or a lawyer.

The knocker was hammered again and Frances scowled in annoyance. 'All right, there's no need to break it down,' she shouted and wrenched open the door.

'Sorry.' Looking suitably contrite, Andrew stood on the step.

Remembering her mortifying experience with the false bosoms, shame lapped over Frances in hot waves and to hide it she stared down at the lino. 'Whadya want?' she mumbled, sullen in her embarrassment.

But Andrew was hardly aware of her. Peering down the passage he asked, 'Kitty. Is she in?'

'No she ain't.' Frances went to close the door, but her mother had already come into the hall.

'Who is it, Frances?'

'Someone wantin' Kitty.' Frances proffered the information with great reluctance.

But Andrew, sensing an opportunity, shoved his head round the door. 'I'm Andrew Seymour, and I met Kitty at the party the other night, Mrs Henderson.'

Liking his polite, well-spoken manner, Edna moved forward to inspect him more closely.

'You remember me, don't you?'

For the first time in his life Andrew's heart had been exposed to the sweet, illogical madness of love; the exhilaration and doubt. He was a highly romantic young man who worshipped beauty and since meeting Kitty he'd spent sleepless hours tramping the midnight streets. Now, having plucked up the courage to call, he was determined nothing would stop him from seeing his beloved. Wedging his foot in the door he smiled boyishly.

Edna found it difficult to keep track of Kitty's love life, but she was sure she'd never set eyes on this particular admirer before. He seemed like a nice young man though, and having no wish to hurt his feelings she said kindly, 'Yes I seem to remember you. She's not back yet, Andrew, but you're welcome to come in and wait.'

'I wouldn't be barging in?' Andrew asked, already half-way along the hall.

'Of course not,' replied Edna and Frances watched in voiceless fury as Andrew followed her mother into the kitchen.

The room was small and appeared to get very little daylight, but he immediately felt enveloped in its family warmth and gazed around with a sense of satisfaction. Small, shabby but clean he thought. But then these were real people, the salt of the earth. People he wanted to be with, fight for.

'It's Kitty's friend Andrew from the other night, come to pay her a visit,' he heard Mrs Henderson say to her husband as a form of introduction.

'Kitty won't be home for a wee while, Andrew, she's at an evening class.'

'Oh, what for?' asked Andrew, wanting to know every tiny detail of his beloved's life.

'Shorthand. She's a great one for improving herself, our

lass.' He spoke with fatherly pride. 'But while you're waiting you might as well pull up a chair. There's not a lot but you're welcome to share it with us.' Tom Henderson pushed a cheese dish and a jar of pickled onions towards him.

Enjoying their unaffected hospitality, Andrew watched Edna cut more bread and remembered his own house, so neat and sterile, and the cramped conformity of his parents' lives. His father was chief clerk in a bank and his mother's every thought and action was censored by the desperate fear of unwittingly committing some dreadful social *faux pas* which would cause her to be banished for ever to the outer limits of polite Chelmsford society. And he'd been brought up in exactly the same way. With much scrimping and scraping (holidays were never taken anywhere but in Clacton and always, Andrew seemed to remember, in the pouring rain), his parents had managed to buy their only child a private education. Only friends deemed to be suitable were allowed, that is of the same background, and even his play was regulated. Riff-raff was what his mother called council house kids and she would shudder visibly if ever she had the misfortune to set eyes on one. Yet to Andrew, their lives had seemed ten times more exciting than his and, imprisoned behind a privet hedge, he would watch with envy as they went by, dirty, scabby-kneed and with their backsides hanging out of their trousers, but happy as pigs in clover. He longed to unbolt the gate then, break free and follow them into the woods, to build camp fires, go bird-nesting or perhaps even bear home frog spawn in a jam jar, pursuits all strictly forbidden to a well-brought-up child like him.

To his parents, their sacrifice had all seemed worthwhile when he'd gained a scholarship to university. But Andrew was as eager as any healthy young man to kick over the traces. Away from their influence, the years of conformity were sloughed off. He made friends of his own choosing, drank beer for the first time, discovered that girls found him attractive and experienced his first sexual fumblings. Exhilarated by it all, Andrew stayed up half the night listening to wide-ranging and deeply philosophical discussions on art, religion and the meaning of life. It was a girl who dragged him along to his first political meeting. Only communism, it was generally agreed, could fight fascism and inequality, so carried along by the enthusiasm of his more politically experienced girlfriend, Andrew had joined the Communist Party and embraced it with the fervour of the convert.

Perhaps it was a subconscious act of rebellion, but Andrew didn't think so – he genuinely wanted to right the world's wrongs.

Of course his parents were aghast.

His mother had agitatedly fingered the string of imitation pearls round her neck and wondered how she could keep such dire news from her friends. His father had received the news silently. His pipe sending up smoke signals of suppressed fury, he'd paced the small sitting-room, back and forth, back and forth across the Axminster carpet. Andrew waited, his shoulders tense, and finally his father removed the pipe from his mouth, wheeled round and barked, 'And what will the customers think, eh, knowing my son is a commie?'

Trying not to show his nervousness, Andrew had answered reasonably enough, 'You don't have to tell them, Father.'

'I've no intention of telling them, but it could get out.' He banged the bowl of the pipe against the fireplace. 'I don't know what Head Office will have to say about it either. It'll put paid to any promotion.' Against the evidence of his eyes, Mr Seymour still entertained a faint hope that one day he might be made assistant manager. 'The sooner this damn silly nonsense passes, the better. We made sacrifices and sent you to university to be educated, not pick up crack-pot ideas.'

71

'They're not crack-pot.'

'Are you trying to break our hearts, Andrew?' His mother was on her knees sweeping up shreds of tobacco from the hearth and she looked up at him with a hurt expression in her pale blue eyes.

'No, Mother, I just want to help people less fortunate than myself and fight fascism. I can't see what's so wrong about that. Love thy neighbour and fight evil, just like the vicar says in church every Sunday.'

Phyllis Seymour, who'd always had her suspicions about the vicar's political affiliations, ignored her son's remark. 'You could at least think of me. I'll be thrown off the fête committee. And supposing Mrs Clarke finds out?' Mrs Clarke was the bank manager's wife and absurdly aware of her position in the town. 'She can hardly bring herself to speak to me now. If this comes out she'll cut me dead.' His mother stood up, found a handkerchief in the sleeve of her cardigan and began dabbing her eyes.

Since it had distressed Andrew as a small boy to see her cry, his mother could easily blackmail him into obedience with her tears. But he was no longer a child. He'd grown up, was stronger, had ideas of his own, and although he didn't blame her entirely for it, he was also more critical of the narrowness of his mother's aspirations. 'Oh to hell with Mrs Clarke, she's just stupid and provincial,' he burst out, angered that she was still prepared to use tears to bring him to heel.

His father's face and neck turned dark red. 'How dare you speak to your mother like that!' he thundered.

'Please, please, Reginald, my head.' Phyllis Seymour's fluttering fingers flew to her temples.

'All right, my dear.' Reginald Seymour went to his wife, put his arm round her shoulders and led her to a chair. 'Now see what you've done.' He glared at his son. Raised voices could send his mother to bed with a migraine for a week so no one in the house was ever allowed to really

72

express their anger, which meant that resentment festered away just below the surface.

'Eat up, yer at yer aunty's,' joked Roy, nudging his elbow. Andrew looked down and saw that while he'd been reflecting on the unsatisfactory nature of his relationship with his parents these days, a cup of cocoa and a slice of bread had been placed in front of him.

'Thank you.' Trying not to feel guilty at imposing on their good will, Andrew cut himself a wedge of cheese.

'Like to try some of this?' Mr Henderson had spooned some piccalilli on to his own plate and was now offering the jar to Andrew.

Piccalilli was considered 'common' at home, so Andrew had never eaten it before. Unwisely he took a large mouthful of the mustardy pickle, sweat broke out on his brow, his eyes watered then he started to cough. 'Gosh,' he managed at last with a shake of his head, 'hot stuff,' and heard Roy snigger.

Tom glared at his son but knowing it would only make matters worse, didn't reprimand him. Instead, anxious to put the young man at his ease, he asked, 'What's your line of business then, Andrew?' He'd already worked out from his accent and well-kept nails that it certainly wasn't anything manual.

'I'm a teacher, at Lakemead Elementary,' Andrew replied, wiping the sweat from his forehead with a hankie.

'Fancy workin' in that dump.' Frances's tone was scathing.

'You went there,' her brother pointed out.

'Yeah, and a fat lot of good it did me.' Kitty, of course, being cleverer, had gone on to the Central School where she'd had the advantage of being taught to type.

'I admit there are plenty of problems. What we need is a new building. The one we have at present is falling down.'

Tom Henderson shook his head. 'Well you won't get that, things being the way they are.'

'No I don't suppose we will, that's why I'm so angry at all the money that was wasted on that jamboree for the Royals.'

'Aye, it was a waste, but sometimes folks need to take their minds off things. But you'll no be from these parts,' Tom Henderson pursued.

'Chelmsford's my home town.'

'So what brought you to Stepney?'

'My political beliefs,' replied Andrew with such youthful pomposity Tom Henderson, anxious not to hurt him further, had to struggle to hide a smile.

'Father wanted me to go into the City but I despise the sort of capitalist society where some people make millions and others starve. The sooner it's gone the better.'

'Maybe, maybe not,' answered Tom diplomatically.

Remembering the long recriminating silences at home if ever he touched on political matters, Andrew looked around the table. He bet that didn't happen here. If something needed saying out it would come, which was the best way, it cleared the air. He wished Frances wouldn't stare at him in that sullen way, though. Maybe she'd mistaken his dancing with her for something more, but she was only a kid for heaven's sake. Give it a couple of years, then he might be a bit more interested.

It was now almost dark in the room and when Mr Henderson rose and lit the gas, Andrew saw that it was past nine. He supposed he ought to be going, but he was desperate to see Kitty.

Frances started to clear away the supper things, clattering the plates noisily – a definite hint this – and Andrew knew good manners demanded that he should take his leave. He was about to rise from his chair when Roy went over to where some shelves had been put up for books and ornaments between the wall and chimney-breast. With great care he lifted down a balsawood aeroplane and placed it in front of Andrew.

'Did you make this, Roy?'

'Yeah.'

Grabbing at any opportunity to delay his departure, Andrew picked up the fragile model, examined it with a critical eye and recognized a master craftsman. It had been glued together with great precision. 'I'm impressed, it's very good.'

'I know,' said Roy, who wasn't one to waste time on false modesty. 'It's a Handley Page twin-engined biplane and I'm gonna be a pilot when I grow up.'

'Are you now? But have you ever been up in an aeroplane?'

As Roy shook his head an idea took shape in Andrew's mind. An ally was always useful and in his wooing of Kitty it would do no harm to have her brother on his side. 'How'd you like to one day, then?' he asked, and ruffled the boy's hair in a friendly manner. 'I've got a friend from university who works at Croydon airport. I could get a cheap fare and take you on a trip to the Isle of Wight. If your parents agree, of course,' he remembered to add.

Roy's eyes widened in hope. 'Fly? Bloomin' 'eck,' then disbelief '. . . d'ya really mean it?'

'Of course I do.'

'I could go, couldn't I Mum? Dad?' Roy danced from one parent to the other, unable to contain his excitement.

'You're like a hen on a hot girdle, keep still,' his father ordered.

'But I can go, can't I, Dad,' Roy pleaded, his face growing anxious as his father mulled over the idea.

'Go where?'

At Kitty's question all eyes were turned to where she stood poised in the doorway. Satisfied she had the attention of the whole room, Kitty pushed the door closed with her foot then sank gracefully into a fireside chair.

Immediately Andrew shot to his feet, his heart pounding in his chest. 'Hello, Kitty.'

75

Kitty cast him an indifferent look. On Monday he'd offered promise, now in comparison to Robert he seemed immature. 'What are you doing here?'

'I've come to see you. I . . . I thought you might like to go somewhere for a drink.'

Kicking off her shoes, Kitty yawned behind her hand. ''Fraid not, I'm absolutely done in.' She closed her eyes and let her arms fall languidly over the arm of the chair.

But her lukewarm response didn't deter Andrew, in fact it enhanced his desire for her. It was privilege enough to stand and gaze at her. The bright lipstick she normally wore had rubbed off, and her mouth seemed somehow more vulnerable and the feathery lashes on the lovely curve of her cheek gave her a child-like air. Without doubt she was the most beautiful creature he'd ever set eyes on and he'd worship her until his dying day.

'Are you hungry? What would you like to drink, Kitty love?' Watching Mrs Henderson bustling around after her daughter and the undisguised pride in her eyes, Andrew felt a passing sympathy for Frances and had an inkling of the hurt it must cause her to be constantly overshadowed by a cleverer, prettier sister.

'Nothing to eat. Just tea, please Mum, with plenty of milk,' Kitty answered, and while her mother went through the ritual of warming the pot, measuring tea into it then filling it with boiling water, Roy shook her arm.

'Hey, Kit, guess what, Andrew's takin' me up in an aeroplane.'

'Is that so?' Kitty tried hard not to sound impressed, but didn't quite manage it.

'You could come too,' Andrew offered.

Her mother handed her a cup of tea and while she sipped, Kitty considered his invitation. For a moment she was tempted, but then Robert's face got in the way. 'Thanks, no. But why don't you take Frances, I'm sure she'd love to go,' she said carelessly.

Andrew looked uncomfortable. That was about the last thing he wanted. 'Well ... uh ...'

Frances had been standing in the shadows and no one thought anything of it when she moved over and stood in front of her sister. Neither did they notice the tremor in her body, nor the compulsive way she flexed her fingers. 'I loathe and despise you, Kitty Henderson.' The words came out like a viper's hiss. Then she brought the flat of her hand up under the saucer and struck it so hard, the cup shot up in the air, saturating Kitty with tea and tealeaves which dribbled down her face and on to her dress.

There was a moment's astonished silence, then before anyone could intervene, Kitty, aware she'd been made to look foolish, leapt to her feet with a look of pure venom in her eyes. 'You bitch! You lousy rotten bitch, I'll kill you, so help me God, I will.' Grabbing Frances, she slapped her hard across both cheeks with the back of her hand.

Knowing he had to accept some responsibility for this drama, Andrew cleared his throat. 'I think I'd better go,' he murmured and aware that no one had heard him, he edged rather furtively towards the door.

7

Kitty whipped the cover off her typewriter, fed paper into it, sat down and typed: FRANCES HENDERSON IS A VILE PIG AND I HATE HER! Then she yanked the paper from the machine, signed it, tore it into shreds, and dropped it piece by piece into the wastepaper bin. She was aware that what she was doing was pointless and childish, but it took the edge off her anger, a destructive emotion which played havoc with a woman's looks, according to a magazine article she'd read recently. But then controlling your temper was probably easier if you didn't have a sister who would test the patience of a saint. And she shuddered to think what damage the tea might have done if it had been scalding hot – perhaps permanent scarring.

To reassure herself, Kitty drew a small mirror from her desk drawer and scrutinized her face. Nothing flawed its perfection except a hint of a frown and the merest tightness around the mouth. Remembering the magazine's strictures, she moistened her lips and practised the smile she would greet Robert with. Slowly, she decided, with just a hint of dimple. Since their chance meeting in the park, he had taken almost exclusive possession of her thoughts, so a cloud had been cast over her day when yesterday Miss Yeo informed her that he'd rung to say he wouldn't be coming into the office. Of course that meant double the correspondence for her today – not that she minded, it would give them more time together and perhaps he'd use it as an opportunity to discuss her future.

Kitty had a fluttery feeling in her stomach at the prospect of seeing Robert again, so to occupy herself she sharpened a dozen pencils for the expected dictation marathon. She had almost finished when Miss Yeo arrived.

'Good morning, Miss Henderson,' the supervisor called over to her as she hung up her hat and jacket.

'Good morning, Miss Yeo.'

As usual her supervisor was wearing a black frock with white collar and cuffs, and looked neat and businesslike. But Kitty, who had an observant eye, noticed that the dress had been carefully darned in many places.

Even though it still wasn't nine o'clock, Kitty knew it gave the right impression to look busy. Opening a file, she pretended to flick through some insurance claims, although really she was watching her supervisor. Because she was such a creature of habit, Kitty knew exactly what she would do, even in what order, and she often wished that Miss Yeo would vary her routine, just to surprise her. First she withdrew a compact from her handbag and gave her nose, which was inclined to redness, a dusting of powder. Next she pulled a comb through her frizzy hair and caused a snowstorm of dandruff to drift down on to her shoulders. This had to be flicked away with a small clothes brush, then, because she was given to dyspepsia, Miss Yeo unwrapped an indigestion tablet and popped it in her mouth. Finally, with a glance at the clock, she sat down and fixed her gaze on the door, daring any girl to be late.

In idle moments Kitty sometimes wondered about her. Was her whole life ritualized like that, perhaps to keep loneliness at bay? And how old was she? Forty at a guess, maybe even forty-five. There was no sign of an engagement ring, and probably she didn't even have a boyfriend or a life outside work. She had a look of ill-health about her as if she never had enough fresh air, and Kitty had two scenarios for Miss Yeo. One was a bed-sit with a single plate, cup and saucer set out on a small table, the other was her caring for an elderly housebound parent. Either way she was sure it was a lonely existence. Kitty was ambitious herself, and she saw no harm in it, but the last thing she wanted was to end up one of the Miss Yeos of this world, unmarried and saving every farthing against the penury of old age.

What, Kitty wondered, would her supervisor's reaction be when she was promoted. And Rose? Would her friend be pleased or envious? She herself might feel entirely confident about her ability to cope with the responsibilities of a secretary, but others would look at her and just see a seventeen-year-old.

Gradually the other girls trickled in, then finally Rose, red-cheeked and panting and with a second to spare. Miss Yeo eyed the clock, gave her cuffs a telling twitch but said nothing. Quickly the room settled down to its daily rhythm and there was no sound other than the rapid tap of the keys of twenty typewriters. By and large the work was undemanding, repetitive and boring – memos, reports and claims – and being summoned to take dictation came as a welcome relief. On tenterhooks, Kitty kept glancing up at the clock. Robert Travis must call for her soon. The hands moved to ten, then ten-thirty, and although Kitty's heart gave a small leap of hope every time the internal phone tinkled on the supervisor's desk, it was never for her. By a quarter to eleven her fingers had lost their nimbleness and she started making mistakes. I must concentrate, she thought, but her mind kept returning to Robert Travis. Surely he hadn't forgotten. After the half promises he'd made, she'd been confident the call would come through for her to go up to his office the minute he'd hung his bowler and umbrella on the hatstand. Unless, dreadful thought, he hadn't meant a word of what he said.

By eleven her concentration had gone and Kitty felt hot, sick and betrayed. She stood up. 'May I be excused, please, Miss Yeo?' she asked, and when the supervisor nodded her assent, she fled to the ladies' room.

Talking was strictly forbidden but as Kitty passed her desk, Rose hissed, 'What's wrong? You look awful,' and for her trouble got a stern, 'Miss Bumford, quiet please,' from Miss Yeo.

Being told she looked awful made Kitty even more depressed, although she had to concede that her friend was right. Her skin, in the cloakroom mirror, looked pasty, her hair dull, her eyes without sparkle. Deciding to buck herself up with a recently purchased lipstick called Luscious Red, she was drawing a careful bow on her mouth when Rose's head appeared round the door.

'Skates on, love. Mr Gorgeous has phoned down for you and Yo-Yo is getting her knickers in a twist, wondering where you've got to.'

Kitty's heart missed a beat. 'D'you mean Mr Travis?'

'Who else?'

Quickly Kitty finished outlining her mouth, shoved the lipstick back into her handbag and followed her friend out of the cloakroom.

Hurrying along the corridor, Rose, always one for a bit of gossip, said, 'Hey, have you noticed how Yo-Yo goes all of a doo-da when she talks to Mr Robert on the phone?'

'No, I haven't,' answered Kitty, whose mind was preoccupied with other matters.

'You watch next time, her neck goes all red.'

Miss Yeo was definitely looking flushed when they got back to the typing pool. And tetchy. She glanced at the clock. 'Mr Travis has now been kept waiting for over five minutes. Will you please go up immediately, Miss Henderson.'

Abasing herself, Kitty answered, 'Yes, Miss Yeo, sorry, Miss Yeo,' even though she longed to skip across the room and up the stairs. Her self-control held until she came to a glass panelled door, but as she pushed it open Kitty couldn't resist giving her reflection a small, pleased smile. Her worries had been groundless, this was it: now, instead of boss and typist, there would be a new intimacy between them, a breaking down of barriers.

Glad she'd had the chance to refresh her make-up, Kitty tapped on the door, heard him call, 'Come in,' and bounced in with an air of happy expectancy. 'Good morning, Mr Travis,' she said brightly, and sat down and waited for him to respond with that slow smile of his, which would lighten his sometimes sombre expression and add an extra dimension to her own day. This morning, though, he was writing and didn't even look up. Instead, mumbling, 'Morning, Miss Henderson,' he continued to scribble away with the air of a man with much on his mind.

A fly buzzed against a windowpane, there was the faint scratch of pen over paper, a door slammed along the corridor, but apart from that, silence. A small, perplexed frown wrinkled Kitty's smooth brow. Something wasn't quite right. Was it perhaps a problem in his personal life? Maybe the reason he was away yesterday, or, awful thought, was it her? After what seemed like an age, he finished writing, scribbled his signature, blotted it, screwed the top back on his fountain pen and eased back in his chair. 'Now where were we? Ah, here.' Still managing to avoid Kitty's eye he started to dictate, and at a speed which suggested he might be questioning the claims she'd made for herself. Piqued, she thought, well I'll show you, and when an hour later Robert Travis had dictated the last letter, there was only one word she needed to query.

Laden with files, Kitty struggled to her feet, by now not even expecting him to hold the door open for her. But whatever else might have deserted him he still remembered his manners, although as she looked up and thanked him, she was surprised at the stony impassivity of his face. Bewildered, she stumbled down the stairs.

Kitty expected the best from the world and its inhabitants and usually they obliged, so she was totally thrown by Robert Travis's coldness. Obviously she'd offended him in some way. Had she been too pushy – men didn't like that in a woman – sounded too ambitious? Perhaps he felt she'd manoeuvred him into making promises he'd no hope of being able to fulfil and were now a source of embarrassment to him.

Kitty tried to keep her mind on her work, but something unheard of, at the end of the day, several of his letters were returned to be retyped. When the supervisor, who'd always regarded her favourably, put them down on the table, she studied Kitty closely. 'Are you ill, Miss Henderson? It's so unlike you to make errors.'

Kitty rubbed her forehead with a weary gesture. 'I've got a bit of a headache.'

'Is . . . is it your woman's trouble?' Miss Yeo asked solicitously, being herself a martyr to monthly cramps.

'No, just my head,' said Kitty, who, during the day had felt the tension in her shoulders gradually work its way up into her neck and skull.

'I'll get you a glass of water and aspirin,' said Miss Yeo kindly. She picked up the letters. 'These will have to wait until tomorrow. Finish the one you are doing and go home.'

Kitty thanked her, swallowed the aspirin and drank the water she brought. However, she didn't go straight home. Instead she went and sat in the square, in exactly the same seat as on the previous occasion. Her vision was too blurred to read, so she just sat there, holding her head up with effort because of the pain. She waited for an hour but Robert Travis never came, and in the end she was driven from the gardens by a headache now so severe she felt it might crack her skull in two.

But there was worse to come. The following morning the internal phone rang, Miss Yeo picked it up and Kitty heard her say, 'All right, Mr Travis, I'll send her up.' Automatically Kitty picked up her pad and pencils, but Miss Yeo was looking past her to one of the other typists. 'Miss Dawson, will you please go up to Mr Robert Travis, he wants you for dictation,' she called, and gave Kitty a curious glance but didn't say anything.

Stunned, Kitty watched Olive search for pencils. The girl looked flustered and well she might, because Kitty knew she wasn't a patch on her. And serve him right if her letters are full of mistakes, she thought spitefully. It was shabby treatment by someone she admired, and deliberate enough to be insulting. Rejection was an experience quite foreign to her and Kitty could easily have succumbed to tears. Instead a hardness grew round her heart and, berating herself for misjudging his character, she set her mind against Robert Travis and determined on a plan of action.

The evening paper had several secretarial vacancies and Kitty pencilled a ring round the most promising. Not one to waste time, immediately she got home she sat down with ink bottle, pen and writing paper and composed several glowing testimonials about herself. No firm could help but be impressed she decided as she addressed the envelopes and stuck stamps on them. She walked down the road to post her applications, and as she pushed the letters into the box, she said out loud, 'Right, that'll show you, Robert Travis. No one treats me like dirt and gets away with it.'

For once in her life, Kitty had failed to understand the full power of her beauty.

8

Frances fingered the locket that Gloria had loaned her and peered across the road from the safety of a shop doorway. The cinema queues were long, there was no sign of Norman and she she could feel a tight knot of anxiety in the pit of her stomach. First of all she hadn't wanted to come, now she was worried he wouldn't turn up. What had decided her was Kitty's expression of disbelief when she'd mistakenly confided that she had a date. Now it looked as if she was going to be stood up. That'd give Kitty a chance to gloat, particularly after the rumpus the other night. She'd really enjoyed that, though, watching Kitty lose her rag in front of Andrew – it almost made amends for the indignities she'd suffered at Kitty's hands. Tit for tat, Frances thought. They were about even now, she and Kitty.

Across the road the queues continued to grow at a spectacular rate and now stretched right round to the back of the cinema. With a self-important air and almost as if bestowing a favour, the commissionaire came out and allowed a few people to shuffle forward to the box office. Chewing her nails she muttered, 'Get a move on, Norman,' then wondered if she should go over and join the queue. But which seats, the stalls or the balcony? Having a choice, making a decision, it was all too much, and her young face folded into deep lines of anxiety.

Frances dithered for several moments, then with the brave but doomed air of an explorer taking that first step on to uncharted territory, she left the shelter of the doorway. She had reached the edge of the pavement when she saw him, striding up and down both queues and obviously searching

85

for her. Her relief was so intense, she waved to gain his attention. 'Norman, I'm here,' she yelled then, with a total disregard for life or limb, she dashed across the busy road.

'Coom on,' he said when she reached him, 'let's get in the queue quickly.' Taking her arm in a masterful way, he led her to the back stalls queue, where other young couples and women with tired faces stood waiting patiently to be taken out of themselves for a few hours; to enter the magic world of the silver screen, where misunderstandings were only ever of a temporary nature and love won through in the end.

'Sorry about bein' so late, but Mr Freeman, me boss, has taken a bit o' a shine to me and he kept me back at work. We were discussing me future. He said if I want to get on in the wine business I've got ter think about learning a foreign language, either French or German.'

'Coo blimey,' said Frances, overwhelmed by such a notion, 'are you goin' to?'

'Yeah, of course. I want to keep ma job, and France and Germany are where we do most of our business. People phone up and we get letters which don't mean nothin' to me. It wouldn't do no harm, having a go at German. In fact I know a few words already.'

'Say somethin', then.'

'*Guten Tag.*'

'What does that mean?'

'Good day. *Ein, zwei, drei, vier, funf.* I've joost counted up to five,' he informed her.

Frances was impressed. 'Is that so?'

'Yeah, and Mr Freeman's always popping off to Germany to see wine growers and he's hinted that he might take me with 'im one day, maybe in the autumn. Have you ever tasted wine?'

Frances shook her head.

'He makes me taste it, and smell it. He says I've got to find out about the bouquet and the like. You'd be surprised

86

at the difference there is. Some wine's so sweet it tastes like honey.'

Although they were unaware of it, while Norman had been talking they'd been slowly edging forward and had now almost reached the head of the queue. The commissionaire let the couple in front of them through and Frances had just murmured to Norman with a sense of anticipation, 'Us next,' when, looking immensely pleased with himself, he came out and plonked the 'House Full' sign down in front of them.

'Oh no!' wailed Frances and a collective groan of disappointment rose from the crowd.

'Sorry, folks,' said the commissionaire, but Frances knew by his face he wasn't really. And watching him as the queue broke up and people drifted away grumbling, she realized that it was something to do with his military uniform. The epaulettes and gold braiding gave him a sense of power and she glared at the man with dislike for denying her an evening at her favourite place on earth, and worse, gloating over the fact.

At a bit of a loss, Norman and Frances stared at each other. 'What we gonna do now?' Norman asked.

Frances shrugged. 'Dunno. Go home I expect.'

'It's Friday night, we can't. Look, d'you fancy goin' to a dance?'

'Where?'

'Well there's one on at the Rex ballroom tonight, I saw it advertised. Johnny Doakes and the Doughboys are playing and they're supposed to be pretty hot.'

'Yeah, all right, I wouldn't mind,' Frances answered, deciding there was nothing to be lost. It would be a real sign of defeat, going home at half past seven on a Friday night, particularly if Kitty was there.

Frances had never been to a proper dance before and she spent a long time in the cloakroom fixing her hair and listening to groups of girls, who rushed in to repair their make-up between dances. They lined up in front of the mirror, chirpy as starlings on a telegraph wire, and savaged the band, their boyfriends and any girl unfortunate enough not to be present. No one was spared. However, immediately the music started again they gave excited squeals of pleasure and crowded out through the door, leaving behind the lingering smell of their cheap Woolworth scent.

When they'd gone Frances studied her reflection with an even more critical eye than usual. Was her hairstyle on the old-fashioned side? Was her petticoat showing? Were the seams in her stockings straight? Dare she venture into the dance hall and risk being skewered on the tongues of those spiteful girls? If only she'd thought to cadge a cigarette off Gloria, it would help steady her nerves and give her something to do with her hands. Frances's arms had gone all goose-pimply and as she rubbed them and tried to put herself in the frame of mind where she could walk casually into the dance hall, a girl's head appeared round the cloak-room door.

'You Frances?'

'Yeah.'

'There's a bloke out here wants ter know if you're gonna be all night.'

'I'm coming, tell him.' Frances took a deep breath, moistened her lips, walked out into the hall and saw her fears were groundless. No one was the slightest bit interested in her. The lights were dim, the band was playing a waltz and the couples gliding around the floor only had eyes for each other. On the ceiling a mirrored ball spun slowly, creating lozenge-shaped patterns of light.

'You took yer time,' grumbled Norman.

'Sorry.'

'Coom on, there's two chairs empty over by the stage, but we'd better bag 'em quick.' Grabbing her hand, he wove his way between the dancing couples.

'That bloke playing the saxophone is Johnny Doakes, he's the band leader,' Norman explained, once they were seated.

'Is he?' More at ease with herself now, Frances studied the rest of the the band. There were five musicians – drummer, pianist, clarinettist and trumpet player, plus Johnny on the saxophone. They had a smooth, easy tempo and were nattily turned out in cream trousers, dark green jackets, bow ties and two-toned shoes, and by the crush on the floor they were obviously popular. The dance finished, couples drew apart and Johnny Doakes, with a flash of white teeth, announced a quickstep.

Norman pulled her to her feet. 'Coom on, let's have a go at this.'

Norman might not have had much to say for himself but he surprised Frances by being pretty nifty on his feet and soon they were up on the floor for almost every dance. If they didn't dance, Frances sat tapping her feet and humming quietly in tune to the music.

'Enjoyin' yerself?' Norman asked.

'Yeah, I am. Mind you I'd like to have seen Ginger and Fred.'

'Well we could always go another time.' Norman said it casually, but there was an assumption that they were now a pair, and Frances wasn't sure if she wanted that.

In the interval Norman bought them both a lemonade shandy and when they went back into the hall, Johnny Doakes was making an announcement. 'As you'll have read on the board outside, we've got a singing contest tonight so I hope all you warblers have been gargling and practising your notes. Now who's first?' He gazed with a hopeful expression at the various groups spaced out around the hall 'Remember, there's a cash prize of five pounds and that's not to be sneezed at in these hard times,' he added as an inducement, when no one moved.

There was a bit of shuffling and giggling, then a young man, protesting and self-conscious, was pushed forward by his mates. The band leader, grateful that his bright idea wasn't going to fall flat, beckoned to him and the young man climbed to the stage.

'What's your name, son?'

'Cyril West.'

'So what you going to sing for us then, Cyril?

Cyril coughed nervously. ' "The Blue of the Night".'

'Right, I think we can manage that, can't we lads?' he asked, addressing the band. They nodded, sorted through their music, found the piece, and Johnny lifted his hand. 'One, two three,' he intoned, tapping his foot. The band began to play and Cyril started to sing, coming in at almost the right bar. Someone, probably his mum, must have told him he sang like Bing Crosby, but although his crooning might have sounded all right in the bath, really he was pretty dire. Frances saw a couple of girls sniggering behind their hands and wondered why anyone would want to risk making themselves a laughing stock. He wobbled uncertainly to the end of the song and, although his mates cheered him loyally, the clapping was pretty half-hearted. The next contestant was a girl with a thin, tuneless voice who thought she was Jessie Matthews. And it went on like this, one after the other, Gracie Fields, Al Bowlly, some indifferent, some downright awful, but all pale imitations of the real stars.

Finally what looked likely to be the last contestant was thanked by Johnny and climbed down from the stage.

'Well, who d'you think should win?' asked Frances, trying to be diplomatic.

'None, they all sounded like screeching moggies to me.'

'I can sing better than any one of them lot,' Frances announced with unusual confidence.

'You?' Norman said, disbelieving. 'Show us then. Have a go.'

'No fear.' Looking panic-stricken, Frances tried to dissolve into the wall.

'Anyone else game to try before we decide on a winner?'

Johnny Doakes shielded his eyes with a hand, pretending to search out one last hopeful.

'Yes, here.' Norman grabbed Frances and before she had time to protest, he was on his feet, yanking her up with him. As everyone in the hall turned to stare, Frances sought with terrified eyes for means of escape. But Norman's fingers were clamped tight round her wrist.

Frantically she tried to prise them off. 'Let go, you're hurting me,' she hissed.

'You said you could sing, didn't you? Well prove it.'

'What's your name, love?' Johnny called, deciding to intervene in the dispute.

'Her name's Frances. Frances Henderson,' Norman answered on her behalf.

Johnny, enjoying the challenge of an unwilling contestant, leapt down off the stage. 'Come along, Frances,' he cajoled. Since he'd sat up in a pram women had fallen for his smile and Johnny didn't expect it to fail him now.

But Frances was in no state to be swayed by his charm and she saw the only way out of this horrible predicament was to make a scene. Except that she'd draw even more attention to herself. Silently swearing revenge on Norman, she allowed Johnny to lead her up on to the stage, where she stood stiff with fear and staring down at a blur of faces. Through the swirling panic and confusion of her mind, she heard dimly a round of applause. The band was clapping its encouragement as well and as Frances half turned to acknowledge it, the pianist, who was just to the left of her, smiled and winked. For some reason she felt she had an ally and and her terror subsided a fraction.

'What you singing for us then, Frances?' enquired Johnny.

'"Smoke Gets in Your Eyes".' It was the first song that came into her head but she knew most popular songs by heart anyway. Frances looked across at the pianist and he smiled at her again. 'With piano accompaniment only,' she added with a firmness that surprised her as well as Johnny.

It was laughable, a kid with no sex appeal stating terms and she was going to be bloody awful like the rest. Still, he'd better get it over with. 'Okay, sweetie.' Johnny stood back. 'Take it away, Paul.'

'What key do you want, dear?' asked the pianist.

'B flat, please.' Frances ran her tongue over her dry lips, rubbed the palms of her hands down her dress, dragged air deep into her lungs, then moved over to stand by Paul. She nodded that she was ready to start, and he began to play.

Immediately she began to sing the last vestige of fear vanished, the outside world faded, and she surrendered to the bitter-sweet lyrics of the song. It was a number that allowed Frances to demonstrate her true range, and her voice somehow captured all the longing, poignancy and heartache of lost love. There wasn't a sound from the crowd, not a shuffle, not a cough and at that moment Frances had an inkling of the power of her talent and stretched out to meet it. When she came to the final verse, hardly knowing why, she clasped her arms around her waist, threw back her head, closed her eyes and sang it very slowly, her voice husky with emotion. She allowed the last plaintive note to float away into the darkness, there was a brief hush, then the crowd went wild. En masse, they rose to their feet, clapping, whistling and stamping their appreciation.

Paul stood up and gazed at her with frank admiration. 'My, you really did something with that song. You wowed the audience and got me right here.' He pressed his hand rather dramatically to his heart.

A little dazed, Frances smiled back, warming to his flattery and wanting to hear more, except that Johnny was now laying claim to her.

'Come on, my little nightingale, enjoy your fame, you've got them eating out of your hand.' He led her to the middle of the stage and called to the audience, 'Well I don't think there's any question who the winner is tonight, do you folks?'

'No,' someone yelled back. 'Give 'er the money, Johnny, and let's 'ave another song.'

Was it some trick, a fluke, the band leader asked himself, finding it hard to make the connection between this gawky kid, hardly out of ankle socks, and the amazing maturity of her voice. Husky yet strong and no straining, not even on the high notes. A real natural. Of course the test was whether she could bring it off again. 'Would you like to sing for us a bit more, dear?' Johnny asked, still nursing doubts.

'I don't mind.' The faces staring up at Frances radiated approval and she wanted to give them more. She'd discovered where she belonged. This was her world. Up here she wasn't boring Frances Henderson whom no one noticed. Up here she was glamorous, adored like a film star. Up here she was in another dimension, untouchable, secure.

And Johnny was left in no doubt about her talent when the crowd started shouting up requests. He saw, too, that when the girl sang she had the chameleon-like quality of the true star. Normally a timid little thing, a spotlight, a crowd, would always transform her. On stage, he sensed, was where she would be in control and where she would always come truly alive. God, they had a winner here, and a band needed a good vocalist these days. He shouldn't have too much trouble persuading her to join them, then they'd be made. He could see it already, his name in lights, engagements at posh West End hotels, contracts with the BBC; money, fame.

The clamour for yet more songs went on and on, for she could make even the tritest lyrics sound like poetry. Frances forgot Norman, forgot everything except the need to please her audience.

But Johnny was enough of a professional to see that talent like hers had to be nurtured. After a while, he put up his hand. 'We don't want to tire this very talented young lady, do we? So I'm going to be firm and say I think she has sung enough for tonight. But what I shall also say and I want this on record, is that I hope Frances will come back and sing with the band again, and soon as well.'

They didn't want her to go, but Johnny was adamant. First, though, he counted out five one-pound notes into her hand. And as he closed her fingers over them, he said in a confidential tone. 'And there's more where that came from. A pound for you every Saturday, love, if you come and sing with us.'

Frances felt the crisp notes between her fingers and, anticipating her family's surprise, recited to herself: a pound each for Mum and Dad, ten shillings for Roy and the rest to put away for a rainy day. It was incredible: for doing something that came as naturally as breathing she'd made more money in one evening than in two months at the shop. And there could be more, Johnny said so.

Her head whirling from the intoxicating cocktail of attention, applause and new-found wealth, Frances was about to step down from the platform, when Paul, half rising from the piano, called to her, 'Promise you'll come and sing for us again, Frances.'

Frances smiled back at him. 'I'll try.' Flattery was all very well, but in the end it depended on Dad and there wasn't much point in making promises she might not be able to keep.

She had all but forgotten about Norman when she saw him at the far end of the ballroom, leaning against a pillar and looking cheesed off. Well it had been his idea, so if she was supposed to feel guilty he could think again. But he had brought her and paid for her so she'd better make her peace, Frances decided and was pushing her way through the dancers when a hand gripped her shoulder. 'Well aren't you the dark horse.'

Frances spun round. 'Andrew!' Then seeing Kitty, added, 'What are you two doing here?'

'We could ask you the same thing,' answered Kitty, quick

as a flash. 'The last I heard you were going to the pictures. And that's where Mum and Dad think you are. Not making a spectacle of yourself in a dance hall.'

'Well if I was making a spectacle of meself, at least I got paid for it.' Frances held out her hand. 'Five pounds, not bad, eh? And he wants me to sing every Saturday.' Kitty had a real gift for making her feel inferior, but her perception of herself had changed over the past couple of hours and she fought to hold on to it. Turning to Andrew she asked, 'I didn't make a fool of meself, did I?'

'With a voice like that? Certainly not. I thought you were brilliant.'

'There's no need to go on about it, you'll make her big-headed, you know,' Kitty snapped.

'I doubt it,' Andrew answered, and as Kitty shot him a look sour as green apples, Frances felt a surge of triumph. Kitty was jealous! Of her! She had the limelight and her sister couldn't stand it.

The band had been taking a five-minute break but now Johnny came forward and announced the next dance and Kitty took Andrew's hand. 'Come on, let's dance,' she said and pulled him away.

'See you later,' Andrew called, and Frances watched them for a moment, amused at Kitty's antics, the way she acted all lovey-dovey with Andrew, gazing up into his eyes, sliding her arms around his neck. And all for my benefit, thought Frances.

Norman hadn't moved from his spot by the pillar and she stood in front of him so that he couldn't avoid her eyes.

'Hello.'

He gave her a grudging nod.

Feeling a dormant aggression surface, she asked, 'What's wrong wiv you? You've got a face as long as next week.'

'Actually if you want to know I'm tired of holding up this pillar. I thought we'd coom here to dance.'

'So we did, but let me jog your memory. It was your

95

idea, me goin' in for the singin' contest and you practically dragged me up on the stage.'

Norman shifted uncomfortably. 'I know, but I didn't think you'd spend the whole bloomin' evening up there.'

'You thought I wasn't going to be any good, didn't you?'

'No,' he lied.

'So what did you think of my singing, eh?' Frances pursued.

'I've heard worse.'

'Is that a compliment?'

'The nearest you'll get from me.'

'Well everyone else liked me so I don't care.' But Frances had had enough of falling out. 'Anyway some good came out of it. I'm in the money, so what do you say to me treating you to a fish and chip supper on the way home?'

Mum and Dad liked the wireless on in the evenings, especially the dance bands – Harry Roy or Carroll Gibbons and the Savoy Orpheans. Often Frances would arrive home and find them dancing round the small room together, cheek to cheek like a courting couple. However, tonight when she opened the door, instead of the usual syncopated dance tune there was silence, which could mean only one thing: Nan was there with Donald. Frances's spirits took a nosedive. She felt desperately sorry for poor old Uncle Donald, a husk of a man, whose life to all intents and purposes had ended in some rat-infested crater in Flanders, and she knew she should love her grandmother. But it was hard to when she was such a misery. Her only pleasure seemed to be putting a damper on everyone else's enjoyment, which probably accounted for the silence tonight.

Mum, who had one of Roy's socks stretched over a wooden mushroom and was darning it, looked up and smiled when she opened the door. 'Hello, love.'

Dad briefly lowered his *Daily Chronicle*. 'Nice evening?'

'Yes thanks, Dad.'

She was itching to tell her parents of her triumph but Donald, a shadow against the wallpaper, and Nan, sipping a glass of stout, put her off.

'Hello, Nan.'

'You're late.' It was an accusation.

Frances looked at the clock. 'It's not eleven yet.'

'That's too late for a girl of your age. Where 'ave you bin?'

Deliberately ignoring her grandmother, Frances went over and switched on the wireless.

'She's been to the pictures, that's all Mum, and we don't mind her being a little late Friday nights if we know where she is.' Trying not to let her mother rattle her, Edna snipped the darning wool, folded the finished sock, rubbed her tired eyes, then picked up another from the pile beside her. How could Roy wear out so many socks, she thought wearily, scuff so many holes in his shoes?

'I don't know why you allow it. There's no telling what she'll get up to, out until all hours.'

To save herself answering, Edna sucked the end of the wool and concentrated on threading the needle.

Frances, who'd been twiddling the nob through the stations, finally found some music and with a sly grin, turned it up to full volume.

Gran put her fingers in her ears. 'For gawd's sake, do we have to have that jungle music?' she shouted.

Frances looked across to her mother.

'Turn it off, love.'

Frances sighed, but did as she was told then into the silence said, 'As a matter of fact I ain't been to the pictures, we couldn't get in. Norman took me to a dance instead.'

'See what I mean!' Nan was triumphant. Her grand-daughter had fulfilled her worst prophecies.

'And that's not all.' Frances produced the notes with the flourish of a magician whipping a rabbit from a hat. 'Look what I got.'

Dad let his paper fall in surprise. Edna leaned forward to examine the money. 'Blimey, where'd you get that from?'

'Did you find it?' her dad asked. 'If you did, someone will be looking for it, so you'd better take it down to the police station straight away.'

'No, I earned it, it's mine, every single penny.'

'What did I tell you, up to no good,' Maud Atkins interjected darkly from her corner of the room.

'Don't look so worried, Dad, I came by it honestly.' Frances handed a pound note to her mother and one to her father. 'That's for you and there's more to come.'

'More to come?' Dad held the pound note gingerly between his thumb and forefinger.

'As I said, me and Norman couldn't get in the flicks so we went dancin' at the Rex instead. They had a singing contest, I went in for it and won.' She paused, waiting for their reaction.

Her father's face broke into a smile and he pulled her down on his lap and ruffled her hair affectionately. 'Good for you, lass. I always said you had a voice which you shouldn't be shy of using, now didn't I?'

'Johnny Doakes, he's the band leader, says if I sing with 'is band on Saturday nights he'll pay me a pound a week.'

'A pound?' repeated Edna, trying to work out how many pairs of socks that would buy for Roy.

'Now hold on a minute,' said Tom Henderson. 'You're only fifteen.'

'I'm sixteen in October,' Frances reminded him.

'Still too young to go singing in dance halls.'

'Dens of iniquity,' muttered Nan like a Greek chorus.

Frances stared at her father in dismay. 'But think of the money. It's more than Mr Jacobs pays me in a fortnight!' She turned with pleading eyes to her mother.

'The money would be a help, Tom,' said Edna eyeing the pile of mending.

'Edna, she's far too young and in that line of business

98

you've got to know how to look after yourself. Musicians get up to all sorts of tricks, they smoke too much and drink too much and it's not a healthy life. Take my word for it.'

'One night a week wouldn't hurt, Dad,' Frances pleaded. 'And what will I tell Johnny Doakes?'

Relenting a little, her father answered, 'Tell him we'll discuss it again when you're eighteen.'

'Eighteen?' Frances wailed. 'That's years away.'

'What's years away?' Gloria stood framed in the doorway smiling and as the family turned, over her shoulder they saw a tall man with greying hair and a wary expression, whom none of them recognized. With pride of ownership, Gloria pulled him forward. 'This is Walter, everyone, and we're going to be married,' she announced and so there would be no doubt she waved her left hand on which a ring sparkled.

Uncertain of his reception, Walter stood there, his face stiff and defensive while they all stared at him. Then into the stunned silence, Nan's voice rang out, shrill and accusing. 'And what's poor Harry gonna say about this, that's what I'd like to know, you baggage you!'

Gloria stared back at them with a white, stricken face, then wailing, 'I don't know!' she threw herself down in a chair and burst into loud anguished sobs.

9

At twelve-thirty sharp on Saturdays all work ceased at Pennywise Assurance. Phones stopped ringing, memos which a minute before had been in need of urgent attention were slung into trays, desks were cleared, typewriters covered and by twenty to one the building looked like an abandoned ship. The girls in the typing pool, eager to taste the weekend's pleasures, grabbed their handbags, called to their supervisor, 'Have a nice weekend, Miss Yeo,' then clattered off down the stairs in their high-heeled shoes.

That is, everyone except Kitty and Rose. For the girls had got into the habit of going to an occasional matinee together, and it was important they looked their best for their afternoon at the theatre.

'Time's getting on, so we'd better decide pretty quickly what we're going to see,' said Kitty, when they reached the cloakroom.

'Hold on a sec, I must go to the lav, I'm bursting,' answered Rose, and shot into a toilet.

'I don't know about you, but I really fancy *Love on the Dole*,' Kitty called to her friend over the partition.

The chain was pulled, Rose came out, ran water into a basin, soaped her hands and pretended to consider her friend's choice. Finally she answered, 'I've heard *Night Must Fall* is heaps better.'

'Really?' Kitty sounded surprised.

Rose, who was rather grateful that out of all the girls in the typing pool Kitty had chosen her as a friend, was usually inclined to fall in with her wishes. However today she'd set her heart on seeing Emlyn Williams and didn't intend to give in without a fight. 'Tell you what, why don't we toss for it?' she suggested.

'Oh all right,' said Kitty, a touch reluctantly.

'It's the fairest way, isn't it, if we can't agree?' Rose's tone was placatory for she didn't want to upset her friend. But that's what she noticed about pretty girls: not satisfied with all the advantages nature had provided, they expected their own way too. Well, an occasional disappointment did no harm, Rose decided as she hunted around in her purse for a coin. She found a penny and was about to tell Kitty to call, when the cloakroom door was thumped vigorously.

'I should get a move on in there, or it'll be two young ladies locked in the lavatory, and for the whole weekend,' the caretaker called jovially.

'Ooh, don't lock us in,' they giggled, and gathering up their belongings the two girls raced down the stairs. They'd reached the last flight when the lift doors opened and Kitty saw, with a missed heartbeat, Robert Travis follow Sir Sidney Travis and a young woman into the main hall. The woman was no mere underling either, for she was wearing a severe but beautifully cut dress, which Kitty, who had an eye for such things, knew was haute couture.

Sir Sidney, stern and lantern-jawed, was well over six foot and his height was emphasized by the top hat and tail coat he invariably wore. They paused to talk and out of deference, staff skirted around the small group and Kitty saw the young woman laugh at something Robert said, then touch his arm in a rather familiar manner.

The dart of jealousy she felt surprised even Kitty and, wondering if it was possibly his wife, she nudged Rose.

'Who's that woman?'

'Miss Alice, Sir Sidney's daughter. His only child since the accident.'

Although it happened well before her time, like everyone else in the firm Kitty knew the story, the tragedy of Sir Sidney's only son, being groomed to take over the firm but overturning his small sports car on a wild rocky coast road in Cornwall and plunging to his death in the sea.

The two friends crossed the hall and pushed through the doors into September sunshine. Sir Sidney's black and yellow Rolls Royce waited at the curb and his chauffeur Percy, smart in brown livery, stood to attention, ready to leap and open the door the moment his employer stepped out on to the pavement.

As they walked past, Rose called, 'Hello, Perce,' and gave him a friendly wave. But the chauffeur stared straight ahead with a stony expression.

'What's wrong with our Perce?' asked Kitty.

'I got fed up with being made use of and told him where to go, so he took my advice and turned his attention elsewhere. It's one of the telephonists at the moment, so I hear.'

'Never mind, there are more fish in the sea.'

'For the likes of you, maybe, but not me. But I have got my pride and he likes a few strings to his bow. I want a chap I can rely on, someone who really likes me. Is that too much to ask?' Rose appealed to her friend.

'It shouldn't be,' answered Kitty, who'd always wondered why Rose hadn't set her sights a bit higher than a chauffeur, even if Percy was a good source of gossip. 'But never mind about men, tell me about Miss Alice, I've never seen her here before.'

'I've heard on the grapevine that she's decided she wants to come in to the firm and learn the business.'

'What, and take over eventually?'

'Probably.'

'But a woman can't do that.'

Rose looked at her strangely. 'Why not?'

Kitty shrugged. Indeed, why not, although amongst the staff it was assumed that Robert was heir apparent, and if he had been led to think so too, he wouldn't care to know a woman might be coming in to steal his position.

While they waited for a bus Rose tossed the penny, Kitty

called heads and lost. '*Night Must Fall* it is, then,' said Rose, trying not to sound too pleased with herself, 'and here's a bus going to the Strand.'

The bus was so crowded the girls were forced to separate, Rose staying downstairs, Kitty going on the top deck. Staring out of the window, she mulled over what Rose had just told her. If Miss Alice did come into the firm, as the boss's daughter she would certainly have her own private secretary. Kitty wasn't sure how she'd feel working for a woman, but if the job came up she would apply for it, she decided, although for the time being, she would keep her plan under her hat.

'Aldwych.' The conductor's voice brought her out of her reverie, and Kitty tore down the stairs and leapt off just as the bus started to move away.

'Idiot, ringing the bell like that, I could have broken my neck.'

'Well you didn't, so come on, we want to get a decent seat. Emlyn Williams is supposed to be really sinister,' said Rose, and arms linked, the two girls made their way round the Aldwych and up into Catherine Street to the Duchess Theatre.

Having found out that the play started at two-thirty, they paid their sixpence for a stool, got a numbered ticket in return, then, assured of a place in the queue for the gods, decided to look for somewhere to eat.

'Let's try Covent Garden,' suggested Rose. 'There are plenty of cheap caffs there.'

But walking through the market had its hazards. Tomatoes and oranges squelched underfoot; baskets of rosy red apples just up from Kent were set down on the ground like booby traps; sacks of Lincolnshire cabbages, potatoes and onions, were piled one on top of the other and leaned like the Tower of Pisa; rough wooden boxes of bananas with 'West Indies' stamped on the lids threatened to ladder their stockings. Then all the time porters, pulling overloaded barrows, yelled at them, 'Mind yer backs, ladies,' so that they hardly knew which way to jump. Kitty didn't care for the language either, it offended her ears to hear flower girls cursing and haggling over prices with the wholesalers. Once the women had made their purchase, they'd divide the flowers into smaller posies, then with them prettily displayed in their wicker baskets, they would find a busy pitch like Eros or St Paul's and, with luck, some gullible young men keen to impress their girlfriends.

Unlike most people, Kitty, with her fastidious nature, didn't find Covent Garden colourful and interesting. To her it was just noisy and vulgar, and the stink of horse muck and decaying vegetables really turned her stomach. But what she disliked most of all was the way they were continuously chi-iked and whistled at by the porters.

Taking it in good part, Rose giggled, but it infuriated Kitty. 'I don't know why you laugh, Rose,' she admonished her friend. 'It just makes me feel cheap.'

'The time to worry is the day you stop getting wolf whistles, love,' answered Rose, a pleasant-looking, good-natured girl who had to fight plumpness and who wasn't in the least jealous of her friend's beauty. She was happy that Kitty was the bright star, she the satellite, and settled for the extra attention from men she enjoyed in Kitty's company.

'Gotta kiss for us then, girls?' a young man lounging with a group of his workmates called out to them, and thinking him no end of a cheeky fellow, his friends laughed.

'Oafs,' muttered Kitty, and having had enough of this attention, without checking first as to its suitability, she pushed Rose through the door of the next café they came to.

Although a menu on the wall offered a choice of hot pies, faggots and sausage and mash, they knew they'd made a mistake as soon as they crossed the threshold. A fly paper hung from a bare light bulb, a large woman in a gravy-stained overall stood guard over a steaming tea urn and on a plate lay a few curling cheese sandwiches on which all the flies of Covent Garden appeared to be eating their fill.

Kitty glanced at Rose, saw her face and muttered, 'Let's go.' But as they turned to leave the proprietress called in an ingratiating tone, 'What can I get you young ladies?'

Losing their nerve, the friends sat down. 'Just tea, I think,' Rose called over to her.

'Nothing to eat? A nice cheese sandwich, perhaps?' she suggested.

'No thanks. A fly sandwich, more like it,' Kitty muttered.

'Righty-o, ladies.' Cheerful in spite of her lack of trade, the woman came shuffling round the counter in carpet slippers so hairy and dirty they looked like two dead dogs. Placing two thick white cracked cups of tarry tea in front of the girls, she smiled at them. 'Enjoy it,' she ordered and went back to her position behind the counter.

Kitty took a sip and wrinkled her nose, for it was heavily laced with condensed milk. 'This is disgusting,' she muttered, resenting the fact that she was wasting good money on something almost undrinkable.

'Never mind,' said Rose, 'let's treat ourselves to poached egg on toast at the Corner House after the theatre. It's more expensive but at least it's clean. Anyway,' she went on, 'tell us about your job search. How many months has it been?'

'Four,' Kitty admitted reluctantly. Four months of coolness between her and Robert, four months of tramping hot pavements in her dinner hour and being interviewed in small, mean offices where the wages offered were almost half of what she was earning now.

'Nothing doing, then?'

'Seems not.'

Rose sighed. 'We live in hard times.'

'I've signed on at an agency, though,' Kitty answered, determined to remain optimistic in spite of these set-backs.

'Frankly I can't understand why you want to leave Pennywise. Yo-Yo's not a bad old stick, the money's reasonable and you'd be lucky to find a better firm to work for.'

'I want to be a private secretary, don't you?'

'Yeah, but I'm prepared to wait for a vacancy to come up at Pennywise.'

'For how long?'

Rose shrugged. 'Until I'm twenty. Twenty-two perhaps.'

'Where's your ambition, Rose?' Kitty admonished sternly. She'd never let on to her friend about her true motives for wanting to leave, and anyway, as she guessed would happen, Robert Travis soon got fed up with Olive Dawson's sloppy attitude, her typing errors and inability to read her own shorthand, and in a couple of days she was sent packing. The next girl was none too particular about her hygiene and, trying hard not to feel smug, Kitty had watched and waited. Within four days she was back in his office with her shorthand pad and several well-sharpened pencils. However, never once did Robert Travis relax into informality, neither did he allude to their conversation in the gardens, so that sometimes Kitty found herself wondering if she'd actually imagined it.

'My real ambition if you want to know is to find a husband, give up work and have some babies,' Kitty heard Rose reply to her question.

'Well we all want that, don't we?' said Kitty, although she wasn't so sure about motherhood. 'What I'd like in the meantime is a little bed-sit of my own, convenient to work. But I need to earn more.'

'Would your parents let you move out?'

Kitty looked surprised. 'I can't see how they can stop me. I'm eighteen in January, it's cramped at home, and I'm fed up with sharing a bedroom. There's my aunt moping about undecided about whether she should marry Walter or go on putting up with Harry and I've a sister who's convinced she'd be as famous as Gracie Fields if it wasn't for Dad. It's hard, I can tell you, and there's not a moment's privacy. It's all right for you, you're an only child.'

'It's not all right for me, not with Mum widowed and dependent on me.'

'Perhaps we could get a room together,' suggested Kitty. 'It would be a bit cheaper.'

Rose cupped her chin on her hand and looked wistful. 'I'd really love that, but Mum would have one of her turns if I even suggested it.'

Kitty had heard about these 'turns', how if Mrs Mumford was crossed in any way, her whole body would shake so violently she would have to be put to bed and the doctor called. 'Life's not easy is it?' she said, staring down at her tea with its brown puddle of scum. She made a face and pushed it away. 'Come on, we'd better pay for this bilge-water and go.'

The play was atmospheric and Emlyn Williams, both sinister and charming, had everyone on the edge of their seats. What with the hard benches and everyone squeezed up thigh to thigh, the only advantage of sitting in the gods was the price, so the girls were glad to get up and stretch their legs during the interval. In the stalls tea and biscuits could be ordered and, looking down, Kitty watched harassed usherettes hurrying up and down the aisles with trays. 'Do you think we'll ever be able to afford that?' she asked Rose, because it seemed to her like the epitome of luxury, tea on your lap in the interval.

'What you and me have got to do, duckie, is find ourselves rich husbands, then we can have whatever we want.'

'At least I'd dress better than that dowdy bunch,' said Kitty casting a critical eye over the matinee audience.

The interval bell went, usherettes started collecting the trays so that rattling tea-cups wouldn't disturb the actors, and people began drifting back to their seats. The girls were about to return to their own places when Rose nudged Kitty and hissed, 'Do you see who I see? Robert Travis, and with a different woman this time. My he gets around.'

'Where?'

'Down there in the stalls, six rows back. Just getting into their seats.'

Rashly sacrificing sixpence, Kitty purchased the use of some opera glasses and trained them on the woman. The lenses were poor, but she had sufficient time before the auditorium lights were lowered to see that she was a true beauty. Kitty was comfortable enough with her own looks not to envy many women, but this girl was outstanding – in a class of her own. And the small intimate gestures, the special way in which Robert Travis guided her to her seat, his arm protectively round her shoulder, demonstrated to Kitty that the young woman was his wife. Not in a hundred years would a man with a wife of such astonishing beauty look elsewhere, it would hardly be worth his while. A conclusion that for some reason made Kitty feel unutterably depressed.

10

The flat faced west and briefly, like the headlights of a car, the setting sun's rays pierced the grey cloud, illuminating Imogen's auburn hair and creating a glorious, golden nimbus of light. Then it was gone and shadows quickly invaded the corniced, high-ceilinged room, making the Victorian furniture his wife preferred to the more fashionable sharp-angled chrome, seem oppressively heavy. Just like life really, thought Robert, a few sunlit days, the rest all shadow. In a sombre, reflective mood, he leaned his head against the wingback chair and tried to listen to the Chopin étude Imogen was playing. But much as he struggled to concentrate on the music his thoughts always returned to Kitty.

Except for the occasional urge to reach out and lightly stroke the peach-like down on her forearm and feel her warm skin through his fingertips, in the structured atmosphere of the office he managed to keep his sexual itch under control. But that unexpected glimpse of her today at the theatre had thrown him off course and he recognized a symptom which, if he didn't control it, could develop into a full-blown, perhaps fatal sickness. Kitty wasn't the sort of girl to sell herself cheap so she'd be a virgin, he bet any money on it. Indulging himself, Robert allowed his thoughts to drift into a dangerous erotic domain where he'd been given access to that wonderful body and he was lying between those long legs, gently caressing her into a response. Breathing a little erratically, Robert closed his eyes. Oh, how they would make love!

There was flourish of chords as the music reached its climax and, disturbed from his fantasy, Robert gave a guilty start and opened his eyes. Aware of the effect these lustful thoughts were having on his body, he quickly crossed his legs. Robert sighed. That was how it must remain between him and Kitty, a vague ache in the groin. If he tried, he could probably woo and win her, but he wasn't a cad, he had his responsibilities and it wasn't worth the all-round unhappiness it would cause. He'd made his bed, such as it was, and he must lie on it; and there was always a chance that things could improve between him and Imogen.

Robert glanced across at his wife. She never seemed to feel the heat, neither did she make any concessions to fashion. Tonight she wore a dress of green crushed velvet with long sleeves that went into a point over the back of each hand. Just as her clothes were very much part of her own unique style, so what Imogen chose to play was a reflection of the mood she was in. On bad days it might be music she'd composed herself, jarring, dissonant sounds lacking in harmony, but which he had to pretend to like. Tonight, though, there was no hint of inner turmoil as she went on to play a cheerful mazurka. He watched her fingers, fascinated by the natural ease and fluency with which she manipulated the keys, and thought about might-have-beens. Thought how if things had been different, she could have had a career as a concert pianist. Certainly the talent was there, and with the graceful flowing movements of her body, the long curve of her white throat and her auburn hair which she refused to have cut, she would have charmed any audience. As she'd charmed him that first time he'd set eyes on her. Bewitched him, almost.

The music finished, but with the resonance of it still in her head, Imogen sat quietly, her hands resting on her lap. But only for a moment, then she stood up, went and switched on a lamp, took a cigarette from a silver box, lit it with a matching lighter and began pacing the room.

'Play something else, darling,' Robert urged.

With an edgy gesture she stubbed out her barely smoked

cigarette and turned to face him. 'I've played enough for one evening. Can't we go out?'

Imogen was inclined to be careless with her cigarettes and noticing the tip still glowing in the ashtray, Robert rose to extinguish it, pressing the end between his fingers. 'But we've just been to the theatre, darling,' he protested. Taking a handkerchief from his pocket he wiped his hands clean. 'And we're too late now for an evening performance.'

'We could go to Soho, have a meal.'

'We had dinner less than an hour ago.' In fact Mrs Webb who came in every day to cook and clean, had only just washed up and gone.

'So we have ... Robert.' Imogen swung round to face him.

'Yes, darling.'

'When can we move? This flat, these four walls really get me down. I feel stifled by it sometimes.' She pressed her fingers against her white throat. 'I'm creative, my soul craves for light, a garden, flowers, trees.'

'There are some houses going up in Finchley. We could take a run out and have look at them tomorrow if you like. I could about afford the deposit.'

'Do you mean live in suburbia? In a horrible little semi-detached, with common neighbours? Good heavens, Robert, what do you take me for?' Imogen shuddered. 'No, I mean a house like Angela and Bruce's, somewhere in the country.'

Robert sighed and silently berated Great Aunt Bertha for bringing up her niece with such a unrealistic notion of what she was entitled to in life. 'Darling, I'm not in a position to buy a house of that size and maintain it, I don't earn Bruce's sort of money, you know that. And there's Mother as well, I have to help her out, and she hasn't learnt to stop being extravagant yet.'

'Well when will you start earning a decent salary?'

'Considering I haven't been with the firm five minutes and I'm still learning, I actually think I'm quite well paid.'

'But you're a relative. Speak to Sir Sidney, ask for a rise.'

'No. He's been generous enough to my family. It was good of him to take me on in the first place. If I get anywhere in the firm I want it to be on merit and because I know how to do my job.'

'What about when he retires? He's got no son to take over from him.'

'His daughter Alice is coming into the firm. I was speaking to her today. Perhaps he intends to groom her to run the business.'

'Nonsense!'

'Well I don't mind admitting, I do have hopes of something better eventually, perhaps a directorship, but it never does to assume.'

Imogen drummed her fingers along her arm and in these restless movements Robert saw danger. Taking her hand, he led her back to the piano.

'Play for me, please.'

'Oh all right, what would you like?' Imogen sat down.

'Play some Schumann. "Scenes from Childhood".'

Her rapid mood changes still astonished Robert. She smiled and her face became gentle and dreamy. 'Do you remember?'

'Of course I do, how could I ever forget, my sweet?'

'You must kiss me first, Robert, then I will play for you.'

Beguiling him in that childlike way of hers, she lifted her face and, obedient to her command, he bent and kissed her. But his mouth wasn't allowed to linger on her lips. Turning away, she found the piece she wanted and started to play. Robert poured himself a whisky and soda and sat down again and the music was so evocative of other times, other places that he found his mind drifting back into the past and the twists and turns of fate that led up to that day of their first meeting.

*   *   *

Although he never dwelt on it, Robert was aware enough of the rest of the world's ills to realize that, compared with most people, he had led a privileged life. That he was also blessed with good health and intelligence, he considered a bonus. Home had been a large, solid ivy-covered Victorian house in Kent. In the way of upper middle-class children he and his sister Clare saw little of their parents. Father went up to the City most days and Mother's social calendar seemed too full for her to have much time to spare for her son and daughter. But he and Clare were happy. They had a large garden in which to roam, a doting nanny and later an equally kind governess. When Robert was cruelly wrenched from this paradise and sent away to boarding school, it was Clare and the governess he wept to leave, not his parents.

The first and greatest tragedy of his life was his beloved sister's death at sixteen of meningitis. Clare had been his closest friend and confidante and, only eighteen himself, Robert was almost annihilated by grief. By then he was a fresher at Cambridge, but academically the year was a disaster. He was in his second year and trying hard to pull himself together, when a telegram arrived that would change his life irrevocably. *Regret your father has passed on. Please come home immediately. Mother.*

Stunned, Robert packed. He arrived home to be greeted by a hysterical mother and the news that his father had gone up to his office as usual, locked the door and rather messily blown out his brains, bequeathing them nothing but vast debts from reckless speculations on the stock market.

It was like Troy falling and his known comfortable world collapsed about him with a terrible and dramatic suddenness. There he was, at one moment never having given a thought to money – and the next facing destitution.

All his mother was permitted to keep were her clothes. Everything else, furs, jewellery, porcelain, silver, pictures, furniture, was auctioned. Those were a miserable two days. Robert resented strangers tramping over his house, picking over their belongings like vultures and he stood in a corner and glared at them with loathing.

But there was one item of furniture which Robert was determined to salvage: the piano on which he and Clare had learned to play. So he borrowed the money from a friend and recklessly bid for it without knowing when he would be able to repay his debt.

His mother wasn't pleased. 'Why,' she asked in a petulant voice, 'if you had money to squander, did you waste it on that? You could have just as easily bid for my escritoire.'

'Because I want at least one memory of Clare, Mother, and surely you do too.'

'Yes of course. My lovely Clare, my lovely house, my lovely furs. How can I stand it?' she wailed in her breathy child's voice and broke down in tears.

Robert put an arm round her shoulder, awkwardly trying to comfort her.

'And how could your father have been so cruel as to do this to me. It was so thoughtless,' she sobbed.

'Don't cry, Mother, I'll look after you,' Robert promised.

'Will you, darling?' She gazed up at him with hope. Her eyes were red and swollen and her make-up was disintegrating under the onslaught of her tears. Usually so careful about her appearance, she looked dreadful now and he pitied her. After all was it really his mother's fault she was self-centred and vain? That was the way she'd been brought up and she'd always depended on looks rather than intellect. It was unlikely she would change.

That afternoon they stood and sadly watched the last pantechnicon move off down the drive, then went back to the dreary furnished house he'd managed to rent in Tunbridge Wells. Only nineteen, Robert matured quickly in those weeks following his father's death, for it soon became evident that his mother was going to make little effort to adapt to her new life. Lighting the gas, making a cup of tea, seemed tasks well beyond her capabilities. Unless she

114

remarried he had to accept that his mother would always be financially dependent on him. At his most despondent, Robert did often pause to wonder who would employ him, for he had no professional qualifications and was without any manual skills.

However amidst all this gloom there was one piece of very good news. It came in a letter via the solicitor while they were having breakfast; some of mother's burnt toast, spread sparingly with margarine.

'What is it mother?' Robert asked, for her expression was more animated than he'd seen it in weeks.

Stella Travis replaced the cup in the saucer. 'Listen to this, darling. "Dear Mrs Travis, Sir Sidney Travis, a second cousin of your late husband, wants it to be known that he has heard of your tragic loss and offers his condolences. Your considerably reduced circumstances have also been brought to his notice. Therefore, feeling a responsibility towards you as a member of the family, he wishes, without intruding on your grief, to purchase a house on your behalf, furnish it and offer you an allowance of three hundred pounds per annum." '

She looked up, did a calculation and said, 'Three hundred pounds – that's not enough to live on.'

'Mother!' Robert rebuked her sharply. 'How could you say such a thing?'

'Well it's true.'

'It's a darn sight more than you have now, so just be grateful.'

'Oh I am. But he wouldn't have missed double that amount.'

'It's still a kind act, and he needn't have bothered.'

'I agree. But as your mother, I hope I may be permitted to say that after what I've been used to, it will be hard to manage.'

'It's harder where there's none.' But his mother turned away from brutal truths and although Robert knew he'd never break through that carapace of selfishness, it still irritated him. 'Anyway, who is this second cousin of Father's?'

'Daddy spoke of him sometimes, although the families were never close. He's rich as Croesus apparently, is chairman of a large insurance company in the City and bought his title off Lloyd George. And that's about as much as I know. I'll have to write, of course, and thank him. Should I mention you're looking for work, dear?'

'Certainly not. When I get a job, it will be on my own merits and not because I'm a relative. He's more than fulfilled his duties already.' Although to Robert these handouts smacked of charity, he knew he was in no position to have too many scruples. There was his mother's welfare to consider, and although he'd been diligent in his search for employment, so far he'd failed to find anything, even of the most menial nature.

But one thing Sir Sidney's generosity did give Robert and that was time. While his mother busied herself househunting he took himself off to London and very quickly found a position in a West End showroom as a secondhand car salesman. His mother was horrified, of course, but Robert didn't care; it was work, and work, he discovered, for which he had a natural talent. The old school tie and accent helped, but very quickly he was earning enough commission to rent rooms in London, repay his debts and send a bit home to his still extravagant mother.

Robert also discovered that selling cars brought with it unexpected bonuses. For when wealthy men-about-town sauntered into the showroom, they often had on their arm some dazzling young creature they wished to impress. Robert would explain the merits of the car the man was interested in, then offer to take the couple for a test drive. The first time a young woman came back to the showroom on her own, he was naïve enough to believe her when she leaned against a Hispano-Suiza and said, stroking the bodywork, 'Daddy's thinking of buying me one for my birthday, but I would like to try it out first, so will you take me for a spin?'

But it was more than a spin they went on that day, and that was how Robert came to be initiated into those most enjoyable of diversions: girls, sex, nightclubs and drink.

Robert couldn't credit his good luck when he discovered how sexually free many young women were, and the drink they consumed astonished him. Most of them had rich, indulgent fathers, which enabled them to dance the night away, then sleep until noon. But he needed to have his wits about him and after five years he began to detect an emptiness beneath the frenetic activity. A more permanent relationship was what he was looking for, so he was ready for Imogen that first time he saw her.

He'd been invited to a weekend house-party and he drove through dappled Surrey lanes in his yellow sports car, happily anticipating the weekend ahead: tennis, swimming, cocktails and dancing, finishing off the night in the bed of any one of the half-dozen girls he knew would be there.

Robert was the first to arrive, and his hostess, Angela North, greeted him with a rapturous kiss. 'Darling, lovely to see you, but I'll have to leave you to entertain yourself for a while. One of Bruce's ghastly aunts and a niece have turned up unexpectedly. Lots of airs and graces and quick to boast about the family tree, but poor as church mice. Working is beneath their dignity but scrounging isn't. Anyway, I've got to try and persuade them to move on or they'll put a right damper on our fun and games over the weekend.' She pulled a face. 'They're rather straitlaced, you know. But come what may there'll be drinkies on the terrace at midday.'

The house, he knew, had been built by Lutyens, the lovely drifting garden, with its patterned brick footpaths designed by Gertrude Jekyll. Robert's room was at the back and he went and leaned out of the window. Recently London had been insufferably hot, but here roses and honeysuckle intertwined and climbed the wall and he inhaled their warm scents with indolent pleasure. Below him two gardeners tended the herbaceous borders, further to the left there was a tennis court and swimming pool. No shortage of money here, decided Robert, and wondered what Bruce did for a living. One thing was certain, selling cars would never bring him this sort of life-style. But never mind, he was young and today life seemed pretty enjoyable. He also felt hot and dusty after his journey, and the swimming pool was clean, empty and inviting. Moving away from the window Robert quickly changed into swimming trunks, ran through the cool house, plunged straight into the pool and swam thirty lengths.

He was stretched out in a deck chair, eyes closed and drying off in the sun, when he became aware of a piano being played somewhere in the house. Raising his head he listened. Haunting and lyrical, the music carried with it memories of Clare, for it was a piece she had often played. But although it was tantalizingly familiar, he couldn't put a name to it. Enticed by the liquid beauty of the playing, he tied himself into a bathrobe and went in search of the music.

It was her long auburn hair he saw first, for Imogen sat with her back to him. Intrigued Robert moved round to see if the face did justice to the lovely head of hair. It did. She must have known he was there, but she went on playing with serene indifference to her audience. He didn't mind because it gave him a chance to study her: the pale face, slender nose, small mouth and large dark eyes. What struck him most forcibly, though, was her stillness. She seemed so different from the boisterous, long-legged, suntanned girls of his acquaintance. In fact she reminded him of a fey medieval maiden, the sort found in paintings with turreted castles and by her side a white unicorn wearing a jewelled collar.

She played the final chords, looked up at him and smiled. 'Hello.' The voice was low and melodious.

'Hello. Hope I'm not intruding. My name's Robert Travis.'

She stood up and he noticed the dress she was wearing was slightly old-fashioned. Later he would discover that this was the mode of dress she favoured, usually in crushed velvet or antique lace. 'I'm Imogen D'arcy,' she said and held out cool, long-boned fingers to him.

'May I ask what that music was?' Robert asked, already bewitched.

'*Kinderszenen* by Schumann.'

'Ah yes,' he said, remembering. ' "Scenes from Childhood". You play well.'

'Thank you, but I was just practising. I shall probably be called upon to play for my supper later tonight.'

'Oh, why's that?' asked Robert, puzzled.

'Well you see my Great Aunt Bertha and I are here on sufferance. Aunt Angela doesn't care for poor people, they make her feel uneasy.'

So that was who she was. One of the penurious relatives Angela obviously hadn't succeeded in getting rid of. 'Well there's a lot of us about these days. I'm pretty poor myself, although I do have a job.'

'Great Aunt Bertha would never allow me earn my own living. What is it she says?' Imitating her aunt, she lowered her voice. ' "No one in the D'arcy family has ever dipped a hand in the muddied waters of the commercial world and you will do so over my dead body, Imogen." So there you have it, although I might add that my aunt sees no conflict in enjoying its benefits.' Imogen made a sweeping gesture that encompassed the house and grounds.

He laughed. 'I'm with your aunt there. I enjoy them too. And look, people are having pre-luncheon drinks on the terrace – shall we join them?'

Quiet without being shy, Imogen was so different, so completely herself, that for the rest of the weekend Robert never moved far from her side. He'd been fond of many of the girls he went around with, without loving any of them.

Imogen was an entirely different matter. She captivated him totally and by the Sunday afternoon he'd made several important decisions. Imogen, with her beauty, deserved better than the life of penny-pinching poverty she had with her aunt. However, his present salary, although it kept him comfortably, was inadequate for a married man. The job also lacked status. Great Aunt Bertha, with her undivided bosom and the lorgnette through which she viewed the modern world and its goings-on with thorough disapproval, would never countenance a marriage between her niece and a mere car salesman, and a secondhand one at that. So Robert resolved that as soon as he returned to London, he would put his pride in abeyance and write and ask Sir Sidney Travis if there was a position for him within the firm. If he was fortunate and the answer was yes, he would then ask Imogen to marry him.

Of course it could have slipped their minds, but no one, neither Great Aunt Bertha, Angela nor Bruce, bothered to mention the family habit of cousin marrying cousin. In particular, no one bothered to mention the illness.

11

Apart from the extended hand of an occasional down-and-out seeking enough for oblivion in a bottle of meths, and a horse with its nose in a bag of oats, there was a dinner-hour lull to the streets and few people about. So when Frances, in her usual hurry to get back to work, felt her arm being grabbed and a male voice in her ear demanding, 'Hey, where've you been all my life?' she spun round with an angry scowl.

'You being fresh or something?' she snapped at the young man, her tone making it clear she was no cheap tart any man could pick up.

'Eh . . . no of course not.' As if seared by hot coals, he let his hand fall. 'It *is* Frances, isn't it?'

Frances eyed him warily. 'Yes, that's me.'

'What a relief, I thought I'd got the wrong girl for a minute. Don't you remember me? Paul Harding. The pianist with Johnny Doakes' band.'

'Oh yeah, I do now. The singing contest at the Rex.'

'Why did you never come back? We looked out for you every week. And people kept asking about you, wanting to know when you were going to sing again? It went on like that for ages.'

'Did it?' Frances grew a little taller. 'I wanted to come, I really did, but it was me dad, he wouldn't let me.'

'Why ever not?'

'There were lots of different reasons.' Frances flapped her hand vaguely, but she remembered how she'd pleaded with her father for a week, trying to wear him down with tears and argument and the promise of money. But he'd remained adamant.

'So what were these reasons?' Paul persisted.

'He says I'm too young, an' he thinks I'll be led astray.'

'Who by?'

'Well if you want to know, you lot in the band.'

Paul, amused by her manner, laughed. 'We're not demons, you know. Anyway, how old are you if you don't mind me asking?'

'Sixteen.' Frances had had her birthday the previous week and she announced it with pride. And, something she'd almost despaired of happening, at last she'd started her monthlies and she was equally proud of that. Now she was a fully fledged woman. Even her bosoms were growing. Thirty-four inches when last measured, instead of a measly thirty-two. A couple more inches and she'd have caught up with Kitty.

'So when would he consider it safe to let you join us reprobates?'

'He said he'll think about it when I'm eighteen.'

Paul shook his head at her dad's puritanical attitude. All that talent being wasted. She was such an ordinary little thing and yet that voice of hers had haunted him for days afterwards. 'You could have been earning yourself some good money, too.'

'You don't have to tell me, I know,' answered Frances in a depressed voice and thinking wistfully of all the dresses and hair-dos she was being deprived of.

'What does your pa think we'll do, cart you off to opium dens in Limehouse or something?'

Frances giggled. 'Or sell me into white slavery.'

'Johnny likes the ladies, all right, but he never mixes business with pleasure, so you're safe on that score. And the other blokes have all got wives.'

'What about you? Have you got one?' Frances asked, because although it was difficult to put an age to him he was probably old enough to be married.

Paul looked surprised. 'Me? Good heavens no. I've got

too many plans for myself to want to be saddled with a wife. I'm going to be a songwriter.'

Impressed, Frances asked, 'What sort of songs?'

He shrugged. 'You know, popular ones.' He rarely admitted his ambition to anyone and was already wishing he'd kept his mouth shut, for so far his success rate was nil. He spent every free moment composing and writing lyrics, regularly hawked his work round music publishers in Denmark Street and just as regularly it was rejected. Only an ocasional 'Keep trying, lad' had stopped him from giving up entirely. 'Perhaps one day I'll write one for you,' he suggested.

'That would be nice,' answered Frances, humouring him, but not believing a word he said.

Even as he suggested it, Paul could hear the melody forming in his head and that lovely voice interpreting it. He had to get home and get the notes down before he lost the tune again. 'This is my bus coming,' he said abruptly and held out his hand to wave it down. He jumped on and as the bus pulled away from the kerb called back to her, 'Now remember, if you do change your mind, Johnny – and me too – would be very pleased to see you.'

Although she told herself she didn't take him seriously, Frances still tried to imagine what sort of song Paul might write for her, and it occupied her thoughts all the way to work and at any spare moment during the afternoon. Mr Jacobs didn't go to the synagogue but he kept the Jewish Sabbath for his mother's sake, so Fridays tended to follow a similar pattern, with the shop usually closing early. They could always count on a few last-minute customers, but today at five Mr Jacobs called to her, 'No interruptions please, Frances,' and went into the back to count the takings.

Knowing the sooner she finished the sooner she would get her wages and go home, Frances got a bucket and mop and started washing the floor. Paul's flattering remarks had put her in a cheerful frame of mind and she began to sing, giving full vent to her strong voice and waving the wet mop like a conductor's baton. Finally Mr Jacobs put his head round the door.

'Sing, alvays you sing, Frances, you should be on the stage. But please a little quiet while I do my books.'

'Sorry, Mr Jacobs.' Chastened, Frances clamped her mouth firmly shut. She waited until her employer's door closed again, then leaning on the mop handle, she thought, he's right, I should be on the stage, and it's only Dad with his old-fashioned ideas standing in my way.

She finished washing the floor and was covering it with newspaper, when an advertisement caught her eye and she bent to read it. *Why not come along to the Rex on Friday at 7.30 and dance to Johnny Doakes and his Doughboys.*

Indeed why not? She needn't let on. But she'd be going against Dad's strict orders. Frances felt a nervous fluttering in her stomach at daring to consider such a wilful act of defiance. Filling an enamel bowl with hot soapy water, she started to scrub the counter and marble cutting surfaces. But she couldn't scrub away the idea. It was heady stuff, the love and approval of an audience, and she was dying to taste it again if only for one evening. And Dad needn't find out . . . any awkward questions and she'd say Norman was taking her to the flicks.

Frances had more or less talked herself into the idea when a customer strolled into the shop and looked about him as if weighing the place up. 'Can I help you, sir?' she asked, without pausing in her task.

He stretched his mouth into a smile and his gold teeth gleamed. 'Yes, lady, you can. Who's the owner of this joint? Your old man?'

Frances shook her head. 'No, Mr Jacobs.'

'Well tell 'im I want to see 'im.'

Not caring for his tone, Frances slowly wrung out a cloth

and looked him up and down. 'Come back Monday. Mr Jacobs don't see salesmen this late.'

'I ain't selling anything.'

On closer inspection Frances could see that this must be true: he was no shiny-suited commercial traveller – the creases in his trousers were too sharp for that. Neither did he have the saleman's desperate air of bonhomie. The opposite in fact. This bloke was over-sure of himself and used to giving orders. But not to me, decided Frances. 'Mr Jacobs still can't see you.' To show she considered the matter finished with, she polished the glass top with a concentrated vigour.

He moved closer and lowered his voice. 'I don't like repeating meself, but go and fetch Mr Jacobs.'

Frances resisted stepping backwards. 'It's Friday. We're closing down for the Sabbath.'

'Oh, a Jewboy is 'e?'

Frances eyed him with instinctive dislike. Although she knew it was a remark not even worthy of a reply, she couldn't resist snapping back, 'Is that a crime, then?'

'In some countries it is. But meself, I'm a tolerant man.' He moved even nearer, thrusting his head over the counter. 'Where is 'e?'

'You heard, he ain't available.'

'He will be when 'e knows who it is.' His tone changed slightly and became almost cajoling. 'Now off you go like a good girl and tell 'im Rikki Mantoni wants ter see 'im about a little bit o' business.'

'Ri . . . Rikki Ma . . . ntoni.'

'That's the boy.' Enjoying her reaction, he smiled, but it was a chilling smile.

Frances saw Mr Jacobs in her mind's eye, all unsuspecting, sitting in the back room amongst a pile of empty cardboard boxes, counting the day's takings; separating silver, copper and paper money before locking it away in the safe for the night. Desperate now to protect her elderly employer from

this notorious villain, she stuttered, 'He . . . he's upstairs an'
. . . and I can't leave the . . .' She was still trying to finish
her sentence when Rikki shot round the counter and
grabbed the door handle.

Although he had caught her unawares, Frances lunged
after him. But she was too late and, as the door swung open,
over Rikki's shoulder she saw Mr Jacobs look up with a
startled expression. He had already bagged the coins, but
in front of him were bundles of ten shilling and one pound
notes. Frances had become confused about what was happening but when she saw the notes, she knew Rikki was
about to pull a gun and steal the money, some of it her
wages.

'No you don't,' she screamed and grabbed his arm.

Thoroughly alarmed, Mr Jacobs rose stiffly, holding on
to the edge of the table. 'Vat is going on?'

'Move, Mr Jacobs, or 'e'll kill you, he's after the money,'
she screamed.

'Silly cow, 'course I ain't. Lot a good he'd be dead.' Rikki
shook her off.

'Vat do you vant then, sir?' To give himself something to
do Mr Jacobs removed his spectacles and began polishing
the lens with a hankie. Frances noticed how his small fat
fingers trembled and she was consumed with a silent rage.

'A word in your ear, Manny.'

'My name is Izak, not Manny,' Mr Jacobs said with great
dignity. 'Not that I have given you permission to use my
first name.'

'Okay, I get you. But first of all get rid of this bint, 'cos
my hand's itchin' to give 'er one.'

'Just you try it!' Frances shot back. 'I'm not leavin' Mr
Jacobs alone wiv the likes of you.' Fierce as a lioness protecting her young she went and stood in front of her employer.

Mr Jacobs took her gently by the shoulders and moved
her away. 'I vill be okay, Frances. I do not think this gentle-
man,' his voice was heavy with irony, 'intends to murder

me. You just go upstairs and check that Mudder is all right.'

When she still didn't move, Rikki came up close to her. 'Do as yer boss says, or I'm warning you . . .' The voice was low, the mouth cruel, the meaning explicit.

'Please go, Frances. I don't vant no trouble.'

Mr Jacobs was now wiping the sweat from his forehead with the handkerchief, and she saw she wasn't helping the situation.

'All right, I'll go, but . . .' She turned to Rikki, wagging an admonishing finger at him. '. . . I'll be back, so don't try anything funny, 'cos I know who you are.'

Giving him what she hoped was an intimidating glare, Frances thumped up the dark stairs. Spared by her deafness from knowledge of what was going on below, Mrs Jacobs slept, her lace cap slightly askew and snoring gently.

Porteous, obviously in need of someone to insult did a paso doble along his perch, berated Frances in Polish, then squawked, 'Up them stairs and get yer knickers off.'

But Frances was in no mood to laugh, and hearing the shop door bang she raced back downstairs again. The notes still lay in bundles on the table, but Mr Jacobs sat slumped in a chair looking sick, old and defeated. Crouching down beside him Frances took his hand, questioning him gently. 'What happened, Mr Jacobs?'

'He vants money, lots of money every week, and he's going to send his boys round to collect it and if I do not pay up, there vill be big trouble for me.'

'But 'e can't threaten you like that. You must go to the police, straight away.'

Finding encouragement in her words, Mr Jacobs sat up straight. 'You are right, Frances, I must not give in to that sheiss, he vill not threaten me. I vill go to police.' He banged his fist on the table. 'This is a democratic country and they vill look after me.'

Frances stood up. 'Go now,' she urged. 'This minute.'

But Mr Jacobs shook his head. 'Mudder would not like it. I must vait until tomorrow evening.'

She argued with him for a good ten minutes, but he was a stubborn old man and wouldn't budge. Then he insisted she should leave, so that he could lock up. Exasperated, in the end she had no choice but to do as he said. But Frances worried all the way home. There was no point in him going to the police on his own, either. When he was over-excited Mr Jacobs's grasp of the English language deteriorated rapidly. He would need all the help he could get and her father, with his knowledge of the law, was going to be the person to provide it, Frances decided.

Except for a couple of mongrels sniffing each other's private parts, Tudor Street was empty. There were no children spinning tops or playing leapfrog, no women gossiping on doorsteps, for the annual migration to Kent for the hop picking had taken place. Frances had always fancied going off in a train to an unknown destination and she envied those kids whose parents went each year. Her mother refused point blank even to consider it, saying she had no wish to live like a gipsy for a month. But most families had gone, amongst them the Hoggs, Mitchells and Phippses, all of them glad of the chance to earn a bit of extra cash and at the same time give their kids the benefit of some good Kentish air.

So the scream, blood-chilling in the abnormal quiet, reverberated down the empty street. Frances stood stock still. 'Oh my God, what's that?' she exclaimed, and pressed her hands against her thumping heart. Another scream equal in anguish followed, but her feet seemed cemented to the pavement and she couldn't move.

Then Peggy Flynn came limping out of the house, making strange, almost inhuman noises and dragging her callipered leg and heavy surgical boot after her.

Frances finally managed to put one foot in front of the other, although she felt as if she were walking through a lake of treacle. As she reached her, Peggy collapsed against the gate. 'Whatever's wrong, Peggy? Tell me.' For just behind Peggy she could see Joyce and Dora, a look of terrified incomprehension on their simple faces. Pressed against their skirts were the six younger Flynn girls, all of them sobbing. 'Is it yer pa? Is 'e laying into yer ma?'

'No, no.' The distraught girl shook her head from side to side, her long plait swinging out like rope. 'You've got ter come, Frances,' she sobbed. 'Ma's lying on the floor in a terrible state.'

'Is it the baby? Is she losing it?' Frances asked, all manner of panicky thoughts rushing through her head as she followed the hysterical girls into the house. For if she was, what did they expect her to do? Mrs Mitchell acted as midwife in this street, but she was away and her own mother was still at work. Frances felt a strong and cowardly instinct to run, to leave Peggy to get on with it. But there were terrible groans coming from the kitchen and she couldn't walk away from those.

But she would need help. 'Dora.' Frances spoke carefully to the girl. 'Go and get Mrs Goodbody. Tell her to come immediately. Say it's urgent.'

The girl nodded dumbly and shambled back down the hall. Praying the widow lady would be in, Frances took a deep breath and followed Peggy into the kitchen. The Flynn house was exactly the same as theirs in layout, except that it seemed to lack even basic necessities and Mrs Flynn lay doubled up on cold and carpetless lino.

Frances, feeling totally inadequate, knelt down beside her, and noticed that the woman's lips were blue and encrusted with saliva. She was also sweating profusely. 'Mrs Flynn, tell me what's wrong? Is it the baby?' She reached out to comfort her with a tentative hand.

Mrs Flynn screamed again and her small, thin body started to twitch convulsively. Terrified Frances shot back from the flailing arms and legs while her children whimpered, 'Mama, Mama.'

Hearing footsteps in the passage, Frances stood up and rushed to the door. 'Oh Mrs Goodbody, thank God.'

'It ain't Mrs Goodbody, it's me.' Norman moved into the light. Almost apologetically he added, 'She's gone to her daughter's for the day, and although I couldn't get much sense out of the girl, she looked pretty upset so I thought I'd better coom.'

'Oh I'm glad you did. I just don't know what to do. I thought at first Mrs Flynn was losing her baby. But I'm sure it's something far worse.'

The children continued to sob but Mrs Flynn had now gone very quiet and still. 'Is Ma . . . dead?' Peggy asked in a small, frightened voice.

Norman knelt down beside Mrs Flynn and felt her pulse. 'She's alive but . . .' He prised open her eyelids, smelt her breath, then rose to his feet. Obviously searching for something he went into the scullery, and a moment later called in a urgent voice, 'Someone better go and get a doctor quickly, this is serious. There's a tin of rat poison in here and it's been opened.'

'Oh Mum, you shouldn't 'ave done it,' Peggy sobbed and threw herself upon her mother.

Unable to cope with the tragedy, Frances backed out of the room. 'I'll go,' she said and turned and fled. She never had any recollection afterwards of how she got to the doctor's surgery but she would always remember the startled faces of the patients as she fell into the waiting-room and shrieked to the closed surgery door, 'Dr Field, Dr Field, you've gotta come there's been a terrible accident!'

On the whole his patients were a silent, docile lot, though the occasional row did break out in the waiting-room, usually between drunks. But Dr Field was a large man, able to deal with the miscreants firmly. Hearing now what sounded like an altercation he flung open his door. 'Who's making trouble out here?' he roared.

'No one, Dr Field.' Frances grabbed his white jacket and

tried to pull him towards the door. 'It's Mrs Flynn, she's swallowed rat poison, please come.'

'God almighty!' the doctor exclaimed, and a horrified gasp went round the room. 'Is she still alive?'

'I . . . think so.'

He turned back into his surgery. 'I'll ring the hospital and tell them I'm bringing her in my car.' With quick efficient movements he dialled a number, spoke to someone at the other end in a low voice and at the same time packed his black bag. He made his apologies to his patients as he strode through the waiting-room. 'Sorry, folks, but you'll have to come back tomorrow. As you'll have gathered, this is an emergency.'

His car was parked right outside the door. 'Hop in,' he said to Frances, and with a grim expression drove at great speed to Tudor Street.

'Where is she?' he barked, as he heaved his black bag off the back seat of the car.

'On the kitchen floor when I left.'

'Well I hope someone thought to cover the poor soul with a blanket.' He strode into the house and Frances, not sure what she should do, followed him. Charlie Flynn was there, kneeling beside his wife. 'Hail Mary full of Grace, the Lord is with thee, blessed art thou amongst women . . .' he mumbled piously and Frances felt a powerful urge to kick him up his hypocritical arse.

The small room was now very crowded. The youngest child had fallen asleep, her head on the kitchen table. The others stood huddled against Peggy, staring at their mother. Occasionally there was a hiccuping sob, but otherwise they seemed to have sunk into a bewildered lethargy.

'You'll have to pull yourself together, Mr Flynn, and help me get your wife into the car,' said the doctor, who wasn't going to waste time feeling sorry for the man. He'd warned him often enough about his wife's constant pregnancies, and what they were doing to her health, but the selfish brute would never listen. 'And I'd like everyone else out of here, please.' He turned to Frances. 'Can you take the children to your house for the time being?'

Frances nodded and trying to reassure the girls that their mum would be all right once she got to hospital, with Norman's help she ushered them next door.

Until her parents arrived home, Frances didn't have time to dwell on the traumatic effect of the tragedy on her own body. Now she was aware of a throbbing over her left eye. Succumbing to the pain, she sat down and let her mother take over and sort things out in that practical way of hers.

First of all nine deeply distressed children had to be comforted and reassured. And also fed: gentle probing revealed that there wasn't a scrap of food in the house and none of them had eaten all day.

After this plans had to made about where they would sleep that night. But Peggy had already made her decision. She drank her tea, ate some bread and jam then bravely announced she was going back next door and taking Joyce and Dora with her. 'Someone's got to keep an eye on Dad,' she said, and although she was only twelve, Frances could see she'd already taken on the role of mother.

'I'll come with you, lass,' said Tom, not liking the idea of the girls going back into the house on their own.

But this still left six small girls who needed a bed for the night. 'Roy will have to sleep on the sofa in the front room,' Edna decided. 'It'll be a bit of a squeeze but then Margie, Joan and Coral can go in his bed.' She patted the heads of the three older girls. 'But that still leaves Pat, Ellie and Dawn, doesn't it my lovelies?'

'Couldn't Nan take them?' asked Frances.

Edna looked doubtful. 'They need a bit of loving tonight, some cuddles, and they wouldn't get that much of that from your nan.'

'What about Mrs Goodbody?' suggested Norman. 'She'd

probably help you out. One of her lodgers has just left and the back bedroom's empty.'

'But she's out,' said Frances.

Norman looked at the clock. 'She'll be back by now. She's always there to get our tea.'

'Can you you be a good lad and run and ask her, Norman? Explain what's happened and tell her it's an emergency. She's a kindly soul, so I'm sure she'll do what she can.'

Gradually things were sorted out. After the children had finished eating, Edna took three of them upstairs, listened to them say their prayers, then tucked them up in bed. Roy's bed was made up on the sofa and as a special treat he was allowed to have Tinker in with him.

Norman came back saying Mrs Goodbody would be happy to take the other three girls and off he went with them again to his landlady's house.

Frances now felt as if she had a hammer pounding away in her skull. The Flynn tragedy had extinguished any thoughts of Paul or Mr Jacobs and his problems. All she wanted was to lie down in a darkened room, and she was wondering if she could sneak off up to bed, when her father returned.

With a depressed sigh Tom sat down. 'I've just put Charlie to bed drunk. He'd gone all maudlin, said how much he loved Ivy. A bit late in the day for that, I would have said. Useless character.' He couldn't hide his contempt.

Edna shook her head. 'Poor wee mites, what's going to become of them?'

'Well Charlie's not capable of keeping that family together,' answered her husband. As they all knew, Charlie's work pattern was erratic. When he was feeling exceptionally energetic he sometimes managed to get work as a labourer on building sites. But he was quarrelsome by nature so it usually wasn't long before he'd fallen out with someone, often the gaffer, and been sent packing. At other times he'd hire a barrow, go down to the gasworks, buy coke and hawk it around the streets. But more often than not the family lived on relief, or the charity of the church and other altruistic organizations, for Charlie was an adept scrounger.

'Everything will fall on Peggy, you see. Poor kid, as if she hasn't enough to contend with. She'll probably end up the household drudge, just like her mum. Which is a shame because she's supposed to be good at her school work.'

'Hey, come on now, we're talking as if Ivy is already dead. Let's look on the bright side and remember that the hospital will be doing their best.'

Edna sat staring into the fire. 'Poor woman, she must have been desperate to do such a terrible thing.' She pulled a hankie from the pocket of her pinafore. 'I should have helped her more.'

Tom went to his wife and put his arm round her. 'Now don't go blaming yourself, you did a lot for Ivy. Why they were for ever round borrowing, you know that. Charlie's the one at fault, no one else.'

Edna rubbed her cheek affectionately against her husband's hand. 'You're a good man, Tom Henderson, do you know that?'

Kneeling, Tom kissed her and Edna responded by slipping her arms around his neck. Frances, watching, knew they were no longer aware that she was there. Feeling excluded by their love, their undimmed passion for each other, she slipped from her chair and very quietly, so as not to disturb them, tiptoed up to bed.

Although there'd still been the mundane to deal with, food to buy, the children to dress and feed, they'd waited all Saturday morning tensed for news from the hospital. Later a policeman called to speak to Frances and Norman, and asked what seemed rather personal questions about the Flynns. Norman answered confidently enough, but Frances grew more and more uncomfortable and was relieved when the constable closed his notebook, put it in his pocket and left.

It wasn't voiced, but no one really held out much hope that Ivy would live and on Saturday afternoon when Father O'Brien came to the door, they knew from his solemn expression that she was dead.

Edna invited him into the house and offered him tea.

'You wouldn't be having something a bit stronger would you, Mrs Henderson? It has been a terrible twenty-four hours.'

'I'm afraid not, Father.'

'Well never mind, the tea will do.' He sat down and splayed his legs towards the fire and they waited for him to speak.

'Ivy, may the Lord have mercy on her, died at midday. Her suffering was terrible, poor woman. There was nothing the doctors could do, her liver was destroyed. She went into a coma in the end, which was a blessing.'

Tom wasn't a man to use bad language, particularly not in front of a man of the cloth, but he gave vent to his feelings in an outburst of bitterness. 'With all those children he kept making her have, one way or another that selfish bastard she had for a husband was going to kill her.'

Father O'Brien turned and regarded Tom with a faint air of disapproval. 'Little ones are God's gift to us, Mr Henderson.'

'Not if you can't feed them properly, Father.'

Edna gave her husband a warning look and tried to take the tension out of the atmosphere. 'Well, the pour soul's problems are over now, so let's hope she's at peace.'

The priest supped his tea noisily, then wiped his mouth with a hankie. 'There will have to be a post-mortem, and I'm afraid she will be denied the rites of the Holy Church or burial in consecrated ground.'

Edna's eyes flared with indignation. 'Are you saying, Father, that she can't have a proper funeral?'

'Killing yourself is the sin of despair, the death of the soul. She has put herself out of the reach of forgiveness.' Father O'Brien held out his cup for a refill.

'I've never heard of such a thing. Ivy was a good, religious woman. She went to mass without fail every Sunday.' Edna poured the priest his tea but in her agitation it slopped into the saucer.

'Suicide is a mortal sin, Ivy knew that.'

Frances saw her mother take a deep breath and knew she was making a tremendous effort to control her anger. 'I always thought Christianity was about love.'

'Oh it is, it is, have no doubt about it,' the priest answered complacently.

'I don't know what effect this will have upon the girls. As if they haven't enough to contend with.'

'Ah yes, the children. While we're on the subject, you'd better know that it has been decided that the younger ones are to go to the Sisters of Mercy.'

'Is this Charlie's doing?'

'He's agreed to it, if that's what you mean.'

'And does Peggy know?'

'Not yet.'

'Well I can't see her allowing it. If I know Peggy she'll move heaven and earth to keep her family together.'

Father O'Brien stood up. 'Well, we shall see. I'm afraid it won't be Peggy's decision, but her father's.'

After he'd gone, to relieve her feelings, Edna picked up the poker and rattled the coals furiously, sending sparks detonating up the chimney. 'Religion, what can you say about it? And that man! How can he even think of taking those children away? It would destroy Peggy.'

'You've got to look at it from a practical point of view, love,' said Tom. 'How's a crippled girl not yet thirteen going to manage eight children? And Charlie's useless. No more than a big kid himself. At least with the nuns they'd be fed and clothed.'

'Maybe. Frances and me, we'll go round in a little while and see what we can do to help. I'm blowed if I'm going to let those kids be imprisoned in a convent without a fight.'

12

Harry sank back into the car's black leather upholstery and took a contented puff of his cigar. This beat flogging chipped dinner plates any day, he thought, and gave Arthur a sly nudge and a wink.

'You boys all right in the back there?' Rikki turned and grinned at them.

'We sure is, boss,' Arthur replied.

'Well I've got big plans for you boys, but we'll talk about that later, after you've seen this club of ours we're taking you to. It's quite a place.'

Harry made no bones about it, he envied the brothers' life-style and he'd decided he wanted a slice of the cake. Take this car, for instance, French and a real flash job with its yellow and black bodywork and white-walled tyres. Then there were their clothes. None of yer fifty shilling tailors for Rikki and Giorgio, oh no, but suits straight from Savile Row and hand-made shirts and shoes. He fancied cutting a dash about the neighbourhood, too, seeing respect tinged with fear in people's eyes. Because that was something he'd never had, respect, particularly from that family of Gloria's. Really thought themselves somethin', they did. Remembering the many slights he'd endured, Harry shifted his behind in an aggrieved fashion. Roll up in a jalopy like this, though, and they'd change their tune. He could just imagine it, so impressed, their eyes'd be nearly popping out their bleedin' heads. Gloria was gettin' a bit above herself as well these days, running around with old brown boots Walter, flashing a ring which was probably coloured glass, and goin' on about how she only had to say the word and he'd marry her tomorrow. It was all talk, of course. Mind you, he did feel a bit jealous at times, not that he'd ever tell her. No point in making her even more swollen-headed than she was.

He hoped it was soon, these big plans of Rikki's, because what they were doing right now was kids' stuff, just chasing a few local street bookies, and them bein' illegal, they handed over their protection money without a squeak. But what they collected was peanuts, so him and Arthur's cut didn't amount to anything much.

It started to rain heavily as they drove past the fountains in Trafalgar Square and up Charing Cross Road. Harry watched the Saturday night crowds hurrying to find somewhere to shelter, and in the sealed warmth of the car he felt well content with himself. He'd heard about the engines of cars purring, and this one certainly did, like a contented cat. Shortly after Cambridge Circus, Giorgio turned off into Soho. Prostitutes, some young and pretty, others raddled old bags, were propped against lamp-posts along the length of its narrow streets. Harry wondered how they all made a living. Whatever they earned, their ponces were likely to take most of it off them anyway. But then it was the law of the jungle out there, eat or be eaten, and you had to look after number one in this life.

Rikki and Giorgio hadn't said much about where they were headed, only that it was a private club they ran. 'Not far now, boys,' said Rikki, as Giorgio drew up at a kerb. 'We'll get out here and walk. With all the narks around it's safer. We can't afford to have them raiding us and greasing palms gets to be expensive.'

Arthur and Harry followed the brothers for about a hundred yards along the street until they turned off down a narrow, poorly-lit passage. All the buildings were shuttered and secretive-looking and it was anyone's guess what went on behind their walls. Giorgio knocked at a door, a small shutter slid back, then there was the rattle of a chain and the scrape of a key in the lock. As they filed in and Harry heard the chain going back across the door, he muttered to Arthur, 'Must be some joint.'

With Rikki leading they groped their way in single file down a dark passage and through another door that opened into a crowded, smoky room. Small tables with red lampshades were set in a crescent shape round the edge of a small dance floor and a three-piece band was playing while several couples danced. To Harry it seemed disappointingly small and dingy. He'd expected a much posher set-up than this. But now a large lady with lots of beads looped round her neck was bearing down on them with a wide smile and open arms.

'Darlings!' she kissed Giorgio and Rikki extravagantly. 'Come and sit down.' She led them to one of the tables, snapped her fingers at a waiter and ordered him to bring champagne.

'This is Flo. The three of us is partners, but most of the time we leave 'er to run things 'ere,' said Rikki. 'An' I bet you two boys is thinking: is this all there is?'

Arthur and Harry shook their heads. 'Oh no we're not,' they lied in unison.

'Good, 'cos this lot is all a front.' He waved his arms round the room. 'The real business goes on in the back on the gaming tables. Roulette, baccarat, vingt-et-un.'

Harry's attention was diverted by a blond, slender young man, who'd sauntered over to their table. Ignoring everyone else, he smiled at Giorgio, then went and stood behind him, massaging his neck and shoulders with a slow, sensual movement. Giorgio closed his eyes and let his head fall back in a manner that made Harry feel uncomfortable. However, neither Rikki nor Flo seemed to find anything strange in their behaviour, not even when the young man bent and whispered something in Giorgio's ear. Giorgio gave his girlish giggle and stood up. With their arms round each other the two of them left the room.

'As you see, people can let their hair down 'ere, lads, be what they want and no questions asked. Membership ain't cheap, so that means we get real class: judges, members of parliament, actors, actresses, titles galore. That's Daisy Lamont the actress over there.' Rikki pointed to what until that moment Harry had imagined was a young man dancing with a girl, for she was dressed in white tie and tails and her hair was sleek and flat as sealskin against her well-shaped head. She was also sporting a monocle.

'That's Daisy Lamont?' Astonished, Harry leaned forward to get a better look, for he'd seen her dance her way through many a film to win the heart of the hero. 'Strewth!'

'And the bloke in make-up, he's a high court judge. You get my drift, don't you?'

To show they were men of the world, Arthur and Harry nodded their heads vigorously.

But Harry was confused. It was all a bit cock-eyed; the accents were cut glass, but no one was what they seemed. Of course he knew about pansy men, but he'd never seen so many in one room. And people in public life, too. Imagine this lot being caught and put in the slammer. Why it would bring the government and country to its knees.

'You can 'ave a boy or a girl, Arthur, even three in a bed if you like. We provide for all tastes, just take yer pick. There's rooms upstairs. An' if you like it straight I could even be available myself,' offered Flo, with a wink and obviously taking a bit of a shine to him.

Arthur cleared his throat. 'Er . . . not at the moment, thank you Flo,' he blustered, 'but I might take you up on it another time.'

'Well don't say I ain't generous.' Flo stood up. 'Shall we show them the gaming room, Rikki?'

'We'll be wiv you in a minute, Flo, I just want a word with the boys.' Rikki waited until she'd gone, then poured the last of the champagne into their glasses.

'This is between us and not a word to Flo. She's funny

141

about dope and won't have it on the premises, but there are quite a few of the customers askin' for it. Giorgio an' me can get hold of a fairly regular supply of hashish off the ships, and I want you two boys to deliver it to the houses of certain customers. It's not too risky and there'll be a good cut in it for you both. How does the idea grab you?'

Harry, with visions of a car, answered quickly, 'I'm in, Rikki.'

'Me too,' added Arthur.

Rikki gave a satisfied nod and stood up. 'Right, let's go and see what you can win on the gaming tables.'

Driving home, Harry felt rather pleased with life and himself. The evening had been a great success. Some business had been transacted to the satisfaction of all, he'd done very well for himself at roulette and was richer by twenty quid. But poor old Arthur had been cleaned out again. He wasn't a lucky gambler, which probably accounted for him doing so well wiv women, to make up for it.

Harry was sleepy from the booze and it was late, so he didn't notice they weren't taking their normal route home until they passed the looming, solid edifice of the Tower of London then drove down Royal Mint Street and into Cable Street. At the corner of Cannon Street Road, the car stopped outside a heavily shuttered shop.

'Harry, there's a parcel in the boot I want you to get.'

'Okay, boss.' To show Rikki what a willing lieutenant he was, Harry leapt from the car and bounded round to open the boot. 'Is this it?' He lifted out a heavy brown paper parcel roughly tied with string.

'That's it. Now just put it on the doorstep.'

'Righty-o.' It smelt funny and laying it down Harry wondered what it was. Getting back into the car, mildly curious, he asked, 'What was in the parcel, Rikki? It smelt kinda peculiar.'

Rikki laughed. 'That's 'cos it's going off. Some yid got

awkward yesterday, said he wasn't gonna pay up, so to teach him a lesson we've sent him a present. A pig's head.'

'What's this bloke's name?' asked Harry, a little less bouncily.

'Jacobs.'

'Jacobs,' repeated Harry and tasted a sourness in his mouth.

'Yeah, and the fact is, I might 'ave to send you boys round to sort him out. Get 'im so terrified he'll be shitting his pants. And if he still don't pay up, then we'll have to think very seriously about torching the place.'

In the grim hours following Ivy's suicide, it had been left to Edna to comfort nine grief-stricken children while Tom attempted to keep Charlie sober long enough to make the funeral arrangements. Frances didn't want to dwell on Ivy's tragic end, but she'd never been so close to death before and it made her pause and take stock and recognize that life was a gift that shouldn't be squandered. Bearing this in mind, on Sunday morning she'd risen from her bed with a new sense of purpose. In the mirror she was aware, in a way that she'd never been before, of her glossy hair, clear eyes and youth.

She walked to work observing the familiar with fresh eyes, ran her fingers along the rough stone of walls as if she were touching them for the first time, stooped to stroke cats, gazed up at the sky. Poor Ivy, Frances thought, she'll never again look up and see clouds form themselves into patterns, never enjoy the sun or rain on her skin. Ivy was shortly going to be nailed into a coffin and buried deep in unconsecrated ground. Frances shivered. And yet Ivy had once been young, must have skipped along these pavements, had hopes, maybe had even experienced joy.

Count your blessings, that's what you had to do, Frances decided. Kitty might have the looks, but it was her voice people wanted to hear, so Paul said. Sometimes, though, she thought she'd be prepared to sacrifice her voice, anything, for just one flicker of interest from Andrew. But in spite of the way Kitty misused him, out with him one evening, practically ignoring him the next, he went on foolishly adoring her. Perhaps I'm just not attractive to men, thought Frances. If she was, why had Norman never tried to kiss her? In fact he hadn't even held her hand. Not that she lost any sleep over it, he wasn't the most riveting of companions and all he ever talked about was wine. Apparently he was off soon to Germany with his boss to visit some vineyards, and in all honesty, she couldn't say she'd miss him.

Frances heard the clang of a handbell, then almost collided with a man who came round the corner with a tray balanced on his head and calling to dozing citizens, 'Muffins! Luverly muffins! Come and get 'em!' Cable Street was quieter and even in Cannon Street Road there weren't many people about. It was bound to pick up later, though, Frances knew that. Pretty soon Jewish families who hadn't shopped on the Saturday would emerge from their houses and the street would be as busy as any weekday.

Since Friday her mind had been so occupied with the Flynns that Frances hadn't given a thought to her employer's problems and she'd expected to find the shutters down and the sign on the door turned to OPEN. Instead the window was still barred, the door firmly locked. Puzzled, she rattled the letterbox. There was a slight delay then a shuffling sound and finally the door opened a fraction and Mr Jacobs's frightened face appeared.

'Whatever's the matter, Mr Jacobs?'

He extended his head with the caution of a tortoise and squinted shortsightedly down the street.

'Come in quickly, Frances.' Beckoning, he opened the door sufficiently for Frances to squeeze through, then banged it shut again and shot the bolts across.

'But what is all this about, Mr Jacobs?'

He put a finger to his lips. 'Ssh, I do not vant Mudder to know. It vould kill her. But it is terrible what I haf to tell you, Frances. I came downstairs this morning and vat do I find?' He wrung his hands distractedly. 'A parcel on the step. And vat is in this parcel? Do you know?'

Frances shook her head.

'A pig's head!'

'A pig's head?' Frances repeated with a shudder of disgust. 'How did that get there?'

'Our visitor on Friday I zink, left it.'

'You mean Rikki?'

'Who else vould do such a terrible thing?'

The soft contours of Frances's face hardened. 'Well we don't have to put up with it. That nasty piece of work will not get away with this. It's vile. You and me, Mr Jacobs, are going to the police, straight away.'

'But the shop.' Izak gesticulated with his hands. 'My customers.'

'Don't worry, we'll put a notice up. Go and get your coat while I see to it.' Taking charge, Frances went into the back room and searched amongst an untidy pile of invoices and bills until she found a pencil and a piece of paper. On it in capital letters she printed: DUE TO UNFORSEEN CIRCUM-STANCES THIS SHOP WILL NOT OPEN UNTIL TEN THIRTY THIS MORNING *Signed I. Jacobs*. Rather proud of her effort, Frances read the note through hoping she'd got the spelling right, then on the way out pinned it to the door.

Walking round to the police station Mr Jacobs grew more and more agitated as he talked about the gruesome deed perpetrated against him by the Mantoni brothers. 'Evil men forced us to flee from our country, Frances, but England I tell myself is safe. And now vat happens? I haf that Rikki to deal with who is also very evil. Evil, the world is full of evil.' Growing emotional, he took out his hankie and blew his nose. Frances, uncertain how to comfort her employer, reached out and touched his arm.

'You're not to worry now, Mr Jacobs, the police will sort those Mantoni brothers out good and proper, you'll see.'

'Yes, lock them up where they can do no harm to good people like me.' Mr Jacobs thumped his hand against his chest.

In spite of her brave words, Frances was rather in awe of the police and truly unnerved at the idea of walking into a police station. Making a complaint wasn't the sort of thing people like her ever did. It was even worse than she imagined and her courage almost failed her when she saw the distance between the door and the desk, behind which a police sergeant sat reading a newspaper. Frances didn't have to look at Mr Jacobs to know he felt intimidated too, so she gripped his arm as the pair of them moved towards the desk, their progress marked by the heavy tread of Mr Jacobs's boots on the bare wooden floor.

It was impossible for anyone to fail to hear them, but the policeman was so engrossed in his *News of the World* he didn't even trouble to look up. Mr Jacobs put up with this for about a minute then cleared his throat loudly.

The desk sergeant, who considered that he was entitled to some quiet on a Sunday morning, lowered the newspaper with a bad-tempered gesture. He'd got to a particularly juicy piece about a divorce and a maid in a hotel in Brighton, and the interruption annoyed him. But he was reassured by the couple standing there. Not trouble makers but a young girl and elderly man. They wouldn't take up much of his time. Probably lost their cat or dog, he thought, laying his paper aside.

'Now what can I do for you good people?' he enquired. His tone was mock jovial and slightly condescending.

'You could oblige me vith your attention first of all,' Mr Jacobs answered in a firm voice.

146

The policeman looked slightly taken aback, but said nothing.

'Ve vant you to do something about those Mantoni brothers. Lock zem up.'

'Now why should I do that?'

'Because they are vicked people, zat is why. Rikki he came into my shop and threatened me, did he not Frances?'

Frances nodded.

'He said I must pay him lots of money each week or he vill do terrible zings to my shop.'

'And has he carried out these threats?'

'Yes, last night they left a pig's head on my doorsteps. It vas disgusting!' Mr Jacobs shuddered.

The policeman stroked his ginger moustache and looked thoughtful. 'But can you prove it was the Mantoni brothers who put the porker's head there?'

Growing angry, Mr Jacobs banged his fist down on the counter. 'Of course I cannot. But he threatened me with all sorts of terrible zings. "You'd better bloody pay up, yid, or else" ver his vords.'

'It has to be them, don't it?' Frances intervened with a worried glance at Mr Jacobs, for his face had gone red and sweat had broken out on his forehead.

'It might have been some naughty boys having a lark.'

'That wasn't a lark, and it was the Mantoni brothers, I'm tellin' you. They do what they like round here and no one stops them.'

'Meaning?'

'Meaning you should have them put away, all decent people say so.' Hearing her own voice answer back, Frances was amazed at her own audacity.

'It has to be proved that a crime has been committed, just the same,' the policeman explained patiently. 'You would like to make a statement, sir, I presume.'

'Yes, I vould.'

Mr Jacobs told his story, while the policeman wrote it

down, right from Rikki coming into the shop on Friday evening to finding the pig's head on Sunday morning.

'Haf you got it all down?' Mr Jacobs asked, when he'd finished.

'If you'll just wait a moment, sir, I'll read it back to you.'

'So vat are you going to do now?' asked Mr Jacobs when he'd signed the statement.

'We will look into the matter and make further inquiries. In the meantime you are not to give in to their threats by handing over any money.'

'See zat you come round to my shop then, to keep an eye on zings. I vant no more trouble.'

'We'll do that, I promise you, Mr Jacobs.'

'Goot.'

Mr Jacobs's belief in British justice restored, they walked out into the September morning. The sun's rays caught the glass on his spectacles and pausing on the steps, he rubbed his neck to release the tension, then he gave Frances an avuncular smile. 'What haf I always told you? This is a goot country to live in. Here the law vill protect you, never forget that my young lady.'

'No, Mr Jacobs, I won't,' Frances answered obediently.

13

Norman stood to attention in front of the dressing-table mirror, raised his right arm and at the same time brought his heels together with a sharp click. Not bad, he thought. Almost as good as them blokes in Germany, with their flags, swastikas and marching songs. Hitler Youth they were called and it had been a treat to watch 'em. For they'd seemed to belong, had a common aim, knew where they were going. A uniform like theirs and he'd show Frances what was what.

But then Germany had been a real eye opener. Everything about it had impressed him, from the moment he and Mr Freeman had stepped off the train. His employer had hired a car and they'd driven north along the beautiful, twisting Mosel, catching glimpses of inaccessible castles and marvelling at vineyards rising in steep terraces from the river bank. They stopped for refreshment in medieval villages the names of which, for Norman, had previously only been labels on wine bottles, enjoyed the hospitality of the owners of the great wine estates. In their large, dark houses, they drank cold golden wines that hung on the tongue like nectar. Afterwards, his head spinning, Norman remembered how he'd followed his host with uncertain steps down to the cellars. And standing there amongst the huge wooden casks, he inhaled that special cellar smell he loved, dank, winey and woody.

Nights were spent in spotlessly clean *Gasthöfe* being waited on by red-cheeked girls as round as the dumplings they served. They slept under billowing eiderdowns and woke to the sound of cow bells and the smell of coffee.

There'd been one bit of awkwardness for him and that was on the first evening when they were having supper. 'Hope you don't mind, Norman, but I've booked us a double room, it'll cut down on the expense,' Mr Freeman explained, as he attacked the mountain of food on his plate.

'Er ... oh, no,' Norman mumbled, but for the rest of the meal he'd felt so sick he'd toyed with his food, only pretending to eat. All he could think of was the housemaster, Mr Dean, in the children's home. Norman could still remember his kindess when he first arrived, a lost little boy grieving for his mam, which made what followed such an act of betrayal. Initially he'd welcomed the attention: the hugs, being taken on his knee, the masculine, tobaccoey smell of him. But then the housemaster had started fondling him in places he didn't like. And what followed was even worse, years of horror and pain with threats of beatings if he spoke out. He'd tried, and failed, to blot those years from his mind, but his housemaster's damaged legacy to him was a dislike of being touched by anyone, man or woman. If there was one person in the world he could choose to kill, it would be that Mr Dean. For he knew he would be doing the world, and lots of little boys, an enormous favour. Some people just didn't deserve to live and he was one of them.

Trust in people was another thing he'd lost; but as it turned out he had no need to worry about Mr Freeman, and they'd had single beds anyway. Of course Norman knew he should have guessed this, for his employer had a wife and several children, and so couldn't possibly be like *that*.

As well as encouraging him to use his limited German vocabulary, as they drove along, Mr Freeman also gave him history lessons and explained what a marvellous job Herr Hitler was doing. 'Whatever people say, Norman, and there are a lot who don't care for his methods, he has brought down unemployment. More importantly he's given the German people back their pride, stopped Jewish financiers from getting above themselves and sorted out the communists.

In my book a man who's done that, can't be all bad. And you can see the effect of his policies with your own eyes. New roads, happy citizens.'

Norman had to agree with him; compared with England, the country looked prosperous, its people healthy.

Afterwards Norman knew he would remember that week as perhaps the happiest of his life. He'd fallen in love with Germany and its people and although, normally, he wasn't much of a talker he'd come home full of it and bursting to tell Frances of his experiences. She pretended to listen, but her face soon took on a glazed look of boredom. But then all she ever thought about was films and film stars. In fact he sometimes asked himself why he bothered about Frances. The truth of it was that before he'd met her his loneliness had sometimes made him feel so miserable he'd thought he would die of it and Norman knew he couldn't go back to that, without a friend or relative in the world.

Mr Freeman was the opposite to Frances. He encouraged him to talk about Germany, particularly the Hitler Youth Movement which had so fascinated Norman.

'Have you heard of Sir Oswald Mosley, Norman?' Mr Freeman asked him one afternoon, when they were in the cellars, checking off some recently arrived shipments of claret from Bordeaux.

Norman looked up. 'Yeah, I have. We get speakers spouting their mouths off on street corners and selling their newspapers all the time round our way. Communists and Mosley's bunch in particular.'

'But you've never stopped to listen?'

'No fear. I'm not old enough to vote, there's too much heckling and I've never fancied getting involved in punch-ups.'

'Well you should listen to what Sir Oswald is saying. There are many people in this country who think he would make a strong leader and he greatly admires Hitler. Perhaps you'd like to come along with me one night and hear him speak.'

'Thanks, I would,' answered Norman, flattered by his employer's continued interest in him. It didn't do no harm keeping on his good side either, because he really enjoyed the wine business and intended to stay in it if he could.

He'd mentioned the meeting to Frances without much hope that she'd be interested, and he was right. 'Who wants to sit for hours listening to boring speeches,' she'd retorted, leaving Norman to wonder if 'boring' wasn't perhaps her favourite word.

The meeting was being held in a hall in Shoreditch and people were streaming in as Norman and Mr Freeman arrived. 'Looks like it'll be a full house,' said Mr Freeman as they were shown to their seats by one of several young men in black shirts trying to maintain order. Norman, looking about him, was immediately aware of a dangerous charge in the air which he found both frightening and exhilarating. Several more blackshirted youths stood on the stage, legs apart, hands clasped behind their backs and with an air of great self-importance. Above them was draped a huge Union Jack.

'Who are they?' asked Norman, although he'd already decided that what he wanted more than anything was to be part of this exclusive group and wear their uniform.

'They're British Union of Fascists stewards. Sir Oswald's bodyguards if you like. He has to cope with a lot of abuse,' explained Mr Freeman.

The heat and excitement intensified as all doors were closed and guards placed at every exit. The babble of voices ceased, a tall, straight-backed man with a trim moustache and wearing boots, jodhpurs and a black military-style jacket strode on to the stage and the audience rose and cheered. Gazing about him with an air of patrician superiority, Mosley waited for the noise to die down, then, satisfied he had the complete attention of the audience, his right arm rose in the fascist salute. Every arm shot up in response, including Mr Freeman's, and Norman rather self-consciously followed suit. Mosley now began to speak. His voice was cultured, and rose and fell in pleasing cadences. He spoke first of unemployment and ways in which it could be reduced, then of the communist threat and the world-wide consequences of them gaining power. Fluently and without notes, he went on to talk of the danger of Britain being dragged into conflict with Germany, a situation, he explained, which was being exacerbated by Jewish financiers interested only in personal gain.

Norman listened intently, dazzled by Mosley's charismatic personality. He was thinking yes, this was definitely a man he could follow when, from several parts of the hall a slow, repetitive chant began: 'Smash fascism, smash fascism'. Startled, Norman turned to see groups of men and women leap on chairs, triumphantly waving red flags and with their fists clenched in the communist salute.

Mr Freeman spun round in his seat angrily. 'This disruption always happens. I don't know how these communist thugs get in.'

'Capitalism is to blame, comrades,' a young man's voice rang out, 'not the Jews . . .' But that was as far as he got. The crowd grew threatening, a spotlight picked him out and in a well orchestrated move, he was grabbed by the stewards and manhandled down the aisle towards the door.

'That's Andrew they've got hold of!' exclaimed Norman, standing in the aisle to get a better view.

'Who's Andrew?' asked Mr Freeman.

'Oh, just someone I know,' Norman answered vaguely, and was saved further explanation by Andrew's comrades rushing to his aid. Soon the hall was in an uproar as opinions and punches were exchanged. Exhilarated, Norman watched them. For two pins he'd have joined in, except he wasn't sure who was communist and who was fascist, although it appeared to have got to the stage where it didn't really matter.

By now missiles were being thrown in all directions, but Mosley stood bravely facing his opponents. However, when a chair hurled on to the stage forced him to duck, his stewards quickly formed a protective barrier and hurried him away. It was as well, for the atmosphere had turned nasty. Knuckledusters appeared, cut-throat razors flashed, there were screams of pain, then blood. Norman realized they wouldn't be able to stand there much longer without being drawn into the fray. He could take care of himself, but Mr Freeman wasn't a young man. Then he heard a policeman's whistle and a dozen or so charged into the hall wielding their truncheons.

As the police started hitting out indiscriminately, Mr Freeman grabbed Norman's arm. 'Come on, let's get out of here or we might find ourselves with broken heads, being carted off in the Black Maria.' Struggling against an angry mob, he led the way up on to the stage and out through the wings where Norman was glad to see an emergency exit. Mr Freeman pushed down the bars and Norman followed him outside, in time to see Mosley's open car driving away with two young men balanced on the running board.

'Dash it, we've missed him. I would so like to have congratulated Sir Oswald on his speech and the way in which he stood up to that communist riff-raff.'

Hearing Mr Freeman's comments, a young blackshirt turned. 'He's speaking again tomorrow night in Bow,' he offered. Then, weighing up Norman, he asked, 'You interested in joining our outfit? The BUF is looking for recruits.'

'Do I get to wear a uniform like you?'

'Of course.'

'And march?'

'Yes, we have weekend camps where you get instruction. It'll cost you a shilling a month to be a member. Just go down to a recruiting office and give them your name, buy your uniform and turn up at the next meeting.'

'As easy as that, is it?'

The young man laughed. 'As easy as that. See you in Bow tomorrow night, then?'

'Well maybe.' Excited, Norman turned to Mr Freeman. 'What d'you think? Should I join?'

His employer put a friendly arm round his shoulder. 'I don't see why not. If my ticker was up to the marching I wouldn't have minded joining myself. But rest assured, Norman, if you do it will certainly be with my blessing.'

14

They had no warning of coming events. It all happened quite out of the blue. Like any other day, Dad had come in from work at the usual time, but instead of sitting down with them at the supper table he stood by the door gripping the handle and staring at the far wall with the unseeing gaze of a man in a state of deep shock.

Years of delivering letters in all weathers had given her husband a good colour, but even in the gas light Edna could see Tom's skin had a leaden tinge to it. Alarmed, she rose to her feet, all manner of illogical thoughts running through her head. 'What an earth's the matter, love?'

Tom didn't reply. Instead he slumped down in the fireside chair and covered his face with his hands.

Hastening to his side, Edna knelt and pressed her fingers against his forehead. It felt clammy to her touch. 'Are you ill? In pain? Tell me, please.'

A strange noise came from Tom's throat.

Frightened, Edna shook his hand. 'Tom, speak to me.'

Making a gallant effort Tom looked up. 'No I'm not ill, more's the pity. Because then I'd at least know I was going to get better.'

Frances, Kitty, Gloria and Roy had all stopped eating and were staring at Tom in bewildered silence. None of them had ever seen him like this before. Tom was rock solid, strong, the whole street knew that. Feeling inadequate in the face of his despair, but wanting to show her father how much she loved him, Frances slid from her chair and poured him a cup of tea. 'Here you are, Dad.'

'I couldn't drink it.' He pushed the cup away.

'Please tell us what's wrong, love.' Edna brushed back the thick fair hair, just beginning to show streaks of grey, with a loving, tender gesture.

Tom stared straight at her. 'All right, I'll tell you. I've been suspended from my job. Without pay.'

Edna's stomach gave a queasy lurch. 'Suspended? Whatever for?'

'Accu ... accusations ...' Tom paused. So deep was his humiliation, he could hardly bring himself to say the hateful words. '... have been made against me.'

'I don't know what you're getting at. What sort of accusations?'

'S ... some postal orders have been stolen from envelopes. Si ... signatures forged.'

'What's this got to do with you?' asked Edna still mystified.

'They ... s ... s ... say it's my handwriting.' Like a tale foretold Tom saw his future: a trial, a grim prison cell, shame and near starvation for his family. Then on release, shunned by neighbours and unable to obtain another job.

'But that's ridiculous! You've never stolen as much as a farthing in your life. Everyone knows you're the most honest person alive. How could they even think it, let alone suggest it!' Indignant and angry, Edna began to pace the small room. Her husband cherished his home, loved her and his children deeply, and she knew without a shadow of a doubt that he would never do anything which would jeopardize all he'd striven so hard for. Pausing for a moment, she stared down at his bowed head with a deep sense of outrage at the faceless men who'd brought her husband to this. 'You've worked there, how long is it ... ?' she did a mental calculation '... for over twelve years, they know your character, and yet they're saying you're a common thief. Talk about loyalty. Frances, get my coat. They're not treatin' you like that and gettin' away with it. I'm going down to see them lot at the post office, right now.'

157

Tom put out a restraining hand. 'No don't, Edna, it wouldn't help matters. I've got the union on my side, they're looking into it, and I'll get a bit of money from them each week. It's bad, coming just before Christmas, and we might have to tighten our belts, but I don't suppose we'll starve.' He straightened his shoulders and looked round at his family. 'Frances, get the Bible from the shelf.'

Mystified, Frances did as her father instructed, lifting down the large family Bible in which were written the names, dates of birth and deaths of the Atkins family going right back to the eighteenth century. She carried it over to her father and he took it from her and laying his hand on the black cover, said, 'I swear on this Bible that I did not steal those postal orders. I want you all to know that.'

'Oh Tom, love.' Edna had tears in her eyes, Gloria blew her nose loudly and Roy ran to his father and flung himself against him.

'We know you didn't, Dad.' Roy was now snuffling into his father's shoulder. Comforting him, Tom went on, 'So my conscience is clear, although if there's any justice in this world, someone down at that sorting office won't be sleeping easy tonight.'

'Have you any notion of who it might be?'

'I have my suspicions.'

'Well you must say something, then,' Edna urged.

'I haven't anything to go on, it's just a feeling.'

'But you want your name cleared.'

'Yes, but I've got to be certain first. Flinging accusations around without proof won't serve much purpose.'

The family all rallied around Tom, but there was still a lot of talking to be done, in particular the question of what they were going to live on without Tom's wages.

'I can manage a bit extra, maybe five bob, although it depends on me tips,' offered Gloria.

'And I can let you have half a crown,' said Kitty, who'd failed so far to find a job which she considered both equal to her talents and paid a decent wage. She no longer had any expectations of promotion at Pennywise either. In fact she regretted ever discussing the subject with Robert, because their relationship had never recovered and he remained as stiffly formal as ever.

All Frances could offer was her two shillings pocket money, and her mother refused to take that. But it didn't take her long to realize how she could ease the family finances. Dad had never been in debt or got behind with the rent and he wouldn't want to start now, so it provided her with the perfect excuse to get back to singing. However there was the small matter of her father's pride, so for the time being, Frances wisely decided, she would keep her plans under her hat.

Frances also knew it would be foolish to get over-excited or assume a job with Johnny Doakes was cut and dried. It was well over two months since she'd spoken to Paul, and the band leader could easily have hired another vocalist by now. An added problem was that she would never have the courage to go to the Rex on her own and men weren't exactly queueing up for the privilege of taking her dancing, not even Norman these days. Since he'd got in with the BUF it was all training camps and exercise – he was away most weekends. He certainly looked a lot healthier, but there was another aspect Frances didn't care for at all. When Norman was in uniform his character changed, he strutted and his manner became hard and almost bullying. She could remember too how Andrew had nearly hit the roof when, hardly knowing what the initials stood for, she told him Norman had joined the BUF.

'What, you're telling me that Norman's joined Mosley's gang of fascists?' he raged.

'What's so wrong about that? You're a communist.'

'The communist aim is equality for all, the fascists want to enslave us. And see this?' He pointed to a cut above his left eye. 'I got beaten up at one of their meetings.'

But Frances wasn't inclined to be sympathetic. 'You should have stayed away, then, instead of going looking for trouble.'

Of course, this had set Andrew off on his favourite hobby horse, politics.

Frances's eyes grew glazed and she'd interrupted his flow by asking, 'You wouldn't by any chance like to take me to the Rex on Saturday, would you?'

Needled by her indifference, Andrew muttered darkly, 'Be politically ignorant, then. Wake up when it's too late.'

'I presume the answer's no,' she'd called, as he stomped off.

'Damn right,' he retaliated angrily.

Frances gave a shrug and wondered how anyone could posssibly find politics interesting. As she'd guessed, she had no better luck with Norman.

'Sorry, you'll have to find someone else to take you, I've got training down in Essex this weekend.'

Niggled, she asked, 'What d'ya do down there that's so important?'

Norman shrugged. 'Various things.'

'Can't you miss one weekend?'

'No.' He could have, of course, but he didn't want to, he enjoyed the camps too much. And even if he tried to explain to her, Frances probably wouldn't understand. She'd always had a family, so it wouldn't mean anything to her, that sense of belonging, of being part of a larger group, of having male companionship and real friends. He enjoyed the discipline as well, the marching, the drill and sport, feeling his muscles respond to the exercise and his body become more finely tuned. But the evenings were the best, with all the singing, horseplay and laughter. Norman had never found much to laugh about before. Taking Frances to a dance was nothing compared to the zing he got from that and he wasn't going to give it up for a girl who he sensed was only making use of him.

'See if I care, I'll go on my own.' But Frances felt peeved. Norman was definitely getting too big for those riding boots he strode around in these days.

The Rex Ballroom, with its flashing lights and promise of romance, drew Brylcreemed boys and girls in their best dresses and dancing sandals up the steps and through its doors. Wishing with all her heart that it was as easy for her, Frances dithered outside for several minutes. Do it, walk up those steps, she berated herself and finally, driven by the memory of her father's despair and by the freezing cold, she placed a tentative foot on the bottom step, then the next until she'd reached the top.

She bought her ticket and was still hovering when she found herself being pushed through the swing doors by the weight of an exuberant crowd. This was it. She was in. The die was cast. There was such a crush in the cloakroom Frances couldn't get near the mirror, so she had a quick peek at herself in her compact mirror, dabbed her nose with powder and went out into the dance hall. Having got this far, she began to feel rather pleased with herself, and edging her way round the floor she sat down where she hoped she might catch Paul's eye. But she'd reckoned without two of his female fans, who hovered in front of the stage gazing at him with adoring expressions. Paul obviously knew they were there, but he refused to look up. Eventually two young men came and asked the girls to dance and Frances realized this might be her one opportunity to make herself known before they came back. But the interval came, Paul played a couple of Fats Waller numbers, then stood up and flexed his shoulders. Guessing he was about to leave the stage, and seeing her chance slipping away, Frances leapt to her feet. 'Paul,' she yelled, amazed at her own boldness.

Obviously thinking it was one of his fans, he pretended not to hear. So she called again, a little more desperately. 'Paul, it's me, Frances.'

Paul swung round. 'Well I never! After all this time,' he exclaimed and immediately jumped down off the stage. 'I hope this means you've come to sing for us.'

He looked so genuinely pleased to see her, Frances felt confident enough to bargain. 'It does if Johnny pays me a pound like 'e said he would.'

Paul laughed. 'Well let's go and see, shall we?'

Taking her hand he drew her up the steps, across the stage into the wings. Here Johnny and his boys were relaxing with a glass of beer and Frances was uncomfortably aware, by the way they gave her the once-over, that they assumed she was some free and easy hanger-on come to distribute her favours.

'Look what I've brought for you, Johnny, our little nightingale.'

Peering at her, Johnny stood up. 'Bless me, so it is!'

'And she says she'll sing for us tonight if you give her a pound like you promised.'

'Now hold on,' said Johnny, who was an astute businessman, 'it is half-time. So ten bob for tonight and we'll see how it goes, eh sweetheart?'

Frances knew she was in no position to argue. 'All right.'

'Before we start, we'd better find out which songs you know.'

'Oh I know most of the latest ones by heart,' said Frances confidently.

'Good girl. Look through the music and tell us what you fancy singing, then.'

Frances was careful to choose numbers she knew would be popular with the crowd, but which at the same time suited her voice. When they'd sorted out the running order, Johnny, pleased with his acquisition, led her on to the stage and, beaming and avuncular, introduced her to the audience. 'Now I have a young lady here whose name is Frances. A lot of you will remember her from a few months back when she got up on this stage and not only won the singing

162

contest, but our hearts as well. It has taken a lot of persuading to get her back here to sing for us tonight, so I hope you'll show your appreciation with a big round of applause.'

Frances's self-esteem shot up like a thermometer in a heatwave. This is what I was born for, she thought, as she felt the goodwill of the audience lap over her. All I ever want to do for the rest of my life is stand on a stage and hear that applause. Tonight she could enjoy the illusion of being even more beautiful than Kitty, tonight she felt in complete control of her life.

Johnny, not wanting to damage a voice that might prove a valuable asset to the band, made her sit out every other number and this gave Frances her first real opportunity to study Paul. Sitting crouched over a piano night after night in a smoky atmosphere probably wasn't the healthiest way to make a living, but he appeared to have survived it well. When he smiled, which he did frequently, his features were transformed, otherwise he was remarkably ordinary-looking and he had a face that people, when lost for a description, were inclined to describe as 'pleasant'. A bit like her own, really, Frances decided. Even their hair was the same straight mousy brown. His tended to flop over his eye and he had a boyish way of brushing it back, which women obviously found endearing because there was no shortage of admirers amongst the dancers.

The two brassy young things, as Frances had nicknamed them, were now dancing together, and they waved and called out to Paul every time they went by. It didn't deter them that he still pretended not to see them, and Frances wondered why some girls were prepared to make fools of themselves over a bloke. No self-respect, that's what it was, she decided. She liked Andrew a lot, but she hoped she had the sense not to make a such fool of herself in front of him.

Johnny announced the last waltz, Frances stood up,

smoothed the front of her dress and walked over to the microphone.

The crowd didn't want to let her go and Frances would have willingly stayed there all night. However the caretaker had other ideas. He was newly married, had a lovely missus and wanted to get home to his warm bed. In about a quarter of an hour the hall was empty, and the band had packed away their music and instruments. Johnny took her to one side and pressed fifteen shillings into her hand. 'The extra five bob is a bribe, sweetheart.' He kissed her cheek. 'You sang like an angel and I want you back next Saturday. But I've got to know I can rely on you.'

'It all depends on me dad.'

'Let me know definitely by Wednesday. Leave a note at the desk. Then if you come every Saturday for a month without letting me down, I'll give you a billing. "Our resident nightingale, Miss Frances Henderson." How'd you fancy that? Your name on up hoardings along with the band's. You'll be a local celebrity.'

'Would I really?' Frances gleefully imagined Kitty's reaction. Outshone by her younger sister – God, she'd be livid, and Andrew could hardly fail to be impressed.

'Are you going to get your coat? Otherwise we'll be locked in,' she heard Paul say.

'Half a sec.' Frances hurried off to the cloakroom and Paul was still waiting when she got back.

'Come on, I'll see you home.'

'You don't have to.'

'I certainly do, you're my responsibility and it's far too late for you to be walking home on your own.'

Outside Johnny called goodnight and got into a taxi with a woman. Paul's two young admirers were waiting for him, wearing only thin coats and dance sandals and shivering in the bitter cold.

'Paul.' It was whispered like a sigh and sad with longing. As they passed, the girls reached out to touch him as if he were some good luck talisman and Frances, familiar herself with rejection, suddenly felt sorry for them. These were girls destined always to be passed over in life.

'Goodnight, girls,' Paul called, then in a very obvious way he took Frances's hand and tucked it through his arm. 'It doesn't do to give them any encouragement,' he said quietly. Then as they walked down a narrow passage and into the main street he added, 'Let's get a move on, before we turn into blocks of ice.'

Frances guessed he was trying to shake off the girls, now trailing about a hundred yards behind like rejected puppy dogs. Their envy for her was almost palpable and Frances smiled. If only they knew. Paul's not interested in me and I'm not interested in him.

'Look, it's snowing!' In the lamplight, Frances saw a few feathery snowflakes, and held out her hand.

'Good, that means we'll get rid of them.' Paul looked over his shoulder, and saw that the girls' images had already been whited out in a flurry of snow. 'This looks as if it's going to be heavy.'

As he spoke, from nowhere a wind blew up, turning the snow into a whirling, blinding blizzard. Supporting each other, they fought their way forward. The cold wind scoured their cheeks and numbed their lips and Frances could feel the snow seeping through her shoes. They would be ruined, and they were her best ones too.

Outside her house they stood for a moment without speaking and trying to get their breath back.

'Would you like to come in and warm yourself up?' Frances offered, before remembering her father's low opinion of musicians and the explaining she would have to do.

'Thanks but I'd better get home. The snow's eased off slightly, but we could be in for some more. If the buses stop I'd have to walk all the way to Stratford and I don't fancy the idea on a night like this.'

'Well if you're sure,' answered Frances, feeling rather hypocritical but relieved as well.

'Before you disappear, I want to say I'm really pleased you came tonight. I've never known Johnny so enthusiastic. You could have a great future with the band.' He paused, then went on a bit awkwardly, 'You remember I told you I write songs.'

Frances nodded.

'Well I was wondering if you'd be interested in trying some out with me.'

Frances was deeply flattered. 'Me? Yeah, of course I would.'

'You see I want to find out if I'm kidding myself. If anyone can make the lyrics sound good it's you. If they still sound lousy I'll pack it in, and save myself some heartache.'

'Have you got any particular time in mind?'

'Maybe one Saturday before the rest of the band arrive.'

'I'll have to let you know. Things are a bit dodgy at home at the moment.'

'Any time will suit me.' Paul patted her cheek in a brotherly fashion. 'Now go indoors before you freeze to death.'

Frances had been half hoping her parents would be in bed so that she'd be spared the explanations until morning, but there was a light under the kitchen door. Dad had a skein of wool looped over his fingers and Mum was winding it into a ball and although the wireless was on, neither of them seemed to be listening to it. What struck Frances was how, in a matter of days, her father had aged, shrivelled in stature, lost his spark, and she wondered about the man who was really guilty. Did his conscience trouble him? Did he sleep well knowing a colleague was being made to suffer for his miserable crime?

Edna tried her best to reassure her husband. 'You're innocent, Tom, we all know that and the authorities will find out for themselves soon enough.' But Frances knew her

166

father dreaded every knock on the door, and had resigned himself to going to prison.

It was a struggle but Edna made a great effort to keep cheerful, and she looked up with a smile at her daughter. 'You're wet, love, take your coat off and come and get warm. When I've finished winding this wool we'll have a cup of cocoa.'

Frances got a chair and moved it over to the fire. Tinker lay stretched out in front of it, motionless except for an occasional twitch of a leg or whisker. Leaning forward, she warmed her hands and gradually the blood began to flow through her veins again. She was bursting to tell her parents about her success tonight, but she knew she had to find the right moment.

'Listen to that,' said her mother, as the wind whistled around the chimney pots and rattled the window frames.

'Not a night to be a tramp. Anyway, where's Kitty and Gloria? I'd have thought they'd be in by now.'

'Kitty went to the cinema with Andrew. I don't know if they had a row, but she came in ages ago and went straight to bed. Gloria's gone gaddin' off somewhere with Harry. He turned up in that flashy car again. It really impresses 'er. The trouble is, that sister of mine doesn't know which side her bread's buttered. She should stick to Walter.'

'Perhaps she don't love Walter.'

'Why's she wearing that ring then, eh?' Edna snapped. 'It's takin' advantage of a decent man. Harry's pockets are bulging with money at the moment and she ought to be askin' a few questions, like where's it coming from. But she swallows any cock and bull story he feeds 'er.'

Frances poked the fire and watched flames shoot up the chimney. 'If she still hankers after 'im, what can you do?'

'Walter's dying to marry her. Harry never will. You can't have everything in this life, no matter how hard you try. Still there's no fathoming people sometimes.' Edna sighed, finished winding the ball of grey wool and immediately began casting stitches on to knitting needles. Watching her, it occurred to Frances that her mother never had the luxury of idleness. Always she was busy.

'What you knitting?'

'A school jumper for Roy. He's put both elbows through the one he's wearing. That boy.' Edna shook her head in mock despair and her needles clicked away busily.

Frances removed her shoes, inspected the cheap compressed cardboard soles, then poked them with her finger. They were like pulp. 'Just as I thought, ruined.' She slung them into the hearth.

'Well you won't be gettin' a new pair for a while, not with things as they are.'

'Perhaps I can wiv this.' Seeing her opportunity, Frances tossed the ten shilling note and silver in her mother's lap. 'I've bin to the Rex. I sang,' she said in a defiant rush.

Edna glanced at her husband. 'What did your father say about you goin' there?'

'It's to help us, Mum. If I can earn money singing, why shouldn't I?' She glanced at her father, gauging his reaction. 'Next week if I go, it'll be a pound. You're not going to tell me off are you, Dad? We do need it.'

Tom Henderson, who hadn't spoken since she came in, shook his head. 'How can I? I'm not entitled to see my family starve.'

Frances went and wound her arms around her father's neck. 'So I can go again next Saturday?' she wheedled. 'It'd help us through Christmas.'

'Do what you like, love, do what you like.'

It was so easy, Frances almost felt ashamed. She'd have much preferred to see her dad his old self, angry at her defiance and ready to take a strong line. Anything but this defeated man, his spirit killed, sitting with shoulders hunched in front of her.

*   *   *

When two heavily moustached men wearing black bowlers knocked on the door and asked in authoritative tones for Mr Thomas Henderson, his family feared the worst was about to happen. Tom, looking grave, invited them into the front room and closed the door.

Hovering in the hall, Edna wrung her hands in despair and cried to her daughters, 'He's going to be arrested, dragged off in handcuffs, I know it.'

'He might not be, Mum,' answered Kitty without much conviction, then tiptoed to the door and placed her ear against it. All she could hear was an indistinguishable murmur then suddenly her father's voice rose to a vehement shout of denial. 'I didn't do it, I tell you!' She stepped back as the door was flung open and the detectives strode into the hall, one of them turning before they departed to bark, 'We will require a sample of your handwriting, Mr Henderson. Come down to the station this afternoon.'

Tom was trembling with righteous anger, but he answered with dignity, 'I shall be very pleased to do that. What time?'

'Two o'clock.'

The family stood in a silent group and watched the two men go, then Tom burst out bitterly, 'So much for British justice. You can't believe how those two men tried to browbeat me into making a confession. They put words in my mouth, insinuated that I was in difficulties with money. In their eyes I'm guilty. I don't hold up much hope, Edna; they want a conviction and they don't care how they get it.'

'We'll put up a fight – it's not all over yet, Tom.'

'It's funny how they never touch people like the Mantoni brothers, isn't it?' Frances mused, remembering, in spite of the policeman's promises, a further threatening visit from Rikki, followed by an even more unnerving silence.

'There's quite a few bent coppers around and a backhander will work wonders in any walk of life,' said Gloria knowingly.

'Perhaps that's what I ought to do this afternoon, put something in the police benevolent fund box.' Tom gave a bitter smile.

Edna looked horrified. 'Tom Henderson, you'll do nothing of the sort.'

'Just a joke, love, but you can see how they get to you.'

Later on when Tom went down to the police station, he was informed that his handwriting would be studied against the signature on the postal orders by an expert and the procedure could take some time.

Gloom enveloped the Henderson household like a thick fog and no one, not even Roy, could concentrate on Christmas. Then on the twenty-third of December when the sun was a brief golden globe in a smoky sky, Dad came in carrying a large goose in one hand and a small Christmas tree in the other, although the enormous grin on his face was enough to tell them the news was good.

'It's all over, they checked the handwriting, decided it wasn't mine and the real culprit's confessed.' He did a few dance steps round the room in sheer joy.

'Thank God, it's bin a nightmare.' Edna started to sob.

Tom laid his purchases on the table and put his arms round his wife. 'Hey, come on hen, you should be smiling.'

'Oh I am really,' Edna replied and sobbed even louder, which made her children laugh.

'Was it who you thought it was, Tom?' Edna asked when she'd wiped her eyes.

'Yes. Poor devil, I feel sorry for him really, he must have been desperate and he's got a dying wife.' Tom was prepared to feel charitable now that his ordeal was over.

'He was going to let you take the blame, though,' Edna pointed out. 'He could have wrecked your life remember, lost you your job, had you sent to prison. Don't feel too sorry for him.'

'Well it's his life that is ruined now, whereas I can go back to work tomorrow. And I'll get compensation and back wages so we'll really be able to splash out for Christmas. You go and buy yourself a new dress, love, you deserve it.'

'But we need so much for the house,' Edna protested.

'Do as I say, woman,' he ordered and nuzzled his wife's neck, which made her go pink and laugh girlishly.

On Christmas Day, Edna cooked enough food to share with the Flynns next door. For Charlie, fly character that he was, had decided against sending his kids to the Sisters of Mercy. With charitable institutions anxious to push all sorts of benefits in his direction, he could see it was no disadvantage to be the father of nine motherless children.

Norman was invited round for dinner and for once even Nan, with the help of several eggnogs topped up with Guinness, unbent slightly. And when they all fell into bed at midnight everyone declared it was absolutely the best Christmas ever.

15

Office workers pushed past her wearing black armbands, Union Jacks flapped sadly at half-mast, and a pall of deep gloom hung over the city. Even the street lamps, it seemed to Kitty, glowed with a dimmer light this evening. Pausing on the steps of Pennywise Assurance, she thought to herself: The King is dead and today is my eighteenth birthday. Although she tried, Kitty could not suppress a passing resentment, because in due deference to the late monarch, all places of entertainment were closed.

It was hard to imagine on this bitter January day, that in May, in bright sunshine, they'd celebrated the King's Silver Jubilee. Of course the country had known for some days that his health was 'giving cause for concern', as the newspapers tactfully put it. Then last night in sombre tones the BBC had announced to the country that the King's life was drawing peacefully to its close. And he was hardly cold before the country had a new monarch, Edward VIII, a bachelor still, but who, as everyone pointed out, would have to stop gadding around and find himself a suitable wife. The succession had to be secured, so an heir was his first priority now, not dancing and hunting.

It'll be a state funeral of course, Kitty decided, and she was wondering whether that would mean a day off work when someone brushed past, catching her shoulder and almost pitching her face forward on to the pavement. As she struggled to keep her balance, the man reached out and caught her arm. 'I do apologize,' he said, following it with, 'Oh, it's you Miss Henderson. Are you all right?'

Kitty's heart gave several uneven skips. 'I . . . I think so.'

'All the same it might be a good idea to move,' said Robert Travis, and Kitty found herself being guided down the steps. She expected him to raise his hat and wish her a polite goodnight when they reached the pavement; instead he fell into step beside her.

The King's death pervaded everything, people spoke in low voices, shop windows were draped in black. Robert didn't seem inclined to speak and although Kitty was intensely aware of him walking beside her, for once she was lost for words.

'Sad news, isn't it?' said Robert eventually.

'Yes, it is.'

'But nothing daunted you're off to your studies I imagine.'

'No, not this evening. I don't suppose the college will be open. Besides, it's my birthday, so I reckon I deserve a night off.'

'Oh, congratulations. May I ask how old you are?'

'Eighteen.'

Robert smiled. 'A great age. No doubt you'll be celebrating?' With some young man, he almost added, but didn't dare.

'Fat chance. Everything's closed.'

'You ought to do something to mark the occasion. After all, you're only eighteen once.' Robert paused. 'Do you fancy coming for a drink?'

Astonished, Kitty asked, 'With you?'

'Who else?' He sounded amused. 'There's a nice quiet pub down by the river, we could go there. Of course, if you don't want to . . .' His voice trailed away.

'Oh no, I'd love to,' Kitty assured him hastily, then thought, what did you make of a man like this? For months now in the office, he'd rebuffed her slightest overture, made it clear that she was a humble typist, he the boss. Yet here he was, as charming and approachable as on that long ago evening in the park. Still, she couldn't have wished for a better birthday present so even if he reverted to type tomorrow, she'd treasure every minute of her time with him tonight, store it like a miser in her memory to dream about long afterwards.

'We'll cut through here,' she heard Robert say, and lightly touching her arm, he guided her down a dark side street. The Lord Nelson was a lopsided, half-timbered building that looked as if it had seen its share of smugglers and shady transactions in the past, and so close to the Thames, Kitty could hear the water slapping against the wall.

Kitty was prepared for the disappointment of finding the pub closed like everything else in London. However, not only was it open, but a huge fire burned in the grate, and because the place was practically empty, they were also given a lavish welcome by the landlord.

'Mr Travis, sir, what can I get you?' the man asked, wiping down the counter with a flourish.

'Well I shall have a whisky.' Robert turned to Kitty. 'What would you like, Miss Henderson?'

'A gin and orange, please.'

While Robert waited for the drinks, Kitty went over to a table by the fire. He watched her remove her coat, unwind a scarf from her neck, and shake her blonde hair free from a holly-red beret. It shone golden as a newly minted sovereign in the firelight and her young beauty moved and disturbed him so much he had to turn away. Whatever had induced him to invite her here after the months of keeping her at arm's length, he asked himself. Because he was a bloody fool, that was why, and lonely enough to risk playing with fire. If only he didn't ache for her so. If only things were different between him and Imogen, if only, if only . . . he could go on for ever. He was well aware of the hurt and bewilderment he'd caused Kitty over the past few months, and he didn't want her to misread a genuinely impulsive gesture. After all, what did he have to offer? Nothing except a lot of pain, and one false move and there'd be no going back.

Keep it casual, don't let an ache in the groin commit you to some damn stupid act you'll regret, Robert chided himself as he paid for the drinks and took them over to the table. Removing his own coat, he sat down, smiled at Kitty and raised his glass. 'Happy birthday, Miss Henderson.'

'Thank you, Mr Travis.' Kitty sipped her gin and orange with the studied poise of a young woman about town. Here they were, she and Robert alone together, their knees almost touching under the table. Bliss.

'How does it feel to be an old lady of eighteen?'

'Not so different from yesterday,' Kitty answered, and wondered if he would think her pushy if she used the occasion to discuss her job prospects at Pennywise.

Fortunately she was spared the need by Robert bringing up the subject himself. 'I hope you don't think I've forgotten my promise to you.'

'Oh, what promise was that?' Kitty gave him her most artless smile.

'You remember, the secretarial post. I asked but there just wasn't anything available at the time.'

'Don't worry, Mr Travis, I wasn't expecting anything,' Kitty lied and took another sip of her drink.

'An opportunity might arise shortly, though.'

Kitty put the glass down on the table and gave Robert her full attention.

'As you know, Miss Alice, Sir Sidney's daughter, is now working in the firm. At the moment she's learning the ropes, but she's a clever lady so I imagine she'll be wanting her own secretary soon. I could put in a word for you.'

Kitty leaned forward eagerly. 'Would you?' Then remembered – if she got the job she'd no longer be working for Robert. But she had to be practical. These were hard times and it might be her only chance to move out of the typing pool.

'Of course I can't promise you'll get the job,' Kitty heard

Robert say. 'My influence is limited. I'll do my best, though. You work hard and I think you deserve promotion.'

'Thank you.' She wasn't going to make the mistake this time of allowing herself to be too optimistic, but at least it sounded as if there were possibilities. 'What's Miss Alice like?'

Robert pondered on this question for a moment. What was Alice like? 'Brisk, efficient, and as you'd expect from any daughter of Sir Sidney, she has a good business head.'

'Would I like working for her?'

'That I can't say. And obviously if you didn't hit it off you'd find it difficult to move to another position within the firm. So perhaps you need to think carefully about this.'

'Here you are, Mr Travis, the sandwiches you ordered.' The landlord put a plate down on the table, a selection of chicken, ham and cheese sandwiches garnished with gerkins.

'Thank you, George.' Robert handed Kitty the plate so that she could help herself. 'I thought you might be hungry.'

'Oh I am.' Kitty took one. 'I usually have to wait until I get home.'

'And where is home?'

Kitty considered it unfair, having to admit she was a girl from the East End, particularly after all the trouble she'd taken to iron out her cockney vowels. For a second she was strongly tempted to lie and say Herne Hill, which was where Rose came from. But she knew there was a risk she would get caught out in her deceit and end up looking foolish, which would be even worse. 'Stepney,' she acknowledged with extreme reluctance.

'I'm from Kent originally and my mother still lives there. But my wife and I live in Holland Park.'

Wife. The word hung between them on an invisible thread. 'She's down in Surrey at the moment, staying with a cousin.'

Actually they'd gone to Angela and Bruce's for the

weekend but Imogen had refused to return to London with him, saying she couldn't stand being cooped up in the flat much longer and that he'd better start looking for a house. He had, in fact, already looked at dozens of properties, but not one pleased her. Like his mother, Imogen had no conception of money and turned away when he tried to explain that they had to live within their means. As always when he thought about his marriage, Robert began to feel depressed. He stood up. 'I'm going to have another drink, how about you?'

'Yes please.' Kitty handed him her glass and leaned back with a small purr of contentment. Robert had let her know his wife wasn't at home, so there was no hurry and they could relax and spend the evening here together.

When they finally left the pub at closing time, fog was drifting in from the Thames and a ship's horn sounded its warning to other river traffic. Kitty, who'd had far more to drink than was good for her, didn't notice that the cobbles were treacherous with black ice, and stepping into the street on unsteady legs she felt her feet slip from under her. Arms flailing, she let out a scream and would have taken a tumble if Robert hadn't grabbed her. Holding her in a bearlike hug, he murmured, 'That's the second time tonight I've had to save you,' and stared down at her with a strange, almost resentful expression.

The whisky had made him reckless, Kitty was happily tipsy, the street was dark and deserted. Kissing her would be so easy and Robert had to fight like mad against the temptation. He still had hold of her when he heard voices, and a group of Billingsgate porters on their way to the fish market went by. There was some coarse laughter then remarks were exchanged and, guessing they were at their expense, Robert quickly released Kitty. 'Come on, young lady, I'm taking you home.'

As soon as they reached the main thoroughfare he hailed a taxi and, more sober now, Kitty thought, God, he's going to see the dump where I live. She couldn't bear the idea of Robert associating her with such shabbiness, so before the taxi had a chance to turn into Tudor Street, she tapped on the window and told the driver to stop.

'I'm getting out here.'

'I'll walk down with you.'

'No thanks.' The taxi drew up by the pavement and Kitty jumped out.

'I enjoyed my evening very much, thank you.'

Her gloved hand was resting on the open window and he touched it lightly. 'It was my pleasure, thank you for coming.'

The taxi driver rolled his fag from one side of his mouth to the other and with a hint of impatience, enquired, 'Where to now, Guv?'

'Holland Park, Hobart Mansions,' Kitty heard Robert say. The taxi moved off, she gave a small wave, then turning, floated in a state of euphoria down Tudor Street. She'd almost reached the house when from the opposite direction she noticed another figure weaving an uncertain path home. She and Charlie Flynn arrived at their front gates simultaneously and where normally she wouldn't have given him the time of day, now Kitty called out cheerfully, 'G'night, Charlie.'

But Charlie, who wasn't a person for social niceties, snarled in return, 'I can't get this friggin' key in the lock.'

'Here, let me.' Exuding goodwill, Kitty moved round to his front door and opened it without difficulty. As the door swung back, she saw four of his small daughters standing in the hall and called to them reassuringly, 'It's all right, girls, it's only your pa.'

The sight of their father obviously offered them little comfort, for as he staggered into the house they pressed themselves against the wall. Then whimpering, 'Peggy! Peggy!' they scuttered off down the hall like frightened mice. Kitty heard fear in their voices and she wondered if Charlie had turned to beating his kids now that he no longer had a wife to knock about. Mum's opinion was that it would have been far better if the girls had gone to the Sisters of Mercy, and she was probably right. Peggy, now the household drudge, was struggling to make ends meet and at thirteen her face already wore the weary, defeated expression of a middle-aged woman. Tomorrow, Kitty decided as she let herself in the house, she must have a word with her mother about it.

The following morning Kitty woke with throbbing temples and a mouth that felt as if it was stuffed full of cotton wool. If that wasn't bad enough, when she put her nose above the blankets her breath condensed in the cold air. She hated these dark January mornings when the frosted window panes blanked out what little light there was and the bedroom resembled an igloo. Yielding to her fragile condition and the warm bed, she snuggled down for a further five minutes. But she was too self-disciplined to lie there long. Sliding her feet out on to the cold lino she looked around her with chattering teeth. 'Where the hell are my clothes?' she muttered then saw in the grey half-light, her dress lying on the floor. Misguidedly she stooped to pick it up and felt a screwdriver being driven through her skull. With an agonized groan, Kitty clasped her head and made her way with great care downstairs.

'Headache powders, where the devil does Mum keep them?' As Kitty searched around in a cluttered drawer, Tinker, deciding it was about time she paid him some attention, rose from his basket, yawned, stretched then plodded over to her. Wagging his tail he waited to be acknowledged. When the expected pat on the head failed to materialize, he barked loudly several times.

Kitty's face wrinkled in pain and to punish him she opened the back door. Freezing winter air rushed in and Tinker shrank back. But Kitty gave him a determined shove up the behind with her foot. 'Out!' she ordered.

She finally rescued a powder from the back of the drawer, sprinkled it into a glass of water and drank it with a shudder. After this she made herself a large pot of tea. Tinker was now scratching and whimpering at the door. Relenting, she let him in and together they went and sat by the fire.

For the first time in her life Kitty knew she was going to be late for work, but there was no way she could hurry. Mum always banked the fire up overnight at this time of the year so that it never went out and it was cosy with just the ticking of the clock. Sipping her second cup of tea, Kitty felt the pain in her head ease. How many gins had she had? Four? Five? Far more than she was used to. Robert had certainly loosened up after several whiskies and left her in no doubt that he found her attractive. Kitty shivered, not from cold but with a sexual excitement that trickled right through her body, and she had to force herself to remember that he was married. She stood up. Her headache had all but gone and it was time to be getting ready for work. When she and Robert met this morning his formality would no longer trouble her. Because even if he fought it, and she expected him to, they shared the secret knowledge of their powerful attraction for each other. All she had to do was bide her time.

Because no man had really interested her before Robert, Kitty's own sexuality had never been tested. Although it was propelling her forward now, she was innocent as yet of its terrible power. Usually so level-headed and in control, it didn't cross her mind to ask herself what she was letting herself in for. Even if anyone had warned her, Kitty wouldn't have listened. She'd already gone too far to want to turn back.

16

'But you promised you'd go with me, Kitty!'

'Go where?' Frances asked, coming into the room at the tail end of this conversation.

Andrew turned and Frances saw the crease of displeasure between his eyebrows. 'With my class to Epping Forest for the day on Saturday.'

Kitty didn't look up from the ladder she was meticulously and almost invisibly mending in a stocking. 'Sorry, I've changed my mind.'

'I can't manage the children on my own, you know that, so what do I do now? Let them down?'

'Seems like it,' Kitty answered indifferently, bit off the darning thread and admired her handiwork.

Good, it's taken time, thought Frances smugly, but Andrew's discovering that beneath that attractive surface, it's really all self with Kitty. 'I'll give you a hand,' she offered, quick as lightning.

Andrew swung round. 'Will you?'

'Sure, as long as I'm back in time to get to the Rex.'

Andrew looked so pleased Frances thought he might kiss her. 'You're a brick and don't worry, I'll have you back on the dot. The children don't get many treats and they've really been looking forward to this picnic. And for them to have been let down at this late date . . .' He cast a reproving glance at Kitty, who, without a word, got up and flounced out of the room.

Frances watched her antics with growing pleasure. Kitty was doing herself no favours with her spoilt behaviour. Later, in the bedroom, obviously trying to justify herself, she said, 'I don't envy you, spending the day with a bunch of snotty-nosed delinquents.' Then, rather snidely, she added, 'Still, I don't imagine you're really going for their benefit.'

Frances bristled. 'What exactly do you mean by that?'

'Come on, admit it, you've got a soft spot for Andrew.'

Frances turned away. 'Well, the way you make use of him, you obviously don't give a fig for Andrew,' she countered.

'Yes I do,' Kitty snapped, although in truth she was indifferent to any man but Robert now. These last three months sitting opposite him, taking dictation, maintaining a cool efficient demeanour while her emotions played havoc with her had been a joy and a torture. Joy because she knew he desired her, torture because being an honourable man he would never do anything about it. Kitty's ambition hadn't quite flown out of the window, but now that the secretarial job with Miss Alice had become, after a couple of interviews, a distinct possibility, the prospect of being parted from Robert desolated her. For the time being, however, she wasn't quite ready to drop Andrew. After all, she still needed someone to take her out and he was the only decent man around. He might be none too pleased with her at this precise moment, but she shouldn't have any problem sorting that out and her sister offered no real threat.

Frances had never been hiking before, indeed might never again, but she was determined to look the part for Andrew. So immediately the arrangements were finalized, she recklessly plundered her post office savings account and went out and bought a pair of shorts, an Aertex shirt and stout shoes.

Nowadays, with her earnings from singing, Frances was able to put money away quite regularly, although it had about as much chance of gathering interest as a rolling stone moss. For a start, Johnny had made it clear that her girlish frocks didn't do much for the band's image. 'Fancy yourself

182

up a bit, love,' he said. 'The punters like to see a touch of glam.'

This gave Frances a good excuse to go to the hairdresser for a set every week. She also took herself off to Wickham's, where she exasperated the assistant by trying on at least a dozen dresses. Finally she chose something rather sophisticated in chiffon and boldly patterned with flowers. It left her broke but it was worth it for the change she saw in the toffee-nosed assistant's attitude, particularly when she also purchased gold sandals and a pair of real silk stockings.

Perhaps it was something to do with confidence, but even Frances was aware that her looks and figure had improved. She knew too by Kitty's comments that she was jealous of her small success. 'A load of blinkin' amateurs,' her sister would say of the band in that sniffy way of hers. At one time her remark would have sent Frances spiralling into a mood of self-doubt, but she had her public now, they were her barometer, they told her she was all right.

Obviously anxious to assure themselves that their little girl was in no moral danger, one evening, without letting on, Mum, Dad and Gloria had turned up at the Rex. Paul had immediately charmed their fears away and Tom had pronounced him a well-brought-up, decent sort of young man. However it was obvious he had certain reservations about Johnny: 'A flashy type,' in Tom's opinion. Then, to Frances's astonishment, Johnny had talked him into increasing her singing engagements. 'She's a real crowd-puller your daughter, Mr Henderson. Let her come Friday nights as well, and I'll give her ten bob extra both nights.'

As simply as that it had been arranged and her name was now on posters all over the East End. The first time Frances saw one, she stood staring at it from the other side of the road. *We are pleased to announce that our resident nightingale, Miss Frances Henderson, has now been engaged to appear with Johnny Doakes and the Doughboys both on Friday and Saturday night.* Bursting with pride, Frances had longed to say to passers-by, 'That's me,' but she feared ridicule.

Today, on her way to meet Andrew, Frances kept sneaking glances at herself in shop windows and liking what she saw. Her breasts filled out her shirt nicely, the shorts showed off her slim legs to good advantage. It only remained to be seen whether Andrew was equally appreciative.

As it was, when she reached the station Andrew was in no position to notice her feminine endowments. Two lads were on the ground scrapping and he was trying to prise them apart, with little success.

Frances hadn't asked but somehow she'd imagined the party would consist of about half a dozen children, manageable for a day. But doing a quick head-count she reckoned there was double that, with boys and girls in equal number.

'Tan their backsides,' advised Frances, as she reached Andrew and the two young pugilists.

Andrew looked up. 'I don't believe in striking children,' he answered, somewhat pompously.

Having no such inhibitions, Frances bent down, grabbed the top boy by the scruff of the neck and pulled him to his feet. 'Behave yerself,' she ordered and gave him a shake.

The boy pulled himself free, glowered at her from under his eyebrows, muttered, 'Sod off, yer silly moo,' and swaggered back to his sniggering friends.

Frances's hand itched. So it's going to be that sort of day, is it? she thought, then noticed that the other boy, a small lad of no more than seven, had his head buried in his knees and was making pathetic whimpering noises. Frances touched his shoulder and held out her hand. 'Up you get,' she said, in a no-nonsense sort of way.

'Are you all right, Henry?' asked Andrew, bending so that his eyes were level with the boy's.

Henry ran his nose along the sleeve of his jumper. 'S'pose so.'

'Good.' Andrew straightened again. 'Shall we be getting on, then? I've already bought the tickets.' He shouldered a heavy haversack and handed Frances a brown carrier bag. 'Can you manage that? It's the sandwiches.'

With Henry attached to her like a limpet to a rock, Frances followed Andrew down on to the platform. The train steamed in, the children cheered and somehow between them, Frances and Andrew managed to bundle them into the same carriage. It wasn't a long journey but they were like jack-in-the-boxes, running from one window to the other and exclaiming, 'Look, sir, look,' whenever they saw a horse or cow.

Young Henry didn't join in these antics, but sat close to Frances sucking his thumb, and flinching if anyone so much as touched him. Frances put her arm round his shoulder and drew him close. Life was going to be very difficult for this little chap. He was too sensitive for his own good.

Although they'd been confined for less than half an hour, as soon as the train clanked to a halt, the children shot from the carriage like bullets from a gun. Then, to the annoyance of other passengers, they proceeded to tear up and down the platform like wild things.

Aware of the hostility, Andrew strove to maintain order. Clapping his hands for some quiet, he called out, 'Can you calm down, please. And be warned, if I have too much trouble today, this will be the last outing ever. Is that clear, Douglas?' He gazed sternly at the lad who'd recently been laying into Henry.

'Yes, sir,' Douglas answered with a meekness that didn't fool Frances. The boy had trouble written all over his sly face. Andrew might be taken in by the little blighter, but she was familiar with his kind. Any disruptive behaviour and she'd know where to look.

Checking that he hadn't lost any of his charges, Andrew called, 'Right, let's be on our way. I want you to walk two abreast and follow me without any messing about. Miss

185

Henderson will bring up the rear.' As an afterthought he added, 'Have you got the sandwiches, Frances?'

'Yes.' She held up the carrier bag.

'And I've got the lemonade.' Andrew patted the haversack. When he had the children as organized as they were ever likely to be, he marched them out of the station. They were scruffily dressed, none too clean and had harsh cockney voices: pedestrians skirted round them with such barely disguised disdain, Frances began to feel defensive on the their behalf. They weren't lepers, for God's sake.

The boys appeared incapable of maintaining an orderly file. They shoved each other into the gutter and tugged the girls' plaits, who then cried plaintively, 'Miss, make them stop!' However by now Frances had decided that unless she saw really vicious behaviour, she would let them get on with it. She certainly admired Andrew's dedication, though. He deserved a medal, teaching them all week then bringing them out on a picnic.

The day was humid and the walk through the small village and up a steepish hill gradually quietened the kids. Henry was dragging on her hand, the string handles of the carrier bag bit into her fingers and Frances could feel sweat breaking out under her armpits. Glancing down she saw unsightly damp patches on her new shirt. She was also making the painful discovery that her brogues weren't as comfortable as their price warranted, and she wondered how far Andrew intended to walk.

They soldiered on, passing small cottage gardens crammed with vegetables and flowers, skirted a dilapidated farmyard littered with the rusting skeletons of farm machinery and hummocks of oozing manure. A pig sloshing around in its own filth fascinated the boys, and they leaned over the fence to scratch its floppy ears and exchange grunts and snorts with the beast. But the girls, more fastidious, wrinkled their little noses in disgust. 'Poo, it stinks,' one of them declared, then they all ran off, convulsed with mirth.

Thankfully, Henry had now attached himself to the girls and looked a little happier, so Frances only had the carrier bag to worry about. The footpath turned away from the farm and cut across an untilled field. Weeds and thistles grew through the impoverished soil and even to her untutored eye it was obvious that good husbandry wasn't being employed here. 'Not much of a place, is it?' she called over her shoulder to Andrew, who was walking behind.

'Like everything else at the present time, farming is in a bad way. But it's even worse for labourers in tied cottages. Whole families are being evicted; mothers with babies still at their breasts, thrown out on the street with nothing but their few sticks of furniture. I've stood and watched it happen, and it brings shame on this Government and country.'

Oh dear, thought Frances, not politics. To change the subject she called, 'Are we going the right way?'

Andrew stopped, drew a map from the haversack and studied it. 'Yes. Once we reach the forest, we're nearly there.'

Frances walked on running her fingers over the lacy heads of cow parsley, and releasing its slightly sickly smell. In the forest, shaded by a green parasol of high beech trees, it was much cooler but even so it wasn't long before the children were complaining. 'We're 'ot, sir,' one of the girls moaned. 'An' I'm firsty,' whined another.

'Stop whingeing, you're supposed to be enjoying yourselves. Shoulders back, breathe in this fresh country air,' Andrew chided. 'We've only walked a couple of miles, hardly far enough to get any exercise.'

But nobody minded, least of all Frances, when they came to a break in the trees and there in front of them was a meadow. The sheer wanton display of wild flowers was overwhelming. Buttercups, daisies, delicate blue harebells and to give an added dash of brilliance, poppies.

Something in the untamed souls of the children was touched by the beauty of the scene and in the brief silence Andrew spoke. 'Well was it worth the walk?'

'Yes!' the kids yelled and with a whoop of delight they plunged into the lush vegetation.

Clearly relieved to be rid of his burden, Andrew let the heavy haversack fall to the ground and rubbed his chafed shoulders. With a wide yawn he dropped down on to the ground and, using the haversack for a pillow, stretched out full length and closed his eyes.

Frances allowed herself the small indulgence of studying his features. The skin was lightly tanned, the lashes long and in repose his mouth had a sweet vulnerability – she wondered what would it be like to kiss. Annoyed by his indifference, she picked a buttercup and drew it over Andrew's closed lids.

But he swatted it irritably. 'Don't do that, Frances,' he said and sat up. 'Anyway I'd better get this lot unpacked for the hungry mob.' He started pulling bottles of lemonade from his haversack and sandwiches from the carrier bag, while Frances unlaced her shoes and examined the heel of her left foot.

'I've got a blister,' she announced and prodded it gingerly.

'Never mind, all emergencies are catered for.' Andrew rummaged again in his haversack, and produced some salve and a tin of plasters. 'Here, let me see to it.'

Frances rested her foot on his thigh, and he bent over her smoothing the ointment on in a way that sent a strange but delightful sensation spiralling up her leg. He applied the plaster then leaned back on his haunches. 'You're not going to be able to walk far with that blister so it might be a good idea to leave your shoes off for as long as possible.'

He stood up and held out his hand. Frances took it and he pulled her to her feet. For a moment they stood face to face and she was certain she could feel the beat of his heart through the palm of her hand. Disturbed, she turned away. 'I'll call the children,' she said, and walked off down the field, grateful for the grass damp and cool between her toes.

The kids were entertaining themselves by swinging like

monkeys from the branches of a fallen tree and as she approached, Henry came running up to her with an agitated expression on his small face. 'Miss, we can't stay 'ere,' he panted.

'Why not?'

'There's polar bears in the next field.'

Frances smiled. 'Polar bears? A bit warm for them, I would have thought.'

'Come an' see if you don't believe me.' Henry took Frances's hand and dragged her to a gate. There, munching placidly, was a flock of sheep.

'They're sheep, Henry, and quite harmless.' Frances patted the boy's head to reassure him.

But Henry was still deeply suspicious. 'Well they don't look 'armless ter me,' he muttered as Frances led him back to where Andrew had the picnic spread out on the ground. By now the lemonade was warm, the paste sandwiches beginning to curl and the icing melting on the buns. But none of this bothered the children: to them it was a banquet and in less than ten minutes there was hardly a crumb left.

Andrew had talked of games, but the sun had broken through and the heat was now intense. 'I'm going where it's cooler,' he announced and moved over to lie in the shade of the trees. But Frances stayed put. A nice tan on her legs would save her the expense of stockings for a couple of weeks. From where she sat it was also easy to keep an eye on the kids. Not that the girls looked like being much trouble. They sat in a small circle weaving daisy chains and chatting quietly. For the boys the fallen tree had a strong magnetic pull and it became in turn a tank, an aeroplane and a horse. Frances's eyelids began to droop with the heat and she must have drifted off, but a wail of distress jerked her back to reality. She looked around for Andrew but couldn't see him and, assuming one of the boys had fallen from the tree, stood up. But the noise was coming from the bottom end of the field and the girls were already charging towards it. Anxious now, Frances hurried after them and found Henry, surrounded by a group of interested spectators, standing knee deep in a crater half filled with stagnant water.

Frances, whose patience was wearing thin, glared at each of the boys in turn. 'Right, who did this?'

Silence.

'Was it you, Douglas?'

'No, miss.' He gave her his sly grin.

'They said there was a polar bear ahind me an' I . . . I . . . was so frightened I slipped.' Reliving that moment of terror, Henry's sobs increased in volume.

'Well don't just stand there, get out,' Frances snapped.

'I . . . I can't, miss, me . . . me shoes is stuck.'

'Pull your feet out of them, then.'

'Ooh, I daren't. Me ma would give me a good 'ammering if I lost 'em.'

'Here, take my hand.' Grasping the branch of a small bush, Frances leaned out. As she did a piece of the bank subsided under her and she slid helplessly into the slimy green water beside Henry.

Frances's nerves were now beginning to disintegrate. Where was Andrew? Struggling to stay upright, she managed to pull herself, Henry, and his shoes, free of the sucking mud and on to the grass. Both of them were in a disgusting state and, maybe at the thought of the punishment likely to be meted out to him when he got home, Henry continued to snivel. However, the other children, enjoying themselves enormously, bounced around like excited grasshoppers.

She was just about to send a couple of the children in search of Andrew, when she heard his voice. 'What on earth's happened?' he asked, staring down at them. Then with a hint of amusement in his voice, added, 'My, you do look a mess!'

The thoughtless remark pierced Frances's pride. It was the last thing she needed anyone telling her. She knew for herself. Eyes blazing, she leapt to her feet. 'Thanks for the compliment, I don't get many of those from you. And I actually look like this because you're not doing your job. Where the hell have you been?'

At her attack, Andrew took a step back. 'Sorry, I was just doing a bit of exploring in the woods.'

'These kids are your responsibility. You see to them. I've had enough.'

For the first time that day the children were silent. Frances knew they were all watching her, but she strode back up the meadow with as much dignity as she could muster. She heard Andrew call her name but she refused to look round, and it was only pride that stopped her from bursting into tears.

17

The day hadn't exactly ended on a high note. It took them some time but eventually they found a horse trough where Frances, as best she could, washed the muck off herself and Henry. But even after she'd finished the boy still looked a sight. He stank to high heaven, there was a tear in the backside of his trousers and his hair stood on end like porcupine quills. And no one could weep like Henry; the tears fell from his eyes, copious, unstoppable. As for her own outfit, it was fit for nothing but the dustbin.

Frances placed the blame fairly and squarely on Andrew. If he'd been doing his job it would never have happened. Neither was he, in Frances's opinion, sufficiently penitent. So to drive her message home she maintained an unforgiving silence until they delivered the children up to their parents in the school playground. Henry was dragged away by his mother, a pinch-faced woman whose shrill voice could be heard berating her son all the way down the street.

Andrew watched them, an expression of concern on his face. 'Poor little blighter.'

'Yeah, there'll be a belting for him when he gets home I shouldn't wonder. Still, it could have bin worse I suppose.'

Andrew turned to her. 'What do you mean?'

'He could have drowned,' Frances answered and was gratified to see Andrew's face turn a shade paler.

'But it wasn't deep enough for that.'

'It don't have to be. Supposing he'd fallen in face first? I've heard of kids drowning in a garden pond.'

'Well Henry didn't drown, didn't come anywhere near it, and the other children enjoyed themselves.'

Frances gave him a chilly look. 'Yeah, particularly the sight of me covered in mud.'

'Look, I've said I'm sorry. What else do you want me to do? Grovel?'

'No, but I was made to look a fool.' Frances felt compelled to goad him, almost like a nagging wife. By now the last child had been collected and they were about to move out of the playground when Frances heard music. 'Listen, a band.'

'That'll be Mosley's biff boys on their way to a meeting, I bet. They like to make a lot of noise and stir up trouble, and this is a Jewish area, so we'd better hang on until they've passed in case there are fisticuffs.'

With a roll of drums and blast of trumpets the band turned into the street, and Frances and Andrew moved over to the school gates, closing them as a protection. Doors were flung open and people stood watching with sullen expressions. The air vibrated with such open hostility, Frances knew it would have exploded into open conflict if the fascists hadn't been well protected by an escort of police.

'It makes my blood boil the way those thugs always seem to have the law on their side.' Andrew's voice was harsh with indignation. 'But then, being a toff, I suppose Mosley's got plenty of good friends in high places.'

Behind the band marched the standard bearers, carrying Union Jacks and the fascist flag, and lastly came the foot soldiers, young men and women for the most part. Families, safe from retribution in upstairs windows, showered them with great gobfuls of spit, jeered, 'Go on, sod off you fascist murderers,' and banged loudly on pots and pans. Youngsters lobbed ready prepared bags of flour like hand grenades. Often they missed their mark but when they did make a direct hit, turning a black shirt white, a triumphant yell of 'Bullseye!' went up and everyone cheered.

However, the fascists were too well drilled to respond to the abuse and they kept on marching in a straight line. The kids' antics raised a laugh, though, and eased the growing tension.

'Look, there's that friend of yours, Norman.'

'Where?'

'Last row. I hope he knows what he's doing, stupid idiot. Whatever made him get mixed up with that bunch?'

Frances shrugged. 'It's no good asking me, I don't know nothin' about it.' But seeing him now, immaculately turned out in a black shirt, leather belt, highly polished riding boots and with the fascist insignia displayed on his left arm, it was her bet Norman had joined more for the uniform than the politics. She could see it gave him pride and he walked with the bearing of a professional soldier, back rigid and head held high.

More policemen brought up the rear and trailing along behind them came the usual detritus of the streets: a couple of tramps, a few stray dogs and a bunch of rowdy, anarchic urchins. And their antics, the way they mimicked the fascist salute and goose-stepped in time to the martial music, did more than anything to puncture the blackshirts' self-importance.

At the next corner the unit turned, the incessant drumbeat faded and, the excitement over, people hurled a few final words of abuse at them then went in and slammed their doors.

'Where are they off to?' asked Frances.

'There's a synagogue at the end of the next street, it's my bet they're going to have their meeting outside it.'

'Why don't the police stop them?'

'That's a very good question and one nobody has managed to answer yet.' Andrew took her arm. 'Come on, let's get you home, I can see trouble brewing.'

The surrounding streets were busy with people obviously making their way to the meeting. A van went by with a voice booming out over and over again from a loudspeaker, until Frances's ears rang: 'Sir Oswald Mosley will be speaking at the corner of Heron Street in half an hour. Every true Englishman should be there.'

'Let's turn down here, I can't bear listening to that crew,' said Andrew and directed Frances into a narrow back street of high-walled warehouses linked by gantries. At first Frances thought the street was empty but then at the far end she noticed a young man whose black garb and ringlets marked him out as an Orthodox Jew. It was clear he'd been running, for he was leaning against the wall and painful, rasping sounds came from his throat.

Before they had time to take in what was wrong, a van screeched round the corner on two wheels, slowed down long enough for two thick-necked bruisers to leap out, then in an excess of exhaust, roared on up the narrow street, missing Frances and Andrew by inches.

'Run for it!' shouted Andrew, but it was apparent the young Jew was hypnotized by terror. He was also hampered by his long coat.

Still too far away to help, Frances and Andrew watched the blackshirts closing in on him. 'Christ killer!' one of them taunted and reached out and knocked off his hat.

'Yellow livered scum!' the other spat out, grabbed the young man's glasses, flung them down on the pavement and pulverized them with the heel of his boot.

Savouring his fear, between them the thugs wrestled the youth to the ground. Then standing over him they began a frenzied verbal and physical assault on him. 'Greasy Yid! Hook-nosed unmentionable, get back to the jungle where you came from!' they ranted, aiming vicious kicks with their steel-capped boots at his ribs, stomach and genitals until his screams of pain echoed round the cavernous street.

'Lay off him, you rabble!' With a long running jump, Andrew reached them, pulled the larger one round and socked him hard in the jaw. The blackshirt retaliated, but Andrew ducked and his fist floated harmlessly through the air.

Frances, catching up, screamed, 'Leave 'im alone! Leave 'im alone!' Anger made her reckless and grabbing the other man's shirtsleeve she pulled. There was a tearing sound and sleeve and shirt parted company. Infuriated the man turned his wrath on her. 'Now look what you've done, you stupid bitch, ruined me uniform.' Eyes bulging like green marbles, he advanced towards her, arm raised, fist clenched ready to strike. Knowing she was about to be knocked for six, Frances took a step back into the gutter, stumbled, was trying to right herself when there was a shrill blast from a whistle and a policeman came running up the street.

'Move it, there's a copper,' one of them shouted and they bolted up the street.

Frances and Andrew were kneeling down attending to the young Jew when the policeman reached them. 'What's all this about, then?'

Andrew gave the policeman a cold stare. 'What does it look like? Fascist bastards, as usual, kicking the guts out of some poor devil because he happens to be a Jew. Why don't you go after them, catch them and lock them up? They get away with murder round here and the law doesn't do a thing.'

'Now son, that's no way to talk. I understand how you feel, but we're not all tarred with the same brush and I don't like them lot any more than you do.'

'That makes a change,' Andrew snapped.

But the policeman refused to be provoked. Taking a notebook and pencil from his pocket, he leaned over the young man who was now sitting up. 'How are you feeling, son?'

He spoke kindly but it was a pretty stupid question to ask someone shaking violently from shock and with a bad cut above one eye, as well as a bleeding nose and possibly some cracked ribs.

The young man muttered something in a foreign tongue which Frances recognized as Polish. 'Maybe it's just shock, but it don't sound as if he speaks English, so there's not much point askin' him questions. They smashed his glasses, too, so he can't see either.'

The constable put his notebook away. 'Perhaps the hospital ought to have a look at him.'

'He probably just wants to get home where he's safe. These people have fled from one lot of tyranny to face another. It just makes my blood boil.'

Guessing plans were being made on his behalf, the young man pulled a crumpled piece of paper from his coat pocket, smoothed it and handed it with trembling hands to the constable.

'It's his address. I'll see him home.'

'Mosley's gang are having a meeting not far from here,' Andrew warned.

'Don't worry, they don't cross swords with the law, so he won't come to any harm with me.'

Andrew, who'd been cleaning up the young Jew's wounds with a handkerchief, put out a hand and helped him to his feet. Frances picked up his hat which had rolled in the gutter and dusted off some of the muck. As she handed it to him, his short-sighted brown eyes glowed with gratitude, and he stumbled out a hesitant 'zank you'.

Frances reached out and touched him in a gesture of good fellowship and the constable took the young man's arm. 'Come on, son, I'm taking you home.'

Frances and Andrew waited until they reached the end of the street, then the young man turned and waved.

'Well at least he knows we're not all lousy bastards in this country. But you've seen first hand just what your boyfriend has got himself mixed up with. They're just a bunch of criminals.'

Frances bridled. 'Who said anything about Norman being me boyfriend?' But her eyes had been opened. After the savagery she'd witnessed today, never again would she be quite so indifferent to what Andrew was telling her. And as for Norman, well he could take a running jump. She was quite certain that if they hadn't been there, those two thugs would have kicked the young Jew to death. And for what reason? None other than that he spoke another language and had different religious beliefs. No one with any spark of humanity could behave like that and if it was what Norman was being taught on those camps he went to, she wanted nothing more to do with him.

Why can't Harry ever be on time, Gloria fumed. Irritated and hurt by his casual disregard for her, she thrust her head out of the bedroom window. Needless to say there was no sign of Harry, only Frances and Andrew returning from their day out. But what on earth has Frances been up to, Gloria wondered. She goes out smart as new paint and comes back looking as if she's been dragged through a hedge backwards. There was a relaxed intimacy in their manner that had never been evident before and they were talking animatedly. Gloria's mind skipped around various possibilities and discarded them. Even if they'd felt inclined, there wouldn't have been much opportunity for any hanky-panky, not with a load of kids in tow. And Andrew was still so bewitched by Kitty he probably hadn't even noticed that Frances had grown quite pretty of late. Using that marvellous voice had done wonders for her confidence, too. But Andrew took her so much for granted, she doubted if it would even occur to him to thank Frances for giving up a precious free day. That was men for you. Even the best of them were selfish buggers.

They reached the gate, Frances looked up, saw her and waved. 'Hello, Auntie.'

'Hello, sweetie. Had a good day?'

'An interesting one. I'll tell you all about it later.'

Well as long as you don't pin too many hopes on it, that's all, Gloria thought. But then that was the trouble with love, it was all so topsy turvy. It was supposed to make the world go round, but all it really did was make you miserable. Take her and Walter, for instance. He was a decent man and she only had to say the word and they could be wed. Time was ticking by for her and she'd have liked a couple of kids, but the trouble was she still hankered after Harry. Gloria splayed her fingers, admiring the engagement ring Walter had given her, and turning it so that the large diamond caught the rays of the evening sun. It must have cost a packet. She'd been so surprised that night he slipped it on she'd just left it there, and now she'd grown used to it. The sight of it irritated Harry no end, and he was always on at her to give it back. Not a chance, sunshine, it's staying right there as an insurance policy for the future. Harry talked of the good times being just around the corner, but he dangled promises like a carrot on a stick, and she was less gullible these days.

Gloria noticed that the kids had stopped playing hop-scotch and cricket and were running towards the end of the road. It was as if they had some secret coded message that told them Harry was on the way in his motor car. It turned smoothly into Tudor Street, Harry sounded his klaxon and excited kids ran along beside the car screaming, 'Gis a lift, mister, gis a lift.'

A couple of the more daring boys managed to jump on to the running board and hold on to the open window. 'Ger'orf you little sods.' Harry aimed a swipe at them and picked up speed. But they clung on in spite of the danger, although they were wise enough to be well out of reach of Harry's itching palm by the time the car drew up.

With an anxious expression, Harry got out of the car and inspected it for scratch marks. Finding none he then took out his handkerchief and reverently polished paintwork he could already see his face in.

Gloria smiled, then shouted, 'I'm just coming,' grabbed a jacket and ran downstairs, where Harry stood waiting with the car door open.

'Allow me, madam.' Helping her in, he closed the door and went round to the driver's seat. 'Right, 'ere's my itinerary. I've got to pick the boys up and take them to the club at nine, so that gives us two hours, sweetheart. Just about time for a drink and a bit o' you know what.' Harry gave her a cheeky grin. It never did any harm to try it on, in his opinion.

Gloria responded by giving him a good-natured clip round the ear. 'I like your sauce. I wouldn't mind a drink, but as for the other, well that depends how nice you are to me t'night, then perhaps we'll see.'

Harry hummed contentedly to himself as he drove to pick up Giorgio and Rikki. It did wonders, a bit of sex, really relaxed him, got rid of all the tension. But then one way and another, life was going along pretty nicely on all fronts at the moment, thank you. He was mixing with real toffs, even if some 'em were weirdos, was well in with the brothers and, as a special privilege, allowed to borrow this really peachy jalopy from time to time. Harry patted the steering wheel in a proprietorial manner. Wait till he got one of his own, Gloria would ditch Walter then. Of course, he didn't know what she got up to with old brown boots but she always delivered the goods for him. Gloria pretended to play hard to get but it was dead easy, talkin' her round. To keep her on her toes, he hinted that there were a couple of girls at the club givin' him the old come on. Not that he'd touch them with a barge pole. You never knew who that sort of women had bin with, and he was pretty particular. Picking up some nasty disease for the sake of a bit of nooky didn't strike him as really worth it. Still, Arthur seemed to be gettin' more than his fair share of what was going with Flo. Thick as two thieves they were, these days. Of course, if he was honest with himself, there were certain things in this trade he didn't have much of a stomach for to start with. It was all very well collecting from shopkeepers, bookies' runners and stallholders, who paid their tributes for protection without any trouble, knowing if they didn't pay up for one gang it would be another. But there were some who resisted, and that was when things got nasty. Like the coffee-stall keeper. He'd refused point blank to cough up as much as a farthing.

It was Arthur and him who'd bin sent along to give the bloke one last chance, but he wouldn't budge no matter how much they threatened. Of course being an ex-boxer gave him an unfair advantage. 'I hardly make a livin' as it is. Now sod off afore I give you a bunch of fives and knock yer teeth to the back of yer bleedin' 'eads.' He held up both fists in such a threatening manner, Arthur and Harry beat an undignified retreat down the street.

Discovering they were not the hard men they liked to kid themselves they were, him and Arthur had to resort to telling a few porkies to cover themselves, like how the coffee-stall holder had got a rival gang in. No one could look more malevolent than Rikki when he was riled. His swarthy features darkened and they stood quaking in their shoes, wondering if it was the chop for them. Surprisingly, Rikki seemed to swallow their story. 'Right, we'll scare the shit out that bugger. He'll pay up wivout any trouble after we've done wiv 'im,' he prophesied.

True to his word he gathered together some real heavies and gave Harry a revolver.

Harry handled the gun gingerly. 'What am I supposed to do wiv this?'

'Don't aim it at me for a start, the thing's loaded.'

'Christ!' Harry exclaimed and nearly dropped it.

Rikki studied him with suspicious eyes. 'You know 'ow to handle a gun, I suppose.'

'I sure do, Rikki,' Harry bluffed. But the weapon terrified him so much, he hadn't taken it with him as he'd been ordered to. They were going to rough a bloke up, weren't they? Not kill 'im. So without letting on, he'd hidden it away in his chest of drawers underneath a pile of clothes and deliberately forgotten about it.

It was just as well, too, because things got nasty that night. The other blokes were a right mean-faced bunch and he'd enjoyed being part of it, liked the way the customers had almost choked on their sausage rolls then quickly sked-addled when they turned up. Puttin' the fear of God into people gave you a marvellous feeling, in fact it was almost as good as havin' sex.

The coffee-stall keeper wasn't so easy to scare, though, and he'd taken the precaution of arming himself with an iron bar. You had to hand it to the bloke, he fought like a real champ and one of their number got it right on the skull. They'd had no choice then and following Rikki's instructions they'd rushed forward, overturned the stall and tipped the proprietor into the road. Harry could never remember anything like that almighty crash. The stall bounced several times, there was an explosion of smashed crockery and plates zigzagged across the road. And the mess! Christ, there was food everywhere, coconut cakes, sausage rolls, sand-wiches all swilling around in a cocktail of scalding hot water, milk and blood, and lying unconscious in the middle of it, the owner. Well 'e did ask for it, not paying up, thought Harry self-righteously.

A police patrol car sounding its gong made everyone run for it and the gang quickly dispersed. He and Arthur had legged it down the Mile End Road and jumped on the first bus that came along. The old adrenalin had really been pumping around in their veins that night. Pleased as punch with themselves, they'd been. Too breathless to speak they sat down, grinned and gave each other the thumbs-up sign. At last they'd proved that they were really hard men.

Life was exciting all right and it got easier after that. Well a bit anyway. You'd have thought an old bloke like Jacobs would pay his tributes without a fuss, especially after the threats, but no such luck. And it had to be me, didn't it,

Harry thought aggrievedly, who Rikki sent round to sort things out. He'd got as far as the shop door, saw Frances behind the counter and just couldn't go in. God, he could just imagine what would happen with Gloria if it got back to her he was threatening the old Jew. So him and Arthur had hit upon a brilliant scheme. Out of every packet of dope delivered to customers they extracted a small amount, sold it on when they had enough and pretended the money was Mr Jacobs's tribute.

Pleased with his cleverness, Harry smiled as he pulled the car up outside Giorgio's and Rikki's house. Maybe it was living a bit dangerously, but it made life a bloody sight easier, kept everyone happy and who wanted trouble? Everything would be just okay as long as Rikki and Giorgio didn't find out they were pulling a fast one, for if they did – here Harry shivered as if someone had run over his grave – it would definitely be curtains for both of them.

18

'Mr Travis, whatever have you done to your face!'

Touched by Kitty's expression of tender concern, Robert gingerly fingered the painful wound and bruising on his cheekbone. 'Does it look an awful mess?' he asked.

'Well to be honest, yes,' Kitty admitted.

'Do you know, I did the most stupid thing this morning and caught it on a cabinet door in the kitchen,' Robert lied and wondered what Kitty would say if she knew the miserable truth of his situation, the travesty that was his marriage. 'Probably I should have gone to the hospital and had it stitched, but it didn't seem so bad at the time,' he went on, thinking to himself: Another inch and Imogen might have blinded me. And all because he'd spoken to her sharply. With good cause, too, for her carelessness had gone beyond a joke and when he'd come in from work and found, yet again, a cigarette smouldering on the very expensive Turkish carpet, he made no attempt to hide his annoyance.

'Imogen, for heaven's sake be more careful. Do you want to set this flat on fire?' Picking up the cigarette, he ground it out on the ashtray from where it had fallen.

Imogen, who more or less chain-smoked these days, didn't reply. Instead, deliberately rebuffing him, she took another cigarette from a monogrammed silver box and lit up with the matching table lighter. She did it with slow, precise movements, her pale, elliptical lids lowered against the smoke and on her face an expression he couldn't fathom.

'Are you paying attention to what I'm saying, Imogen?' Robert heard his own voice, sharp and schoolmasterly, as if reprimanding a child.

Weighing the lighter in the palm of her hand, his wife inhaled with an edgy resentment and still didn't answer.

Robert had no warning, didn't see the lighter coming, only felt the heavy metal gouge into his cheekbone with a force that knocked him off his feet and sent him reeling backwards into a chair with a yell of pain. His ears and head were ringing from the impact, his vision was blurred, but he still heard the lighter thump heavily across the parquet floor and was aware of blood dripping on to his trouser leg. 'Christ, what did you do that for?' he exclaimed, shocked by her violence. Nursing his cheek he glanced up and got his answer. His wife stared back at him, trembling and ashen-faced, and there was such unveiled hatred in her dark eyes, Robert hung his head in despair. There was just no hope for them, not now or in the future.

And yet he'd tried so hard. To the best of his ability and where his pocket would allow it, he'd catered for every whim, but he knew he finally had to accept that this woman whom he called his wife remained a stranger to him. And in facing up to this fact, Robert at last felt liberated from the constraints of marriage.

He remembered the start of it all, their wedding, and afterwards driving down to Dorset in his little sports car, his beautiful wife beside him, and full of hope for the future. Then had come the sham of their honeymoon. He was gentle and considerate with Imogen, but she refused to be touched. In fact one night she grew quite hysterical and the strange glances of the other guests the following day had so shamed him, he decided to leave immediately.

During the months that followed, the marriage remained unconsummated and as Imogen's behaviour became more erratic, Robert couldn't quell a growing suspicion. The family, he was certain, must have had some inkling of Imogen's tenuous grip on normality and had kept quiet about it. As he came to the bitter conclusion that he'd been hoodwinked into marriage, Robert grew fearful about their future together. And yet he'd once adored this girl who was his wife in name only, had thought her the most divine creature on earth. Under the circumstances he'd have no trouble getting the marriage annulled, but he had a strong sense of duty. For better or worse Imogen was his responsibility and he couldn't put her fragile personality through the shame of the divorce courts. It would be the end of her, and he could never live with that guilt. So Robert came to a decision. He would continue to care for Imogen as best he could. However, he was a normal man so from now on he would pursue his deepening attraction for Kitty, held in check so far only after intense struggles between conscience and desire.

Robert glanced at Kitty. She was sitting, one leg crossed over the other, doodling on her notepad and waiting for him to start dictating. A dart of longing ran through him and simultaneously an idea. Shuffling his papers, he gave her an apologetic smile. 'I'm sorry, Miss Henderson, could I call you back later? I haven't got quite as many letters as I thought.'

Kitty, who while she was waiting had been idly writing 'I love you' over and over again in shorthand, quickly scored through the symbols and stood up. 'That's all right, Mr Travis. What time do you want me back?'

'About four.'

Kitty looked surprised.

'Is that too late?'

'No, but it means I probably won't have time to get the letters finished today.'

'Don't worry, tomorrow will do.' Convinced that his scheme must look transparently obvious, Robert began to feel foolish.

But Kitty smiled back at him in happy ignorance. 'Oh that's all right, then.'

After Kitty had gone, he gave the telephone operator Aunt Bertha's number in Richmond and held on while she dialled it.

Apart from Imogen, he and Aunt Bertha had nothing in common so their relationship had always remained formal. She never looked particularly pleased to see him and today her voice was cool at the other end of the phone.

'Aunt Bertha, I need to talk to you about Imogen. I'm really concerned about her health and feel she needs medical help.'

'I can't understand that. Imogen might look frail, but when she was with me she never suffered a day's illness.' The criticism was implicit.

This is going to be damn difficult, Robert thought. 'It's not her physical health I'm talking about.'

'I don't think I understand, Robert.' The disembodied voice sounded suddenly wary.

'It isn't easy to say this, Aunt Bertha, but I'm afraid it's Imogen's mental health that concerns me. Her behaviour is very irrational at times and increasingly hard to ignore.'

'How dare you imply that Imogen is unbalanced! My niece is artistic, and all talented people are highly strung and emotional, I thought you would have realized that.'

Robert understood Aunt Bertha's reluctance to acknowledge Imogen's illness: as he'd discovered for himself, it was a painful and frightening fact to have to confront. Neither did he wish to cause her further hurt by going into the details of Imogen's attack; to explain how afterwards he'd pleaded with her to tell him what was wrong, or the inconsolable weeping his questions induced. But he was forced to, stripping his own feelings bare in the process. He also told Aunt Bertha how it took over two hours and a sleeping draught to finally calm Imogen down. Mercifully, she'd still been asleep when he left the flat this morning, her face innocent as an angel's and with no hint of her mental turmoil.

He continued with his explanation, quietly and calmly, hoping to penetrate that inflexible mind, or maybe for her even to show a hint of sympathy for his plight. But he waited in vain. It was sufficient to have married a D'arcy, even if the family tree had diseased roots. But at least there was one thing he could be thankful for in this sorry mess. With the marriage unconsummated, he wouldn't bear the responsibility of some child inheriting that tainted blood.

'I shall go to Holland Park and bring her back here. If you had the faintest understanding of Imogen, you'd realize it's being cooped up in the flat that's causing the problem. She feels stifled in it, she told me so herself. A girl of her sensibilities needs to be in touch with nature and her inner self. She should be living in a house with a garden.'

'We've looked at dozens of houses, but Imogen hasn't liked any of them and I'm not yet in a position to afford the sort of property she's set her heart on, without falling heavily into debt.'

'What the dear poor child needs is a break. I'll see she's properly looked after for a few days.' Her tone implied that here was one more area in which Robert was sadly wanting.

There was a lot Robert could have said, but showing remarkable restraint he kept his mouth shut. Besides, although she'd have been surprised to know it, he felt intensely grateful towards Aunt Bertha. For a short while he would be rid of Imogen and her volatile moods. Because the idea of having to face his wife tonight filled him with a most awful dread. 'Are you quite sure, Aunt Bertha?' he asked, trying not to betray his relief.

'Absolutely sure.'

'Mrs Webb, the housekeeper, should be there by now, she'll let you in. You'll also be able to judge for yourself whether she should see a doctor, then we'll talk about it again. I don't care how much it costs. All I want is for Imogen to be well.'

When Aunt Bertha rang off, Robert replaced the receiver on the cradle, leaned back in his chair and in a great release of tension, stretched his arms high above his head. For a few days he was a free man. A bachelor. As if observing himself from a distance, he was aware of lifting the phone again and asking for a line. He dialled the number of a restaurant with fumbling fingers, got the wrong number and had to try again. On the second, successful, attempt, he booked a table for two for seven o'clock then, shaken by what he'd done, he sat staring at the phone, knowing he was a reckless fool and would surely pay for it.

Kitty returned at four and Robert dictated steadily for an hour. A little after five he rubbed his neck in a weary gesture. 'I think that's enough for today. I expect you'll be wanting to get off to your evening class.' He held his breath and waited for her answer.

Kitty, who was checking her shorthand, looked up. 'Oh no. That finished last week. I got my certificate for a hundred and forty words a minute, like I said I would,' she added with pride.

Robert breathed easily again. This was even better than he hoped. 'Clever girl. How about a drink then, to celebrate your success?'

Her skin flushed pink. 'This evening?'

'Yes. The Lord Nelson where we went before.' Robert spoke quickly to hide his nervousness. 'At six, say. I'll meet you outside.'

'Thank you.' Without another word Kitty stood up and left the room and Robert had a brief crisis of conscience. There was already an inevitability about their relationship and it would move forward now under its own momentum. So for Kitty's sake, should he nip it in the bud? She was only eighteen, after all. Hardly at an age to know what she wanted or even to understand what a risky voyage she was embarking upon. Well she still had a chance to change her mind, Robert told himself as a salve to his doubts. There would be no hurrying her, tonight they would drink, talk and eat, that was all. At least he no longer had to agonize

209

over his own behaviour, for he could hardly stand accused of being unfaithful to a wife he'd never had a sexual relationship with.

Robert gave a pleased glance around the small restaurant. With individual booths to protect them from prying eyes, he'd chosen well. And it was expensive enough to impress Kitty without being intimidating. He smiled at her over the wine list.

'Shall we have the hock?' he suggested.

Kitty hadn't the foggiest idea what hock was, but she would have died rather than admit it to Robert. 'That would be lovely,' she answered and went back to studying the menu, which, thank heavens, was in English, then blanched when she noticed the cost of each dish. Lobster thermidor at that price! Kitty blinked in astonishment. Why it would pay her wages for a week. Still Robert must be able to afford it and it was the sort of restaurant she'd always dreamed of being taken to . . . and, she glanced across at Robert, with a man like this. She didn't want to spoil the evening by asking herself too many questions, such as why had he brought her here, and where was his wife. In case she never got the chance again of this glimpse of another way of life, she wanted to savour every precious moment: the starched table linen, the cutlery set out in precise order of use, the solicitous waiters.

'Have you chosen yet, Kitty?' she heard Robert say.

Kitty glanced down the menu for the cheapest dish. 'Lamb cutlets, please.'

'I'll have the same,' said Robert to the hovering waiter, and as he went another came over with a slim brown bottle. The wine waiter presented the label to Robert to read before removing the cork and pouring a small amount into his glass. Robert tasted the wine, nodded his approval and the waiter then moved round and filled Kitty's glass. As he poured, the glass misted over and when Kitty tasted it, the wine was so cold and sweet on her tongue she immediately took several more sips.

'What do you think?'

'Mmm, it's delicious.'

So are you, Robert wanted to say, but curbed himself. There must be no rushing.

The wine helped Kitty relax and by the time they were having liqueur with their coffee, she was leaning back surveying the other diners and thinking to herself, I was made for this way of life. When earlier, in the Lord Nelson, Robert had casually suggested they go somewhere for dinner she'd been so flustered at the idea she'd almost said no. He probably mistook her hesitation, imagining she would feel out of her depth in a posh restaurant. But really it was more to do with being in an intimate situation with Robert, facing him across a table and still unsure where their relationship was heading. Kitty herself was now quite clear what she wanted and had stopped thinking about the consequences. Married or not, there was no man for her but Robert. He was so at ease with himself, so masculine, so deeply attractive.

They didn't discuss what was on both their minds or where it would lead. Instead they kept to safe topics, talked about the theatre and plays they'd seen.

'I saw you at the theatre once,' Kitty dared to say. 'With your wife.'

'Oh.' He gave her a guarded look.

'She's very, very beautiful,' Kitty ventured, deciding it was time the subject was brought out into the open.

Robert twisted the stem of his brandy glass. 'Yes and talented. She could have been a professional pianist.'

So why are you with me tonight instead of her? was the question that hung between them. But instead of giving Kitty the answer she wanted, Robert called the waiter for the bill.

Outside on the pavement, they stood looking at each

other, then Kitty held out her hand formally. 'Thank you for a lovely evening. I've really enjoyed myself, but I must go.'

Robert held on to her hand, his eyes lingering on her lips and imagining their softness. 'No, don't go yet,' he pleaded, his good intentions flying out of the window. He'd been starved of a woman's body for so long, he wanted to take this girl in his arms now, here in the street, to touch the warm skin and inhale the womanly essence of her.

'My parents will be worried if I'm too late.'

'Yes, of course.' He let go of her hand. 'But let me take you home.'

Over his shoulder Kitty saw a bus approaching that would take her to the top of Tudor Street. 'It's all right, I'll catch this,' she said, and leapt on as the bus pulled up. She waved to him, called again, 'Thank you,' then, congratulating herself, went and sat down. She'd found the strength to walk away from him and Kitty, being the girl she was, knew that once you were sure you'd safely hooked a man, it never did any harm to keep him dangling.

He dreamed about her that night, vivid, erotic, disturbing dreams that stayed with him when he woke and well on into the day. 'Damn and blast it,' Robert swore and, unable to concentrate, hurled a book at the wall. Later, when Alice came into his office to discuss a claim put in by an almost bankrupt businessman whose factory had conveniently gone up in flames, Robert stared at her blankly when she put a question to him.

'Robert, whatever is the matter with you? You're not listening to me.'

'Sorry, Alice, but I've quite a lot on my mind at present. Imogen isn't well.'

'I'm sorry to hear that. What's the problem?'

'Her nerves.'

'Oh dear. We must arrange for you to bring her down to

Leyborne for the weekend soon. I'm sure she'd find it very relaxing. Does she ride?'

'No, but I'm certain she'd enjoy it just the same. Thank you, Alice.' In fact Robert knew Imogen would adore a weekend away. In true D'arcy fashion she was in her element in large country houses. The only problem was, it often made her restless when she got back home, making it clear he wasn't the good provider she'd been led to believe he was. Still, it might help him. His career prospects looked pretty stagnant at the moment and a weekend with Sir Sidney and his daughter might nudge the old man into considering him for something better, a directorship perhaps. After all they shared a surname, and he could certainly do with the extra cash. His mother continued to make calls on his pocket in spite of the allowance Sir Sidney made to her, and if, as it looked at present, Imogen was going to need some sort of psychiatric help, well that wouldn't come cheap. With a larger salary he might even be able to afford a decent sized house.

'I'll talk to Father, sort out some dates. Oh and another thing, Father tells me I'll be having my own office soon. I've also more or less decided on that young Miss Henderson you recommended as my secretary. I interviewed several girls but she seemed far and away the best.'

Robert swallowed. God, he was going to lose her. 'I'm sure you'll find her extremely efficient, Alice, I always have.'

'I'll arrange one final interview with her as soon as I'm settled.'

Robert didn't mention his conversation with Alice when he rang down for Kitty a little later. In fact he didn't even bother to give her any dictation. All he said, was: 'A drink? At the same place?' Kitty replied with the merest nod and Robert thought, it can't go on like this or I'll explode.

The Lord Nelson was crowded and noisy and Robert was impatient to be on his own with Kitty so after one drink he grabbed her hand and said, 'Come on, let's get out of here.'

It was a warm evening so they strolled along by the river and through the Embankment Gardens where the trees and shrubs had the dusty look of late summer. They walked apart saying nothing, but the space between throbbed with sexual tension. This seemed to be the place where courting couples came and the gardens were busy with most of the benches occupied. After a while Robert finally found what he was searching for, a secluded spot behind a tree and here he pulled Kitty to him. Looking down at her he murmured, 'Oh Kitty my love, you don't know how long I've been waiting to do this,' and tilting her chin he bent his mouth hungrily to hers.

Kitty, all her senses on fire, moulded her body to his. Through her thin summer dress she could feel his need for her with a mixture of excitement and fear and all the while a pulse beat in her ears like a warning. He's married, and not like your usual young lads. He won't be satisfied with kisses and romance. He'll want more, lots more. But she was already too deeply and hopelessly ensnared to heed these warnings.

A polite cough made them leap apart. A policeman was standing there. 'Oh good evening, constable,' said Robert with an embarrassed smile and he and Kitty were forced to walk sedately on.

Although dizzy with lust, the following day Robert managed to dictate about six letters in a fairly businesslike manner. At five-thirty, when he was sure the offices had emptied, he got up and went and turned the key in the lock. He had stopped asking himself if what he was doing was right. He didn't even ask himself if he loved Kitty, he was just driven by the desperate, primitive urge to lay claim to her ripe, peachy-soft body. Standing in front of her he began to undo the buttons on her blouse with fumbling, unsteady fingers.

Kitty had never permitted a man to touch her breasts

before, and she kept very still as he pulled down the straps on her petticoat. She could hear his jagged breathing and her own heart was pounding violently against her ribcage as he pulled her to her feet. With hungry kisses he lifted her on to the desk, then cupping her breasts in his hands he bent and gently took a nipple in his mouth. Almost swooning with ecstasy, Kitty closed her eyes. Then just down the corridor she heard women's voices and the clatter of buckets. In a panic she pushed Robert away. 'It's the cleaners!' she whispered and hurriedly buttoned her blouse. 'They'll be wanting to get in here in a minute.'

'Christ almighty,' Robert raged in frustration.

'I'd better go.' Supposing they were caught like this, she with her clothes in disarray and being made love to by her boss. If word got around they'd both be out on their ears.

'No, sit down and keep calm,' ordered Robert, taking control of the situation. 'Open your pad, pretend you're taking dictation. If they come in I'll say we're working late.' He went and unlocked the door, straightened his tie, adjusted himself below, then sat down behind his own desk. 'Kitty, listen to me. Would you come to my flat?'

'Your flat?' She gave him a startled look. Had he gone mad? 'But what about your wife?'

'Imogen's not there. She's gone to visit her aunt in Richmond for a few days.' He spoke quickly and urgently, trying not to think what he was doing. 'Please, please say you'll come.'

Kitty hesitated. Although she was certain of her own feelings for Robert, she would have never dared to imagine their relationship reaching this stage. But now matters were suddenly careering along at a frightening pace and she was finding it hard to cope with all the unfamiliar emotions of love, fear and guilt raging through her. And although more than anything in the world she wanted to please him, Robert seemed to be asking her to take more and more risks. 'What will happen when we get there?'

He reached over the desk for her hand, a tender expression in his brown eyes. 'Nothing you don't want to happen, my love. I'm just desperate to hold you in my arms, that's all.'

It was an irresistible combination: tenderness plus his need for her. Kitty gave up trying to hold out. 'All right, I'll come, but only for a little while.' By laying emphasis on the little while, she was able to deal with any lingering doubts she had about going to a married man's flat.

She loved to see him smile and he did now. His eyes lost their sombre look and the corners of his mouth lifted. 'Good girl. Get the Underground to Holland Park and wait for me outside the station.'

Feeling as if she were on a switchback and couldn't get off, Kitty ran downstairs to the typing pool, collected her handbag and jacket and walked to the Underground. Waiting on the platform she could hear in her head the insistent voice of common sense. Take the train east, not west, go home, it said. What and be denied all the excitement, this delicious terror? No fear, the reckless part of her nature answered and when the next train west came in, Kitty jumped on.

Hanging around the exit at Holland Park made her feel like some cheap pick-up, and when two smirking young men called out to her, 'Hello, dolly,' Kitty was so offended, she would have gone home if Robert hadn't just then come up the steps. Taking her arm, he hailed a taxi and soon they were clanking up in the lift of a rather smart block of flats. As it ascended the thought niggled away at Kitty again that this wasn't part of the life plan she had drawn up for herself. There could be no future with a man who already had a wife and if she had an ounce of sense, she'd tell Robert here and now that she wanted to end it. But she lacked the willpower and anyway, she was too hopelessly committed to him.

The lift squeaked to a halt and Robert opened the gates.

'Supposing one of your neighbours sees us?' Kitty asked, in a frightened voice.

Sensing she was on the verge of making a bolt for it, Robert took her hand and squeezed it reassuringly. 'That's very unlikely. Apart from the caretaker, you never see a soul here. I'd be surprised if they even recognized me.'

Still uneasy, Kitty kept casting glances over her shoulder while Robert unlocked the flat door. By the time she stepped over the threshold her mouth was dry with apprehension and she expected to be confronted by a wrathful wife, rolling pin in hand. Robert pushed the door shut and stood leaning against it while Kitty took a cautious look around her. No wife, thank heavens. Growing more brave she moved further into the room. She really knew very little about Robert, but maybe this flat would offer up some clues. Had he any children, for instance? Toys, those were the things to look for: a Dinky car left under a table, a rag doll abandoned on a chair. But a quick scan revealed nothing. In fact the room was abnormally tidy and had a rather gloomy, unlived-in look. Magazines were laid out on a coffee table in precise date order and she certainly didn't care for the heavy furniture. Her taste was for modern decor. To give herself more time, Kitty moved over to the bookshelf and inspected the titles. As well as leather-bound classics there were also popular writers like A. J. Cronin and J. B. Priestley. The lid was up on the piano and she went and stood in front of it. 'Is this your wife's?' Kitty could never bring herself to say her name.

'Yes. Do you play?'

'Only Chopsticks.'

He laughed. 'I can do a little better than that.'

Robert realized that all this prowling about the room was to hide her nervousness. In fact, having got her here, he felt pretty much on edge himself. He did so want her, but if he wasn't careful he still might frighten her away. Moving over to the sideboard he mixed them both a cocktail. 'Come and sit down and drink this.' He handed her a glass with a green olive on a stick in it and patted the sofa.

Kitty did as she was bid, but when he went to put an arm round her shoulder, she pulled away.

'Are you sure your wife won't come back?'

'Quite sure.' He had in fact taken the precaution of ringing Aunt Bertha before he left the office. Imogen refused to speak to him, but her aunt had informed him she was looking a picture of health and they were shortly going to supper with friends.

'Oh.' Kitty drank her cocktail in almost one go and handed him her glass. 'Can I have another?' With two drinks inside her she was certain she'd feel a lot braver.

'Certainly.'

And sure enough, by the time Kitty had finished the second drink all the things she felt nervous about no longer mattered. She moved closer to Robert, rested her head on his shoulder and allowed him to unbutton her blouse. When he'd removed it, Robert pressed her back on the sofa and carefully eased her skirt up her legs until the soft white flesh between her french knickers and her stocking tops was revealed.

Kitty didn't protest when he undid her suspenders and rolled her stockings down her legs, but a pulse beat in her ear and her head and heart were locked in mortal conflict. One had to win. Should she let Robert go the whole way? Rose had told her that when men put it in you the first time it hurt so much, you screamed out in agony. Although she loved Robert more than anyone in the world, she wasn't sure if she was prepared to go as far as endure pain. But he had her skirt off now and was leading her into the bedroom. She allowed him to remove her petticoat and press her down on the bed, but while he hurriedly pulled off his clothes, Kitty turned her head away. She'd never seen a man naked, except Roy and he didn't count. When he lay down beside her she shyly covered her breasts with her arms.

'Don't do that, my darling.' Robert gently pulled her arms away. 'I want to look at your lovely body. You can't imagine how often I've dreamed of doing this.'

She raised her head slightly. 'Have you? How often?'

'Twenty times a day, every time I see you. My sweet girl, you fill my mind, my soul, don't you realize that?'

She had to know. 'But your wife, what about her? Don't you love her?'

'Not in this way, never this way.' Gently he allowed his hands to roam across her breasts and down over her stomach. She was perfectly proportioned, full-breasted with a slim waist and long legs.

'What do you mean?'

'Kitty, I want to tell you something. Imogen and I haven't got what you call a proper marriage. Do you understand what I'm getting at?'

Kitty looked puzzled. 'Not exactly.'

'What I'm saying is we've never lived as most husbands and wives do.' Robert felt ashamed making such a confession, as if the fault lay with him. It also put his manhood in question.

'You mean . . . ?'

'I mean the marriage has never been consummated.' There, he'd said it. 'I've never told that to a living soul before, Kitty.'

'Not consummated?' It was so astonishing, Kitty took a little time to absorb it. How could anyone possibly resist Robert? He was the most sexually attractive man she'd met in her life. And she wasn't the only one who thought this. From discussions she'd overheard, quite a few girls in the typing pool would have been more than willing to drop their knickers if he'd asked. 'But why not?'

'I can only suppose she doesn't love me.' Robert's sense of loyalty wouldn't allow him to discuss Imogen's mental state with Kitty at this stage in their relationship.

'Why did she marry you, then?'

'Because I asked her, I imagine. And I probably looked a good prospect.'

'You poor, poor dear.' Just imagine, forced to live like a monk. But not for much longer. Kitty reached up and wound her arms round his neck. She no longer felt a sense of guilt and she was ready now to make her great sacrifice.

It was so long since he'd made love to a woman, Robert was worried that in his feverish, desperate need for her, he would be clumsy. He managed to control himself, though, taking pleasure in the silky texture of her skin and skilfully bringing her to a moist receptiveness, although she still stared up at him with large frightened eyes when he entered her. 'Will it hurt?' she asked.

'No, I shall be very gentle, my darling.'

'Supposing I have a baby?' she continued, as he moved above her.

'You won't. Trust me.' He kissed her. 'Just relax, darling, there is nothing in the world better than making love.'

Kitty wasn't so sure and it did hurt, but not as much as she had imagined. Then very quickly and with a groan Robert expelled something sticky on to her stomach. He didn't move but lay very still on top of her, holding her very tight and breathing heavily. So that's what it's like, thought Kitty. Rose had exaggerated the pain, books the rapture. She wasn't disappointed, but there again she wasn't sure what all the fuss was about. What she did feel, though, was a sense of triumph. She was Robert's true wife now, not that other sexless creature. If she could go on giving him this, it would bind him to her, and so tight, he would never leave.

They were dozing in each other's arms when the phone rang. Robert lay a long time before padding naked into the other room to answer it. His voice was too low for Kitty to catch what he was saying but he wasn't gone long.

'Who was it?' she asked pulling him back possessively

into her arms and stroking his dark hair back from his forehead.

His eyes had a dull, hopeless look and his voice was expressionless as he answered her. 'It was Imogen and she says she's coming back tomorrow.'

19

It was the horrifying attack on the young Jew that finally shamed Frances into confronting the depth of her ignorance about what was happening in the world around her. So in an attempt to rectify this she listened more carefully to what Andrew was saying, read her dad's paper and at the first opportunity, confronted Norman. 'I saw you the other night, marching with those thugs.'

'We ain't thugs,' Norman countered. 'Sir Oswald believes in order. If there's trouble at our meetings it's always commies like Andrew who start it.'

'So how do you account for two of your lot nearly kicking a young Jew to death that same night?'

Norman looked uneasy. 'I don't know nothing about that.'

'Well you should,' Frances retorted. 'If Andrew and me hadn't rescued him they'd have probably kicked his brains in.'

'Jews don't understand our ways and they shouldn't be 'ere.'

'So you think that's a good enough reason for killing someone, do you?' asked Frances, her voice growing high with indignation.

'Don't put words into my mouth. But it's gettin' so our streets don't belong to us any more. And Sir Oswald says the Jews haven't got any sense of loyalty.'

'You're talking about people like Mr Jacobs. I can't see what harm he does anyone and he loves England.' Frances put a hand on his arm and her tone became more persuasive. 'Give it up Norman, please.'

But he shrugged her hand off. 'No,' he answered and

walked away. How could he ever explain to Frances it wasn't just about politics, it was far more than that, it was about camaraderie and friendship and wearing a uniform.

The tension continued to grow all over the East End that summer. Rowdy meetings, both Fascist and Communist, were held almost daily on street corners and Frances was continually being solicited to buy copies of either the *Daily Worker* or *Blackshirt*. It got so that no one could avoid taking sides and whole streets, families even, were polarized by their beliefs.

Frances had never wasted time listening to soap-box oratory. However, when one evening she came across Mosley speaking to a large audience from the roof of a van, she decided to stop to listen, wondering what it was the man had that drew people such as Norman to him.

The meeting was highly organized, with the police, as usual, well in evidence. What struck Frances, though, was how easily Mosley dominated the crowd. But then he had the sort of accent that was used to giving orders and expected to be obeyed. However, his lower jaw moved rather in the manner of a ventriloquist's dummy, which struck Frances as faintly comical, although there was nothing amusing about what he was saying. Stabbing the air with his index finger to make his point, he spewed forth his hate.

'Jews are an alien people,' he shouted through the loudspeaker. 'They come here and take over shops and small businesses and by undercutting and using sweated labour, deprive the native Englishman of his livelihood.' All the country's ills were the fault of the Jew, it seemed, and he went on to blame the Jewish landlord for pushing up rents and forcing the poor into even more inadequate housing. 'In fact,' he thundered, 'the British are becoming strangers in their own country.'

Mosley gestured and postured and the more outrageous

his statements, the more rousing the cheers. Any hecklers were quickly silenced. As he went on to talk of the cleansing spirit of fascism, Frances tried to move away, but she found herself hemmed in by a dense crowd. After what seemed an eternity, Mosley came to the end of his tirade and several rousing verses of 'We are the Boys of the Bull Dog Breed' followed. To demonstrate their patriotism his supporters sang the National Anthem, concluding with the fascist salute, and it interested Frances to see how many arms went up, some belonging to people she recognized.

Norman had always been a strange one, but fancy getting involved with this dangerous bunch, she thought, and walking home, her heart felt heavy on his behalf. No good could come of it at all.

It started off like any normal Sunday morning. The shop was busy and Frances was slicing hot salt beef for a customer when she heard slow chants and stampeding feet further along the street. Before she had time to even wonder what the commotion was about, she looked up and saw several prancing, leering figures in front of the shop window. At the sight of these apparitions she gave a terrified scream, the knife slipped and she just missed cutting off her finger.

'Alien scum! Hail Mosley! Down with Yids!' the youths chorused, then a brick came spinning through the window. Simultaneously there were cries of terror and the explosive sound of glass splintering into hundreds of spiked shards. Women threw themselves down on the floor, but the glass flew about the shop, embedding itself into meats, pickled herring and the heads and legs of customers. Then suddenly it was quiet except for the odd Yiddish expletive and frantic prayers.

Frances and Mr Jacobs, who'd ducked down behind the counter, stared at each other mutely. As if it wasn't enough that a threat of an attack from the Mantoni brothers hung over them, they now had fascist thugs to cope with.

Frances, who could hear several women sobbing, cautiously raised her head above the counter. Her leg muscles had liquefied but seeing the women needed help, she managed to lever herself up. 'It's . . . all . . . all right, Mr Jacobs, they've gone.' Her teeth were still chattering with shock and she had difficulty talking.

Mr Jacobs struggled to stand as well, but was defeated by his rheumatism and the trauma of the situation. Bending down to assist him, Frances wondered how many more shocks his ageing heart could stand.

'Stay where you are, Mr Jacobs, I'll get you a chair.'

But her employer waved her away. 'No, no, see to the customers, Frances. My Gott, I thought I had left this all behind in Poland.' After a couple of attempts he had managed to struggle to his feet and was now surveying the destruction. 'Is nowhere safe for us Jews? Is it true ve vill be forced to vander the face of the earth for ever?' A tear trickled down his tired face, and Frances's heart was smitten with pity.

She reached out and touched his old veined hands. 'No, Mr Jacobs, you are safe in England and the authorities will sort them lot out, you'll see, so don't you worry yerself.' She wanted to offer him more words of comfort, but several deeply distressed, bleeding customers were needing her help.

Frances had no idea if she was doing the right thing, but she washed the cuts, fortunately only superficial, with warm salty water. When she'd cleaned the women up, she suggested they go along to the London Hospital outpatients just to check that there were no glass splinters left in the wounds. By the time they'd drunk a couple of cups of hot sweet tea and sampled the various biscuit assortments, the women were all much more cheerful and went off discussing the incident which, now it was behind them, had turned into something of an adventure.

When they'd gone and before she started on the job of

clearing up the mess, Frances went outside to investigate
further.

Glass crunched under her feet like ice and Frances had
to pick her way with care through the debris. Down the
length of the street, every single Jewish shop window had
been wantonly attacked: the greengrocers, the bakery, the
kosher butchers and the tailors. Frightened families had run
from tenements, children were crying and a lone bobby was
trying to calm gesticulating, angry shopkeepers.

'Come on, let's go and sort those bastards out,' Frances
heard a young man shout. The policeman tried to talk them
out of it, but a group of Jewish youths marched off down
the road, wielding large sticks and chanting the familiar
anti-fascist slogans. Frances was so angry herself, she would
like to have gone with them. She certainly understood their
desire for retribution, but feared that if their fury was
unleashed it could go beyond broken heads and black eyes
to killings.

Depressed at human nature and puzzled why anyone's
political beliefs could matter to them so much they had
to destroy another person's livelihood, Frances went back
inside.

Mr Jacobs stopped sweeping up glass and leaned on the
broom handle. 'Vas it Mosley's biff boys, my dear?'

'Seems like it. Only the Jewish shops were attacked.'

'Vy people haf so much hate in them for the Jew, I do
not understand, Frances.'

'Neither do I, Mr Jacobs, although I think some of these
lads smash things up for the hell of it.'

'But it vasn't the Mantoni boys.'

'No, it wasn't,' Frances agreed, and wondered when they
could expect the brothers. After witnessing the way in which
the police had treated her dad, her confidence in them had
faltered, and Rikki and Giorgio's silence made her feel
extremely edgy. They had no understanding of the word
humanity and would arrange a killing as casually as they

ordered a new suit. So Frances and Mr Jacobs were constantly on their guard, but as the weeks passed and still nothing happened they grew more fearful. For although neither said so, it occurred to them both that the brothers must be planning something truly diabolical.

The sticky humidity and hot pavements didn't help the violence, which continued unabated through that summer, building up in the autumn to a highly explosive situation. People saw their streets being taken over by gangs of lawless youths, and it was no place for the old and frail to be. 'We've gotta get rid of the Yids, we've gotta get rid of the Yids,' they'd taunt, and rush down the street pushing anyone who got in their way into the gutter. It was now a common sight to see boarded-up windows; shops were looted, stalls wrecked, faces slashed and a Jewish child was hurled through a plate-glass window and blinded. The police never seemed to be around to protect the vulnerable, and yet people saw how Mosley could always depend on their support at his meetings. An atmosphere of hate and fear prevailed, although some Jewish shopkeepers refused to be cowed by the bully-boy tactics. Finding a dark humour from somewhere, they would scrawl 'Smashing business done here' across their boarded-up windows after each attack. Mr Jacobs took the precaution of keeping his strong wooden shutters up at all times now, although for the benefit of his customers he chalked on them in defiantly large letters, THIS ESTABLISHMENT REMAINS OPEN FOR BUSINESS.

Then whitewashed messages began to appear on walls and kerbstones. 'Bar the road to fascism,' said one. 'All to rally at Gardiners Corner 12 o'clock Sunday October 4th,' exhorted another. On her way home from work, Frances had leaflets pushed in her hand, urging her to help form a human wall against Mosley. Not sure what it was all leading to and with only a few days to go, she asked Andrew.

'Mosley and his storm troopers are planning a big march through the East End on Sunday. The Government are doing nothing to stop them, so the people have decided they will. My advice is, stay away from work that day, there's likely to be trouble and you don't want to get mixed up in it.'

But Andrew's warning made Frances doubly determined to go to work. If the enemy was at the gates, Mr Jacobs would need her there more than ever.

Three women in the cramped space of a bedroom, all trying to get ready to go out at the same time, wasn't a good arrangement. So relaxing on the bed, Frances smoked one of Gloria's Abdulla cigarettes and waited for her aunt and sister to finish. Saturdays were busy at the restaurant and Gloria looked dog-tired. Frances knew she'd like nothing better than to fall on to the bed beside her and have a fag and a gossip. But juggling two boyfriends was complicated and she had to get herself ready in double-quick time for the hour allotted by Harry.

'You seein' Walter afterwards, Auntie?' Frances asked.

'Yeah, we're going to the music hall. Second house.'

A klaxon sounded. Gloria shouted, 'Coming love,' picked up her handbag and gave her hair a pat. 'Do I look all right?' she asked, but didn't have time to wait for an answer.

Kitty padded to the window to make sure the car had gone, then sat down on the bed and tucked cotton wool between her toes. 'She wants her head examining, putting up with that crook.' Kitty offered this judgement while painting her toenails bright scarlet.

'She loves him.'

Kitty's reply was a derisive snort.

'You ever bin in love, Kit?' Frances watched her sister's face closely and sure enough she coloured slightly. She'd bet her bottom dollar it wasn't Andrew who was responsible for that girlish blush, though, or the physical changes in her; the ripeness of her body, some secret knowledge in her eyes when she came home from the book-keeping classes she was supposed to have enrolled for.

'No.' Kitty stood up abruptly and went to the mirror.

'So you don't love Andrew, then?'

'Don't make me laugh.'

'Has he ever kissed you?'

'None of your business!'

'Where's Andrew takin' you tonight?'

Kitty shrugged irritably. 'I don't know, do I?' She turned and looked at her sister lounging on the bed. 'Shouldn't you be getting ready?'

'In a minute. Paul's written a song for me and we spent all afternoon trying it out.'

'A song? For you?'

Frances refused to be stung by the mixture of amusement and disbelief in her sister's voice. She could deride all she liked but, beautiful as she was, no one was ever going to write a song for Kitty and she knew it. 'He's written several for me before, actually, but he's such a perfectionist most of them go in the bin.' Intent on needling Kitty, Frances went on, 'This is the first one, he says, that does true credit to my remarkable voice. It still needs working on, but when it's finished he's going to ask Johnny if I can give it its first airing at the Rex. I'll let you know when, then you and Andrew could come and hear for yourself how good it is.'

'I'll think about it. It depends what I'm doing.'

Or who you're seeing, thought Frances slyly, and decided to do some detective work to find out who the mystery man was. 'I knew you'd make some excuse, you always do.'

'It's nothing personal, just that the Rex isn't really my cup of tea.'

'It used to be, so what's changed about it so suddenly?'

'I've grown out of it, I suppose.' Kitty checked that the polish on her toenails was dry then rolled a pair of stockings up her legs.

'A bit beneath you, you mean.'

'I never said that.'

'Or a bit common, like me,' Frances goaded.

'Don't talk stupid. Anyway I must go.'

Frances heard the click of Kitty's heels on the pavement outside and, still smarting, thought, she's jealous of me and my success – that's why she won't come to the Rex. So why did she allow herself to get steamed up? What did Kitty matter when she had the adulation of the crowd at the Rex? Because, she supposed, she'd been seeking the good opinion of her sister and failing to get it since she was a small girl and it still had the power to hurt.

20

It was marvellous to be part of it all and Andrew gazed around him with a sense of elation and gratitude, knowing he would remember the fourth of October for the rest of his life. Hundreds had been expected, but he could hardly believe it: thousands, perhaps a quarter of a million East Enders had answered the call and they swirled around him like shifting sand. From all points of the compass they came to converge on Gardiners Corner, waving banners and flags and chanting 'They shall not pass' until there was one solid mass of human flesh from Aldgate Pump in one direction to Whitechapel High Street in the other. To further deter Mosley, several roads were blocked by trams deliberately abandoned by their drivers, and Andrew silently saluted his comrades in arms.

Leman Street was no less congested and although Andrew's instructions were to make his way down to Cable Street, he knew that getting there would be like swimming against an incoming tide. Well, no point in standing about, might as well get on with it, he said to himself and began elbowing his way through the crowd. As far as the eye could see it was the same story. Every side street and alley was choc-a-bloc. Irish dockers, Somali seamen, orthodox Jews and housewives stood shoulder to shoulder in their determination to stop Mosley and his thugs. Andrew allowed himself a quiet smile and looked at his watch. Right now the fascist leader would be marshalling his troops in Royal Mint Street. If the police had any sense, they'd be telling him he was wasting his time. There wasn't the faintest chance of him and his biff boys getting through this hostile crowd, not in one piece anyway.

The crowd was growing more dense by the minute as people from other parts of London poured in to give their support. Shove as he might, it was one step forward two back. The more prudent shopowners, Andrew noticed, had taken the precaution of boarding up their premises and across one frontage flapped a banner on which someone had drawn a crude cartoon of Mosley, trousers round his ankles and squatting on a chamber pot. Coming out of his backside like a fart were the words: *I talk a load of crap*. Andrews smiled to himself. If only ridicule could do the trick.

Families in upstairs tenements sat with their legs dangling over windowsills, looking for all the world as if they were viewing a play from the dress circle of a theatre. Hearing cat-calls and whistling Andrew's gaze carried on upward. As he'd guessed, some of the wilder element, young men in the main, were perched like crows on the rooftops, no doubt with various missiles at the ready.

With cockney defiance that said 'Up yours' to Mosley and the police the East Enders swayed and sang and chanted, and Andrew loved them for their courage. It remained a bone of contention between him and his parents, this concern for people without either power or education. However, he was sensitive enough to his mother and father's feelings to realize that it must have been one of the great disappointments of their lives to see all their high hopes for their only child dashed. His mother would love to be able to boast to friends that her son was something important in the City. It would move her at least one rung up the Chelmsford social ladder. But this was the person he was and he doubted if he'd ever change.

He'd thought sometimes of taking Kitty down to meet his parents. They shared similar values and somehow he felt sure Kitty would approve of their respectable, dull lives.

Maybe it would even help her to regard him with a more kindly eye. Andrew sighed. Fat chance, although he was damned if he would give up hope. He and Kitty had little in common, he was well aware of that; he'd also worked out a long time ago that she was self-centred and didn't treat Frances all that nicely. So he'd kept quiet about it when he eventually took Roy for a flight. But he was in awe of her beauty: the slim line of her body, the dewy skin, the graceful, lovely tilt of her neck, and the occasional smile she bestowed on him which would make him catch his breath in wonder. He wouldn't defile his feelings for her with thoughts of sex. He wanted his love for her to be pure, romantic, and he knew no other woman would ever touch his heart in the way Kitty did.

Andrew was about to give up the struggle to reach Cable Street when he was disturbed to see what looked like a cavalry of mounted police moving up Leman Street. Clearly it was a deliberate act of provocation, since it could be for no other reason than to carve a path through for Mosley. Andrew watched them with a growing sense of outrage. Surely they must know the danger of forcing horses through such a dense crowd. They were taking no heed, either, of the fact that every nook and cranny, every doorway, was so jam-packed with people there was no ecape route. On they ploughed, powerful and arrogant on their huge mounts.

But although the tension was rising, it remained peaceful enough until the taunting started on the roof. Then tiles started to crash down amongst the horses, causing them to rear and almost throwing the policemen from their saddles.

People looking on cheered and the mood of the police turned ugly. Angered at being made to look stupid, they charged, laying about them brutally and indiscriminately with their staves and batons. As people shrank from the flailing truncheons the scene turned to one of terror and mayhem. Frantic, hysterical women tried to claw their way to safety, others stumbled, fell and were trampled on. Men shouted, 'Hey, what the friggin' hell d'yer think yer doin'?' and were silenced by blows.

Andrew heard pounding hooves, screams, the crack of batons on heads, saw blood, smelt fear and dust. In a state of uncomprehending panic, the crowd pushed this way and that and Andrew found himself pressed helplessly against a lamp-post, with the air being expelled from his lungs and in danger of being asphyxiated.

But the police didn't let up on their assault. The horses mounted the pavement and with their heavy bodies forced the crowd further and further back. Enraged, Andrew shinned up the lamp-post. 'These are our streets,' he yelled, 'don't let them push you back, come forward!' He waved his arm like a general mobilizing his troops and the crowd rallied. But they stood no chance against horses and truncheons. The flow was checked and they were pressed back against shop windows, which cracked under their weight. Broken glass lacerated legs and arms and more blood flowed. Seeing several distressed people in need of help, Andrew scrambled down the lamp-post. He was struggling to get to them when a mounted policeman began beating an elderly man about the head and shoulders with his truncheon.

'Pack it up, mate,' the terrified man pleaded, attempting to protect himself with his arms. But the policeman continued with his vicious attack until blood was spattering down the man's face.

Andrew ran up and grabbed the horse's reins. 'Stop it before you kill him!' He shouted his command in anger and despair. 'This is England, for God's sake, a democracy, not Hitler's Germany or Franco's Spain.'

The policeman's reply was to charge his great horse straight at Andrew. He was agile enough to leap out of the animal's path, but his foot caught against the kerbstone, he stumbled, couldn't right himself and fell flat on his back in the gutter. Petrified, he saw the huge black polished hooves paw the air above him, and knew his brains were going to be crushed to pulp. But his sense of survival came to his aid and he rolled away. Scrambling to his feet, Andrew smelt the animal's sweat, and saw his own fear reflected in the poor beast's eyes.

Horribly shaken and aware that he'd escaped serious injury by a hair's-breadth, he looked around for somewhere to lean. Men and women were being arrested and man-handled down to the police station, and a hot-headed young lad who wouldn't go willingly was being carried screaming and fighting between four policemen.

But they couldn't arrest everyone and although most of London's police force had been brought in it was apparent that they were losing control of the situation.

'Come an' get us,' youths taunted. They scattered ball-bearings and marbles under the horses' feet and flung whizzbangs which caused them to rear back into the crowd in fright. Tiles continued to smash down from above, paving stones were being ripped up. The more frustrated and angry the police became, the more menacing they grew and, notic-ing a copper striding in his direction swinging a truncheon, Andrew decided to make a run for it.

He didn't realize how shaky his legs were until he turned into Cable Street and paused to size up the situation. The street was narrow and consisted mainly of lock-up shops with tenements above. Parked broadside across the road was a lorry, clearly put there to deter Mosley if he decided to chance his luck.

A young man in a flat cap bobbed up from behind the vehicle and beckoned him impatiently. 'Get a move on, com-rade, we need all the 'elp we can get 'ere.'

'Okay, I'm coming.' Andrew took a quick look round then made a dash for it. Squeezing round the defences, he found himself in the company of several dozen more men and a great deal of fevered activity. He recognized a few faces, but many of them were strangers to him.

'Don't touch workers shop' was chalked across a door, but no one was taking any heed of this rather optimistic plea and men were forcing open the lock-ups and scrambling to help themselves to the contents with the energy of worker bees. Carts, crates, planks of wood, corrugated roofing and old doors, were commandeered and piled on top and around the lorry to form what they hoped was an impregnable barricade.

'Should they be doing that?' asked middle-class, law-abiding Andrew. 'After all, the stuff doesn't belong to us.'

The young man in the flat cap gazed at him in mild puzzlement. 'This ain't the time to be worryin' about it bein' legal. We're doin' this for democracy, me old cock. To stop the advance of fascism. The narks won't get through 'ere. We'll man the barricades and fight to the death.' Rather taken with his own high-flown rhetoric, the young man paused and his dark brown eyes grew serious as he contemplated his imminent demise. Then brushing such thoughts aside he gave a cheery smile and asked, 'What's yer name, brother?'

'Andrew.'

'I'm Herbie, nice to meet yer.' He prised a sett out of the road with a crowbar and handed it to Andrew. 'A present for you and don't be worried about usin' it – there's plenty more where they came from.' He laughed. 'Here they come, a whole bloody army of 'em. Let's see who can be the first to clobber a nark.'

Andrew weighed the sett in his hand. Never in his life had he used violence against anyone. But it was a just cause, he told himself as he hesitated. It helped to remember the old man covered in blood and the countless other acts of police brutality he'd witnessed today. It was almost like civil war. With a gush of anger, Andrew watched the police charge forward. In the class war those policemen, who were workers after all, should be on their side. There didn't seem much hope for the world if they were willing to support fascism and turn against their own kind.

When the call 'Now!' came, Andrew responded without a qualm. His arm jerked up, a rip of excitement shot through him and he took aim, and those police nearest the barricade were bombarded with setts and chunks of paving stone.

'Fascist arse-lickers!' they taunted.

'Bolshevik scum!' the police retaliated, and lobbed the missiles back.

The combination of excitement and fear curdled Andrew's stomach, but although there was something shameful in admitting it, he realized that he'd never felt so keenly alive as at this moment. So this is why men kill, he thought, picked up a piece of paving stone, flicked it over the barricade with the obligatory 'Bastards!', then hastily retreated to a safe distance. Or so he thought. For he wasn't quick enough and a sharp object caught him on the back of the head and he let out a yelp of pain. Slightly stunned, he staggered to the shelter of a doorway.

Immediately Herbie was at his side. 'You all right, brother?'

Andrew tested his head. He could feel his hair sticky with blood. 'Just a bump,' he lied, not wanting to make a fuss when there were men with far worse injuries than his lying on the ground being attended to by first aid workers.

'Back to the battle then, we've got to stop them buggers.'

'Christ, the narks are dismantling the barricades! Move the injured!'

At the shouted command, a few, anxious to save their own skins, bolted, but between them, Herbie and Andrew lifted an unconscious man and dragged him by his arms to another barricade further along the street. They managed to fetch a second casualty to safety and were trying to get their breath back, when Herbie muttered, 'Here them bastards come again.'

Mentally gearing himself up, Andrew watched police and

reinforcements come charging along the narrow street.

But then came a most unexpected and extraordinary turn of events.

Apart from an occasional lewd comment, until now the women in the tenements above the lock-ups had appeared content to observe rather than participate, which was out of character for they were a tough bunch, normally prepared to take on anybody. What they did next, though, must have taken time and a considerable amount of planning. In fact the whole thing was so well co-ordinated it was like a scene in a Keystone Kops film, but visually twice as entertaining. For as the unsuspecting bobbies rushed forward, the women leaned out of their windows and with balletic precision emptied the contents of their chamberpots over the unfortunate constables' heads.

The police, pee dripping down their helmets and faces, spluttered, swore and danced around in impotent rage. 'You cows'll get three months for this, attacking police officers,' one of them threatened with a shake of his fist.

'Piss-pots!' the women yelled back, and cackled like witches.

From behind the barricades, the besieged men were whooping their approval and support. 'Give it to 'em, gels,' they shouted. But the women were in no need of their encouragement. Store cupboards had already been raided and bottles of vinegar, camphor, ammonia, eucalyptus and anything else they could lay their hands on, exploded around the feet of the luckless policemen.

The combined smells were were enough to knock anyone senseless and by now the terrified and demoralized policemen only had one thought: to escape these screaming viragos while they were still in one piece. Followed by taunts and jeers, they made a rush for one of the sheds, crammed themselves inside and slammed shut the door.

Truly in their stride and with wild catcalls the women, going for the kill, rushed downstairs and into the street.

'Come out of there, you yellow-livered bastards!' they shrieked, and hammered and kicked on the door.

'Gawd almighty,' muttered Herbie, 'I almost feel sorry for the poor sods. Those women look about ready to bite their balls off.'

And they didn't let up on their terrifying onslaught until the door slowly edged open and the ashen-faced coppers filed out, arms raised above their heads in abject surrender and sheepishly aware that they'd been defeated by mere women.

The defenders of the barricades all stared at each other. 'This is a turn-up for the book. What the hell are we supposed to do now?' asked Herbie. 'Arrest 'em?'

The problem was solved when one of the communist leaders went over to the coppers. 'Give us yer helmets and truncheons, lads. You've bin cracking open heads like eggs all day, this'll put paid to your antics for a while.'

Their bombast gone and without any protest, the coppers did as they were ordered.

'Now shove off,' the man ordered and they were sent on their way with a slow hand clap. But everyone recognized that it was the women who were the true heroines of the hour. And a force to be reckoned with. Certainly Mosley would be wise to think twice before trying to push his way through Cable Street.

With the police gone it all became a bit aimless. Some men hung around looking for guidance, others drifted away. 'Looks as if we've won,' observed Herbie.

'Yep. Seems so.' Seeing no point in staying, Andrew started to walk on down the street, away from the barricade, the torn-up paving stones, the blood and mess and smells.

'Where you goin'?' asked Herbie, following close behind.

Andrew shrugged. 'Don't know.' After the great surge of adrenalin it all seemed an anticlimax. 'Perhaps I'll make my way back round to Gardiners Corner, see what's going on there.'

'Mind if I join you?'

'Be my guest.' Andrew had hardly spoken when he heard pounding hooves. 'They're back. Run!' he yelled to Herbie and tore up the street. A figure was standing in the middle of the road and when a girl's voice called 'Andrew' he stopped briefly. 'Christ, what are you doing here?' Then without waiting for a reply he grabbed Frances and pulled her along behind him.

Panting, they turned the corner. 'In here,' Frances ordered and pulled him into the shop.

'Herbie.' Andrew could hardly speak, but he reached out and hooked his new friend into the shop. Slamming the door they both leaned against it.

'Blimey, that was a close one,' said Herbie, then they started to laugh hysterically.

Mr Jacobs, hearing their laughter from the back of the shop, looked round the door. 'I vould not haf thought there was much to laugh about today.' He sounded censorious.

'Sorry.' Andrew and Herbie both made a courageous effort to stop, looked at each other and were off again.

'They've been in the fighting, Mr Jacobs.' Frances apologized for them. 'I think they're just letting off steam.'

Mr Jacobs's expression changed. Beaming, he pumped their hands up and down in gratitude. 'So you boys haf been in the thick of it? Zat is very brave of you. Now you must haf some food. Hot salt beef on rye bread. Do you like ze idea?'

Andrew's stomach rumbled at the mention of food and he remembered he hadn't eaten since early that morning. 'Very much, Mr Jacobs.'

'Goot.'

Frances went to make tea and when she came back, Mr Jacobs was questioning Andrew and Herbie closely, wanting to know every detail of their day. 'You young men are heroes and ze King should give you both a medal.'

Andrew laughed. 'We're more likely to be locked up than

get a medal. Anyway, I didn't do much,' he added, brushing aside his part in the battle.

Herbie, who wasn't troubled by modesty, was fairly wallowing in all the attention. So much so, he wanted to hold on to it. 'Actually I'm thinkin' of joinin' the International Brigade and goin' to Spain,' he announced, took a slurp of his tea and looked around at his audience, waiting for their reaction.

His statement made very little impression on Frances. She had no idea what the International Brigade was, and to her Spain was a distant and mysterious land. But Mr Jacobs stood up and slapped him on the back. 'It makes me proud to know you, Herbie my boy,' he beamed.

Andrew's attitude, however, was a little more circumspect, and he regarded Herbie with a trace of doubt in his eyes. 'When are you going and how are you getting there?'

Herbie, aware that his boasts wouldn't stand up to cross-examination, huffed and puffed a little. 'I've got contacts, ways and means.'

'But when exactly are you going?' Andrew persisted, trying to pin him down.

'About the end of the month,' he answered vaguely.

'Before you go, come and see me, Herbie. I vill give you a little money. You vill need it.'

'That's all right, Mr Jacobs, don't you worry about me.' Herbie waved the offer aside. In fact he was beginning to wish he'd kept his mouth shut. Bleedin' hell, the last thing he wanted was to go to Spain. The trouble was he could never resist indulging in occasional flights of fancy – or lies as his ma called them – and they got him into no end of trouble. Ma swore it would be the death of him one day, and this tale was collapsing round him like a house of straw. Still, there was one way out of this dilemma.

Trying to look nonchalant, Herbie stood up. 'Thanks for the refreshments, Mr Jacobs, but I'd better be on me way.

Me ma is a worrier and she'll be wondering where I am if I'm not 'ome soon.'

'I'll come with you,' said Andrew, rising to his feet as well.

'Don't go yet, Andrew,' Frances pleaded, adding as a bribe, 'Stay and have some more tea ... and another sandwich.'

'Thanks but I've got to go. And on your way home, see to it that you keep clear of Gardiners Corner.' He lightly touched her face. 'Do you hear me? Things are still a bit volatile out there.'

'Yes, I hear you. Are you comin' around this evening? Dad'll want to hear all about the day.'

'Will Kitty be there?'

Frances hid a sigh. 'I expect so. We're all expected to play cards with Nan on Sunday nights.'

'I'll try and make it.'

Well it was better than nothing, Frances supposed, taking a philosophical view. She showed the pair of them out then watched as they ambled up the street together, Andrew tall and slim, Herbie, his new friend, short-legged and stocky. Definitely an ill-matched pair, she thought, heard Mr Jacobs calling and turned back into the shop.

By the time they reached the Commercial Road, Andrew had decided he would give Gardiners Corner a miss after all. His head throbbed, his shirt collar was caked with dried blood, his suit covered in dust, and – he looked down – there was a rip in his trouser leg. He'd done his bit for democracy, and his mind was more on the evening with Kitty now. She wouldn't be impressed if she saw him like this. He was in need of a good wash and he wanted to spruce himself up for her. 'If you don't mind, I'll leave you here,' he said to Herbie when they came out on to the main road.

'Righty-o, old son.' Herbie held out his hand. 'Hope we

meet again. I'll think I'll pop along and have a gander at what's goin' on, but I won't stay. The crowd's thinned out but there still seems to be plenty of coppers around. You'd think they 'ad no homes to go to.'

It certainly seemed to Andrew that the steam had gone out of the day until he glanced over Herbie's shoulder. The girl caught his eye initially because she was a real looker, a little like Kitty in fact. She was moving along the pavement towards them, laughing amd chatting to a friend in a happy, carefree way. The girl was not more than a couple of feet from where he and Herbie stood when someone pushed her against a policeman. It was purely accidental and Andrew watched in disbelief, as the nark, his temper and nerves frayed by the day, swung round, truncheon raised to strike the girl.

'Oh no you don't!' Andrew wasn't going to stand by and see him wantonly destroy such beauty. Reacting instinctively, he leapt towards the constable, wrested the truncheon from his hand, spun him round and smashed his fist right in his face.

'Stone a crow!' Herbie exclaimed as the policeman, his helmet all askew, staggered back with blood spurting from his nose. Then through his white hot anger, Andrew was aware of whistles being blown, and of Herbie yelling, 'Run for it, mate!'

But the warning came too late – already he was surrounded by police officers, in an ugly mood and moving in on him. Unwisely, Andrew tried to smash through the cordon and make a dash for freedom. But this was just the excuse they needed and as he rushed at them, a blow on the head sent him reeling. The world spun, his legs crumpled, then with both arms locked behind his back he was dragged, half-conscious, to Leman Street police station. Here he was charged and thrown into an overcrowded cell where he blacked out.

When he came round he was crouched against a wall,

hemmed in by fifty pairs of legs. He shook his head to try and clear it, and found Herbie kneeling beside him.

'What are you doing here?'

'They called me a Jew bastard, said I was an accessory and arrested me too.'

'It's not fair you being involved, Herbie.'

'Think nothing of it, mate,' answered Herbie, whose cheerfulness, even in extreme circumstances, never seemed to desert him. 'They can't get me for much, I ain't done nuthin'. Not that they know of, anyway.'

The heat in the small crowded cell, his pounding head and the smell of sweating bodies made Andrew want to retch and he wondered how long he could last without vomiting. There was no space to move, so he just sat, feeling ill and wondering about his parents. They always had people round for bridge on Sunday evenings. Imagine their reaction if they knew their son was in prison.

The afternoon dragged on with nothing to break the monotony except the arrival of another batch of prisoners. At six, a sour-faced police sergeant came and informed them that Sir Philip Game, Chief Commissioner of Police, had ordered Mosley to abandon his march. Before the policeman had even finished, the inmates let rip. They rattled the bars of their cell doors, stamped, cheered and sang. This was the news they'd been waiting for and made up for their injuries and imprisonment. The people of the East End had achieved what they'd set out to do, stopped the Blackshirts in their tracks; taken on authority and won.

Shortly after this a trickle of prisoners were released, but Andrew and Herbie were kept locked up until gone eight then rough-handled to the desk. Lined up on the counter were ball-bearings, pieces of brick and a file.

'What have you got to say about this little lot, eh? Found 'em in your pockets, we did,' said the desk sergeant, looking mighty pleased with himself.

Andrew had never had any brushes with the law before

and he was so shocked at this blatant tampering with the truth, he was rendered speechless. But fuelled by anger and a sense of injustice, he found his voice. 'You did no such thing!'

The sergeant leaned over the desk. 'Are you accusin' me of being a liar, Sonny Jim?'

'What I'm saying is you planted them,' Andrew retorted bravely.

The policeman chortled. 'Well we'll soon see what the magistrate 'as to say about that. I'm releasing both of you on bail, I want yer addresses and don't try anything funny, 'cos we'll soon catch up with you and the charges are pretty serious. Carrying dangerous weapons, incitement to riot and assault on a policeman. With a bit o' luck the magistrate will put the pair of you away for three months.'

Herbie wasn't good at silence but he managed it for five minutes on the way home while he contemplated his future. Then, with it all bottled up inside him, he had to speak. 'I don't know about you but I'm not keen to be banged up for three months. Shall we do a runner? Go to Spain.'

'We won't get three months, not when we tell the magistrate that the police are lying,' answered Andrew confidently.

'You did clock a copper, though,' Herbie reminded him.

'Serves him right, it was an unprovoked attack on an innocent girl.'

'What about your parents? What will they say if you get sent down?'

Andrew thought about it. 'I don't suppose I will, but if I did I think there's a pretty good chance my parents would disown me.'

As far as Norman was concerned it had been a frustrating, pointless day. He'd spent ages making himself look immaculate and all for nothing. Several thousand of them, with flags and bands, had lined up in Royal Mint Street waiting for orders to march. It was their annual rally, and a big day for the organization. They'd looked like a real army, too, and he'd felt tremendously proud to be part of it.

But of course the bloody communists had gone and spoilt it all. The police had done their best to try and find a route through and occasionally a rumour would come up the line that people were being injured and killed not far from where they stood. That made him feel a bit queasy, but he still wanted to march. Sir Oswald's arrival in an open car was heralded by cheering and Norman's hopes soared briefly. But still nothing happened and eventually even the most well-drilled of them grew restless. Then came the great disappointment as news filtered through that the police had ordered their leader to call off the march.

And this Mosley did. 'Because I am an upholder of law and order,' he told his troops, 'although I consider that the police have given in to mob rule.'

Thoroughly disgruntled, instead of marching to Westminster with the other members, Norman went back to the flat Mr Freeman kept above his business premises. He'd promised to wait there to hear about the day.

Later, after too many glasses of wine, Mr Freeman said, 'There might still be trouble on the streets, Norman, so why don't you stay tonight?'

Unable to think of a reason not to, Norman answered, 'Thank you, Mr Freeman.'

'Call me Cyril,' his employer suggested quietly and reached out and took Norman's hand.

21

'All shadows fly away/when I remember yesterday/when love came to me/to you and me. The sun upon the lake/ my heart for you to take/when love set us free/both you and me. Now shadows fall across my path again/and I recall the pain/the day you left/the day you went from me . . .' sang Frances, her own pain lending an extra dimension to the simple phrases.

Frances didn't like the word blackmail, but it had taken some serious arm twisting before Johnny could be convinced that Paul's composition was of a high enough standard to please a Saturday night crowd. 'It's good Johnny, take my word for it.' Then, confident enough of her own popularity, she pressed on, 'Of course there are always other bands . . .'

Knowing the battle was lost, Johnny held up his hands in capitulation. 'All right, all right. I'll let him give it a try. But I've got my reputation to think of, so he only gets one chance.'

Frances had trotted off to Paul rather pleased at the way she'd manipulated Johnny, only to find that instead of being delighted Paul was overcome with doubts, convinced that his song was rubbish and that the audience would hate it. Which was why Frances knew she had to give the song all she'd got, for Paul's future as a songwriter was at stake. Tonight she had no need to fake the emotion, though, every word of the song rent her heart. She was also reassured by the blur of faces gazing up from the semi-darkness of the hall, because with the true performer's instinct, Frances could feel approbation flowing from them to her. Paul's got a winner here, she thought, and remembered the hours of rehearsal they'd both put in. Not that she minded. In fact for a few weeks she'd been grateful for anything that kept her mind occupied.

She came to the end of the song, heard the slight pause, like a sigh almost, then the tumultuous applause and she turned to Paul with a smile. But instead of giving her the thumbs up sign and happy grin she expected, he sat hunched over the piano as if all the creative energy had drained out of him. He'd sworn to pack it all in if he failed this time, and the strain of the past week showed on his face. He seemed unaware of the applause, so Frances went over and took his hand. 'Listen to that, Paul, it's for you. You're a success, come and take your bow.'

With a dazed expression he allowed Frances to pull him to the front of the stage. 'Paul Harding, songwriter and a new talent, folks,' Johnny announced, happy to take his share of the credit now that the success of the song was assured. 'And remember, you heard "All Shadows Fly Away" for the first time here, played by the composer and sung most wonderfully by Frances.'

Paul, who had at last come out of his trance, took Frances's hand, squeezed it, murmured, 'Thanks, you were great,' kissed her lightly on the cheek then went back to the piano.

For the benefit of the wallflowers, Johnny announced an excuse me waltz and Frances sat down. She puzzled over Paul's behaviour for a little while, but inevitably her thoughts drifted back to Andrew. What had possessed him to run off like that with Herbie to Spain? It was about the stupidest thing anyone could do. And why? To fight in some pointless war. She supposed they'd been planning it in jail. Three months would give them heaps of time. Also, although out of shame she'd refused to admit it for a long time, Frances knew her own incautious words had played some part in driving him out of England.

The fourth of October hadn't put an end to the trouble

with the fascists. Outbreaks of violence continued through-out the autumn and Norman had his collarbone broken at one meeting. However at the end of the year the wearing of uniforms was banned. Consequently some of the steam went out of the BUF and quite a few of its members, including Norman, deserted the organization.

None of this had been of much help to Andrew and Herbie, though, who were both sentenced to three months' hard labour for incitement to riot and for punching a police-man. His shocked parents more or less disowned Andrew, and callous-hearted Kitty refused point blank to be seen anywhere near Wormwood Scrubs. So Frances found herself trailing across London regularly with second-hand books she'd bought in the market and chocolate from Mr Jacobs.

There was no question about it, Kitty was the object of Andrew's love, and because of this Frances had never dared scrutinize her own emotions too carefully, but her heart was pierced by pity whenever she saw him, caged like an animal in a zoo and made bitter by what Andrew saw as a terrible miscarriage of justice. Slowly, too, Frances began to recog-nize in herself the difference between the immature infatu-ation of a fifteen-year-old and the breathless joy that swept over her whenever she saw Andrew now. The prison visits, dreary as they were, became a fixed point in her life and she hoped Andrew looked forward to seeing her with the same sense of anticipation. But all he did was brood over Kitty's indifference. 'Please ask her to come and see me, Frances,' he entreated, as she was about to leave one day.

'I'll see what I can do.' She'd tried so many times before, one more wouldn't make any difference, she supposed.

Kitty came in late that night, in a touchy mood, and undressed without a word.

'Where you been?' asked Frances from the bed.

'To the pictures with Rose.'

Liar, thought Frances. Kitty was clever at covering her tracks, so her investigations into her sister's love life hadn't progressed far. In fact she hadn't even established the identity of the man, although she had a strong hunch that he was married. She had no positive proof, but Kitty's secretiveness, the irregular hours she kept, all pointed to it. 'Andrew wants to know why you won't go and see him.'

'I'm not visiting any jailbird,' Kitty snapped rolling down her stockings and examining them for ladders. Today at work she and Robert had indulged in some hectic lovemaking in the stationery cupboard.

'Shall I tell him that?'

'Tell him anything you please,' Kitty answered indifferently and Frances thought, right I will, you cold-hearted bitch, that'll finish you in Andrew's eyes. But when she repeated it word for word, he didn't react with anger. Instead a look of desolation swept over his face and he buried his head in his hands.

'And another thing,' Frances went on in a jealous outburst. 'I should say you're pretty much wasting your time with Kitty. She's got other fish to fry these days.'

Andrew's head jerked up. His skin, pale enough anyway from lack of sunlight, took on the colour of tissue paper. 'What do you mean?'

'She's going out with someone else.' Frances considered adding that Kitty's suitor was married but rejected it.

She did herself no favours with her outburst because when Andrew was released from prison he didn't come near the house and it was Mr Jacobs who told her that he and Herbie had gone to Spain. It hurt like hell that he didn't trouble to say goodbye and there'd been no contact since, no letter, and in the deep, instinctive recesses of her heart, Frances was convinced she would never see Andrew again, that already he was dead on some dusty foreign plain.

Johnny went into a new number and Frances stood up and moved to the microphone. As she began to croon 'Lover Come Back To Me' she was struck by the irony of the words.

To Frances's relief, by the end of the evening Paul had come out of his depression and appeared to be in a mood to celebrate. 'Tonight, my girl, we're going to live dangerously. I'm taking you for a fish and chip supper, double helping of chips,' he grinned.

Sparing no expense, Paul also ordered them a plate of bread and butter each and two glasses of sasparilla. Lifting his glass he smiled and said, 'I should be toasting you with champagne, and one day I will, I promise you that. You're my good luck charm, do you know that, Frances?'

'Nonsense. You wrote the song, Paul, I only sang it.' Frances picked up her knife and fork and pierced the crisp brown batter on her haddock.

Paul leaned back in his chair. 'Yes, but it was the *way* you sang it, with your soul.' He pressed his hand to his heart. Getting carried away, he went on, 'I'm going to write another one for you. Dozens, in fact. I've got all this music in my head, I hear it all the time.' He picked up a chip, waved it like a baton, shoved it in his mouth, swallowed, then said excitedly, 'We're going places, you and me. I can feel it in my bones.'

It would have been awful to deflate Paul's sudden rush of optimism, so Frances picked up her glass. 'What about a toast to that, then? The future.'

'And the fabulous duo,' said Paul, then clinking glasses they grinned happily at each other across the table.

'I wish you'd give up this game with the Mantoni boys, Harry. The way you're goin' it's only a question of time before you're nicked and sent down.'

'Nonsense, love. Me and Arthur knows exactly what we are up to.' Harry took a swig of his beer, looked around the pub and lowered his voice to a more confidential level. 'Now I don't want you to breathe a word of what I'm gonna tell you to anyone, d'you understand, Gloria? It's for your ears only.'

With her index finger, Gloria made the sign of the cross over her left breast. 'Cross me heart, Harry.'

'You see the pair of us 'ave got quite a clever dodge goin' at the moment.'

'Oh!' Gloria looked at Harry doubtfully. That was one thing Harry and Arthur weren't: clever, not by a long chalk.

'Come nearer.'

Gloria edged her chair right up against Harry's and he went on in a low voice, 'You see, it's like this, we 'ave to deliver hashish all over the West End to the boys' customers.'

'Hashish?' Gloria squeaked.

'Keep yer voice down, love, for gawd's sake. Yeah dope. Cor, you should see some of those houses we goes to in Mayfair, they're like palaces. Fair makes yer tongue hang out, I can tell you. Dripping wiv money and jewels they are, lucky sods. Made me think about what Andrew said, how it's wrong that some folks have everythin', others bugger all. Anyway to get back to my story. What me and Arthur does is this. When we gets the dope from the boys, we take a little bit out of each package.'

'Oh Harry, you don't!'

'Only the tiniest bit, honest, Gloria. Then when we've got enough, we sell that and keep the money for ourselves. I'll soon have a fair bit stashed away. Then what I reckon I'll do is get out of the game, move away down to Eastbourne and maybe buy a garage.' Of course there was the largish chunk of money that found its way back to the brothers as part of Mr Jacobs's so-called tribute, but Harry knew he had to keep his mouth shut about that.

'On your own?' asked Gloria in a small voice.

Harry reached out, pulled her to him and kissed her neck, inhaling the warm powdery smell of her. ''Course not, you'd come too. You'd have to ditch Walter, though. Mind you, I think you ought to give 'im the old heave-ho anyway. Admit it, he ain't your sort, Gloria. Give him back his ring. You and me belong tergether, you know that, don't you?'

But Gloria was getting wise to Harry. 'I'd feel a bit naked without a ring now. Will you buy me another one?'

'Of course, love. Twice the size, with three diamonds that'll twinkle like the stars in the heavens.'

'Put yer money where your mouth is, then, and let's see it. This ring ain't going back, it's me insurance policy for when I can't stand another day of that bloody restaurant and them tight-fisted customers.'

'You just pop along to the jewellers next week and see if there's anythin' takes yer fancy.'

'If a couple are gonna get engaged, Harry, either the man buys the ring or they go together,' Gloria explained with a touch of asperity.

'Ah well, it's time, you see, I ain't got a lot to spare.' Harry glanced at his wristwatch, an expensive Swiss one, Gloria noticed. 'Blimey, eight o'clock. I'd better be gettin' along to the club, sweetheart.'

'I don't know how you've got the nerve, Harry. You can't even spend a whole evening with me, and yet you expect me to give up Walter.'

Harry patted her cheek and stood up. 'We'll talk about it another time, I promise.'

Oh no we won't thought Gloria. Walter had asked her to name the day and when she saw him tomorrow night, she'd do just that!

22

'Happy, Mrs Hurst?' It was a warm afternoon, the hood was down and the air was soft and scented on Kitty's face. The lane they were driving along was steeply banked and thick with wild flowers. Stippled light pierced the dense summer foliage and Kitty felt as if she was in a world of pure enchantment. At Robert's question, she turned with a languid movement of her head and smiled at him. 'Totally, thank you, Mr Hurst.'

He squeezed her hand. 'Good.'

But a snatched happiness, thought Kitty a trifle sadly, twisting the recently purchased Woolworth's ring round her finger. If only it was the real thing, gold and not brass, and she and Robert were off on their honeymoon. To protect themselves they had to use false names, she understood that, but it made their love seem like a hole-in-the-corner affair. Kitty wanted them to be able to declare their passion for each other openly, not hide away as if it was something sordid. But she'd quickly discovered there was a high price to pay for loving a married man, because you immediately entered a world of evasion and deceit. For instance she'd had to lie to her parents about this weekend. First of all she'd had to pluck up courage to mention it, and that had taken a whole week. Even then she'd sweated with nerves as she spun her carefully rehearsed tale of Rose inviting her to stay overnight at her house at Herne Hill. Dad hated untruths and she'd waited, jumpy as a rabbit, knowing her story wouldn't stand up to cross-examination and she'd be revealed as that most despised of people, a liar. But astonishingly both Mum and Dad had accepted it without question.

That sister of hers was a different matter of course. She was always ferreting around, asking questions that were no concern of hers, and Kitty had a horrible feeling that she guessed something. Which meant she had to be on her guard all the time. Because if Frances did find out about Robert it would go straight back to Mum and Dad, then all hell would be let loose.

Take this morning, for instance. She was arranging her new hat at a jaunty angle over one eye as dictated by the fashion magazines, when Frances, who was watching her, started one of her interrogations. 'Where you goin', all done up like a dog's dinner?'

'Me and Rose are going to the theatre this evening.'

'Seems to me you're taking a lot of trouble for Rose.'

Ignoring this comment, Kitty turned so that Frances could get a better view of her blue linen suit with its contrasting check jacket. 'What do you think of my new outfit?'

Frances considered for a minute then delivered her opinion. 'The suit's okay, but that hat don't half look daft.'

The desire to slap Frances hard across the face was almost overpowering, but Kitty drew a deep breath, snapped the suitcase shut and recited to herself, Don't lose your temper, remember how it ruins your looks. But she couldn't resist one parting shot before she swept off down the stairs. 'Your trouble is, you're jealous because you can't get a bloke!'

'Have you got one, then?' Frances called after her. 'Is that why you're all tarted up?'

Kitty had ground her teeth and ignored the gibe, but she'd taken an instant dislike to the hat and it was now stuffed away in her suitcase. The next pay rise she had she was going to get a room of her own, away from Frances and her constant prying. A place where she and Robert would have more time together. Meetings were often very snatched and his excuse today to Imogen was that he was on an overnight visit to his mother in Tunbridge Wells.

They slowed down for a herd of cows, then a little further on for a hay wagon. Kitty glanced at Robert's profile and while they waited slowly stroked his thigh, moving her hands up to his groin until she was pleasuring him with her fingers. He was hard in an instant and she gave a small, feline smile. She constantly needed the reassurance of her sexual hold on him.

'That's exquisitely enjoyable, my love, but if you don't stop I'll crash into that wagon then we'll literally be having a roll in the hay ... Of course ...' he put his foot on the brake, 'we could pause here for a moment or two in the woods ...'

'But I haven't got that thing in.'

'Get it in as soon as we arrive at the hotel. I want you before dinner, after dinner, and probably six times during the night.'

'That thing' was a dutch cap. And what an ordeal that had been, first plucking up courage to go along to a birth control clinic, then claiming she was a married woman and the even greater indignity of having the cap fitted. Lying there on a hard bench while a white-coated nurse examined her most private parts. And the trouble she had getting the blasted thing in. It needed practice, there was no privacy at home and if you spent too much time in the lavatory, some-one was bound to come banging on the door. Then, because she was terrified of her mother or Frances finding it, she had to carry this giant jellyfish around in her handbag all the time. But Robert was right, they needed to take proper precautions because in the first flush of their love they'd been careless at times.

Kitty leaned back and gazed up through the arching branches of the trees. But we should be making lots of babies together, Robert and me, I should be giving him a son and heir. After all that wife of his wouldn't ever. She was so glad there was nothing in the way of sex between them, she couldn't have borne it, knowing Robert was doing with Imogen what they did together. She wouldn't press him on the matter of leaving Imogen yet, but she was hanged if she was going to spend the rest of her days as his mistress. She wanted the trappings and recognition that went with being Mrs Robert Travis. Robert had the choice now, and he couldn't possibly want to remain tied to a frigid woman who dared to call herself his wife. Robert was loyal, and he never said a great deal about his life with Imogen, but reading between the lines, it was obvious he was pretty miserable with her.

Kitty rested her head on Robert's shoulder and felt the roughness of his jacket against her cheek. She loved it that he couldn't leave her alone. She smiled remembering the times they'd made love in Miss Alice's office, knowing the cleaners were only a few yards down the corridor. They'd done it on the priceless Persian carpet, Robert had had her across the desk, sitting in a swivel chair and up against the filing cabinet. It wasn't love-making, just quick, feverish sex and although Kitty felt rather guilty about it, she was deeply aroused by the element of danger.

She often wondered if she had done the right thing going to work for 'sour chops' as she called Alice. It took her away from Robert, and Miss Alice found fault with her work, was unfriendly and kept her late just to show who was boss. Kitty had imagined she'd be pleased to have a secretary who was fairly clued up on the workings on the firm – instead it annoyed her. Still, for all the disadvantages, at least she got that promotion she'd been dying for and was earning reasonable wages now.

'Here we are.' A discreet sign said Arlington House Hotel and Robert manoeuvred the car up the short gravelled drive. Lawns, smooth and green as the baize on a billiard table, were laid out on either side, nude Grecian figures were placed discreetly about the garden, petunias and geraniums tumbled over stone urns.

'Gosh!' Lost for words, Kitty fought a sense of awe. Her aspirations had always been on the ambitious side, but she'd never dared dream of getting to stay in a place like this.

'Do you like it?'

'It's beautiful.'

Robert brought the car to a halt in front of a charming Georgian house, its warm brick obscured by sweetly scented climbing roses. Leaning over, he kissed her. 'I want only the best for my lady.'

Robert also had another motive. Because the hotel was small and discreet, there was little risk of bumping into someone he knew. It was costing him a king's ransom, but what the hell . . . He tried not to think too often of the parlous state of his bank balance. Kitty's love for him had turned his life around, given him back his pride in his manhood, and he wanted to return it by taking her to expensive places and watching her unsophisticated delight. Add to that a wife who thought any discussion about money common and an extravagant mother and he knew he was sorely in need of a hefty salary increase. He did have hopes of putting wheels in motion soon, though. Robert guessed that Alice had engineered the invitation he and Imogen had received from Sir Sidney, a long weekend at Leyborne at the beginning of next month. He'd have to see he used his time there constructively, charm the old man, and Alice too, because if he got the signals right, she was showing an interest that went rather beyond mere business. Not that it was reciprocated: thin, sharp-angled women weren't to his taste. Only Kitty's round young softness could satisfy his needs and he wanted her all the time.

Robert was opening the car door for Kitty, when a bellboy ran down the steps and greeted them with a small salute. 'Afternoon sir, madam,' he said and bent to pick up their suitcases. Immediately Kitty was aware of how shoddy hers looked, pressed cardboard against Robert's real leather. His was bashed about a bit, but it was covered with labels that spoke of cruises and exotic holidays abroad. It was said you could always tell true toffs by the quality of their luggage.

Robert smiled, squeezed her hand and said, 'This is it, Mrs Hurst,' and together they walked up the steps into the cool black-and-white-tiled hall.

Kitty's stomach felt queasy, her palms damp. She was sure she had Scarlet Woman stamped all over her and that the receptionist would guess immediately she had no legal right to be wearing a wedding ring and show her the door. But as Robert signed the register and the girl handed him the key, she was smiling at them. 'Enjoy your stay, Mr and Mrs Hurst, Sam will show you to your room.'

Kitty felt brave enough to respond with a 'Thank you', and as she followed the boy up to the first floor, she made a decision. I'm going to make the most of this weekend, enjoy every single moment, instead of wasting precious time either feeling inadequate or worrying about people guessing our secret.

In the bedroom Kitty looked about her and gave a sigh of pleasure. I was born for this, she thought. With its antique furniture, fresh flowers and fourposter bed, it struck her as being more like a bedroom in a country house than a hotel. The curtains moved slightly in the breeze and, going over to the open window, she saw they overlooked another vast lawn at the back of the house. Below, some of the hotel guests played croquet, while others were being served afternoon tea in the shade of a huge cedar. All understated, but reeking of privilege and wealth and a world away from Stepney.

Robert tipped the lad lavishly, almost pushed him out the door and locked it. 'The honeymoon suite – what do you think, Kitten?'

'I don't know what to say, it's all so marvellous.'

'Come and thank me properly, then.'

Kitty ran to Robert, threw her arms round his neck and kissed him. 'Thank you, darling, for everything.'

Holding her around the waist he carried her to the bed and said with a tender smile, 'Shall I ravish you now or wait?'

Kitty lifted up her dress immodestly, showing her suspenders and French knickers. 'Now, please sir.'

He kissed the soft skin of her thighs, undid the suspenders with his teeth and rolled down her stockings. Kitty quickly divested herself of her clothes, throwing them untidily on the floor, then pulling off his braces, she unbuttoned his flies.

'Hussy,' he smiled and pressed her back on the bed. She was still sometimes shy naked, but when she went to cover her breasts with her arms, he pulled them away and holding her wrists, kissed her mouth, then her neck, then her breasts, gradually moving down her body. She squirmed and gave little moans of desire. With his fingers he rubbed her to response until she was pleading, 'Now, now,' and when he entered her she was so moist and warm, Robert had trouble controlling himself. You've got all the time in the world, remember, he told himself, and moved slowly on top of her. 'Quicker, harder,' she demanded. Gripped in the pincer of her arms and legs, he willingly obliged until the bed was rocking like a ship in a storm and she came with a great shuddering cry. Sweating and replete they fell apart, arms spreadeagled and panting.

Kitty lay staring up at the canopy of the fourposter then she started to giggle. 'I hope the ceiling's still in one piece in the room down below.'

'If it is now, it won't be by the time the weekend's over, my love. But maybe, this being the honeymoon suite, the hotel has reinforced the joists.' Kissing her lightly, Robert sat up. 'I'm going to fill the tub and have a long soak, care to join me?'

At home it was often a question of sharing the bathwater,

but bathing with a man struck Kitty as pretty daring. She still carried with her, too, a working-class modesty and she could never stroll around unselfconsciously naked like Robert did. Slipping into a white towelling dressing-gown provided by the hotel, she stood up.

Robert laughed. 'Why do you do that, Kitten? Be proud of that beautiful body of yours.' A trifle reluctantly Kitty parted with the wrap.

'That's better.' He kissed her and went and ran the bath. Soon steam, carrying with it the scent of carnations, was billowing out of the door. Kitty could hear Robert singing in a pleasant baritone as he sloshed the water about. I've done that, made Robert happy. It was an awesome thought.

'The water's lovely, Kat, come on in,' Robert called and Kitty padded naked into the bathroom. It was a huge, old-fashioned bath with brass taps and claw feet, and Robert was lying submerged in bubbles and steam. His eyes were closed but when Kitty slipped into the other end of the bath, he opened them and said, 'Come here, my little mermaid,' and pulling her towards him he began soaping her all over. He watched her until her eyes dilated with desire and her mouth opened slightly, then pulling her to her feet, he wrapped a towel round her and carried her to the bed. They made love, rested then made love again.

Although Kitty did wonder where Robert had learned all the tricks that could bring her to the peak of desire so quickly, jealousy prevented her from asking. There must have been other girls, lots of them, before he was married, but she didn't want to know about them. What did surprise her was that since he'd married Imogen there'd been no other women in his life until their affair started. For a physical person like Robert it must have been hell. Still, he was making up for lost time, Kitty thought with a smile.

Robert's eyes were closed and she leaned over and kissed his lids, then traced her finger over his well-shaped mouth and the cleft in his chin. 'Do you love me, Robert?'

261

He opened his eyes and gazed at her tenderly. 'More than anything or anyone in the world.'

'You'll never leave me?'

'My silly little Kat, who for?'

Kitty shrugged. 'I don't know. Someone perhaps.' This was always a vague but persistent fear, that some girl belonging more to his world would come along and take him from her.

'I'll love you till the day I die. Now come here and let me show you.'

Later, as they lay in each other's arms, on a nearby tree a blackbird started to sing. The sun was sliding below the trees, but the still evening air heightened every sound. Kitty heard the click of wooden mallet against ball, then a well-bred girl's voice complained, 'Oh you are a beast, Alastair,' following it with a laugh to show she didn't mean it.

Robert had dark hairs on his chest and Kitty curled one lovingly round her finger and sighed with pure contentment. She had everything she could possibly want. Theirs was a deep and perfect love and would go on for ever. Shortly they'd have to dress and go down to dinner, act like a dull married couple or, Kitty smiled to herself, perhaps they wouldn't bother and instead stay here and make love again. As she snuggled up to Robert, Kitty suddenly remembered that the dutch cap she'd gone to so much trouble to obtain, still lay unused in her suitcase.

23

Harry couldn't put his finger on it, but there was definitely a strange atmosphere in the club that evening. According to his instructions, he wandered amongst the customers, introducing them to others of similar sexual tastes, smiling and pressing them with, 'A drink, sir?' or 'Some champagne, madam?' Bloomin' extortionate the prices were, too. Talk about a fool and his money being easily parted. Well, in this establishment there were a good few of those, particularly at the gaming tables. It seemed some of them couldn't wait to rid themselves of the family wealth. But then you didn't join a club like this unless you were pretty well-heeled to start with.

Harry went about his business of keeping the customers happy and laughing at their feeble jokes with one eye on the door. Where the devil had Arthur got to? He should be here by now. Again he was beset with a vague disquiet.

When he saw Flo come in, all beads and bosom, and sit down at a table and order a drink, Harry made his way over to her. 'Where's me mate, then?'

'Oh, ain't 'e arrived yet?' Flo countered.

'I thought he'd be wiv you?' Arthur often stayed overnight in Flo's flat upstairs.

Flo drummed her heavily ringed fingers on the table top and avoided his gaze. 'No, he had a message to go home. It seems his ma ain't well.'

'That so? Funny he never said nothin' to me about Queenie bein' poorly.'

'It came on sudden like,' Flo answered and ended the conversation by rising to greet a newly arrived member.

As the evening wore on and it looked as if neither Rikki nor Giorgio was going to turn up either, Harry's unease grew. They kept a very close eye on the running of the club and one of them was always around. Then there was Flo's behaviour, her shifty look. A sudden dreadful dawning of why she couldn't look him in the eye made Harry swallow hard. Then his heart started to pound erratically against his ribcage and he felt a vital need to visit the bog. Christ, had the brothers found out about their little scam with the hashish and lettin' old man Jacobs off his toll? Arthur hadn't got much up top, and it would be just like the stupid sod to go blabbing to Flo after a drink too many. And she'd shopped them! That was it! To the Mantoni brothers, and no one crossed them and got away with it. It all seemed so obvious – Harry shivered and looked about the dimly lit, smoky room. He'd better get out of here PDQ. Knowing there was a back way out, he sidled towards the kitchen. It was kept in case there was a police raid, as a getaway for club members whose careers would never survive exposure in the press of their colourful sex lives. Harry found the door easily, but it was locked and the bolts were rusty. 'Come on you buggers, move,' he muttered and, struggling against his growing terror and with sweating, shaking hands, Harry tried to ease the bolts. They wouldn't budge, though, and he expected at any second to hear a sinister voice behind him demanding to know what he was up to.

Harry was about to give up and surrender to his fate, when the bolts suddenly shot back. With a great gasp of relief he unlocked the door. It swung open and, savouring the fresh air on his face, he started to walk down the alleyway and away from the club. His feet and head told him to run, but Harry knew that might arouse suspicion. If you want to get out of this alive, act natural, an inner voice said, and finding enough spittle to wet his dry lips he began whistling a popular tune.

A prostitute standing on a street corner called, 'Like a

nice time, love?' and beckoned him over. For a moment Harry was tempted. Anything to help him enjoy a few minutes' oblivion.

'How much?' he asked and moved nearer.

'A quid to you, sweetheart.'

Under the lamplight the face was raddled and Harry's fastidious nature was repelled. She should be paying him with a moosh like that. 'Sorry,' he lied to spare her feelings, 'I ain't got that much on me.'

'Fifteen bob, then.'

Harry shook his head.

'Ten bob,' the desperate woman bargained, and as he walked away, Harry thought, poor cow, what a life.

By the time he reached the Charing Cross Road, Harry's panic had subsided enough for him to make some plans. He would return to his room, collect the money he had stashed away under the floorboards, pack and make himself scarce, for good if necessary.

But supposing the brothers had a contract out on him, and one of their hitmen was waiting back at his place? The fear Harry had tried so hard to keep at bay returned. Sweat trickled down his spine and the backs of his legs like raindrops. Keep calm, Harry lad, he ordered himself, you're gettin' yerself in a right muck sweat and all this might be nothing more than your imagination. And if it ain't, well you'll do yerself no good falling to pieces. With an enormous effort, he managed to empty his mind of dismembered bodies and a shallow grave in Epping Forest. First things first, and he needed to go and check that Arthur was okay.

Just in case anyone was on his trail, Harry caught a bus to the City, then hailed a taxi and gave the driver Arthur's address. 'Myrtle Street, please, mate,' he said then sat back and prayed for the first time in his life. A premonition that his prayers would probably go unanswered was confirmed when a speeding police patrol car, its bells ringing, overtook them, closely followed by an ambulance.

'They're turnin' into Myrtle Street,' the taxi driver informed Harry unnecessarily. 'Looks as if something's wrong.'

He wriggled his behind in anticipation and increased his speed.

'You can stop 'ere,' Harry called, when they reached the corner. 'I'll walk the rest of the way.'

He paid the driver, turned into Myrtle Street and his heart seemed to stop and the breath leave his body. Although he knew he was walking towards his own doom, Harry kept moving, the whole nightmarish scene of police cars, policemen and spectators crowding around Arthur's house, acting like a magnet and drawing him forward. He had to know the worst.

He could feel the tension, the ghoulish curiosity of the onlookers, as police moved in and out of the house. Stopping short of the main crowd he forced himself to speak. 'What's happened here?' he asked a spectator.

The man turned, glad to be able to pass on the grisly details. 'Seems someone's been bumped off, although the rumour is it might be a double murder, a bloke and his mum. Look, they're bringin' them out now.' The man nudged Harry eagerly.

As the two bodies, each covered by a blanket, were carried out on stretchers, Harry vomited, down his jacket and trousers and all over his shoes.

The other man looked at him strangely. 'You all right, mate?'

In reply Harry broke into wild sobs and turned and stumbled blindly down the street. Arthur, his best mate since they were kids and closer than a brother, dead, killed by those gangsters. Queenie, too, and what harm had she ever done anyone? Harry stopped, leaned against a wall, blew his nose and wiped his eyes. His mouth tasted sour and he could smell the dry vomit on his clothes, but his grief and fear had turned into a consuming anger that cast out reason. He wanted revenge. Tonight.

'What's happened up there?' The voice belonged to the taxi driver, standing by his cab and maybe hopeful of getting another fare.

'Those bastards the Mantoni brothers killed my . . . my best mate an . . . and 'is mum.' Harry choked back the tears and straightened up. 'And now I'm gonna get them before they get me.'

'I wish you luck, mate. The world will be a better place without them two evil specimens. Can I drop you off somewhere?'

Harry waved him aside. 'No thanks,' he answered, his mind preoccupied with hitmen. They'd be aiming to flush him out now and the first place they'd look was the club, which was where they'd expect to find him at this time of night.

Harry roomed with a Mrs Bryant who never allowed visitors, male or female, under any circumstances. She refused to explain why, but if asked, would mutter darkly, 'I have me reasons.' Harry knew, therefore, that she'd have to be forcibly restrained before anyone could get access to his room. Nevertheless, as he approached the house, his nerves were taut as a bowstring. He jumped at every shadow and constantly cast frightened glances over his shoulder.

Only when he was safely indoors did Harry relax and knock on Mrs Bryant's kitchen door. Eventually it opened a quarter of an inch. He could hear a high keening noise, which was the only sound her simple daughter could make, accompanied by dance music playing on the wireless. The music made him think of Gloria and all their evenings out together. And her warnings. God how he wished he'd listened to her now.

'What is you want, Mr Watts?' the woman asked, through the crack in the door.

'Has anyone called asking to see me tonight, Mrs Bryant?'

'Not a soul,' his landlady replied and shut the door on his face.

'Thank you for nothing,' Harry muttered, but taking no chances, he edged up the stairs with a cat-like caution, flung open his door and threw himself back against the wall. When no one leapt out on him, he bravely ventured into his room, slammed the door and turned the key. Moving with speed he turned up the gas, went to the corner of the room, lifted the lino and a floor board and pulled out a wad of notes. Fifty quid, that would see him nicely for a while. He peeled off a note to leave for his rent then poured some water from a jug into a basin to wash his hands and face. He gargled away the sour taste in his mouth, changed his clothes, went to his chest of drawers and pulled out the gun Rikki had given him. At last he was going to find a use for it, he thought, as he packed a suitcase.

Harry stuffed the bank notes in his breast pocket, the gun in his jacket pocket. Unlocking the door he paused and listened. The wireless was still playing dance music, the girl still making her strange noises. Hugging his suitcase against his chest, Harry crept down the stairs and out of the front door, closing it quietly behind him.

At a brisk pace, and coldly in charge of himself, he set off in the direction of the Mantoni establishment, aware of the revolver heavy against his hip bone. He'd never fired a gun in his life but he was a pretty good darts player, and that's what you needed, an accurate eye and a gut full of hate.

He had a good mile to walk and time to prepare himself and make his plans. After the job was done, he'd make for a big city like Birmingham or Manchester, dye his hair, grow a beard, and become an anonymous face amongst thousands.

In a small park a couple of streets away from where the brothers lived, Harry hid his suitcase in some bushes. What he hadn't prepared himself for, though, was a police car parked outside the house, and the shock of it stopped him in his tracks. 'Bloody hell,' he swore, 'don't say they're

arresting them and depriving me of my chance to get even.'
At that moment the front door opened and hearing voices,
Harry ducked behind a wall.

'Let me know if you want any more help wiv the case,
officer. I'd be more than willing to oblige. But as you saw,
me and Giorgio have had a couple of broads here all
evening, and you've got their addresses if you want to talk
to them again.' This was Rikki at his most unctuous, the
police at their most disbelieving.

'Thank you, Mr Mantoni, we intend to. We'll also be wanting to interview you and your brother again, so don't make
any plans to leave town,' the policeman answered and got
into his car.

As he drove off Harry stood up. Moving quickly, he called
softly, 'A word, Rikki,' and thrust his hand in his pocket.
Rikki turned, with a look of genuine astonishment, Harry
was gratified to see. 'You look surprised to see me, old son.'

As Harry moved forward, Rikki backed up the path. 'Yeah
. . . a bit.'

'Thought I'd be in my coffin by now, like Arthur and
Queenie, didn't you? Except the blokes you sent to do your
dirty work, got it wrong.'

In the street lights, Harry could see that sweat had broken
out on Rikki's forehead and his bottom lip had developed
a nervous twitch. 'I . . . don't know what yer gettin' at.'

'What I'm gettin at is that you killed my best mate Arthur
and 'is mum, you frigging bastard.'

'I ain't moved from this house all evening,' Rikki protested.

'No, and next time you do it'll be in a box – and that's a
promise.'

Harry raised his arm, there was a glint of metal and Rikki
screamed in high terror, 'Giorgio!'

Quite calmly, Harry squeezed the trigger, aiming for the
heart. 'This is for Arthur.' He felt the recoil, Rikki staggered
back and he fired again. 'And this is for Queenie.'

Rikki collapsed in slow motion grasping his breast, the blood spurting through his fingers and staining his dark blue smoking jacket black. His eyes remained open and he stared at Harry in disbelief.

Giorgio had now come to the door and seeing his brother lying on the ground, he began to whimper with terror.

Harry called his name. Giorgio looked up and Harry took aim a third time. But this shot wasn't so accurate, probably because he was trembling so violently and although Giorgio screamed the bullet only grazed his shoulder.

'What a pity, I missed.' Harry spat in the gutter, threw down the gun and waving victoriously to neighbours now appearing at windows and doors, he strolled off down the street.

'Didn't I always tell Gloria that low life would come to a sticky end? He ain't got the sense he was born with, Harry Watts.' Gratified at the accuracy of her predictions, Gran took a pinch of snuff from a small tin and inhaled it up both notrils with noisy gusto.

Edna stared at her mother with a cold dislike. Sensitivity had never been her strong point, but she was appalled by her mother's total lack of compassion, even for her own daughter. It didn't matter that this was a tragedy of unparalleled proportions, only that she had been proved right.

'You've said enough, Mum,' Edna rebuked her mother sharply. 'I don't know how Gloria's managed to get up and go to work each day. It must be a living hell for her without you adding to her grief, so be good enough to keep your opinions to yerself in this house.'

'If that's how you feel I'll go then,' Maud Atkins huffed.

Edna closed her eyes and rubbed her forehead with a weary gesture. 'Yes, perhaps you'd better. I don't make good company these days. Me nerves are shot to pieces and I feel as if I've aged twenty years.'

'And whose fault is that, eh? Not mine. But I know when

I'm not wanted.' Deeply affronted, Maud Atkins gathered up her coat and Donald.

Edna was in no mood to placate or apologize or press her to stay. A word out of place and her mother was immediately on her high horse, and yet she was always so free with her own opinions. 'See yer nan out,' she instructed Frances.

Kitty could barely hide her own irritation as Maud stomped out of the house. Just like Nan to spread ill feeling, she had a gift for it, and now she'd put Mum thoroughly out of temper when she'd been bracing herself all day to put a tricky proposition of her own.

'Don't let Nan upset you, Mum, sit down and I'll put the kettle on,' Kitty said, hopeful that a cup of tea might ease her path.

'Thank you, dear.' Edna gave her daughter a grateful smile and sank into a chair.

Frances had obviously walked some of the way home with Nan and Donald, and while she was in the scullery Kitty heard her return. Placing three cups and saucers on a tray, she carried it into the small back room. Her mother had her eyes closed, and studying her exhausted features Kitty noticed how the strain of the last weeks had deepened the lines on her face.

'Here you are, Mum.' Kitty shook her gently and handed her a cup.

Edna opened her eyes, took the tea and stirred it. 'Thank you, dear.' Her thoughts still on the spat she'd had with her own mother, she went on, 'You know, I try hard, but I'm afraid I often find it difficult to like Mum, let alone love her. She was almost gloating about Harry. And she's so totally self-centred it takes my breath away at times. She doesn't even seem aware that these past weeks have been a nightmare for Gloria.'

'It's been a terrible time for everyone,' Kitty said quietly. In fact the repercussions of the murder had affected all their lives, sometimes in unexpected ways. Because of their close connection with someone who'd dared to kill a Mantoni, the family were minor celebrities in the area, while Harry was a hero, a real Robin Hood who'd done all small businesses an enormous favour. The general opinion was that it was good riddance to a real bad 'un. The only pity was that Harry hadn't managed to do both the brothers in while he was at it. Outside the East End, fortunately, it was nothing more than a gangland killing and so far Kitty had managed to keep the whole horrible affair from Robert – for how much longer she wasn't sure. Which accounted for her need to speak to her mother urgently. Steeling herself, Kitty drew her chair up beside Edna.

'Mum, I don't want to add to your worries, but the trial starts on Monday so the papers will be full of the murder. With Gloria a witness, they're bound to find out where she lives and our names and photographs are going to be splashed all over the front pages. I've been giving it a lot of thought, and if you don't mind I'd like to move out and get a place of my own.'

Her mother took a sip of tea and put her cup back down on the saucer before replying. 'You want to desert us, is that it?'

But Kitty had her future to think about, and she refused to allow her mother to make her feel guilty. 'I'm not deserting you, but if it comes out that I'm connected in some way with a crook and a murderer, they're never going to keep me on at Pennywise. I might even find it difficult to get another job.'

'Have you spoken to your father about this?'

'No, I hoped you would.'

'And how are you going to look after yourself in this room?'

'Mum, I'm nearly twenty. Plenty of girls are married with kids at my age. In a year I'll have the key of the door anyway.'

'Where will you go?' asked Edna, too defeated to argue with her self-willed daughter.

'I've been looking at rooms near where I work,' Kitty answered, sensing she had won but trying hard to hide her elation. 'There's one vacant, and the landlady says I can have it, but I've got to make up my mind quickly.'

Frances, who was reading a magazine, hadn't paid much attention to the conversation, but as her mother continued her questioning, her ears pricked up.

'Are you sure you'll be able to afford it? It's not just the room, there'll be food to buy as well.'

'I know I'll have to be careful, but with luck I'll get a rise on my birthday.'

'When you goin'?' asked Frances. She knew losing Kitty would add to her mother's distress, but personally, she was delighted. The luxury of a bed all to herself and extra drawer space were just two of the benefits that sprang to mind. Imagine being able to stretch out at night and not have Kitty complaining about her cold feet.

'If I go and put a deposit on the room tomorrow, I can start moving my things in immediately,' said Kitty, assuming that the matter was settled. 'In fact I might as well go and start packing now.'

Kitty suppressed her jubilation until she was out of the room, then tore up the stairs like a young gazelle. It was utterly selfish of her, she accepted that, but the sooner she got out of this doom-laden house, the better. She felt sorry for her aunt, who wouldn't?, but she shared her nan's opinion of Harry. He was a no-hoper and Gloria should have dumped him years ago. And because he was a liability, why should she be penalized, Kitty asked herself. She'd worked damn hard to get where she was in the firm and she was blowed if some small-time crook was going to ruin it for her.

Even the murder was a cock-up. Trust Harry to shoot Rikki with half the street looking on then leave the evidence behind. And does he lie low like anyone sensible would do? No, with his description in all the papers he gets on a train to Manchester. No wonder the police caught up with him the next day.

When Kitty had stuffed as many clothes as she could into one suitcase, she filled a carrier bag with books. Staring down at her worldly possessions, she thought: why waste time? I might as well take this lot round to my new lodgings now, pay a week's rent and move in tomorrow.

Kitty fell in love with her little room immediately. It was at the top of the house, with a sloping ceiling and a view of the gardens and trees. Imagine, a place of her own: space, freedom, privacy. Jubilant, she bounced up and down on the narrow bed. All her clothes had been hung up in the wardrobe or put away in the chest of drawers. Her books were in the bookcase, her few ornaments displayed on the mantelpiece over the gas fire. Slightly at a loose end, she sat with her hands folded on her lap, wondering what to do next. She'd have a bath, that was it, even though it cost threepence. She was changing into her dressing-gown when there was a knock at the door.

Quickly tying the cord, she opened the door to a buxom, cheerful-looking girl with a burning bush of frizzy red hair. 'Hello, I'm Felicity Turner. I'm in the room next to yours.' She held out her hand and Kitty shook it.

'How do you do. My name's Kitty Henderson. Won't you come in and have a cup of tea?' Kitty asked politely, playing hostess for the first time in her life.

'Are you sure?' But Felicity was already edging her way through the door and glancing around her with a bright curiosity.

'Do sit down,' said Kitty and searched in her purse for pennies to feed into the meter before lighting the gas ring.

'That meter gobbles up money,' Felicity warned. 'As you'll find when you've got the gas fire on in the winter.'

Kitty, who didn't want to know the bad news this early, smiled and said, 'Well never mind.' Anyway, Robert had hinted that if she found it hard going financially, he might be able to help her out.

'Tell you what, why don't we have something a bit stronger to celebrate your arrival?' Felicity jumped up. 'I've got some booze in my room.' She dashed out and came back a couple of minutes later clutching two bottles, one with gin in it, the other lime juice. Pouring what looked like a generous measure into the tea cups, Felicity raised hers in the air. 'Here's to your new life.'

'Thanks.'

'First time away from home?'

'Yes,' Kitty admitted.

'You'll be able to kick over the traces now.'

'I suppose so.' Although she had taken a liking to Felicity, Kitty had no intention of giving away any secrets.

'You'll have noticed the list of do's and don't's pinned to the back of your door.'

Kitty nodded. One in particular stood out in her mind: NO MEN IN ROOMS, in capitals and underlined three times in red ink as a dire warning, had come as quite a blow.

'I ignore most of them, particularly no men in rooms.'

Intrigued by this free spirit, Kitty asked, 'How d'you do that?'

Felicity smiled. 'Easy peasy. There's a fire escape on the landing, need I say more?'

In fact, as Kitty was to discover from the noisy love-making she could hear through the walls, Felicity had a man in almost every night. Not always the same one, either, which rather shocked her, although she knew she was in no position to moralize about other people's behaviour. Besides, when Robert came to her room, she'd at least be able to count on Felicity's discretion. Perhaps now too, they'd be able to snatch an hour together at the weekends, if he could find an excuse to slip away from Imogen.

That first weekend away from home was a testing time for Kitty. Felicity had gone to stay with friends, and Robert was down at Leyborne. He and Imogen were invited down there quite regularly now and it made Kitty feel so miserably jealous she'd even rowed with Robert about it. But as he explained, he was rather indebted to Sir Sidney. 'He's been very generous to my mother, provided me with a job, for which I'm grateful and he's taken a shine to Imogen and is charmed by her piano playing. That makes her happy and she loves the house.' Apparently a directorship had been hinted at, which Robert, with his present inadequate salary and the large fees he had to pay to various doctors treating Imogen's nerves, desperately wanted.

In the office, too, Kitty was often instructed by Alice to phone and book tickets for places such as Glyndebourne in summer and Covent Garden in winter. Always it was four tickets and a chauffeur-driven car, always it meant Robert spent less time with her.

On the Sunday morning, church bells and rain gurgling in the gutters woke Kitty. She drew back the curtains. The bare November branches dripped with rain, the gardens looked bedraggled, the street below was wet and empty. Kitty made tea and got back into bed. At the thought of the long Sunday hours to be filled, she was tempted to go home to Mum's roast beef, Yorkshire pudding and apple pie. But balancing her loneliness against Gloria's misery, she knew which she preferred.

She tried to pass the time by sleeping, but that made her feel headachy, so she got up and lit the gas fire. She was soon so alarmed at the way the meter swallowed up the pennies, she dressed and went out, wrapping up well against the rain, and taking an umbrella with her. She walked until she came to the only building that was open, an art gallery, and to get out of the rain, she went in.

But Kitty had no eye for art and she soon tired of staring

at saints and angels, slaughtered animals and fruit. Hell, what should she do? She couldn't just trudge around in the rain and her money had to last the week so she didn't dare spend any, not even on a comforting poached egg on toast. Suddenly she had an idea. Jumping on a bus to Holland Park, she walked to where Robert lived and stood on the opposite side of the road, staring up at his flat, which was as physically near as she was allowed. The November day was drawing in, lamps glowed in windows, but Robert and Imogen's flat remained dark. The rain pounded off her umbrella, but Kitty didn't move and eventually Sir Sidney's limousine glided up the road. It came to a halt and Percy jumped out and opened the back door. Robert emerged first and turned to assist Imogen, then Alice, out of the car. Alice was laughing at something Robert said, and Kitty's heart was stricken with pain and jealousy. They went inside and a few minutes later the lights went on in the flat and Kitty remembered the hours she'd lain there in Robert's arms. A figure came to the window and drew the curtains, shutting out the night, and for Kitty it was like being excluded from Robert's love.

24

Harry had been committed for trial at the Central Criminal Court, the Old Bailey, and the first thing Frances did when she left work that Monday evening was to head with anxious steps for the news-stand at the top of the street. 'Read all about it! Read all about it!' the news vendor exhorted as she hurried towards him. 'Watts changes plea to guilty!'

Frances stopped dead. 'No, he couldn't have!' she protested, unaware she'd spoken out loud.

'Well 'e has, gel, an' it's all there as you'll see for yerself.' With a quick flick of the wrist, the man folded the newspaper and handed it to Frances in exchange for her pennies. As she opened the paper and read the stark headline, WATTS CHANGES PLEA TO GUILTY, her fingers trembled as if she'd been struck down with the palsy. Underneath was a photograph of Harry, smiling and well-groomed, taken some years previously. What possessed you, Harry? Frances raged silently, and her eyes skimmed the page, searching for an answer.

The judge, it was reported, had said it was unusual to alter the plea in a murder trial, but the prisoner was aware of the consequences and he saw no reason why he should not permit it. There followed a strong plea for mercy from his defending counsel. Harold Watts, he stated, had shot Rikki Mantoni, a known criminal, in self-defence believing his own life to be in peril after his friend and business associate Arthur Challis, and Queenie Challis his mother, had been found bludgeoned to death in their own home.

The judge then advised the jury that it was their duty to return a formal verdict of guilty on Watts, which the foreman did. Donning his black cap the judge passed a sentence of death, ending with chilling finality, 'And may the Lord have mercy upon your soul.' As the words rang round the court, the accused, Harold Watts, aged 32, closed his eyes and looked as if he might collapse. But he pulled himself together and marched unaided to the cells below.

By the time Frances reached the end of the report, the typeface was a wavering black line. She forgot the careless way in which Harry had often treated Gloria and her memories reached back into a happier past; the shilling pressed into her hand as a child, the conspiratorial wink, the whispered, 'Don't tell yer ma.'

She screwed up the paper and pushed it into a rubbish bin, then walked blindly down the street. Indifferent to the icy drizzle or her own safety, she trudged on through dark, unfamiliar streets, thinking of her aunt who must at this moment be in the deepest pit of despair. It wasn't until her teeth started to chatter that Frances realized the drizzle had become a steady downpour. She should go home, she knew. It was the darkest hour of Gloria's life and she needed her. But she dreaded the awkwardness and her own clumsy inability to find the proper words of comfort.

Deeply ashamed of her cowardice, Frances nevertheless kept walking until she came to a cinema. Here she stopped to study the stills of a Deanna Durbin film. Tempted by its bright lights and the promise of music and warmth, she went in and sat through the main film and a cartoon twice, but the images on the screen remained unfocused and Deanna Durbin's sweet voice came from a long way off. During the newsreel she saw nothing of the posturing Il Duce, Lord Halifax's meeting with Hitler or the fighting in Spain. The bombed cities, the terrified fleeing citizens, didn't even bring Andrew to mind.

When the cinema turned out at half past ten it was still raining hard, which left Frances with no choice but to make for home. With the dead weight of sorrow on her shoulders, she dragged herself up the street. She couldn't put it off for much longer, but what did she say to her aunt? When someone died under normal circumstances you mouthed the familiar clichés of regret, but hanging was hardly a normal situation. How would she even meet Gloria's eye?

As she approached the house Frances saw that her mother was showing someone out. Curious, she increased her speed and recognized Dr Field getting into his car.

'What's he doing here?'

'Not surprisingly, Gloria's been pretty hysterical. He's given her a sedative to calm her down and help her sleep,' Edna answered, locking the door and following Frances down the hall.

'There's no point in asking how she's bearing up, then?'

'No, and yer nan came round, which didn't help.'

'She didn't make one of her famous remarks, I hope.'

'No, she spared us that. We've given Gloria our room for tonight. She needs to be on her own right now. I'll come in with you, Dad will have to make up a bed in the front room.' To keep herself occupied, Edna put on the kettle. 'Do you want something to eat?'

Frances shook her head. Food would stick in her gullet.

Not another word was said by anyone and they went silently to bed. In the dark it was worse; all Frances could see was Harry, hands tied behind his back, a hood over his head, a rope round his neck and choking to death.

However the local people weren't going to give up their hero to the gallows without a fight. A petition was organized, signed by thousands and presented to the Home Secretary with a plea for mercy. Right until the last day, Gloria clung on to that one small hope, an eleventh-hour reprieve, but the Home Secretary decided against it.

When Harry asked to see Gloria, her family tried to talk her out of it. But she was adamant. 'It's the last thing I'll ever do for him and I'm going.'

Bravely Gloria powdered away the dark shadows under her eyes, rouged her cheeks to hide their pallor, put on her highest heels and jauntiest hat and set out for Pentonville Prison. It was a huge, grim place and Gloria's mind was so gripped by the horror of Harry's execution, her body went into involuntary spasms as she approached it. 'No, I can't,' she cried and, blinded by tears, backed away. The temptation to turn and run was overpowering, but although Harry had failed her often in the past, Gloria knew she couldn't desert him in his final hours. So with leaden feet she moved forward, forced her name out through numb lips, stepped through the portals and heard the doom-laden slam of the gate behind her.

Gloria was shown into a room with dark green painted walls and bare floorboards. An atmosphere of terror clung to the room, the smell of bowels out of control that no amount of disinfectant could scrub away. Two warders stood guard and Gloria thought: What's going on behind those impassive features, how do they cope with the anguish of mothers, wives and sweethearts saying their last farewells? Perhaps to survive, they became inured to it and the suffering passed over their heads. Harry was already waiting. His prison clothes hung loosely on his thin frame and his unbrilliantined hair was streaked with grey. Even though this was their last meeting, a wire screen divided them, cruelly denying Harry the comfort of a final embrace. But he made fleshly contact by forcing his little finger through the tight mesh and linking it with Gloria's. 'Hello, love. Nice of you to come.'

Gloria's lips trembled. 'Hello, Harry.' She'd sworn she'd be brave, but she knew she was making a hash of it and when Harry attempted a smile for her benefit, her eyes filled with tears.

'Hey, don't cry.'

'Oh why did you do it, Harry?' she asked in a choked voice.

''Cos of what Rikki did to my best mate and Queenie. I'm only sorry I didn't get Giorgio while I was about it. After all they can only 'ang me once.'

'No, I don't mean that. Why did you change your plea to guilty? You might have stood a chance if you hadn't.'

Harry shook his head. 'No I wouldn't. It was an open and shut case, love. Half the street saw me shoot the bugger, but I wanted to do one decent thing in me life and spare you the ordeal of goin' in the witness box and bein' cross-examined. Having the past raked over and written up in the papers was something you didn't deserve. You've had to put up wiv enough from me and you warned me about the Mantonis an' I was a stupid sod and wouldn't listen. I've only one regret an' that's that I didn't always treat you proper. I should have married you a long time ago and then I wouldn't be in this bleedin' mess. Still, too late for regrets.'

'Oh, Harry.' Gloria tried a weak smile.

'But I want you to make me a promise.'

Gloria wiped her eyes. 'I'll do anything you say.'

'Marry Walter.'

It was too much and Gloria's body shook with convulsive sobs. 'I couldn't, not now.'

'You must, he's a good man, he'll treat you well and you need someone to look after you. And that's what you want, isn't it? A home and a family, and I never gave it to you.'

A warder tapped Gloria on the shoulder. 'Time's up I'm afraid, miss.'

The blood seemed to drain from her body and the world momentarily receded. For God's sake don't faint, Gloria reprimanded herself, you'll only make it worse for him. 'Goodbye, Harry.' She put her mouth to the wire and their lips touched. Harry's were cold as death. Releasing her finger from his she turned and stumbled out of the room.

'Goodbye, sweetheart. Always try and think of me kindly,' Harry called.

Gloria turned for one last look at him, but the door had

already slammed behind her. She was escorted across the prison yard by a silent warder, but her legs would barely support her and she wobbled on her high heels. The warder gripped her arm and swooning against him she sobbed hysterically, 'They can't do it to my Harry, they can't!'

'There, there, miss,' were the only words of comfort the man could offer her. Then, stony-faced, he let her out through the massive gates where a framed notice of Harry's execution at nine o' clock the following morning had already been posted.

In May, with a strong breeze blowing the blossom off the trees, Gloria became Mrs Walter Powell. It was a quiet register office wedding with just the family and a brother and sister on Walter's side. Gloria had lost a good deal of weight, but everyone remarked on how pretty the bride looked in her powder blue costume, and how handsome Walter suddenly seemed. 'And a tower of strength,' Maud Atkins muttered out of the corner of her mouth to Edna, 'over that other business. I'm surprised 'e stuck by her. Most men wouldn't.'

Edna gave her mother a withering look. 'I'm not. Walter's a good man. He also happens to love Gloria, and she committed no crime, wasn't on trial.'

Maud folded her arms and hitched up her bosoms. 'Mud sticks, though.'

'Shut up, Mum, for this day at least. I want it to be a happy occasion. Gloria deserves it after what she's been through.'

Frances, listening to this exchange of views, saw her mother fighting to control her anger, and wondered if Nan resented the secure future that awaited Gloria. For Walter had a good job in a solicitor's office, owned his own house and had made it clear that his wife would no longer need to go out to work. But was she the only one who noticed that a light had gone out in Gloria, Frances wondered. The old cheeky Gloria with her ability to cock a snook at life, had all but vanished, although maybe now with Walter she'd be able to put the past months behind her and achieve a measure of peace. Frances prayed so.

Confetti was being thrown at the bride and groom and the photographer was bustling about, organizing everyone into a group and instructing them to smile while he captured the happy event through his lens. When this was done to his satisfaction Gloria called, 'catch' to Frances and threw her niece her small posy of jewel-bright anemones. But before Frances had a chance, Kitty, quick as lightning, made a grab for the posy and clutched it triumphantly against her breast.

Gloria looked annoyed but Frances thought: Who's she trying to get to the altar? No point in asking – Kitty was still as close as an oyster, and her living away from home had severely curtailed her own detective work. But Frances thought she wouldn't have minded being a fly on the wall in that room of Kitty's sometimes, just to find out exactly what she got up to.

The photographs taken, and with the bride and groom leading the way, the family trooped back in procession to Tudor Street where Mum had laid on tea, beer, sandwiches and a small wedding cake.

Gloria and Walter were spending their honeymoon in Eastbourne and just before the hired car came to take them and their luggage to the station, Frances went and sat down on the floor beside her aunt and rested her head on her lap.

'I'm gonna miss you and the chats in bed at night.' If she wasn't careful, Frances knew she would cry.

Gloria stroked her niece's cheek fondly. 'I'll miss our talks too, love. But you can come round whenever you like and bring that nice lad Paul with you when you do.'

Frances sat up. 'Why Paul?'

'He's got a bit of a soft spot for you, but I don't suppose

you've even noticed. Yer head's still full of Andrew, isn't it?'

Frances didn't bother to deny it. 'Do you think Andrew's been killed? It's so long since anyone heard from him I sometimes think he must be dead. I couldn't bear it if he was.'

'I'm afraid you'd have to,' answered Gloria quietly. 'But don't worry, as they say, bad news travels fast. You'd have heard if he was. Anyway, isn't there some way you can find out? He must have parents.'

'Yeah, in Chelmsford. But he might not be in contact with them. When he went to prison, they were so ashamed, they refused to visit him.'

'He'll turn up one of these days, but you shouldn't waste your youth pining for Andrew. He loves your sister, that's not going to change.'

'He will love me one day, I'll make him.' Frances's face had a determined set to it.

'Paul's a nice lad, more your own background too, and you've got so much in common, both being musical and those lovely songs he writes for you.'

'Paul's my friend, nothing more,' Frances insisted.

Gloria shook her head. 'Why are we human beings always so contrary and want what we can't have?' she wondered out loud.

Walter was signalling and she smiled across to him, then got up to go.

'Tell you what, the first Sunday after we get home I want you to bring Paul round to Stuart Street for tea. You'll be our first guests. Will you do that?'

Frances kissed Gloria with great affection. 'Of course I will. I want to see your lovely new home, don't I? I do love you, Auntie, and I know you're going to be ever so happy with Walter.'

Gloria hugged Frances tight and fought back a tear. 'And I love you too sweetheart, very much.'

285

25

During those first months after she moved in, Robert climbed the fire escape to her room under the eaves as often as he could. It was hard for Kitty to flout convention with the same cheerful disregard as Felicity and she found the narrow bed, with its squeaking springs, embarrassing and inhibiting. So together she and Robert would haul the mattress on to the floor and make love in front of the gas fire. The house wasn't overlooked, which did away with the need to draw the curtains, and sometimes a full moon would shine down on their naked bodies as they lay curled in each other's arms languid and content from love-making. On summer mornings, birds in the garden woke Kitty with their song and on stormy nights the great trees creaked and heaved and threw up shadows on the wall that reminded her of galleons tossing on a turbulent sea.

Snug in our own small world, skin on skin, Kitty would think, sigh with contentment and press herself even closer to Robert. But he could never stay long and tonight, like every other one, he unwound himself from Kitty's arms and started to dress.

'Don't go yet,' Kitty pleaded and tried to pull him back.

'There's Imogen, darling. I must.'

'Leave Imogen. Divorce her.' Kitty had grown bolder in her demands of late.

'Kitten, you know I can't. It would destroy her. Would you want to build your happiness on someone else's misery?'

Actually Kitty thought she would find it quite easy. But she was canny enough not to say as much to Robert, sensing it might do little to forward her cause. Hugging her knees, she watched him sit down on the bed, pull on his socks and shoes and tie his laces. In a minute he would be gone. Was it always to be like this, her happiness rationed out in meagre portions? She'd surrendered totally to Robert. Her heart, her body, her soul belonged to him and it was right and proper that they should be joined together as man and wife.

Robert was now knotting his tie in the mirror. 'You know there's going to be a war, don't you Kat? And that will change all our lives. Irrevocably.'

'You're not to frighten me with such talk, Robert,' answered Kitty fretfully. 'Mr Chamberlain has promised us there won't be.'

'Don't believe that ineffectual fool. Our Prime Minister is behaving like an ostrich. He comes home waving a piece of paper with Hitler's signature on it and bleating about peace with honour. There's nothing honourable about what he's done and I don't think much of his statesmanship if he believes for one minute that maniac will abide by any agreement. In the meantime he allows Hitler and his gang of thugs to get away with murder. First they walk into Austria, now the Sudetenland. You see, next it will be the whole of Czechoslovakia. If we don't soon wake up, all Europe will be under the heel of the Nazi jackboot. This country ought to be praying that the government comes to its senses before the German army reaches our shores.'

Kitty listened to him with growing dismay. 'Is it really as bad as that?'

'Yes. Because while the government tries to fool us with optimistic talk, it is also preparing to issue gas masks and make arrangements for the evacuation of children.' Done with knotting his tie, Robert turned to face Kitty with a sombre expression. 'I reckon that by this time next year most able-bodied young men will be in uniform.'

'Not you, Robert. Not you. I couldn't bear it if you left

me.' His words chilled Kitty's heart and she ran to him to be comforted.

Robert held her to him, leaning his chin on her head. 'Well perhaps I'm just being a pessimist. Maybe by some miracle the world will be spared a full-scale war,' he answered, but there was a definite lack of conviction in his voice.

That evening Robert couldn't shake off his vague depression, it stayed with him after he left Kitty and all the way home. However it wasn't war but his financial problems that weighed most heavily upon him. His overdraft at the bank was frightening and the manager was making threatening noises. But without a directorship and a huge jump in salary he saw no way out of the crisis. Imogen was having psychotherapy regularly and although the fees were horrendous he didn't dare stop them while they appeared to be helping her. And he had to admit it, it was due to Imogen's ability to charm Sir Sidney that he'd recently had a small salary rise. But it wasn't enough. Not with a spend-thrift mother, and a mistress who'd become used to decent restaurants and good hotels.

It was curious, but Imogen's whole character changed when she was down at Leyborne. She positively revelled in the vast grounds and army of servants, although she often paid him back with petulance when they returned to the flat. Actually, he would have preferred to spend less time down there, but Alice was insistent and if he demurred she always had Imogen as an ally. And really he couldn't afford to get on the wrong side of the boss's daughter, she had too much influence with the old man. An added problem was that she had also made it pretty evident she was attracted to him. She would engineer situations so that they were alone together and Robert wondered idly what would happen if he allowed it to go further. It would be so easy out riding one morning. He smiled grimly. His body in exchange for a directorship, and that would solve his monetary problems. But imagine the complications! Appalled at the avenues he'd allowed his thoughts to stray down, Robert called himself to task. He'd never be unfaithful to his Kat. Never.

Pushing open the heavy doors of Hobart Mansions, Robert gave a deep and heartfelt sigh. Joining the army and disappearing into an all-male environment, perhaps even abroad, was suddenly an enticing idea. Armed combat wouldn't solve his problems, unless he was killed, but it would certainly focus his mind and distance him from some of his more pressing problems.

Robert was halfway up in the lift when he sniffed and thought, What's that, someone burning their dinner? But as the lift rose to his floor and he pulled open the gates, there was a haziness in the atmosphere and a smell of smoke that disturbed him. Then, the horror already envisaged, he remembered Imogen's carelessness with her cigarettes. 'Christ!' he yelled and shot forward. Throwing himself against the front door, Robert struggled to insert the key in the lock, then fell into the hall. Here the smoke caught in his throat and made him cough violently. Robert could hear his heart thumping in his ears and he was so engulfed by dread, he had to force himself to keep moving. 'Imogen, are you there?' he called. Without any hope of her answering, he edged his way forward and saw with an awful sense of inevitability, smoke curling out from under his wife's bedroom door.

'Oh no!' With a dry sob he grabbed the handle, pushed open the door and was immediately thrown back by the blast of heat and swirling clouds of thick, black, acrid smoke. Robert clamped his handkerchief over his mouth and crouching low, inched his way forward. Flames crackled round the bed and up the curtains, but Imogen must have woken and made some attempt to escape for he found her lying unconscious on the floor. Choking on the fumes,

Robert grabbed her ankles and dragged his wife towards the door. Her nightdress had rucked up round her waist so he pulled it down to preserve her modesty then, cradling her in his arms, he stumbled out of the bedroom and out of the flat, retaining enough presence of mind to close the heavy oak doors after him.

Outside on the landing, with Imogen still in his arms, Robert collapsed against the wall, eyes streaming and trying to drag air into his lungs. When at last he was able to breathe he stared down at his wife. Her long hair was singed, the pink satin nightdress blackened with grime, the raw burns on her arms and legs already beginning to blister. But by some miracle, her beautiful face was unmarked. In fact she looked to be asleep and, laying her gently on the bare floor, Robert sought for her pulse. He couldn't find it and knowing his brain was in danger of becoming fogged by panic, he struggled to get a grip on himself. What to do? What to do? Get an ambulance, and the fire brigade, before the whole building ignited. In the confusion of his mind, Robert suddenly remembered that his neighbour was a doctor. In one step he was at his door, thumping on it frantically with both fists. 'Dr Swanson! Dr Swanson!'

'What an earth . . . !' Confronted by Robert, smeared with soot and sweat, the doctor's face wore a startled expression.

'Call the fire brigade and an ambulance. Our flat's on fire and my wife is unconscious. You must come and see to her, quickly.'

'Good heavens, a fire you say?'

'Yes, yes.' Robert spoke sharply, impatient that the man should need convincing.

'Just a moment.' The doctor disappeared and returned with his black bag. 'My wife is phoning the fire brigade and an ambulance.' Professional and in charge now, the doctor bent to examine Imogen, pushing back her eyelids then listening to her heart through his stethoscope. It didn't take him long. He stood up and removed the stethoscope from his ears. 'I'm terribly, terribly sorry, Mr Travis, but your wife is dead. Smoke inhalation, I'm afraid. It happens very quickly.'

'No.' In the distance, Robert heard the jangle of the fire engine bell.

'We must get her into my flat. The police will have to be informed.'

With the doctor's help Robert carried Imogen into the flat. The fire engine had now arrived, instructions were being shouted, hoses unwound, ladders erected. Robert, sitting with his head in his hands, heard glass breaking and thought, It's my fault Imogen is dead. If I'd been here instead of with Kitty she would still be alive. I would have found that fatal cigarette and stubbed it out like I always do.

The ambulance followed quickly behind the fire engine, and as Imogen's body was carried out on a stretcher, the building was being evacuated. Some of the elderly residents who'd already gone to bed were standing shivering in their nightclothes and clutching their pets. There was a great deal of excited discussion going on, but as the cortege passed Robert was aware of a sympathetic silence.

Everyone was kind at the hospital, the police interview was done with a tactful regard for his grief, but Robert had no idea what they asked him or what his answers were. It was hours before officialdom had finished with him and as he walked home through the dim, early morning streets, revived slightly by the cold November air, he was aware of an unfamiliar world. A milkman on his rounds chatted companionably to his horse, men slouched to work, mufflers round their necks, hands thrust deep into pockets, the Woodbines clamped in their mouths shining with the luminosity of glowworms. All the normal, mundane things of everyday life still carried on while his wife, the girl he'd once worshipped, lay dead on a cold slab.

This time yesterday she'd been alive and the worst wasn't even over. Now he had to convey the tragic news to Aunt

Bertha. 'And where were you?' he could hear her asking.

Making love to my mistress while your niece's lungs filled with deadly fumes and she slowly choked to death. Robert let out a great gasping sob.

The fire had been extinguished, the residents were in their beds. Three storeys up a curtain flapped in a black gaping hole. But supposing he hadn't come home when he did. Robert saw the conflagration in his mind's eye, the whole building a funeral pyre, and he shuddered with horror.

Although he was dog-tired, he wanted to put off as long as possible entering the flat, for he feared his own reaction. So he took the stairs instead of the lift, dragging himself up by the handrail. Although, miraculously the fire had been contained, probably by the heavy oak bedroom door, a haze still hung around the rooms and a greasy soot covered everything. In Imogen's bedroom all that was left of the bed was the springs. Ceiling and walls were blackened, furniture and carpets saturated and there was a persistent drip, drip of water. A tattered, scorched piece of curtain hung lopsidedly from buckled curtain rings, ornaments lay smashed on the floor and there was an unpleasant charred smell. Overwhelmed by a crushing guilt and the sense that the tragedy need never have happened, Robert covered his face with his hands, slid to the floor and sobbed unrestrainedly.

And this was where Alice found him, curled up and rocking backwards and forwards on his heels. He didn't hear her footsteps, and her hand touching his shoulder startled him.

'Robert, come along, I've got the car outside and I'm taking you back to Leyborne. You need a bath, then a long sleep.' Her voice was calm and reassuring. She bent and wiped his haggard face, then taking both his hands she helped him to his feet. Glad to have someone else take charge, Robert surrendered his weary body to her and he went obediently as a child, allowing Alice to draw him away from the bedroom, out of the flat and down the stairs.

Percy was waiting by the car and he touched his cap and murmured sympathetically, 'Sorry about Mrs Travis, sir.'

Robert's face began to work again and Alice pushed him quickly in the car. Percy slammed the door and got into the driver's seat and as they moved off, Alice feared Robert might turn and look back. But he didn't. Instead, his head fell against the upholstery and he closed his eyes.

She gazed fondly at his exhausted features. 'That's it, rest.'

Robert opened his eyes again. 'But how can I? The news must be broken to Aunt Bertha. Then there's the inquest. After that . . .' his voice choked, '. . . the funeral.'

Alice reached out and touched his hand lightly. 'I'll take care of everything, Robert, try not to worry.'

'Thank you. It was good of you to come, Alice, but how did you find out about the fire . . . ab . . . about Imogen?'

'The police phoned Leyborne, told me of the tragedy, said you were in deep shock and might be in need of help. I came immediately.'

'How did they know your number?'

'You must have given it to them.'

'Yes, I suppose I must.' Glad of her calm presence, Robert's eyes closed again, and his head slipped down on her shoulder. 'Thank you, Alice, for coming, you saved my sanity.' He yawned once then fell into a deep sleep. He stayed like that for the rest of the journey and although her shoulder became cramped and stiff, Alice didn't move. Instead she sat with the faintest suggestion of a smile upon her lips, while making plans for the future in her head.

Kitty was filing letters when Rose put her head round the door.

'You on your own?'

Kitty nodded. Miss Alice wasn't in yet, which was unusual for her.

'Have you heard?'

293

Kitty pushed the filing cabinet drawer closed. 'Heard what?'

'The terrible news.' Rose's eyes were round with the effort of containing herself.

'Well spill it, then.'

'Mr Robert's wife is dead.'

Kitty didn't move or speak.

'There was a fire last night at their flat. Mr Robert got there too late.'

Managing to sound calm, Kitty asked, 'Who told you this?'

'Don't you think it's a terrible tragedy? Poor man.' Rose shook her head and her features drooped in sympathy.

'Yes, of course, but who told you?' Kitty persisted and wondered if Rose noticed that her hands were shaking.

'Percy. He had to drive up and collect Mr Robert this morning. Saw all the damage and everything. Percy says he's in a bad way, so Miss Alice has taken him down to Leyborne.'

The phone rang on Kitty's desk and as she picked it up, Rose mouthed 'See you later' and left.

As Kitty had expected, it was Miss Alice. She made no mention of the fire or Imogen's death, just informed Kitty that she wouldn't be in that day, or the next. After this she gave instructions about letters that needed to be typed, followed by a list of people she wanted Kitty to phone. Then, telling Kitty she would call the following day, she rang off.

Kitty's head rang with the questions she'd wanted to ask Alice about Robert, but daren't. And I should be with him at this time, she thought fretfully, not Alice, because what could that vinegary spinster do to ease the poor dear's pain? Certainly not offer him the solace of her body.

Kitty sat for a long time staring into space and slowly the implications of Imogen's death percolated through her to her conscious mind. Robert was a widower now. Free! Yes of course it was terrible that Imogen was dead, and in such a tragic way, but she'd only ever caught glimpses of her and she'd never made Robert happy, so to pretend grief would have been hypocritical.

Kitty studied her left hand. She'd have a proper wedding ring on there soon, not a brass curtain ring. A suitable time would have to elapse, of course, because there had to be a period of mourning and due respect for the dead. But there was no reason why by this time next year she shouldn't be Mrs Robert Travis. And just let Miss Alice look down her snooty nose at her then!

26

The whole family was in the front parlour helping Dad put up paper chains and sprigs of holly when Paul came round absolutely bursting with news. Frances could tell by his expression, as soon as she opened the door, but she was also familiar enough with Paul's ways to know he'd want an audience. So she curbed her curiosity while he knocked the snow off his boots then followed her into the front room, which tonight, because of the extreme cold, luxuriously sported a fire.

'That's a welcome sight.' Unwinding his scarf, and pulling off his gloves, Paul went over and extended his hands to the flames.

By now Frances was growing impatient. 'Come on, what have you got to tell us?'

'Tell you? Who said I had anything to tell you?' Paul teased.

'You can certainly milk a situation for all it's worth. Just put us out of our misery.'

'Try and guess what it is.'

'Paul Harding, I'll throttle you,' Frances threatened.

'Oh all right . . . well,' he paused. 'Johnny's got us a gig in a West End hotel for New Year's Eve. How about that?'

Frances stared at him speechless, Tom Henderson stopped hammering and spat the tacks out of his mouth on to the palm of his hand. 'Has he, by jove. How'd he manage that?'

'The band they'd engaged dropped out for some reason. I suppose there was a panic and they asked Johnny if he could stand in. We're getting quite a name for ourselves you know, Mr Henderson. If this goes well there might be other offers. Imagine, the West End.' Paul put an arm round Frances and gave her an affectionate hug. 'Hey, you're not saying much – aren't you pleased?'

'Of course I am, but I'm still trying to take it in,' answered Frances, who couldn't decide whether to be thrilled or terrified at the idea of entertaining a posh West End audience. Then she started to panic. 'But what about rehearsals? Christmas is only five days away.'

Paul placed his hands on her shoulders and looked at her with a mock-serious expression. 'Now look here, my girl, stop getting yourself all worked up about nothing.' He shook his head. 'What a worrier you are, Frances. It'll be New Year's Eve and everyone will be boozed to the gills. Johnny's keen for you and me to do a couple of numbers on our own to warm up the audience, but we can decide on those and go over them together beforehand.'

'It makes me feel sick just thinking about it.'

'Don't think, then. We'll go down a treat, so stop being so nervous. Oh, and another thing, Johnny says you've to wear an evening dress.'

'But I haven't got an evening dress.'

'Well, you'll have to go out and buy one then.'

'What, just for one evening?'

Paul tapped Frances on her head. 'Get it into that noodle of yours, it won't be. This is the start of something big, kiddo.'

'Get the glasses out, Edna,' said Dad. 'If this daughter of ours is going to be famous, we might as well drink to it.'

When Kitty came home on Christmas Eve it was still snowing heavily and although it caused chaos, a white Christmas was such a novelty in London people were prepared to put up with the inconvenience and cold.

Roy and all the other kids were out making slides in the road or tobogganing with dustbin lids in the park. Mum was busy all day preparing stuffing, mince pies and trifle and fretting, as she did every year, about there being enough to eat and how she was going to get everyone round the table. But even with an extra place having to be set for Walter, they all squeezed in. Looking round at her family with paper hats stuck on their heads and happy and flushed from an excess of food and drink, Frances felt a deep love for them all, even Nan and Kitty. But she was aware, too, of something slipping away from her, a feeling that this might be the last time they'd sit round the table as a family. Talk of war and gas and bombs frightened Frances, but it excited Roy, who saw it as an opportunity to join the air force and become a pilot, although thank God, at the moment he was far too young. Dad tried to reassure her, but he was training as an air raid warden, and in all the London parks deep trenches were being dug.

Since it was Gloria's first Christmas as a married woman, she was entertaining the family on Boxing Day. But Kitty refused to go. It annoyed Mum but she wouldn't budge.

'There's a thaw setting in, but I want to get back in case it freezes again tonight and I've got work tomorrow.'

'Are you all right? You look very peaky.'

'I'm fine.'

'Well you weren't this morning,' Frances put in. 'I heard you being sick in the lav.'

'Were you, Kitty?' Edna studied her daughter with even more concern.

Kitty gave her sister a withering look. 'It was only an overloaded stomach, that's all. I've taken some Liver Salts and I'm fine now.'

'Gloria's so happy with Walter and she wants to show it all off, her new house and her cooking. I thought you might have made the effort after all she's been through.'

'I'll go round and see her next time I'm home, I promise.'

'And when will that be? We don't see you from one week's end to the other.'

'She's too busy living it up to bother about us,' interjected Frances.

'Shut up,' Kitty snapped, then went all hot and cold. Frances and her big mouth, she could slaughter her sometimes. 'Anyway, I must pack.' Kitty pushed past her mother and sister and not long after left the house laden down with mince pies, slices of cold pork and Christmas cake. It was such a relief to get away from the stifling family atmosphere. The festive jollity, the songs round the piano and games such as charades and consequences that her father loved to organize, only intensified her own misery.

In spite of the thaw, Kitty's room was icy cold. Stuffing pennies into the meter's hungry maw, she pulled a blanket off the bed, made a cup of tea and sat huddled over the fire nursing her unhappiness. None of the other lodgers was back yet and the house was silent. The gas popped, a wedge of snow slipped with a thud off the roof and every muscle in her body ached with nausea and fear. She'd always considered herself a person in control of life, had never had much time for women like Gloria who insisted on loving unsuitable men, and yet here she was in a similar dreadful situation.

Robert hadn't been into the office since the night Imogen died, neither had he made any attempt to get in touch with her. In normal circumstances it would have been bad enough, but now she was carrying his child. He had suffered a dreadful shock, his wife dying in such terrible circumstances, there was no denying it, but she'd imagined that after the funeral it would be only a question of time before he was back behind his desk. But the days passed and he still didn't return and what had been a vague unease became a reality and she discovered she was pregnant. At first she thought it rather well-timed. With a child on the way, they could marry immediately without observing a period of mourning.

The days became weeks, but she never dared ask after

him. Then one day through the partition that divided her small office from Miss Alice's she heard her discussing him on the phone. Kitty stopped typing and listened intently. 'Yes,' she heard Alice tell the other person, 'he collapsed completely when he reached Leyborne, poor boy. Then he had a nasty attack of flu which developed into pleurisy then pneumonia. I feared for his life for a few days. He's recuperating now, though, and well on the way to recovery.'

Poor Robert, I should have been looking after him, not Alice, Kitty brooded, and felt a rush of guilt at her own lack of faith in him when he'd been so ill. A couple of weeks before Christmas her spirits had risen even more when a memo went round every office informing staff that Mr Robert Travis had been made a Director. That means he'll be back soon, thought Kitty, and stared down at her expanding waistline. He'd better hurry too, for sharp-eyed Rose had already commented on her weight.

Christmas came and with still no sign of Robert her hopes plummeted again. A fear crept over Kitty that he had stopped loving her and she felt betrayed, abandoned and frightened. She had no idea what she should do, either. There were women who did abortions, she knew that, but how did she find one and where would the money come from? She'd be forced to give up work soon, her parents would have to be told and the thought of her father's anger terrified her. Robert in the meantime just walks away from his responsibilities, thought Kitty bitterly.

Downstairs she heard Felicity's voice. In a moment she'd be banging on the door asking what sort of Christmas she'd had and wanting to come in for a natter. Quickly Kitty locked her door, turned off the gas and light, and jumped into bed fully clothed. She couldn't face anyone tonight, particularly not anyone as determinedly cheerful as Felicity. But as she lay in bed, Kitty came to a decision. Robert wasn't going to be allowed to get away scot free. They'd made a child together and he must be told. At the weekend she would go down to Leyborne, walk up to the front door and demand to speak to him, and she wouldn't flinch from making a scene if necessary.

In spite of aching stomach muscles, after having spent half an hour retching down the lavatory, Kitty was still at her desk by eight-thirty the following morning, for Miss Alice never lost an opportunity to criticize. In Kitty's opinion jealousy was at the root of it, her being so plain. Well dressed, though, and Kitty certainly coveted many of her designer clothes.

With a definite plan, Kitty was in a calmer frame of mind this morning. Once Robert knew about the baby her life would be on an even keel again and she could tell Miss Alice where to stick her job. Kitty busied herself opening the post until quarter to nine when she heard Robert's voice and her heart lifted. He was back! Her worries were over. Alice said something Kitty didn't quite catch, then she went into her office and closed the door. Eager to speak to Robert, Kitty gave her five minutes then took in the mail and placed it on her desk. 'Good morning, Miss Alice. Quite a large postbag this morning.'

Alice, who was pulling off galoshes, looked up. 'Good morning, Miss Henderson.' She straightened the collar of her cherry wool dress, moved over to the desk and flicked through the pile of correspondence. 'Did you have a good Christmas?'

'Yes thank you,' Kitty lied. 'And you, Miss Alice?'

'Oh yes.' Her normally sallow skin glowed. 'Father Christmas brought me a very special present.'

'Oh, what was that?' Kitty enquired, as she knew she was expected to.

Alice looked almost coy. 'A husband.'

'A husband, Miss Alice?' Kitty repeated uneasily.

'Yes, and no more "Miss Alice", please. In future you

must call me by my married name. I'm Mrs Robert Travis now.'

Alice's face went out of focus and Kitty had to clutch the desk for support.

'Miss Henderson, are you all right?'

'A bug, I must go to the toilet.' Feeling as if she might indeed throw up there, Kitty turned and fled down the corridor. She didn't knock. Robert was sitting at his desk, but he stood when she entered.

'Hel ... hello ... Kitty.'

'Why did you do it?'

'I ... had no choice.'

'No choice?' she screeched.

'I was deeply in debt.'

'I've heard some excuses ...' Kitty stared at him with unveiled loathing.

'Please, I don't want a scene.' Disturbed by her hatred he turned away.

Kitty's fury was like Vesuvius erupting. This was the man who professed to love her, they'd made a child together, now he wouldn't even look at her. How dare he! 'Don't want a scene? Well how's this for a start?' Kitty's arm swept across his desk. Pens, letters, memos, files and the inkstand went flying, the ink splattering a black spidery design across the wall and carpet.

Robert, staring at the mess, didn't see Kitty turn to the bookcase until a heavy book on company law struck him hard on the chest. Winded, he staggered back, but before he could right himself another hefty tome came flying across the room and he had to duck.

'How could you!' she screamed, lobbing another book at him.

'Kitty! Calm down! You'll have the whole building in here in a minute.' Robert went to restrain her but a solid leather cover jabbed spitefully into his forehead.

'Good. Then I can tell them all about us and how I'm

pregnant.' Her voice was strident with anguish and rushing at him, she pummelled at his chest with both fists.

'What on earth is going on here?' Alice, who was standing in the doorway, stared at the wreckage, at Kitty's ravaged, tear-stained face and Robert gripping her wrists, then wisely closed the door.

'This . . . this husband of yours is the father of my child. How's that for a surprise wedding present?'

Even in the depths of her gut-wrenching misery Kitty was gratified to see the appalled look on Alice's face. 'Is this true, Robert?'

'I didn't know about the baby . . . I'm sorry.' Robert turned away with hunched shoulders.

'But you admit to an affair.'

'Yes.'

'I had no idea.'

'No, I don't suppose he bothered to tell you. Or where he was the night Imogen died.' Kitty sank sobbing into a chair. 'What's to become of me now, and the baby?'

'Be quiet, please. The staff are arriving for work. If this scandal got out . . .'

'Do you think I care?' Kitty's voice rose several octaves. 'I've nothing to lose, my life is ruined anyway.'

Attempting to take control of the situation, Alice said in a quiet tone, 'Look, let's try and talk sensibly about this. First of all, Robert, it would probably be better if you left the room.'

'Yes, all right.' Avoiding Kitty's venomous glance, Robert fled from the devastation he'd caused.

'I loathe and despise you!' Kitty screamed after him.

'Hush, my dear. I understand your feelings, but we are not going to get anywhere in an atmosphere of recrimination. How many months gone are you?'

'I don't know. Maybe three.'

'Have you seen a doctor?'

'No.'

'Do you want the baby?'

'Not now. How can I look after a child? I've got a living to earn. You'll have to give me the money so that I can get rid of it.'

'No, you can't do that. The child is a Travis after all. I'm not having it flushed down some sluice. But obviously you can't be left to go through this on your own.'

'It's me he should have married, not you!'

'Marrying a typist would hardly be appropriate; there would have been no future for Robert here if he had. And he was in deep waters financially.'

'Does he love you?'

Alice shook her head. 'I assume not, he's never said so.'

'Well he loved me, so there!'

'And look where it got you,' Alice couldn't resist saying, then felt ashamed of herself when Kitty's shoulders started to heave again. 'There, there, don't take on so.' She put a tentative arm round the girl. 'It might seem like the end of the world, but it isn't.' Not even for me, she thought. She stared down at the top of Kitty's bowed head and tried to sort out her own feelings. Although outwardly she might appear calm, she was horribly shaken by these sordid revelations, particularly coming so soon after their marriage. She'd guessed Robert wasn't happy with Imogen, but she'd never dreamed there was another woman in his life. But of course Kitty had worked for him and she was pretty. She could understand the temptation, but if he was going to have an affair with a working-class girl, he really shouldn't have been so careless as to get her pregnant. But having struggled so hard to get him, there must be no recriminations otherwise he might walk away from her. Somehow she would cope; smooth over, patch up, organize, she was good at that. Already making plans, Alice composed her mind then after careful thought said, 'If the money was found so that you could go away and live comfortably until the baby was born, would you be agreeable to Robert and me adopting it?'

'I'm having it killed. I don't want the thing in my womb. I hate it, like I hate him!'

'I'm afraid I can't permit you to do that. If you had an abortion, I would have no choice but to report you to the police.'

'I'll go where you can't find me.'

'Come now, be sensible. If you do what I suggest I would settle a very generous sum on you once the child was handed over. It would all be done legally, through a solicitor. I suggest you think about it carefully.'

Kitty picked at the embroidered rose on her handkerchief. This was the worst nightmare of her life. But what choice had she? The thought of a woman putting a sharp instrument up inside her made her feel physically sick and she had no intention of struggling to bring up a bastard child on her own. She was sure she would hate it anyway. It was more than love and sexual attraction that she'd felt for Robert, she'd idolized him. For her he was the perfect man, yet in the space of an hour he'd tumbled from that pedestal. Now he was no longer someone to look up to, but just an ordinary fallible man capable of betrayal and deceit. And the child was his as much as it was hers. So he could have it, and for the rest of his life be reminded of how he'd violated her love and be scoured daily by guilt.

Kitty managed to stem the flow of tears and ask, 'What about my parents?'

'Do you have to tell them?'

'How can I avoid it? I can't not go home for six months. They're always complaining now I don't bother to visit them enough.'

'You could tell them you're working with me down at Leyborne for a while. I could be the one who is pregnant and rather sickly. Would that satisfy them?'

'Maybe.'

'Do you want a day or two to think about it?'

'There's no point. I'll do what you say,' Kitty mumbled in a defeated voice.

'Good,' said Alice briskly. 'You go home for today. This might take a couple of weeks to organize. I'll have to get in touch with some mother and baby homes and inspect them first. We want to get you settled in a nice one don't we?'

Kitty looked at Alice with bemused puzzlement. How can she act so coolly when she's had this bombshell presented to her a few days after her wedding? I bet it's all show, I bet inside she's all churned up and going through hell. I hope she puts Robert through the mincer too, it'll serve him right.

'There are just a couple of conditions. You must not breathe a word about this business to a living soul in the office. Neither, under any circumstances whatsoever, are you to contact Robert. The relationship between you is severed, for all time. Is that clear?'

Desolated, Kitty could only nod.

'If anyone asks, I'll say you've gone down with an attack of flu. You live nearby, I believe?'

'Yes. Cardigan Square.'

'Go back there now and wait and as soon as everything is fixed up I'll come round and see you.' Alice bent and started picking up books. 'In the meantime I'd better get this room cleared up.'

27

'Turn around and let's have a proper look at you, then,' ordered Johnny.

Confident in her white crepe evening dress, with its sequinned epaulettes and clever cut that moulded itself flatteringly to the lines of her body, Frances did an obliging twirl for the band leader.

Johnny kissed her on both cheeks. 'What do you think, Paul? Sensational, isn't she?'

'That's a fact,' Paul agreed, and took the opportunity to kiss Frances too. He wasn't quite so astonished by the glamorous girl in front of him, though. He'd watched her slow metamorphosis from the shy kid who had to be almost dragged on to the stage, to a pretty nineteen-year-old whose charm for him lay in the fact that she still really had no idea how attractive or how talented she was, although no doubt that was about to change.

'Clothes make a difference,' Frances pointed out, but she liked the way Paul was regarding her, slowly and with a look she'd often seen men give Kitty, and which sent a shiver of excitement and apprehension down her spine. She was far more confident about herself these days, too. Probably because there was no Kitty around as an unfair comparison, she was allowed to be judged on her own merits.

Frances had let her hair grow and she wore it tonight in a new style, swept up at the sides and fixed with two diamante hair clips in the shape of butterflies. But although Frances knew she looked thoroughly sophisticated and composed, inside her stomach was churning. Normally an audience didn't bother her, but this wasn't called the Grand

Hotel for nothing and out there were people who'd forked out good money to see in the New Year and would expect value in return. Johnny had also made it clear that they were all on trial; if the guests took a fancy to them, there was no knowing what might come from it. Maybe that big time he kept promising them.

'We're here until one o'clock, it's going to be a long evening, so pace yourself Frances. Give it your best, but don't go straining that voice. Three numbers will do for a start. Paul can tinkle away on the old ivories until they've eaten their grub, then the boys and me will go on and the dancing can begin. You both ready?'

Paul and Frances nodded and Johnny walked out on to the small stage behind which, picked out in fairy lights and decorated with balloons was the sign: A HAPPY, PROSPEROUS AND PEACEFUL NEW YEAR TO ALL OUR PATRONS AND WELCOME TO 1939.

Paul gripped her hand. 'Chin up,' he said.

'You nervous?' Frances asked.

He nodded. 'And you?'

'A bit.'

'You've no need to worry, you'll knock 'em for six – you always do.'

'Touch wood when you say that.' Frances tapped her head superstitiously. 'Pride comes before a fall.'

'Rubbish!' Paul retorted, then before this discussion could develop, Johnny began to address the audience.

'Good evening, ladies and gentlemen, I hope you will enjoy swinging in the New Year with me and my band. Dancing will commence a little later, but in the meantime here to entertain you while you dine is our beautiful chanteuse, Miss Frances Henderson, and accompanying her on the piano, the talented songwriter, Mr Paul Harding.' Johnny turned to present them, but his well-oiled charm had apparently failed to win the audience over because Frances and Paul entered to tepid applause.

Paul sat down at the piano, massaged his fingers, then put his hand to his mouth and coughed nervously. Frances gripped the microphone for support and glanced around the restaurant, weighing up the audience. The lighting was subdued and flattering, diamonds glittered on crepy necks and slim young arms alike and the smell of expensive perfume, hothouse flowers and wealth wafted across the room to her. Real society types, she thought, drowning in money and hard to please. Well we'll see.

She and Paul had decided to kick off with 'Smoke Gets in Your Eyes', but they had to compete with the clatter of cutlery, loud conversation and an inattentive audience. With ebbing confidence Frances got through the number, aware that she wasn't giving anywhere near her best. Wisely, Paul didn't wait for applause, and as soon as they finished he went straight into 'These Foolish Things'.

In the small world of the Rex, Frances was quite a star with a devoted group of fans, so this rich crowd's indifference began to annoy her, although she hid it well behind a professional smile. How dare they ignore us? We might not be big names, but Paul and me are talented. Taking refuge in derision she thought, and look at them stuffing their faces. Seven courses when there are women in Stepney without the money to give their kids one square meal a day.

This time when they finished, Paul gave the audience the opportunity to applaud. A group at one table managed a few desultory handclaps but even this was interrupted by a burst of loud laughter from another table. Bloody snobs, Frances fumed, with no manners, who think because they're loaded they can treat people like dirt. She exchanged glances with Paul then went up to the mike. 'This next song,' she announced in a firm clear voice, 'was written by my accompanist, Mr Paul Harding. It's called "All Shadows Fly Away", and I hope you enjoy it.'

Frances stood back and gazed around her in an imperious manner, daring them not to listen. As Paul began to play she closed her eyes and swayed in time to the slow, beautiful melody. The words, which always put her so much in mind of Andrew, flowed from her effortlessly. Her young voice was in the full flower of its perfection and Frances knew she'd finally gained the fickle crowd's attention when even harassed waiters hurtling in and out of the kitchens paused to listen.

At the end of their three numbers, when she and Paul took their bow together, Frances was certain she heard a faint 'Bravo', but coming off she muttered, 'I don't know about you, but I feel as if I've already earned my night's money.'

'Well they're certainly the worst damned audience I've ever played for,' Paul conceded. 'I think we won them over, though. And by the way the champagne's flowing, they'll soon be too oiled to care what we play.'

Fortunately for Johnny, Paul was right. Drink quickly put everyone in the right mood and once the band got going with its easy rhythm and popular tunes, the small dance floor was soon crowded with couples.

At one minute to twelve, Johnny went to the front of the stage. 'Will everyone link hands for "Auld Lang Syne" please.'

A piper entered and to the skirl of bagpipes, everyone joined in singing Rabbie Burns's familiar words, which tonight took on an extra poignancy. Never far from anyone's minds was war and what it might bring with it. By this time next year London, its churches, monuments, fine buildings and citizens could be cinder.

But balloons descending from the ceiling, whistles, streamers, funny hats, even a stranger's kiss, helped dispel their fear for an hour or two. Caught up in the frantic gaiety, Frances was aware of someone handing her a glass of champagne, then of Paul taking her in his arms and kissing her. 'Happy New Year, darling,' he murmured, but their brief intimacy was interrupted by a portly drunk who had staggered up on to the stage. 'How about a New Year's kiss for me as well, little lady?' he leered, made a grab at Frances and before she could stop him, his lips were attached to hers like a suction pad.

Quickly Paul intervened. 'That'll be enough of that, sir.' His tone was polite but firm.

Frances, in a gesture of disgust, wiped her hand across her mouth, but the drunk, whose wits had deserted him, glowered at Paul belligerently. 'Want to fight for the lady?' Bunching his fists, he staggered around the stage shadow-boxing, tripped over the microphone wire and went arse over elbow on to the polished dance floor, then tobogganed on his stomach right into the middle of the dancing couples.

Highly entertained, they formed a laughing circle round him. However Frances, who knew it would never do to be seen mocking a guest's downfall, no matter how obnoxious his behaviour, clapped her hand over her mouth to still her giggles and watched an irate woman thump across the floor. 'For heaven's sake get up, Hubert,' the woman barked, her voice heavy with contempt. 'You're making an absolute fool of yourself as usual.'

Someone offered Hubert a hand and he rose obediently and followed his wife, meek as a lapdog, back to their table.

They'd hardly sat down when the manager entered, now in the guise of Old Father Time and bearing on his shoulder a scythe. In his wake came two chimney sweeps with soot-blackened faces, who wove in and out of the tables wishing the patrons a happy New Year and doling out freshly minted pennies for luck.

'Here you are, sweetheart, keep it safe and I give you my word, it'll bring you love, happiness and prosperity.' With a pink smile, one of the sweeps handed Frances a coin. Thanking him, she took it and put it in her purse. It probably wouldn't but she'd keep it anyway, Frances decided, if only in memory of a rather special night.

Later, when she and Paul came out into the street to look

for a taxi a great, swaying, roistering crowd was spilling out from Trafalgar Square along the Strand. In the crush Frances found herself with a glass in her hand, which a passing stranger obligingly filled with champagne, then Paul grabbed her and whirled around in a crazy dance until her head spun.

'Stop,' Frances protested at last. She leaned against a door, laughing and gasping for breath. 'It's been a marvellous evening, hasn't it, Paul?'

'Indeed it has. But you could make it even better.'

'How?'

'By falling in love with me.'

More than half-drunk Frances giggled foolishly. 'You are joking, aren't you?'

Paul kissed her lightly. 'You know me, a real joker,' he answered and kissed her again.

Three days into the New Year a letter addressed to Frances dropped through the letterbox. Roy brought it in and as she turned it over in her hand, he stood watching her, wriggling with curiosity.

'Who's it from then, Frances?'

'Mind your own business.' With no idea herself she studied the handwriting, then peered at the postmark. It was smudged and faint but she thought she could make out Chelmsford. Her heart thumping agitatedly, she tore open the envelope then gave her brother a brilliant smile. 'It's from Andrew. Imagine, after all this time.'

'So he ain't dead.'

'Of course not, idiot, he's at home. Hush now while I read what he's got to say.'

Dear Frances

It seems such a long time since I saw you and I'm wondering how you all are? I got back from Spain last October in a pretty bad way, so wasn't able to get in touch. Mother's been nursing and feeding me, though, and I'm a whole lot better now. Poor old Herbie copped it and it was all rather terrible, and I'm afraid my ideals rather went out the window when I saw the brutality on both sides of the war. There's nothing noble about it, believe me, although it looks as if we all might be fighting another one soon.

I'd like to see you Frances but I'm not quite up to moving far just yet so I was wondering if there's any chance of you coming down here to Chelmsford to visit me. I know you get Saturday off, and if you can come, I'll meet you at the station. Please let me know by return what train you are catching. I'm dying to hear all the news.

Best wishes
Andrew

Frances finished the letter and read it through again. No mention of Kitty. Was that a good or a bad sign? Had he finally got over her? Well it's me he's written to, Frances told herself. Me, after all this time, he wants to see.

'Well, what's 'is nibs got to say for 'imself? Does 'e mention the fighting?' asked Roy.

Holding the letter to her breast, Frances turned to him with shining eyes. 'He's invited me to go down to Chelmsford on Saturday.'

'Is that all?' Roy answered with brotherly disdain.

Frances leapt up. 'What do you mean, is that all? I'm going this instant to find out the train times, then come straight back here, answer the letter and post it. It's cutting it a bit fine, but I reckon he'll get it tomorrow.'

Frances knew she looked good, and so she should: she'd spent all morning trying on and discarding clothes, until she finally settled on a dress of dark blue wool and her new tweed coat. But her legs felt jittery, the heels of her shoes too high as walked along the platform and down the stairs. What would Andrew make of her? After all, they hadn't set eyes on each other in nearly two years.

Frances handed over her ticket and quickly scanned the faces of the few people waiting in the booking hall. Seeing no one she recognized, she was hovering uncertainly when a voice she knew called her name and she swung round with a wide smile.

But the smile quickly faded. 'Andrew?' she queried, and hoped her reaction didn't show, for she was totally unprepared for the pale, gaunt young man standing in front of her.

'You're shocked, aren't you? I can see,' Andrew challenged.

'N . . . no I'm not,' Frances lied.

'You should have seen me when I first got back from Spain. I looked like a scarecrow. But I'm really on the mend now. Putting on weight every day.' Andrew stood back and surveyed her. 'You look grand, though.'

'But what's happened to you?'

'I managed to dodge all the bullets and bombs, unlike poor old Herbie, but I picked up something rather nasty which has taken it out of me. But I'll tell you more about it another time.' He linked her arm in his. 'Come on, my father's waiting outside with the car. We're going back to our place for tea.'

Frances paused. 'I didn't know we were doing that. I'm working tonight, you know, so I can't stay long.'

'Don't fret, I'll get you back in time. Still at the Rex?'

'Yes, but not for much longer. Johnny's negotiating with the Grand Hotel, you know just off the Strand. We played there on New Year's Eve and they were so pleased with us the manager has offered us Friday and Saturday nights.'

'My, you are going up in the world. It'll cost tuppence to talk to you soon. But what about Mr Jacobs?'

'He knows. I'll stay on with him for a while. But I shan't

work on Sundays. Roy's going in to help and maybe learn the trade, then there'll be a job for him when he leaves school.'

'How old is Roy now?'

'Eleven and a bit.'

'He's not going to get to be a pilot, then?'

Frances gave him a sideways glance. 'People from our background don't get to fly aeroplanes, you should know that.'

'They do if there's a war.'

'I wish people would just stop talking about war, I'm fed up with it. I thought you would be as well.'

'Yes, it's hardly to be recommended.'

'You all right?' Frances asked in concern, because Andrew had stopped and was leaning heavily against her. She also noticed that though the day was cold his forehead was beaded with perspiration and his breathing was laboured.

'I will be in a sec. I have a mother who is determined to molly-coddle me so I haven't been out much, and it's more of an effort than I thought.'

'Take your time, I'll help you.'

'By the way, my parents don't like to be reminded of me going to Spain. In fact my mother gets quite hysterical at the mere mention. So don't ask me anything about it when we get home.'

'I won't say a word.' Supporting Andrew, Frances moved out of the station and a short plump man standing by an Austin Seven, seeing the situation, walked fussily towards them tut-tutting loudly.

'I thought as much, you aren't up to this excursion.'

'Yes I am, Father,' Andrew answered firmly. 'I can't remain an invalid for ever. Anyway, let me introduce Miss Frances Henderson, a good friend of mine.'

'How do you do, Miss Henderson.' Mr Seymour held out his hand.

'Pleased to meet you, Mr Seymour,' answered Frances, a trifle unnerved by his formality.

Mr Seymour banged his gloved hands against his thick crombie coat. 'Let's get going, then, it's too cold for you to be standing around, Andrew.'

Andrew indicated to Frances by a raised eyebrow that he found his father's solicitude embarrassing. Frances smiled back, making it clear she understood, before climbing into the car beside him. They drove a little way through the town then turned off into a tree-lined avenue of semi-detached houses built in mock Tudor style. All the houses had names and Mr Seymour pulled up outside one rather grandly called Balmoral. Frances saw a face hovering at the window and as they walked up the short crazy paving path from which no weeds, she was sure, would ever be permitted to sprout, a woman opened the door. She stood worrying the pearls round her neck with restless fingers and Frances was aware of her less than friendly scrutiny.

Andrew introduced her and his mother said, 'Let me take your coat, Miss Henderson.'

'Thank you. But call me Frances, please, Mrs Seymour, I'd much prefer it.'

'Oh ... all right.' The smile was glassy, with a hint of condescension in it. 'Would you like to come through to the drawing-room?'

Bloomin' hell, thought Frances, drawing-room, who do they think they are, putting on such airs and graces? Until this minute both of Andrew's parents had managed to make her feel ill at ease, now all she wanted to do was giggle.

A tea trolley was laid out with rose-patterned china and tiny crustless sandwiches, sponge cake and gingerbread nestled on paper doilies. My sister would have loved this, Frances mused, it's just up her street.

'Do have a seat Miss ... er ... Frances.' Mr Seymour indicated a fireside chair covered in grey uncut moquette.

She sat down and looked about her. The room was rigidly

tidy, the furniture waxed to an ice rink shine. Not a room to relax in, Frances decided and thought of the ramshackle friendliness of her own home. No wonder Andrew used to spend so much time there. No wonder too that he'd kicked over the traces, joined the Communist Party and gone to Spain. A child was almost duty bound to rebel against such conventional parents. Imagining her hostess sweeping up around her feet if she dared drop any crumbs, Frances began to worry about how she was going to manage to eat. To her relief Mrs Seymour separated a nest of tables and placed one beside Frances's chair, along with a lace napkin and plate. 'A sandwich, Frances?' She held the egg and cress triangles towards her.

After she'd poured the tea and Frances had struggled with sugar cubes and tongs, Mrs Seymour sat down and sipped her own tea but didn't eat. 'Andrew tells me you sing. In a band.' She managed to make this sound like a thoroughly reprehensible activity.

'Only on a Friday and Saturday at the moment.'

'Frances will be moving on to greater things soon. The band has been engaged to play at the Grand Hotel in the West End,' Andrew intervened.

Frances could see that Mrs Seymour was impressed, even though she fought hard against it. 'Don't they broadcast on the wireless sometimes?'

'Yes, I think so.'

'So we might hear you in the future?' Phyllis Seymour suggested, wondering if this piece of information could be usefully employed to impress the bank manager's wife.

'Maybe.'

Warming slightly towards the girl, she cut her a slice of the gingerbread she had considered saving.

'Well at least Andrew has decided not to go back to teaching in Stepney,' said Mr Seymour, speaking for the first time.

'I haven't made any decisions about my future yet,

Father.' Andrew sounded slightly exasperated. 'The world's in too much turmoil.'

'Andrew, please don't mention war or I shall have one of my migraines.' Mrs Seymour pressed the back of her hand dramatically against her forehead.

'Sorry, Mother.'

Frances saw him stare at his shoes, heard the placatory child speaking, and felt sorry for him. His mother had probably blackmailed him like this all her life. Her glance went to the clock, she saw with relief that she could decently leave and stood up. 'I'm afraid I'll have to go or I'll miss my train. You don't need to worry, Mr Seymour, I can walk,' she went on when Andrew's father rose from his chair.

'I wouldn't think of it, my dear girl.' In the hall, he helped Frances into her coat. 'No need for you to come, Andrew.'

'But I want to. In fact I insist. Frances is my guest.' Andrew's voice was firm enough for his father not to argue.

Frances thanked Mrs Seymour for the tea and said politely that it had been nice meeting her.

Mrs Seymour didn't return the compliment, neither did Mr Seymour when she got out of the car, after thanking him for the lift.

'I'll see you on to the train,' said Andrew, buying a platform ticket. 'Sorry about my parents,' he apologized as they walked slowly up the stairs. 'Believe me, it's nothing personal, they're like it with almost everyone.'

'Well I realize I'm not quite your class.'

'Don't talk such rot, please Frances. My mother lives her life in terror of committing some social gaffe, it's all she's got to think about, and I can't wait to get away. I feel sorry for them and I love them, but they suffocate me with their concern.'

'Is it true what your father said about you not coming back to London?' Frances asked as they waited for the train.

'I've been in prison, don't forget, it'll go against me when I'm looking for a job, particularly in teaching. Anyway I

318

might be in uniform before long, much as my mother detests the idea.'

'You'll come and see Mum and Dad and Roy, though, as soon as you're up to the journey? They're all dying to see you again.'

'What about Kitty, is she dying to see me?'

Frances, her hopes dashed that her sister's name wouldn't be mentioned, gave an indifferent shrug. 'You'll have to ask her that yourself. She's moved into a bedsit and we don't see much of her these days.'

'Has she still got that boyfriend?'

'Perhaps. Perhaps not. Kitty's such a close one you never know what she's up to. Is that why you went to Spain?'

'One of the reasons, although I think prison addled our brains. Herbie and I had some romantic notion about fighting for democracy. Lot of good it did him, poor devil.' Honouring his friend's memory, Andrew was silent for a moment.

The train pulled in and the noise of slamming doors and hissing steam limited conversation. Frances got into a carriage, letting the window down to say goodbye, but as the train moved off Andrew thrust an envelope into her hand. 'Could you give this to Kitty for me please, Frances?' he shouted, trying to keep pace with the train. Frances's instinct was to yell, 'No!' and hurl the letter back at him, but by now he was no more than a dim shape on the platform. Throwing herself down on the seat she stared with a dark anger at her sister's name scrawled across the envelope. So is this the reason he asked me down here? So that I could act as postman. But for the middle-aged couple sitting opposite and watching her with deep interest, Frances would have shredded the letter into confetti and cast it to the four winds. But slowly, out of her resentment the seed of an idea began to germinate, take root and grow. This gave her the ideal excuse to pay a call on her sister and find out what she was up to. Before that, though, when she got home she would steam open the envelope. Frances had no scruples; as letter carrier she felt entitled to know exactly what it was that Andrew had to say to Kitty.

Frances stepped down from the bus, fingered the letter in her pocket and looked about her. She knew that Cardigan Square where Kitty lived was just off Holborn, but it was a wet, dark Sunday night and there wasn't a soul about to ask the way. Taking a chance, she walked on a few yards checking street names until she came to Cardigan Lane. Assuming this would lead into Cardigan Square, she turned down it. Here it was even more silent, and her echoing footsteps on the cobbles made Frances cast several nervous glances over her shoulder. Relieved finally to reach a small square surrounded by tall houses, she checked off the numbers, stopped at number nine, climbed the steps and rang the bell. A light went on in the hall and the door was opened by a thin woman with a froth of blonde curls tied up with a red ribbon. She was nursing a small poodle and its little topknot was teased up in exactly the same manner as his mistress's. It also sported a red bow and Frances was struck by the uncanny resemblance between owner and dog. By way of a greeting, the poodle bared its teeth at Frances.

'It's all right, Pepi won't harm you,' the woman assured her as she took a frightened step back. 'Now who is it you want, dear?'

'Is Miss Kitty Henderson in, please?'

'And may I ask who are you?'

'I'm her sister.'

The woman moved closer and studied Frances's face. 'Yes, there's a resemblance.' She pulled the door open and as Frances edged past, Pepi gave a warning snarl.

'Good house dog,' observed Frances with a thin smile.

'He has to be, there are some queer types about these days. That's why I'm careful who I let in. Anyway you'll find your sister on the second floor, first door on your left.

She might be pleased to see you, she's been off work sick.'

The woman left her and Frances climbed the stairs, but before she had reached the second flight, the light went out and she had to fumble the rest of the way up as best she could.

She was directed to Kitty's room by a crack of light under the door and was about to tap, when she heard a snuffling noise. Holding her ear against the door, Frances listened. It was definitely the sound of someone crying. She must be pretty poorly, Frances decided, for Kitty wasn't one for tears.

Frances rapped on the door and heard Kitty blow her nose and clear her throat. 'Who is it?'

'Me. Frances.'

'Frances? What the . . . Go away.'

'Are you all right, Kitty? The landlady says you're ill. Perhaps I should go and get Mum.'

'No, don't do that.' There was hurried movement on the other side of the door, then it was flung open. Even with her back to the light, Kitty looked a sorry mess. Her hair lay lank against her scalp, her eyes were puffy and the woollen jumper she was wearing was in need of a wash.

This was so unlike her fastidious sister, Frances just stood and stared. Downstairs she heard the front door open and shut, then as footsteps began to ascend the stairs, Kitty pulled her into the room and closed the door.

It was obvious Kitty was on the move. A half-packed suitcase lay open on the bed, bookshelves had been emptied into a tea chest and ornaments lay wrapped in newspaper. 'You leaving here?' Frances asked unnecessarily.

'Yes, tomorrow.' Kitty turned away, lit a small gas ring and put the kettle on.

Frances looked about her. 'It seems quite a nice room. Why you doing that?'

At this question, Kitty slumped on the bed and started to howl.

By now totally bewildered, Frances sat down and put an

arm around her sister's heaving shoulders. 'What's wrong, Kitty? Tell me.'

'I'm pregnant.' The sobs grew even louder.

'Pregnant?' Frances repeated foolishly. 'You?'

'Yes, me.'

'Oh my God!' Frances clapped her hand over her mouth. 'Are you getting married?' This could account for Kitty moving.

'No.'

'Why not? Is he married?'

The increase in volume of Kitty's sobs told her she'd guessed correctly. But although her long-held suspicions had finally been confirmed, it brought Frances no pleasure.

The tears trailed down her sister's face. 'You've no idea how badly I've been treated.'

'Do you want to tell me about it?'

Kitty shook her head.

'What about Mum and Dad? What will you tell them?'

Kitty rubbed her fingers across her cheeks to check the tears. 'They're never going to find out, and you'd better not tell them. In fact you'd better not tell a living soul, not even Gloria.'

'I won't, I promise.'

'Do you swear on Mum and Dad's lives?'

'I swear it,' Frances repeated solemnly. 'What you going to do, get rid of it?' As far as Frances could see this was the only possible solution.

'No. As soon as it's born, it will be adopted. Everything's arranged. Tomorrow I'm going down to Kent to a convent. I'll be looked after by nuns until the birth.'

'But how are you going to explain away such a long absence to Mum and Dad?'

'I've got it worked out. I shall write and tell them that I'm going to work for Miss Alice down at Leyborne for a few months.'

Frances shook her head. 'Well they're always complaining

322

they don't see much of you, so they might swallow it. But can't you tell me who the father is?'

'I've told you all you're going to know. Do you want some tea?'

'Yes please.'

With a weary, heavy movement, Kitty stood up. 'Take my advice, give men a miss, they make you pregnant then ditch you. And don't have kids. You're sick all the time. This'll be my first and last one, I promise.' She set a selection of biscuits out on a plate and offered them to Frances. 'The next few months are going to be pretty lonely. I don't suppose you would consider coming to visit me sometimes.'

Frances hid her surprise by biting into a chocolate digestive. 'Yes, of course I would. Just give me your address.' But she did pause to wonder if she was allowing herself to be made use of: Kitty had never had much need of her in the past. However with the circumstances she found herself in and the support she would need, that could change. They might even grow close, like real sisters.

It wasn't until later, walking to catch the bus, that Frances remembered Andrew's letter, still in her pocket, with his proposal of marriage to Kitty. Well he wouldn't want her now, she was soiled goods, Frances decided, and drew it out, ready to drop into the first litter bin she came to. But then she paused. If a sisterly affection was to develop between her and Kitty, she could hardly start with such a breach of trust, she reflected, and stuffing the letter back in her coat pocket she walked on.

28

As well as their normal weekend gigs the band was now being booked for functions and twenty-first birthday parties, so Frances's free time was limited. In spite of this she stuck to her promise to visit Kitty, even though it took the good part of a day to get to the home and back. Instead of the grim Victorian establishment she'd expected, Frances was surprised to find comfortable rooms and discreet, smiling nuns. In God's eyes these girls might have fallen by the wayside, but since most of them appeared to be from good families, money was obviously cushioning them against the harsher realities of an unwanted pregnancy.

However Kitty didn't appear to appreciate her good fortune. She was touchy, found it hard to resign herself to her condition and fretted constantly. 'I had so many plans and look at me now.' She lifted up her slim legs and studied them. 'I'll die if I get varicose veins. Why can't we be like birds and sit on eggs, then we wouldn't end up all gross and disfigured.'

'You might not think so at present, but there will be a life after the baby, you know.'

'I doubt it.'

'Yes there will. Be positive. Look, I should have given you this before. It's from Andrew and why I came to Cardigan Square that night. But what with everything else it got overlooked.' Frances drew the letter from her handbag and handed it to Kitty. 'He's back from Spain and I've been to visit him.'

Kitty took the letter and turned it over in her hand.

'Crumbs, I'd almost forgotten about Andrew ... perhaps I should have stuck with him.'

'Open it, see what he has to say,' urged Frances, although she already knew its contents.

Kitty slit open the envelope, read the letter and gave a tiny smile. In a better humour she said, 'He wants to marry me. Imagine, after all this time.'

'There you are.'

'He wouldn't if he saw me like this.'

Well it would certainly test his love, thought Frances. 'You could write to him, explain, he might.'

'I couldn't marry Andrew, not in a million years.' Kitty tossed the letter aside with a peeved expression and stood up. 'I'm tired, I'm going to lie down.'

'I'll be off, then.' Frances stood as well. 'Johnny's got more work than he can cope with, so it might be a couple of weeks before I can manage another visit. But the months are flying past and it'll be over quicker than you think.' Less than tactful she added, 'Do you want a boy or a girl?'

'It's something I don't care to think about, thank you,' Kitty retorted in a frosty tone. 'And don't worry if you can't come down. When I'm really huge I won't want to see anyone.'

'I'm not anyone, I'm your sister, but if that's what you want . . .' Frances shrugged, but she was deeply hurt. She might as well give up: she and Kitty would never be close, never. 'What about afterwards, when the baby is born? I will be its aunt.'

'Oh no, not then. Definitely not then. You might start cooing over it, and I couldn't stand that. All I want is to get the adoption over and done with and the creature out of my life.'

After a long exhausting labour, on 14 June 1939, Kitty gave birth to a boy. She called him David and for six weeks she held his small, sturdy body to her breast, breathed his baby smell, bathed him, saw his eyes begin to focus. She'd felt nothing but resentment as he grew and moved inside her, so it caught Kitty totally unawares, the strength of her love for her son. But she'd heard other girls sobbing at night when their babies were taken from them, so she tried to harden her heart against his baby perfection: the tiny fingers with their prehensile grip, his first smile, his blond fluff of hair, his brown eyes. But it was hopeless, there was too much of Robert in this baby they'd made together for her not to adore him.

The day she so dreaded approached and towards the end of July, Alice came down to the convent with a solicitor, who had with him lots of legal-looking papers for Kitty to sign.

'I'm not signing anything. I've changed my mind. I'm keeping my baby.' Kitty pushed the documents back across the desk.

Alice was aghast. 'But you can't. How will you look after him? You won't be able to support yourself alone and no one will marry a girl with an illegitimate child.'

'I don't care. He's my baby and I love him,' Kitty answered back valiantly.

They were in a small bare room with just a table and a few chairs. The solicitor coughed and gazed at her with a severe expression. 'Miss Henderson, half the agreed amount of money has already been placed in a bank for you and I have the balance here in an envelope. This money was on condition that you hand over the child to Mr and Mrs Travis six weeks after the birth. You have also enjoyed a degree of comfort here at the convent a girl in your situation wouldn't normally expect. Therefore I urge you to think seriously before you go back on your agreement, for it could prove expensive.'

'I don't care about your money,' Kitty sobbed. 'I just want my baby.' Hugging her stomach she started to rock backwards and forwards on the chair.

'But where will you go?' asked Alice.

'Back home.' But Kitty knew she couldn't. What, back to Tudor Street with a bastard child, to the sneers of the neighbours who'd always accused her of being hoity-toity and would delight in seeing her brought down a peg or two? 'Go! Take him now. Don't let me see him again.'

The solicitor slid a document, an envelope and a fountain pen across the table. 'If you'd just sign that, Miss Henderson.'

Kitty's hand shook as she took up the pen and signed her son away and her desperate sobs almost broke Alice's will. 'We'll look after him, really love him, I promise you that, my dear.' Alice laid a hand upon Kitty's shoulder in a futile attempt to comfort her. 'He will be the only one, too. It appears I can't have children of my own, so I want to thank you, Kitty, for a precious gift.'

'Leave me alone!' With a sob of deep anguish, Kitty's head fell forward on her arms. Not another word was said and she heard the door open and close, voices in the corridor then a baby's cry which almost tore her apart. As the car drove off, Sister Bernadette came and helped her back to her room, but wisely didn't try and offer any platitudinous words of solace. Unfortunately it was all too sadly familiar. The pain would ease in time, but the nun doubted if Kitty would ever rid herself of the guilt of abandoning her son to another woman. How women suffered at the hands of men. How glad she was she'd given her life to God.

The next day, feeling as if she'd had her heart ripped out of her, Kitty left the convent and for no good reason bought a train ticket to Brighton. She booked into a hotel, and immediately went on a shopping spree, buying dresses recklessly, only to find when she got back to her room and tried them on that she hated every single one.

The hotel was expensive, the food good but it tasted of nothing. In the evening, hoping to anaesthetize the pain, Kitty sat in the bar sipping gin and orange, but her grief was like a suppurating wound. She'd never found it easy to get close to people, envied Gloria and Frances their easy relationship, and now she'd lost for ever the one human being she loved unequivocally. *I'll never see my son take his first stumbling steps, hear his first words, but Robert will. He'll enjoy all the pleasures of fatherhood, see him off on his first day at school, watch him grow into manhood, play cricket, have girlfriends.* She was the one who was suffering for loving unwisely, not Robert, all was well with him. He had his son, wealth and power, whereas for her there was just an aching loneliness. *And what of the future?* Here she was, twenty-one, bitter and discouraged and with all the hopes she had for herself come to nothing. She had enough money to tide her over for the time being, but she was damned if she'd go back to an office.

Kitty's brooding introspection was interrupted by a flashy-looking individual sporting a diamond ring on his small finger, who plonked himself down beside her. 'On your own, dear?'

Kitty stared at him with unfriendly eyes and stood up. 'No I'm not, actually. My husband's upstairs, and I think it's time I joined him.'

The following morning after breakfast Kitty took a stroll down to the front. It was crowded with holidaying families apparently determined to ignore the grim reminder of war everywhere: hotels and boarding houses sandbagged, great rolls of barbed wire at the ready in case of invasion. She'd been worrying about her future last night, but would there be one if the Germans invaded? She'd seen the newsreels, the steel-helmeted men with fixed bayonets cutting a swathe through Czechoslovakia. Her future could be rape or death. Although the day was warm, goose-pimples rose on Kitty's arms. In the faint hope that there might be good news, she bought a newspaper, paid for a deck chair and sat down. The sea was calm, childish screams and laughter came up from the beach, and large ships moved along the flat rim of the horizon like carboard cut-outs. Were they German warships, Kitty wondered, perhaps with their guns pointing in this direction? Stop it! she rebuked herself and determinedly opened her newspaper. She skimmed the pages, hoping to find something halfway cheerful to read and in the centre spread of photographs a crowded recruiting office and the caption underneath caught her eye. 'Patriotic young women in London yesterday queued in their thousands for the chance to serve their country by volunteering for the Women's Auxiliary Air Force.'

With a sense of purpose she hadn't felt in months, Kitty folded the newspaper and stood up. Suddenly it seemed so clear and simple. That's what she'd do, go back to London today and join up, do her bit to defeat Hitler. Kitty knew she probably hadn't any right to feel optimistic, not with a war imminent, but if she joined one of the services, for the foreseeable future at least someone else would make all the decisions affecting her life. She'd be told what to wear, what to eat, what job she was going to do, what time to get up and go to bed. After the heartache of the past months Kitty knew that was exactly what she needed right now.

On 1 September, with identifying labels tied to buttonholes, gas masks slung across shoulders and clutching beloved teddy bears and brown paper parcels, the children of Tudor Street joined the great exodus from London. All any parent knew was that they were going to the safety of the country, and mothers tried hard to be brave. However for most it was a struggle to contain their tears and they watched wan-faced as the crocodile of children marched off down the street to goodness knows where. Some of the little ones sobbed in bewilderment, but for many of the older children it was a great adventure. Peggy Flynn kissed her younger sisters with a hungry love and watched their departure with sad red eyes. They, however, looked positively joyous at the prospect of leaving behind their father's drunken tempers and leather belt and waved happily to everyone.

After Roy had gone the house fell silent. Edna was too bereft to speak and concentrated on putting up blackout curtains and pasting strips of brown paper on to the windows. Tinker lay under the table with his paws over his ears and Dad spent hours in the Anderson shelter, trying to make it habitable, so he said.

Two days later war was declared. Great silver barrage balloons, looking like inflated fish, hung over London and almost immediately the air-raid siren went. They all rushed to the shelter in panic, thinking German war planes were about to blast them into oblivion, only to discover later that it was a false alarm.

On the Monday a postcard arrived from Roy and Edna sniffed noisily as she read it.

Dear Mum and Dad
   Arrived here 6.50 at 6.55 I fell down stairs. I am staying at Mrs Williams 14 West Street Braintree. I am sleeping with the school Lunyatic David Edwards. Am having a good time. Love Roy. Kiss Tinker for me a hundred times.

The card was written in indelible pencil and badly smudged as if from tears.

'There you are, he's fine,' said Frances encouragingly, when her mother handed it to her to read.

Edna turned away and blew her nose. 'I just miss m' little lad, that's all.'

'We can always go down and visit him and see how he's getting on, it's not too far. The main thing is that he's safe from bombs.'

Edna, struggling to pull herself together, thought of women all over the country waving goodbye to husbands and sons. 'Yeah, I should thank God Roy's too young to be called up and yer dad's too old.'

And so began the great disruption of war. Kitty wrote from Gloucestershire with the news that she'd joined the WAAF, was loving it and would be home as soon as she'd finished her basic training.

'She's supposed to be in Kent working, then suddenly she springs this on me. Why does Kitty never tell us anything?' Edna demanded and slammed the letter down angrily on the table. 'But perhaps her family aren't good enough for her these days.'

If only you knew the true story, thought Frances. My God the roof would come off. 'That's Kitty all over, Mum, she's always been a close one.' She nearly added, 'and self-centred, too,' but thought better of it. Frances soon had her own worries anyway. In a fit of panic, the Government closed down all places of entertainment, Johnny lost the whole of his band to the air force in one day and Paul came to tell her he was due to go for his medical the following Monday.

'Damn Hitler,' Frances cursed, 'he's ruined my career, and just when it had started to get going.'

'Don't talk rot, of course he hasn't. Entertainers will be needed for the troops. There are artistes out on the road already, well-known ones too. They're auditioning at Drury Lane, you could go along.'

As it was Frances didn't have to, because a week or so later after fierce criticism, the Government allowed dance halls, football grounds, cinemas and theatres to reopen. Paul also failed his medical.

'Apparently I'm puny and weak-chested, and not up to long route marches,' Paul explained, hiding his humiliation at not being allowed to die for his country with a wry smile.

But Frances hardly bothered to listen. 'So nothing's changed? We can go on exactly as we were?'

'Absolutely.'

'Oh that's marvellous.' Frances clapped her hands in delight, then went over and hugged him.

*   *   *

London was packed with servicemen and -women, most of them young people freed from the restrictions of home life for the first time ever. The danger and uncertainty of war, the sense of there being no tomorrow fuelled their recklessness. Throwing their bonnets over the windmill and ignoring their parents' warnings about sex, booze and VD, they got down with singular determination to the business of having a high old time. The Grand Hotel, anticipating this, was anxious to have the band, Paul and Frances back on very generous terms and with a contract for six nights a week. In record time Johnny collected together replacement musicians, knocked them into shape and soon they were back in business. Now when Frances walked into the hotel she passed a very glamorous portrait of herself, taken by a famous society photographer. At last, Frances felt, she was entitled to call herself a professional singer.

A couple of weeks later, coming out of her gate she saw, further down the road, a man in army uniform. 'Norman?' she called, but her voice held a question mark, then he turned round and sure enough it was him.

'Hello, Frances, long time no see.'

Norman had moved out of Mrs Goodbody's about two years before to live in a flat above where he worked. Their friendship had cooled after Cable Street anyway. Frances had made it clear that as long as Norman remained in the BUF she wanted nothing to do with him. But that was in the past and now she found herself quite pleased to see him. 'So you're in the army?' she said, looking him up and down.

Norman stood tall and proud. His boots were bulled to perfection, the creases in the rough khaki serge were razor thin and he wore his cap at exactly the right angle. 'Yeah, I volunteered.'

He must know he'll be fighting Germans, thought Frances, people he spoke of with admiration, but then she realized that wasn't the point; the uniform was the attraction for Norman, just like it had been in the BUF.

'So where are you off to?'

'To say goodbye to Mrs Goodbody. Our regiment's being posted south. But you're quite a local celebrity now. I even saw a bit about you in the paper. It said you were one of the hottest singers in town.'

'I'm doing all right,' Frances answered modestly.

'I don't suppose you could let me have an autographed photograph of you? It'd make the blokes in the billet green with envy.'

'I am flattered. Give me your address and I'll send it.'

'Would you consider writing to me occasionally, as well?'

Frances looked doubtful. 'I'm not much of a letter writer, Norman.'

'That doesn't matter. You see . . . everyone else gets letters but me.'

Frances's heart was smitten. Poor Norman, she'd forgotten how he hadn't got a relative in the world. So he gave her his address and, feeling like a film star, she sent him a photograph, signing it with a flourish in black ink: from Frances to Norman, with love. His letter of thanks came back heavily censored from France.

Life was now in a state of permanent flux. Kitty turned up, showing off in her WAAF uniform. 'Where's Dad?' she asked as she removed her greatcoat and cap.

'Gone down to the British Legion for a pint and game of darts. If you'd bothered to let us know you were coming, he'd have stayed in.'

'Never mind, the next forty-eight-hour pass I get I'll come and stay.'

'That's good of you, I'm sure,' Edna remarked tartly. 'You don't seem to have much time for your family these days.'

Kitty's face reddened. 'I have been busy, Mum, and I was in the wilds of Gloucestershire.'

'I'm talking about before that.'

333

This not being a line of conversation Kitty had any wish to pursue, she turned quickly to her sister. 'Why don't you join up? It would broaden your horizons.'

'That's enough of that,' Edna warned. 'I don't want to lose all my children. As it is this is going to be a street of old people soon, with the kids all gone and now the young men.'

'What about Andrew? Do you hear much from him?'

Wondering at her renewal of interest, Frances gave her sister a sharp look.

'If you came home more you might see him,' Edna answered. 'He's been to visit us several times, hasn't he Frances?'

Frances bit hard into her toast and didn't answer.

'Always asks after you.'

'Does he? After all this time.' Kitty made a neat pile of the crumbs on her plate with her index finger.

'He's talking of joining the RAF. More toast anyone?' asked Edna and without waiting for a reply she stuck a slice of bread on the end of a toasting fork and held it in front of the hot coals. Continuing her meditation she went on, 'All our young men going off to war like this was something I hoped I'd never see again in my lifetime.'

'Well if he comes round give him my regards,' said Kitty. 'Anyway I must be off. I don't like being out late on my own in the blackout.'

'Next time you come, we'll have a real family get-together, kill the fatted calf and Gloria can show off her little boy Terry,' said Edna, helping Kitty into her heavy overcoat.

'Oh, I'm not that interested in kids, Mum,' Kitty answered quickly.

'How can you say that, he's your cousin and a lovely little chap, and the apple of his parents' eye, particularly when they'd almost given up hope. Gloria deserves some happiness after that awful business she had to go through with Harry. I'm surprised she didn't crack.'

'Try not to dwell on it, Mum. You can't change the past,

334

so it's best to try and forget it,' Kitty advised, then, turning to Frances, surprised her by saying, 'Fancy walking to the bus stop with me?'

With nothing better to do, and some questions she wanted to ask, Frances picked up her coat. Seeing them out, the security conscious Edna was careful to switch off the hall light before pulling back the heavy army blanket covering the front door. 'Quickly, before we have a warden yelling at us and I'm fined,' and she pushed her daughters through the door before Kitty even had time to give her a quick peck.

Frances switched on her torch, which gave off a tiny prism of light, flickered and went out. She shook it, but nothing happened. 'Blast, the batteries have gone flat and they're like gold dust to buy.'

Fumbling around in the dark they missed the kerb and found themselves in the gutter. Kitty giggled. 'Here, take my arm.'

But their eyes soon adjusted and with arms linked companionably, Frances asked, 'How are you now, Kitty?'

'I'm bearing up.'

'And the baby?'

'The baby died.'

Frances stopped. 'Died?'

'Yes, he was stillborn.' Neither Kitty's profile nor her voice displayed any emotion.

'Poor little thing. Why didn't you write and tell me? It must have been awful for you, all on your own.'

'I'm over it now.' Kitty turned to Frances. 'You swore you'd never breathe a word of this to anyone so I can trust you, can't I?'

'I don't know why you keep asking. I've told you umpteen times, my lips are sealed.'

'That's okay then, because I want to put it behind me and get on with my life, so I'd prefer it if you never mentioned the subject again.'

Frances shrugged. 'Just as you say.'

This put paid to any further intimacies and they didn't speak again until they'd joined the queue at the bus stop. Then while they stood waiting, Kitty said, 'There's a chap I know keeps pestering me to go out with him. Perhaps I'll get him to bring me along to the Grand Hotel next time I get a twenty-four-hour pass.'

'He'd better have a full wallet: it's pricey.'

'Don't worry – he's loaded, this one.'

The bus, with its headlights dimmed, loomed spectrally out of the darkness, the queue shuffled forward and Kitty just managed to get on. Hurrying to get a seat, she didn't have time to wave and walking home, Frances thought of the dead baby. Poor wee mite. Although she didn't give any impression of grief, Kitty must feel something surely after carrying him for nine months. But then that was her sister all over, difficult to fathom and now to add to that, it looked as if she'd turned into a pretty hard case as well.

29

Those who said the war would be over by Christmas found their optimism misplaced. Instead, along with the uncertainty and rationing, Britain was gripped by the most bitterly cold winter in living memory. Winter over, there then came the humiliation of defeat at Dunkirk and a gloomy acceptance that invasion was inevitable. With most of Europe conquered the British Isles, standing alone and vulnerable, had to be next on Hitler's list.

If this wasn't enough, Mrs Goodbody heard through the Red Cross that Norman had been captured at the fall of Dunkirk and was now a prisoner of war in Germany.

'Well at least he's out of the fighting,' said Edna, viewing it philosophically, 'and he speaks some German.'

Andrew, brave but foolhardy, came round to tell them he was joining the RAF and applying to train as a fighter pilot. Frances felt nauseous, but she refrained from saying anything and during that late summer in the blue skies of southern England, people watched, hearts in mouths, as high above them the RAF and Luftwaffe fought it out for air supremacy. Burning Spitfires and Messerschmitts would spiral to earth and after each combat newspaper vendors would chalk up British and German casualty figures as if they were cricket scores. Reading them, Frances knew Andrew's chance of survival was pretty slim. She took to saying a small prayer before she went to sleep at night and God must have heard her because by great good fortune, soon after he joined up, Andrew was accidentally run down by a Bedford truck in the blackout and sustained a broken arm and leg.

*　　*　　*

'I'm bored, come and see me, please.' The order was scrawled on a postcard and obediently Frances trotted down to visit him in hospital. She'd had her hair lightened a shade in a West End salon and she walked down the ward to some appreciative comments from other patients. But Andrew seemed not to notice her changed appearance nor to hear the wolf whistles. He was also in the foulest of moods. 'Do you know what?' were his first words. 'I've just been told I can forget about becoming a fighter pilot, and they don't consider I'm officer material either. I reckon they've found out I was in the Communist Party,' he muttered darkly.

'Well your mum will be pleased you're not going to become another casualty figure.'

'Oh she'll think it marvellous, me spending the rest of the war as a bloody pen-pusher.' His grey, dark-lashed eyes looked sullen.

'You're her only child. Can't you put yourself in her shoes for once? It beats me why you're always wanting to put your life at risk anyway.'

'Probably a psychoanalyst would say it's a reaction against my mother. I was never allowed to indulge in any of the normal schoolboy pursuits. I'm a classic case of arrested development.'

Frances reached out and took his hand. 'I'm pleased you're not going to fly, too.'

But her confession seemed not to touch his heart. Instead, as he was bound to sooner or later, he asked, 'How's Kitty getting on in the WAAF? She never answered my letter, you know.'

'Didn't she? Well she's been posted to Lincolnshire and not liking it much. Flat and boring is how she describes it and too far from the bright lights.'

'It would be funny if we ended up on the same air base,' Andrew reflected.

Hilarious, thought Frances. I'd split my sides laughing.

'She could drop me a line if she feels like it.'

'I'll mention it if I see her.' Your love, pure as the driven slush, thought Frances cattily. If only he knew . . . that would get Kitty out of his system good and proper. Pity she was sworn to secrecy, for the temptation to spill the beans was almost overwhelming.

Before she left, Frances, very daring, leaned over and kissed Andrew on the lips which evoked some jocular comments from the other beds but little response from Andrew. On the train going home she felt truly disconsolate: five years and she was no further forward than on that evening they'd first met. The brutal truth, of course, was that she was part of the fixtures and fittings of Andrew's life and she made herself too readily available. If she could forget about him how much simpler life would be. Gloria was for ever dropping hints about how much she and Paul had in common and how obvious his feelings were for her, and she did so want to be loved, like Dad loved Mum. Here she was almost twenty-one, not bad looking, and yet she'd never had the excitement of a proper romance. Because of Andrew she'd turned aside all other men, had hardly kissed one – and there was a war on. She was probably the only virgin left in London and she could be dead tomorrow. Frances stared hard out of the train window. What an epitaph. She died a virgin. Well perhaps the time had come to rectify that state of affairs.

Reichsmarschall Goering, having failed in his battle for control of the skies, changed his tactics and decided instead to bomb London into submission.

The customers in the Grand Hotel restaurant these days were quite a different bunch from pre-war crowds. More democratic, and certainly livelier, Frances decided. Although a few evening dresses and fur coats had been brought out of mothballs, the predominant colours were khaki and the light and dark blue of the air force and navy.

About every ally was also represented: Free French, Norwegians, Poles, Canadians. Johnny, with his new band knocked into shape, was playing all the favourite numbers and bestowing his Gibbs Dentifrice smile upon the dancers. It was wiped off his face a second later, though. Frances was moving to the mike to sing 'The Touch of Your Lips' when the air raid warning sounded. The music stopped and everyone stood stock still and listened to the throb of engines overhead. Almost simultaneously they heard the pounding of anti-aircraft guns followed a heartbeat later by an enormous explosion. Frances felt the floor slip from under her, the whole building seemed to move several degrees and the walls implode. Amid screams and panic and people diving for shelter under tables, windows fractured, plaster fell from the ceiling and the lights went out. Frances, struck rigid with terror, was amazed to find she was still standing and clinging to the microphone.

Miraculously the building righted itself and the manager appeared with a hurricane lamp. Holding it high, he said in a voice with only a suggestion of a tremor in it, 'Will you all, as calmly as possible, clasp hands and follow me to the cellars. We'll be quite safe down there.'

Paul grabbed Frances. 'Come on, before this lot descends on us.' Coughing with the dust, he pulled her after him.

The cellars were vast and cavernous. Wine was shelved in racks, and it was cobwebby and cold. There was a sort of hysterical bonhomie, and men tried to make light of the situation with silly jokes. Overcome with claustrophobia, Frances imagined the huge, five-storey building collapsing and burying them alive and her teeth started to chatter with fear.

Paul took off his jacket and placed it on her shoulders, then put his arm round her. 'Snuggle up,' he advised. 'It might be a long night.'

'Thanks.' Gratefully Frances moved closer to him, comforted by his body warmth. An army officer, obviously feeling the need to organize people, stood up. 'Right, how about a sing-song?' No one seemed able to summon up any enthusiasm so Frances, ashamed of her own cowardice, got them going with 'One Man Went to Mow'. They continued in this vein with songs like 'Green Grow the Rushes-o' and 'Ten Green Bottles', silly but reassuring and remembered from childhood.

'What about "All Shadows Fly Away", Frances?' a voice suggested after a while.

'All right.' Not moving from Paul's side she sang it unaccompanied, her voice echoing around the cellar, and in the anonymous dimness she was aware of a woman sobbing quietly. As she finished, the all clear went, there was a collective sigh of relief and people started to move back upstairs.

Wan and exhausted, they came up into a grey dawn filtered through a thick pall of smoke. The whole of London appeared to be smouldering and in stupefied silence people gazed about them at the destruction: the huge crater in the middle of the road, an office building sliced in half with desks and chairs dangling precariously over the edge and charred files and documents floating in the sea of water.

'Christ!' exclaimed someone speaking for them all. 'If I could get my hands on that sodding Hitler, I'd have his bloody bollocks off!'

'It could have been worse,' Paul observed. 'It looks as if the hotel had a very near miss.'

An ARP warden, his features grimy and exhausted under his tin hat, turned on hearing Paul's comment. 'You're right there, mate. But this ain't nuthin'. You should see the docks, they've taken a real 'ammering. The whole area's in flames.'

Frances was filled with such an awful sense of dread, that for a moment faces misted over and voices receded.

'Hey. You all right?' Paul had hold of her. 'You look a bit queasy.'

Getting a grip on herself, Frances answered, 'Mum, Dad

341

– I've got to get home.' She moved away from his arms and began to pace up and down. 'Where can I get a taxi?'

The warden laughed. 'They're about as rare as hens' teeth just now, love. You'd be lucky even to find a bus. I advise Shanks's pony, it'll get you there quicker – that is if they let you through.'

Without waiting for Paul, Frances lifted up the hem of her long dress and set off down the street.

'Where exactly do you think you're going?' asked Paul, running after her and grabbing her arm.

'Home, like I said.'

'Not on your own. I'm coming with you.'

They didn't speak after this but as they moved deeper into the City and were confronted with the full horror of the devastation, Frances's fears for her parents' safety multiplied. A beautiful Wren church had crumpled like a pack of cards, water cascaded from fractured water mains, ambulances clanged along dodging craters and trying to get the injured to hospital. At the top of one street they found their way barred by special constables. 'Sorry, but you can't go down there, a building's likely to collapse at any moment.'

Forced to take a tortuously long detour, Frances stumbled over rubble and shattered glass. Her dress was torn and dirty, her feet in the flimsy silver sandals cut and bleeding.

Passing an open café, Paul stopped. 'Let's have a cuppa. We've been up all night and need it.' He looked pale and coughed a lot.

'You can have one if you want, but I shall keep going,' she answered, dogged in her determination to get home.

'Oh all ri . . .' Another bout of coughing forced Paul to lean against a wall to regain his breath. However, Frances had already walked on and didn't notice.

When they reached Aldgate Pump, Frances felt she was almost home. But here it was far worse than anything she could have imagined. Fleeing families pushed prams containing all their earthly belongings in front of them, crying children ran behind clasping beloved pets in their arms and all the streets had great gaps in them like lost teeth. Familiar landmarks had disappeared overnight and as she turned into Tudor Street her heart was racing so violently she could hardly breathe. She was brought up short by chaos. Mattresses, tables and wardrobes had been dragged out on to the pavement, fire engines, ambulances and lorries blocked the road. Some people sobbed and called out for husbands and wives, others wandered around in dazed silence. Looking around at the carnage, involuntary spasms shook Frances's body. Paul took her hand: he had already seen the pile of smoking rubble where the Hendersons' house and adjoining ones had once been. Frances must have seen it almost simultaneously for with a wild 'No!' she broke free and stumbled up the road.

Someone tried to hold her back, but she pushed them aside, scrambled over the rubble and began tearing frantically at the bricks with her bare hands. 'Mum, Dad, where are you? Answer me,' she screamed.

Arms went round her waist. 'Frances, come away, it's too late, my dear, they've gone.'

Frances covered her ears with her hands in denial. 'Don't say that! Don't say it, it's not true!' She spun round to Gloria, who was standing with tears streaming down her tired face.

Paul took her into his arms and held her close. 'I'm so sorry, my love.' But she couldn't bear his comfort and pushed him away. Hearing a whimpering Frances looked down. It was Tinker scratching at the rubble. 'Oh, Tinker, where did you come from?' she sobbed, and picking him up, buried her face in his warm, sturdy little body.

Frances insisted she wanted to stay, certain that if she did her parents would rise unharmed from the wreckage and Gloria was almost forced to drag her away. 'Come, dear, we're going home.' Supported by Paul, half swooning with shock and grief, Frances lurched unsteadily down the street. In the space of a few hours the source of her security, everything most dear and familiar, had vanished; her parents, their love, the house where she'd grown up, neighbours and friends. Wiped out like her happiness.

Walter was waiting for them at the end of the street in his little car and Gloria and Paul helped her in to it. 'What about Kitty ... and Roy?' She thought of them both still innocently asleep and unaware of the tragedy and her face puckered with fresh pain.

'Walter and me will deal with everything, don't worry,' Gloria said quietly. 'Kitty will get compassionate leave and tomorrow Walter will take me down to see Roy.'

'But who's going to look after him now? He's still only a boy,' Frances sobbed.

'There'll always be a home for you all with us, you know that. We'll look after Tinker, too. But right now we're going to take you home so that you can have some sleep.'

For a long time after the funeral Frances felt as if her heart had shrivelled to the size of a pea; that she was suspended in some emotional no man's land and incapable of the normal human responses of love, hate, envy or pain. She stopped eating and in the space of a month went from a healthy nine stones to a gaunt seven stones. The money was rolling in, she'd rented a small flat above a bookshop in Covent Garden, but when she sang it was like an automaton.

As the destruction continued to rain down from the skies, ripping the heart out of London, few were untouched by tragedy and loss. To escape the bombs, exhausted families moved out to sleep in Epping Forest or took up residence in the foetid atmosphere of the Underground. But by and large, stirred by Mr Churchill's rousing speeches, Londoners lifted two defiant fingers to the Nazis and life went on. Shops boarded up their broken windows and continued to do business, workers, dazed from lack of sleep, struggled to get in to their offices, and the once hated pea souper was now greeted as a friend: when the thick yellow fog descended, it blanked out the city to German bombers and assured Londoners at least one night's uninterrupted sleep.

The moon, however, was another matter and tonight, as Paul walked Frances back to her flat from the hotel, bombed-out buildings looked ghostly in its cruel, cold light.

'A bomber's moon,' commented Paul, looking up.

'Don't say that, it's asking for trouble,' answered Frances, and as she put the key in the lock, dead on cue, the sirens went and searchlights started criss-crossing the sky.

'What did I tell you? You'd better come in, but don't put any lights on,' Frances warned and ran on up the stairs.

By the time Paul reached her small sitting-room, she'd drawn the heavy blackout curtains and switched on a couple of table lamps and one bar of the electric fire.

It was furnished accommodation and a trifle shabby, but Frances had added homely touches; pictures on the wall, ornaments, bright shawls thrown over the armchairs. Paul was reminded that this was all she had, no souvenirs, no photographs of her parents. Everything she cherished had been taken from her. 'Shouldn't we go to an air raid shelter?' he asked, hearing the distant thud of a bomb, then gunfire.

'You go, I'll take my chance here. I couldn't face a shelter tonight, I'm absolutely done in.' Kicking off her shoes, Frances went through to her small bedroom, lay down on the bed and closed her eyes.

Paul watched her from the door, his heart touched by her stark misery. She'd gone dangerously into herself since the death of her parents and he felt frustrated at being unable to make contact with her now on a personal level. Their relationship was strange, intimate from the years of working together, but no matter how many hints he dropped that he'd like it otherwise, Frances refused to take him seriously. And of course there was that fly in the ointment Andrew. As long as she hankered after him there was little chance for anyone else.

'Frances, would you like some tea?' he called to her.

Frances opened her eyes. 'Oh, yes please, I'm gasping.' She put a pillow behind her head and sat up.

When he'd made the tea, Paul put two cups and saucers on a tray and took it through to the bedroom. Frances's eyes were closed, but tears were streaming down her face.

'My dear, what is it?' Paul moved to the bed, sat down beside her and took her hand. It was cold and he tried to rub the circulation back into it.

Frances leaned against him, crying quietly. 'I'm so unhappy.'

Paul stroked her hair back from her forehead and kissed her as he would a child. 'I know you are, my dear.' What could he say, that eventually the memory of her parents would grow dimmer and her misery recede? She wouldn't want to hear that. So instead he held her close and gradually her tears ceased. In a little while he knew by her breathing that she was asleep. Cautiously Paul shifted away and let her head fall on the pillow. Tiptoeing into the sitting-room, he turned off the electric fire and lights then went back and lay down beside her, covering them both with a blanket.

Paul lay in the darkness, aware of her body tucked into his, then a while later he heard the all clear sounding. He ought to go home, he supposed, but instead he put his arm round Frances and snuggled closer. He had almost drifted off when he was startled by her voice.

'Paul, are you awake?'

'Just about.'

'I've been thinking for some time that I ought to lose my virginity.' She spoke very matter-of-factly.

The blackout curtains kept the room pitch dark and for one confused moment Paul wondered if Frances was talking in her sleep. 'Good Lord! Who to?'

'You.'

Paul's heart thumped. 'Well, I'm flattered.' He sat up and switched on the light. He'd taken off his jacket and shoes but otherwise they were both fully dressed.

'How do you start?' Frances enquired.

'By falling in love,' answered Paul.

'I thought you just took off all your clothes.' Frances stood up, unzipped her evening dress, stepped out of it and lay back down on the bed again.

'Frances, what's this all about?'

'Don't you want to, then?'

'What a daft question, of course I do.'

'Well get on with it.' Eyes squeezed shut, she lay rigid as a marble figure on a tomb.

'I will not get on with it. I'm not a prize bull. Having sex is about love, the flowering of passion, commitment, and you feel none of those things for me. Do you?'

'I'm very fond of you.'

'Gee, thanks.' Paul groped for a cigarette, lit it, started to cough and stubbed it out. 'Frances, I care about you deeply, you must know that by now, but much as I would like to, I couldn't take you without you feeling the same way about me – it would be like a rape. It's probably an old-fashioned attitude, but that's the way I am.' Paul stood up. 'And in case temptation gets the better of me I'll sleep in the other room for the rest of the night.'

When Paul awoke the next morning he could see from the luminous dial that it was eleven o'clock. He sat up feeling ghastly. His clothes smelt of cigarette smoke and his mouth tasted like a sewer. He was padding to the bathroom when he remembered his bizarre conversation with Frances in the small hours and imagined her embarrassment this morning. But what had possessed her, he wondered, as he turned on the geyser. With only the regulation five inches of water there was no temptation to linger, and in about ten minutes he was dressed again. He gargled to clean out his mouth, felt his stubble and decided he'd have to find a barber's, but first of there was a proposition he had to put to Frances.

Breezing into her bedroom, Paul drew back the curtains and called boisterously, 'Wakey, wakey.'

Frances sat up, blinked and looked puzzled. 'What are you doing here?'

'There was an air raid.'

'Oh yes,' then, 'oh God,' as she remembered her stupidity.

Paul sat down on the bed and took her hand. 'Look, there's a perfectly simple solution to all this, we could get married.'

'Is this to spare me any embarrassment?'

'No, it's because I love you, Frances.'

She plucked the bedclothes. 'It's very kind of you, Paul, but I just couldn't, not yet. Anyway I've been doing some thinking myself and this isn't a sudden decision, either. I want to get away from London and the best way to do that is by joining ENSA. In fact as soon as I've washed and dressed I'm going down to the Theatre Royal for an audition.'

'You can't do that. What about me?'

'It's a free country, there's nothing to stop you joining.'

Paul stood up. 'You're right. We'll go as a pair.' He looked excited. 'Henderson and Harding. You get dressed while I go and find a barber's.'

Although it looked as if she was going to have to hold on to her virginity a bit longer, Frances felt as if there was at least some motive to her life again, and she'd changed into a siren suit and tucked her hair into a snood by the time Paul returned. To save on her sparse rations they decided to go for a late breakfast at a nearby café.

'Got any bacon?' Paul asked the waitress hopefully, when after a long wait she came to serve them.

'No.'

'Sausages?'

'All we 'ave is baked beans or scrambled egg.' She licked the end of her pencil impatiently and gazed round at the customers still waiting to be served.

'It's dried egg, I suppose.'

The waitress gave him a withering look. 'There is a war on, love.'

'Let's just have tea and toast,' said Frances, who couldn't stand the sulphurous taste of dried egg.

The utter hopelessness of the past few months was already beginning to shift and later, as she and Paul walked down Drury Lane, Frances gave a slightly guilty giggle. 'Heavens, what's Johnny going to say, losing his singer and pianist in one fell swoop.'

Paul grinned. 'Johnny can't say a bloomin' thing. After all, as the waitress pointed out: "There is a war on, love."'

30

The journey to York was interminable. The train was full to overflowing with servicemen and -women, it juddered, stopped and started and never seemed to get above a speed of twenty-five miles an hour. The corridor put Frances in mind of an assault course and she found it embarrassing having to step over kitbags and prone bodies in order to get to the toilet. The Midlands countryside, small towns and villages, slipped past the window, it grew dark, and a ghostly blue light came on in the ceiling, which was too dim to read by and which made everyone look ill.

Gradually, though, troops disembarked at various stations along the line until at last there was room for Paul and Frances to spread themselves out and get to know their fellow artistes.

They were a mixed bunch, but happy to talk about themselves. One couple, Basil and Bunty, had been in a seaside concert party before the war, Freddie was a ventriloquist, Susie a pretty young soubrette with an innocent air who, whatever her talents, Frances was certain, would be a success with the troops.

'We'll have to decide on order of appearance,' said Basil, a dapper man, not in his first youth and with such ink black hair Frances suspected it must be dyed. Bunty's was such a horrible bright orange, it had to be.

'We don't mind getting the show going, do we Frances?' said Paul.

'It's all the same to me,' Frances replied, not too worried about pecking orders since she rather suspected that she and Paul were going to be the stars of the show anyway.

'With our professional experience, I feel Bunty and I should bring the show to a close,' said Basil.

'Well I don't know about that,' Freddie answered. His lugubrious features took on a petulant look and he had a quick swig at a hip flask.

'Look, why don't we put our names in a hat,' suggested Paul, who could see the discussion collapsing into an undignified squabble – no way to start several months of working and living together.

'I think that's very fair, Paul,' said Susie, giving him a sweet smile.

Paul smiled back. 'Thank you, Susie. Are we all agreed, then?'

The others mumbled their assent, Paul wrote their names on slips of paper and popped them into Freddie's trilby. 'The first out the hat is the last one on, that okay? Would you like to do the draw, Susie?'

Susie's shoulders moved excitedly as she dipped her hand into Freddie's hat and drew out the first slip of paper. 'Frances and Paul,' she squealed and although Basil didn't look too pleased he had the sense to keep his mouth shut. So it was decided: Susie would be the first on stage, followed by Basil and Bunty, then Freddie.

'We can change it around each night, can't we?' said Paul determined to keep it democratic. 'And tell you what, why don't we have a grand finale where we come on together and sing popular war songs. Stuff like "It's a Long Way to Tipperary" and "Goodbye Dolly". Songs the troops can sing-along with.'

'That is an excellent idea, Paul,' said Susie.

'I know we're with ENSA but we could give ourselves a name so that we sound more like a concert party.' At Paul's fairly ordinary suggestion Susie went almost goggle-eyed with admiration and Frances found herself feeling irritated.

Various ideas were bandied about until Frances came up with a name. 'How about The Dominoes?' she suggested, and The Dominoes they became.

There was an army truck waiting for them at York. They all climbed in the back with their luggage and props and bumped along uncomfortably for what seemed like hours in the pitch dark. With its strange country noises, owls hooting, blood-curdling screeches, Frances, a town girl to her toes, found it all rather eerie. She moved closer to Paul, and he put an arm around her.

They knew they'd arrived at the army camp when the lorry was ordered to stop and a sentry came round to inspect them. 'So you're the Every Night Something Awful bunch are you?' he quipped.

'That's a tired old joke,' snapped Basil. 'And we are professionals, you know.'

'Well it's a full house tonight, so you'd better be good or the boys will want their money back.'

'Cheeky young buck, doesn't he know we're doing this for peanuts?' said Freddie and took several more nervous swigs at his hip flask.

'Well, ten quid a week sounds like quite a lot of money to me. I never earned that in the chorus,' Susie admitted with some honesty, as the lorry drove on. 'What do you think, Frances?'

'I'm happy with it,' answered Frances, who knew it would sound like boasting if she admitted she and Paul had been earning double that amount at the Grand Hotel. 'Anyway, money's not the point, we're here to do our bit.'

Fortunately the entertainments officer was more welcoming than the sentry, but then rather spoiled it by going on to tell them that only last week they'd had George Formby and the boys had really loved him and the week before that Jack Buchanan.

Doubting if they could compete with such stars, Frances's confidence took one of its periodic nose dives. The troops, she'd heard, lost no time booing off the stage those acts they thought were lousy.

Overnight accommodation was being provided on camp for them and Frances found that she and Susie were sharing a room.

'Lord, I'm exhausted after that journey,' said Susie falling on the bed.

'You'd better not be, you're on in half an hour,' Frances reminded her. 'Here, have some of these, they'll buck you up.' She handed Susie the plate of slightly stale Spam sandwiches that was obviously intended to be their supper. 'I reckon it's going to be a hard grind for the next few months so we'd better get used to it.'

'I suppose you're right.' Susie sighed, rolled off the bed and got herself into her costume, a short frilly red, white and blue dress with a matching hat which had inscribed across the front, Hi Boys!

'They'll love you,' said Frances admiringly, but was dismayed to see how creased her own evening dress was when she unpacked it. There was no time to put a few desperately needed curlers in her hair, so she made the best of it by piling it on top of her head and fixing it with diamante clips. And knowing how a bit of glitter could buck up an unironed dress, she added a marcasite necklace and bracelet as a finishing touch.

'I reckon we'll both cheer the troops up tonight,' said Susie as she pushed her feet into her tap shoes.

'Don't you think the creases show?' Frances asked, trying to smooth the worst of them out.

'No, and I bet Paul thinks you look nice whatever you're wearing.'

Hint, hint, thought Frances. 'I suppose when you've worked together as long as we have, you stop noticing.'

'You're not engaged, then?'

'Good heavens, no.'

'He's your boyfriend, though,' Susie persisted.

'We're just very good friends.' Forced to remember the exhibition she'd once made of herself, Frances felt her cheeks stain red. If Paul had taken her up on her offer, would they even be that now?

'Is that so?' Susie's pert little face brightened and she took Frances's arm. 'Come on, let's go. I'm not so sure about the others, but here's betting you and me aren't booed off the stage.'

With the aid of a torch, they made their way along a cinder path to the NAAFI hut where the concert was to be held. The others were already there, looking as tense as if they were about to appear at a royal command performance. Susie took a quick peek through the curtains. 'The top brass are in the front row and it's a full house.' She stepped back and held her stomach. 'God, I wish I wasn't on first now. I feel sick.'

'You've no time to be sick. Here, give me your music.' Snatching it out of her hand, Paul went and sat down at the piano and began playing an introduction. Two soldiers on either side of the stage pulled back the curtains, Susie fixed her features into a cheeky smile, ran on to the stage, put her index finger under her chin, curtsied, then gave a saucy wink.

Without her having done a thing, the men cheered their approval and the rest of them gave a sigh of relief. Susie seemed to have an india-rubber body, because not only did she tap dance, she did the splits, backward flips, high kicks and cartwheels. These went down a treat with the troops, and there were approving whistles, particularly when they caught a glimpse of her frilly knickers. Susie, thank God, was a hit and she came off to enthusiastic applause and cries of 'More! More!'

'Good girl,' said Paul and Frances tried not to notice him giving Susie a hug. Basil and Bunty, dressed as matelots, went on next and did various numbers with a nautical flavour, then it was Freddie's turn. The swigs at the hip flask had grown more frequent during the course of the evening and Frances felt herself going tense as he walked on stage with his doll Bertie, like him in evening dress. He hiccuped, stumbled and almost fell. Freddie's speech, or rather the dummy's, was slurred and he had problems with his false teeth but fortunately the audience, thinking this part of the act, laughed uproariously.

Finally it was Frances and Paul's turn. They began with 'All Shadows Fly Away', which was almost their signature tune now, and followed it with 'Begin the Beguine'. To conclude, Frances sang, 'A Nightingale Sang in Berkeley Square'. It was one of the most popular songs around, so when she heard a few accompanying voices, Frances moved forward. 'Shall we all sing this together?' she invited. 'You ladies and gentlemen in the front row as well.' She smiled down encouragingly at the officers and their wives, but they were rather concerned about their dignity and at first refused to join in. However, when the whole ensemble came on stage for the grand finale, and Paul banged out rousing patriotic numbers like 'There'll Always Be An England' and 'Run Rabbit Run' their lips began to move, self-consciously at first, then with a cheerful abandon.

The Dominoes had four curtain calls before they were allowed to go and they came off stage feeling brilliant and talented and glowing like true stars.

Afterwards they were invited over to the officers' mess for drinks. Freddie was soon paralytic in a corner and Susie surrounded by large group of admirers. Paul went to fetch Frances a drink and while she was waiting for him a tall, good-looking captain, who she'd noticed glancing in her direction, came over and spoke to her.

'Miss Henderson, let me say first of all how much I enjoyed your singing tonight. The men get very bored and homesick and a show like your company put on is a great tonic for them.'

'Thank you, we loved doing it.'

355

He twisted his whisky glass, then went on a trifle diffi-
dently, 'Eh . . . uhmm, you wouldn't by any chance have a
sister called Kitty?'

'Yes, I have,' answered Frances, surprised by the question.

'I thought so. When I saw you on stage I was struck by
the resemblance and then of course, there's your surname.'

'The difference between us is that Kitty's a beauty, I'm
not.'

'Nonsense. Anyway let me introduce myself, I'm Robert
Travis. You'll perhaps remember that Kitty worked as my
secretary at Pennywise Assurance some years ago.'

'Oh yes, I remember.'

'How is she?'

'Fine, as far as I know.'

'Oh. Good.'

It was obvious he was waiting for more information so
she added, 'She's a WAAF on an air station in Lincolnshire
now.'

'When you next see her, tell her I asked after her, will
you please?'

Frances nodded. 'Certainly.'

'Thank you, goodnight.'

Frances's face wore a preoccupied expression as she
watched Robert leave. Slowly bits of the jigsaw of Kitty's
past were slotting into place. He had to be the man, it was
so obvious. Her sister had always set her standards high
and Robert Travis was just the type Kitty would fall for.
Handsome, middle-class, not short of the odd bob or two
but also married – and the father of her child. Somehow the
wife had found out, but although they'd been forced to end
their relationship, he didn't caddishly abandon her and it
was his money that saw Kitty through her pregnancy. It
was pretty apparent, too, that in his head the affair wasn't
over for Robert.

'Did I interrupt something? It looked as if you were being
chatted up.' Paul handed her a drink.

'No such luck. He's Kitty's ex-boss. What he did do, though, was answer some questions that have been bothering me for a very long time.'

Over the next year The Dominoes were on the move constantly. They acquired their own van which Basil, Paul and Freddie drove between them. With all the road signs down they frequently got lost or found themselves stuck up to the axle in mud and having to dig themselves out. They endured snow, fog and rain but what really tested their nerves was Freddie's driving, particularly when he drove with one hand nursing his hip flask and the other on the wheel. It was a punishing schedule, tempers became frayed and because they were forced to live in such close proximity, there were frequent squabbles followed by long silences. But they also knew their value as morale boosters, and being real troupers they went on, night after night, playing in hangars, village halls and on ack-ack sites – in fact anywhere they were required. One evening, in a tent with a storm raging outside, they performed to the accompaniment of great claps of thunder and rain pounding off the canvas. That they could hardly make themselves heard didn't appear to bother the audience or dampen their enthusiasm, and the show went on regardless.

Telling herself she wasn't jealous, Frances watched Susie set out to charm Paul. It was obvious by the way he teased her that he wasn't immune to her coquetry, and it might have gone further if it wasn't for the fact that Susie was an outrageous flirt who found any man in an officer's uniform totally irresistible.

Paul had never again referred to her bizarre behaviour on the night of the air raid, and Frances always recalled it herself with great waves of embarrassment. What began to concern her more was Paul's loss of weight. At first she put it down to their life-style and irregular mealtimes, but his persistent cough was worrying. However Paul dismissed her suggestion that he should visit a doctor. 'Don't worry about me, Frances, I'm fit as a fiddle. The trouble is we're all tired and could do with a break.'

They were all exhausted, there was no denying it, nevertheless Frances decided that as soon as they got back to London, she would see that Paul had a check-up. It wasn't for no reason that he'd failed his medical.

So she was glad when they finished touring in the north and turned south again, gradually making their way back down through Lincolnshire where they were booked to perform at the RAF camp where Kitty was stationed. Here was a different kind of landscape, flat and strange with magnificent sunsets and the almost continuous roar of bomber aircraft taking off and landing.

With their lives fractured by war – Mum and Dad gone, the three of them dispersed round the country – Frances knew if they were to endure as a family they must keep in contact, so she wrote regularly to her brother and sister. She'd let Kitty know in good time when the company was arriving and since they hadn't seen each other for over two years, she imagined her sister would be looking forward as much as she was to catching up on the family news and gossip.

However it was another WAAF who greeted her. Popping her head round the door as she was getting ready to go on, 'You Frances?' she asked.

'Yes.'

'A message from Kitty. She says to tell you she's on duty and sorry, but she'll be missing the concert. She'll be round to see you right after the show, though.'

'Thanks.' Frances's smile was affable, but as she arched her brows with dark pencil and applied the heavy make-up needed to accentuate her features over the footlights, she speculated on the true reason for Kitty's absence. It had to be a fairly rare occurrence, your sister turning up to perform in a show, so surely a colleague would have swapped shifts if she'd asked. Frances was making her lips red and luscious as Betty Grable's when a suspicion wormed its way into her mind and pausing, she leaned forward and scrawled across the mirror with her lipstick, JEALOUSY! That was the top and bottom of it. Her voice would make her the centre of attention and Kitty couldn't bear the idea of being overshadowed. Frances shook her head. They both ought to have grown out of their childish jealousies by now, she thought as she erased her handiwork; she was quite sure she had.

Frances undid the scarf protecting her hair, swept it up on top of her head, secured it with two tortoiseshell combs, then stepped into a white chiffon dress. It was pre-war and beginning to show signs of age and as she zipped it up, she studied her finished appearance with a critical eye. Not a bad-looking tart, as Gloria would say, and the reflection smiled back in agreement.

Frances half-expected Kitty not to be there when she and Paul came off after their final number, but she was waiting in the wings and greeted them exuberantly. 'Oh, it's marvellous to see you both after such a long time.' She kissed her sister and Frances was wondering whether perhaps she'd misjudged her when, to her astonishment, over Kitty's shoulder she saw Andrew.

'Good Lord,' she said, stepping away from Kitty's embrace, 'what are you doing here?'

'Well that's a fine welcome,' Andrew laughed. 'I'm stationed here.'

Frances could feel her heart beating like a faulty clock. 'Funny, Kitty's never mentioned you in her letters.'

Kitty smiled vaguely. 'Oh didn't I? I could have sworn I had.'

Frances turned to Paul. 'You remember Andrew, don't you?'

'We've met,' Paul answered curtly and took hold of Frances's hand.

'I'm ever so glad I didn't miss you, because before you leave we're going to celebrate. Look.' Kitty waved her left hand triumphantly under Frances's nose.

Frances stared at the diamond ring, then at Andrew, then back at Kitty, saw their smug expressions and felt a fist of pain in her throat. 'You ... you're engaged?' she managed.

'Right first time.' Andrew drew Kitty possessively towards him. 'Kitty's being posted to RAF Tangmere sometime soon, so we decided to make it official before she went and I feel the luckiest man in the world.'

Well you shouldn't because she doesn't love you, I do, Frances wanted to yell at him. You're being used, can't you see it, you blooming idiot? She watched Andrew bend and kiss Kitty and, unable to stand the pretence any longer, said, 'I'm sorry, we'll have to go, the others will be waiting for us.'

'But we're going to have a drink to celebrate,' Andrew protested.

'Another time perhaps. We've got a long journey tomorrow.'

'You might at least congratulate me,' Kitty pouted.

Claw your eyes out, more like it, Frances thought venomously. 'By the way, Kitty, before I go, I bumped into a friend of yours recently.'

'Oh, who was that?'

'Robert Travis. '

It was gratifying to see Kitty so completely lose her composure. 'Robert?'

'Yes, you worked for him at Pennywise he told me. He wanted to know how you were getting on, what you were doing with yourself these days. Really interested he was. Said I was to be sure to send his fondest regards.' Taking the opportunity to slide the knife between the ribs, Frances turned to Andrew. 'Do you know, Andrew, your fiancée's a real dark horse. There she was all that time working for the most gorgeous-looking man in London and she never let on to a soul. Now I wonder why?'

Kitty's skin had a greenish tinge to it and she was making frantic eye signals. But Frances ignored them. Tasting power, she decided she no longer owed Kitty any loyalty. Andrew would know her for what she was, not the perfect angel he imagined but soiled goods, a girl who'd had an affair with a married man and borne an illegitimate child. That would put paid to any engagement. 'Actually I think there is something you should know Andrew, for your own benefit . . .'

'Frances,' Paul tugged her hand and, annoyed by the interruption, she turned with a frown. 'What is it?'

In reply his body shook with violent coughing, his hand went to his mouth and droplets of blood sprayed between his fingers on to Frances's white chiffon dress.

'Oh my God!' Frances stared down at the spots as they spread and joined and became a red map, then into the silence she heard Paul say with quiet understatement, 'I think there's something wrong with me.'

'You seem to be haemorrhaging. I'll go and fetch the station MO.' Andrew spoke in a calm voice, hoping to allay the sort of fears a word like haemorrhage induced in people. 'Somebody find Paul a chair,' he called over his shoulder and pushed his way through to the exit.

Frances, immobilized by terror, left it to Susie and Kitty to go to Paul's aid and to Bunty to find him a glass of water. No one dared say the dread word tuberculosis and she was locked in by an absolute certainty that Paul was about to die.

Andrew returned quickly with the medical officer, who took one look at Paul's pale, sweating face then said, 'I think we'd better get you across to the sick bay and have a look at you, old chap.'

Frances, ashamed that so far she'd done nothing, rushed to Paul's side. 'I'll help you.'

'No need. And please get your dress disinfected in Lysol immediately, Miss Henderson.' The officer's voice was firm and Frances, rebuffed, went and stood with the rest of the group. But as they watched with sombre expressions Paul being assisted down the steps, Susie voiced what was in all their minds. 'Who's going to play for us now?' she asked tearfully.

'I can bang out a tune if needs be,' answered Bunty, but in their hearts they all knew that this was the end of the line for The Dominoes.

Frances gave up trying to sleep when she heard the thud, thud of engines grow in volume. She knew what it was, the Lancaster bombers returning from a night raid. She got up, slipped into her dressing-gown and went and stood by the window, watching as they swept across the sky like huge cumbersome birds, making the whole building shudder and momentarily blotting out the early morning sun. Bombing raids, for the air crew, meant long hours of boredom followed by periods of great danger and casualties were high. How do young men with everything to live for check their fear, Frances wondered. How, last night, did these same brave young men sit in the audience laughing and cheering, knowing they might be going out on their last mission. Death and destruction fouled the world – and there was Paul too, his life in danger from this killer disease. Oh why hadn't she insisted more vehemently that he see a doctor, then it might not have advanced this far. Blaming herself and crushed under a weight of depression, Frances leaned her cheek against the cold glass of the window and allowed the tears to trickle down her face. God, how she wished this awful war was over, but it just seemed to go on and on, so that sometimes she thought it would last for ever.

The activities of washing, dressing and packing helped pull Frances out of her melancholy. Coming to a decision further aided her recovery. The Dominoes were due to perform at another RAF camp that evening and they had to be on their way soon. Before they left, though, Frances was determined to see Paul and she walked over to the sick bay prepared to do battle with the doctor if necessary. Fortunately he was an understanding man who went to great lengths to put her mind at rest about Paul.

'The x-rays have confirmed tuberculosis and I know the blood frightened you, but it isn't the scourge it once was. We have the drugs these days to deal with the disease and Mr Harding stands a good chance of complete recovery.'

Frances's face was illuminated with such joy at this news, the doctor felt obliged to add a cautionary note. 'Mind you, it will take time. The life he's been leading hasn't helped and Mr Harding needs a year at least of complete rest in a sanatorium. As soon as he's up to the journey, we'll try and get him transferred to one further south to make visiting easier.'

'Can I see him now?'

The doctor looked doubtful.

'Please.'

'All right, but he's very tired so only for a few minutes. And you'll have to wear these.' He handed Frances a voluminous gown and face mask, adding with a twinkle, 'And no physical contact, please.'

Paul was lying propped up on pillows, his eyes closed and his strong, blunt pianist's hands on the counterpane looking as blue-veined and transparent as a newly hatched chick. Frances tiptoed to the end of the bed and called his name quietly.

He opened his eyes, and realizing he must think she was a nurse in her garb, Frances said, 'It's me, Paul.'

'Hello, dear.'

'We're off in a minute, I came to say goodbye.'

'You won't forget me will you, Frances? We've been good mates for a long time, haven't we?'

A tear trickled down Frances's nose and her throat hurt.

'More than that, Paul. Much more.' Her mask gave her courage and she blurted out, 'I love you Paul.'

It was an effort, but he managed a wonderful smile. 'In that case, I'll make jolly sure I get better.'

'I'll write, every day,' Frances promised when the doctor came to tell her her time was up. She managed to say goodbye without crying, but immediately she got outside she broke down and was so busy mopping up her tears she didn't see Kitty until she felt a hand on her arm.

'How is Paul?'

'Not very well. As you probably guessed, he's got TB.'

'I'm terribly sorry.'

'I'm going to miss him so.' Frances blew her nose. 'I'm only just realizing how much I've always depended on him and yet taken him for granted.'

'It happens when you've known people a long time. It's the same in families,' said Kitty, looking wise. 'Frances, about last night. Were you going to tell Andrew about the baby?'

Frances could see the rest of the company loading up the lorry and Susie beckoning to her. Glad of a let-out from this embarrassing question, she answered, 'Look, I must go, everyone's waiting for me.' She started to walk away but Kitty kept determinedly in step with her.

'You always promised you'd never breathe a word to a living soul.'

Frances paused and looked straight at her sister. 'Yes I did, didn't I? And I won't, because that, Kitty, is something I'm going to leave you to tell Andrew yourself.'

31

In a small bookshop opposite the Cross in Chichester, Kitty, after much browsing and indecision, finally treated herself to a second-hand copy of *How Green Was My Valley*. Because she was pretty, the young assistant forgave her for taking such an age to choose one book and when she'd made her purchase, he rushed round the counter, held open the door and wished her a polite 'Good day'.

For his trouble, Kitty bestowed on him her sweetest smile and it still played round her lips as she stepped out on to the pavement. But the smile froze when she saw, walking towards her along West Street, a man in army officer's uniform who, by his stride and height, she recognized immediately as Robert.

Imagining such a moment, over the years she'd fine-tuned the bitter words she would castigate him with. Instead, as he drew nearer, the sentences gagged in her throat and Kitty stood mute, waiting for him to recognize her.

But obviously to him she was just another WAAF in a blue shapeless uniform and unbecoming cap and he might have passed by if she hadn't found her voice. 'Hello, Robert.'

'Kitty!' His face registered several emotions, pleasure, guilt and uncertainty amongst them.

They stood staring at each other, both awkward, both remembering, but at a loss to find the right words. Although Kitty's heart was irretrievably scarred, she was anxious to acquit herself with dignity, to show that despite his abandonment of her she'd survived really rather well. Robert wore his uniform with the distinction she would have expected, but the years had added a few lines round his eyes and mouth and under his peaked cap she could discern grey threading through darker hair. But in spite of all the pain he'd inflicted, it was still a beloved face. Over five years since her world collapsed around her, and yet not a day has gone by when I haven't thought of you or our son, she wanted to say, and drew a deep, sad breath.

'Aah ... uhmm I've just been having a look round the cathedral. A fine building,' said Robert, feeling the need to break the silence.

'Yes, it is,' answered Kitty, unwilling to admit she'd never set foot inside it.

'Anyway, what are you doing in these parts? When I met that sister of yours with the lovely voice, she told me you were in Lincolnshire.'

'I've been stationed at Tangmere quite a while now.'

'For the big build-up, eh?'

Kitty nodded. The whole of the south coast was packed with troops, and with heavily camouflaged tanks and guns, and all leave had been cancelled. It was apparent to all service personnel that an Allied invasion was imminent, the only question was when.

'And you?'

'The same reason. But how are you? I must say you're looking well.' Looking achingly lovely, were actually the words on Robert's lips, but he knew he'd forfeited all right to express such thoughts.

'Thank you. Perhaps that's because I'm engaged to be married.'

'Oh I am glad for you.' Hypocrite, he thought. 'Are you happy?'

'Ecstatically,' Kitty lied in return, with a bright, brave smile.

'May I ask who the lucky man is?'

'Andrew. Someone I've known for a long time.'

'Look, this is no place to talk, Kitty. Have you got time for a cup of tea?'

Kitty hesitated. Why shouldn't she? The future was uncertain, the past gone. 'That would be nice. I'm on night duty at the moment so I've got time.'

'Good.' Taking her arm he guided her across the road to the Dolphin and Anchor. Through the rough serge of her jacket Kitty could feel the pressure of his fingers and, remembering how they'd explored every crease and crevice of her body, a hot tongue of desire shot through her. Perhaps he's gone bald and that will put me off him, she thought desperately. But when they sat down and Robert removed his cap, his hair still sprung back thick and strong from the pronounced widow's peak.

Robert ordered tea, sandwiches and scones which a waitress eventually brought to the table, and while Kitty was occupied pouring tea, she dared to ask, 'And how is our son?'

'He's a fine young lad. The apple of Alice's eye and his resemblance to you is uncanny. Here, let me show you.' Robert drew a wallet from his tunic pocket, pulled out a photo and handed it to Kitty.

She took it with unsteady fingers. After the adoption the raw pain of loss wouldn't leave her and the need to see her baby had been so strong, Kitty had defied Alice and gone down to Leyborne several times in the hope of catching a glimpse of him. But the house was surrounded by acres of garden and grounds and only once had she caught a brief glimpse of a uniformed figure pushing a pram. After several such fruitless visits she realized she was only compounding her misery and stopped going.

'He'll be five soon,' said Robert as she studied the snapshot.

'I gave birth to him, Robert, I do know when his birthday is. Even what hour.'

'Sorry.'

'What do you call him?'

'David. The name you gave him.'

'Thank you.' In the photograph, David was standing holding Robert's hand. A chubby little boy with a head of blond curls, he was smiling up at his daddy, and Kitty was so overwhelmed by her loss, and what might have been that her eyes filled with tears.

Robert leaned forward and grasped her hand. 'Don't cry, darling.'

'Why shouldn't I? I'm the one who lost everything, not you.'

Robert flung himself back in his chair. 'Christ I mucked things up for you, didn't I?'

Kitty wiped her eyes and hoped none of the other guests had noticed her distress. 'You did.' He needn't think she was going to let him off the hook easily. 'Are you happy with Alice?'

'We rub along. I don't love her, I love you, Kitty, and I'll go on loving you until my last breath.'

'Oh Robert, my love,' Kitty whispered, her voice choked with emotion.

He stroked her face tenderly. 'I've often wanted to get in touch with you and try to explain what happened, but I knew how much you must hate me so I could never find the courage.'

'I did hate you, what can you expect? You ruined my life. But why did you marry Alice? I could never understand that – you were supposed to love me.'

'When I tell you it will sound as if I'm making excuses for myself, which I am I suppose. As you might guess I was in a terrible state after Imogen died. I suffered from tremendous guilt because I wasn't there to save her, then when Alice took me down to Leyborne I fell ill with flu, which developed into pneumonia. She took care of everything, saw to the arrangements for Imogen's funeral, made sure I had the best medical treatment available, and of course, I was indebted to her for that. Then Sir Sidney offered me a directorship and a big salary increase. I was

368

horrendously in debt, so this was a very welcome promotion. What I didn't realize was that there were conditions and shortly after this Alice started dropping hints about marriage and how I needed a wife beside me. I was appalled and made it quite clear that since I was only recently widowed it was hardly appropriate for me to be thinking of remarrying.'

'She always had her eye on you, I used to watch her.'

'Yes, I was aware of it too. Anyway she became impatient with me and quite bare-faced in her demands. In fact she made it clear that if I didn't marry her, not only would I find myself out of a job but my mother would also lose her house and allowance. That really frightened me. I couldn't see my mother homeless and reduced to penury once again, which she would be if I was unable to find another position. Then with all my debts to pay off . . .' Robert shrugged. 'So, weak-headed idiot that I was, I went ahead with it. Foolishly I hoped it wouldn't make any difference to you and me. Of course, if I'd known you were pregnant I would have held out and taken my chances and the story might have had a happier ending.'

Too shamefaced to look at Kitty, Robert had told this story staring at the carpet. 'I've made a right bloody mess of everything, haven't I?'

Kitty leaned forward and lightly ran her fingers through his hair, delighting in the thick spring of it. 'You've still got time to put it right, Robert,' she said quietly.

The shame went from Robert's face and his eyes lightened with hope. 'Do you really mean that?'

'Every word.'

'But your fiancé, what about him?'

Kitty very deliberately tugged the engagement ring from her finger and dropped it into her shoulder bag, along with the photograph of her son. 'That's finished, if it ever started. My sister can have him.'

'My dearest darling.' Robert lifted her hand to his lips.

369

'Look, I've got to get back to camp, but is there any chance of us meeting tomorrow?'

'I told you, my days are free this week.'

'Can you be outside here by two o'clock?'

'Try and stop me.'

'Marvellous. I've still got my car, and if I can scrounge some petrol, we could drive up on the Downs. Otherwise we'll just get on a bus, it doesn't matter where to, as long as we're together.' As he stood up to go he leaned over and kissed her with great tenderness. 'I'm so happy, Kitten. I know I don't deserve this second chance you're giving me, but I shan't let you go again. I promise I'll make up for all the wretched years we've been apart and tomorrow we'll discuss our future.'

When Kitty came off duty at eight in the morning, she set her alarm for twelve o'clock and went straight to bed. She woke immediately the alarm went off, got up and dressed in her WAAF uniform, but stuffed into a carrier bag a summer dress, sandals and nylons she'd bought on the black market. She caught the bus into Chichester, went into the Dolphin and Anchor ladies' toilet and changed into her civilian clothes. While she combed her hair down round her shoulders, Kitty prayed she wouldn't bump into an officer who recognized her. What she was doing was strictly forbidden, but to hell with regulations, today she wanted to be her prettiest and most feminine for Robert. When she went back outside he was waiting for her in his car with the hood down. She leapt in and flung her uniform into the back seat.

'Good heavens I hardly recognized you, you look like a real girl.'

'Yes, but can we get out of here before I'm caught?'

'Righty-o.' Robert turned on the ignition, put the car into gear and swept round the Cross, where a policeman stood directing the traffic, then into North Street. They drove up past the hospital and barracks and chugged along for several miles behind convoys of army trucks and armoured cars. Kitty tried to be patient, but she could see the precious afternoon slipping away.

Eventually Robert turned off into a country lane and she could see they were heading for the Downs. American troops were encamped everywhere, and Kitty wondered if they would ever find a quiet spot. After a few miles Robert drew into the side of the road and stopped. 'We'll walk from here,' he said, pulled a tartan rug from behind the seat and put the hood up. Taking Kitty's hand he set off along a track towards a wood. Ox-eye daisies, red campion and small green wild strawberries were tucked into the embankment. Rabbits hopped away at their approach, pigeons cooed softly and Robert pointed out to Kitty a jay, its red breast showing up sharply against the lush greenness of late spring. 'It's hard to think of war, invasion and killing with this peace all around us, isn't it?' Robert sighed and putting his arm around Kitty's shoulder, pulled her towards him.

'Robert, tell me something, will you go?'

'Yes.'

'Can you talk about it?'

'No. Not that I want to. We don't know how much time we have together so let's be selfish and forget the rest of the world for these few hours. Let there be just you and me.'

After a short while they plunged off into the wood, and here, well away from the track and any likelihood of being disturbed, they found a small green glade.

Robert spread the rug on the ground then pulled her down beside him. He was so desperate for her, he just wanted to push her back on the rug, hoist up her dress, unbutton his flies and take her. But although that would satisfy his need, it probably wouldn't give Kitty much pleasure. Kissing her, he unbuttoned her dress and pulled it over her head. But she wouldn't let him remove her precious nylons, so Robert lay back and watched with lustful pleasure as she undid her suspenders and rolled the stockings down her slim legs. When she was naked he quickly divested himself of his uniform.

'Let me look at you.' The sun through the trees dappled her breasts and Robert ran his hands lightly over the pearly texture of her skin and round her pink, hard nipples. Lying side by side, they explored each other with a bemused happiness, the years of separation melting away. Kitty raked her fingers through the hair on his chest and belly and down into his groin. He was already hard, and hungry for him she turned on her back. Holding him she directed him into her, wrapping her legs around him at the same time. As she felt the thrust of him inside her, she closed her eyes. It had been such a long time.

'Open your eyes,' Robert ordered, resting the palms of his hands on the ground. 'I love to watch you when you come, the way your skin goes all rosy and your eyes dilate. Can I come inside you?'

'Yes you must, you must,' she moaned as his thrust became more urgent. Then with a great spasm of release she cried out, and with such abandon, she frightened the birds from their siesta and sent them flapping in panic out of the trees.

'You were always a noisy one,' Robert laughed, and kissed her. Then as she lay resting her head on his chest, he asked, 'By the way, did you have that cap in?'

'Darling, that cap would have rotted away by now.'

'Hasn't there been anyone else? What about your fiancé?'

'The thought of making love to anyone else but you makes me feel physically sick.'

'Supposing you get pregnant again?'

Kitty raised herself on her elbow and ran her index finger across his lips. 'This time I shall keep it and love it like hell.'

Robert was silent for a moment, then he said in a thoughtful voice, 'Kitty, I'm probably not going to be able to divorce Alice, you realize that, don't you? But when this shindig is over, I want us to be together as much as possible. There's no shortage of cash now, so I could afford to buy you a decent house, even a business, a shop perhaps.'

'What about a florist's? You could bring David to see me then,' Kitty daydreamed.

'Maybe I could at that.' They lay together, happily making plans for the future until clouds cut out the sun, it grew cold and began to spit with rain. Hastily they dressed and when they returned to the car, Kitty changed into her heavy WAAF uniform. Robert drove her back to the camp, but before he kissed her goodnight they arranged to meet again the following week. However their meeting was destined not to take place, because shortly after this, all of Southern England became a restricted area, service personnel were confined to camp and on 6 June Operation Overlord began.

At the beginning, no one was certain that the invasion would be successful and it was an exhausting, tense period. Like everyone else, Kitty had little time to think about personal matters, because all she did was eat, sleep and work. She heard fellow WAAFs, some married, others engaged, crying in the night, but she remained determinedly optimistic about Robert and knew he would write to her as soon as he could. June, July passed but not a word, then in August a letter arrived, soiled and crumpled but bearing a French stamp. Kitty sat down on her bed and stared at his handwriting, so dear, so familiar to her, hugged it to her breast and whispered, 'Thank God,' then tore the envelope open with clumsy, eager fingers.

My dearest, darling Kitten

    While I write this letter, I am praying it will never be sent. However, I have asked a fellow officer to post it to you, in the event of my being killed, so when you receive it you will know I am not coming back to you, my darling. The only thing that has kept me sane in the utter madhouse of war, is your dear face before me and the memory of that last perfect day we spent together. At least we shared that and I'm so glad I was able at last to make my peace with you. I ache with the pain of knowing I'll never again feel your pliant body under mine or kiss your sweet lips. The plans we made will now come to nothing, and I grieve our six wasted years apart and my stupidity. But we made David together and he's a grand boy, so try and hold on to that and remember something good came out of it. There is a letter with my solicitor which will tell our son the truth when he is twenty-one. He deserves it, so do you. You were my one true love, believe me Kitty, and I apologize for leaving you like this. I never seemed to get it right, did I? Farewell my darling, my love for ever,

    Robert.

The letter fluttered from Kitty's numb fingers, then with a long wild animal cry of pain, she threw herself down on the bed. Knowing what it was, the other girls in the hut came rushing to her side. But she rejected their words of sympathy and comfort and turning away, she lay staring at the wall dry-eyed and frozen-hearted.

32

Tired of watching a small girl in the train seat opposite pick her nose, Frances pulled out the newspaper she'd bought to take to Paul at the sanatorium and hid behind it.

The news was good these days. The threat from doodle-bugs and V2 rockets had subsided, Allied forces were advancing on all fronts, and a map showed how far the invasion had progressed. Holland and Belgium had been liberated, the German army was retreating across the Rhine and prisoner of war camps were being liberated daily. Poor Norman, Frances thought, five years of captivity. She'd written to him regularly, but only a couple of his letters caught up with her as she toured round the country. Like all prisoners of war, the main problem he'd had to deal with was boredom, although he was proud of his fluency in German.

Never mind, he'd be home soon. Everywhere people were saying to each other, 'It won't be long now.' For the nation was war weary; tired of the shortages, the separations, the fear and loss. They wanted it over quickly so that they could sit round their firesides with loved ones in peace again. Roy was living with Gloria and Walter now, but still had dreams of becoming a pilot. With luck, though, the war would be over before he was called up, for another loss in the family was too terrible to contemplate.

People assumed it was what you wanted to hear when they told you that grief lessened after a time, that the memory of loved ones dimmed. But the last thing Frances wanted was to forget her parents. Dipping back into her memory she saw them dancing, as they'd often done, round the small room together, the gas still not lit and the wireless playing in the background. Tears spurted up involuntarily in her eyes and, sensing curious glances, she held the paper high in front of her, swallowed hard and found her attention caught by a picture of a woman and small boy standing outside Buckingham Palace. The child proudly displayed a medal and underneath the caption read: *Posthumous citation for gallantry. Yesterday Mrs Robert Travis, widow of Captain Robert Travis, went to the Palace with her son David to receive the Military Cross, won posthumously by his father in recognition of gallantry in action.*

'Oh no!' Frances exclaimed and got more strange looks. But she didn't care. Robert dead, too. How many more? Poor Kitty and poor little boy. Tears threatened again. No matter how proud he felt, a medal wasn't really a fair exchange for his daddy. Disturbed by something familiar about the boy's features, Frances studied the photo more closely. How old would he be? Five, getting on for six. With a quickening interest, she did some mental arithmetic. Kitty had told her the baby was stillborn and yet here the boy was as large as life and her sister to a T. Staggered by her discovery and with her mind working furiously, Frances let the paper fall and stared out of the window. There it was, the final clue, the mystery was now solved, the complications of Kitty's life unravelled. Well, perhaps not the full story, but as much as she was ever likely to know. It was conjecture on her part, but Frances assumed Robert had legally adopted his own son, and she marvelled at his saintly, understanding wife. There couldn't be many women who would be prepared to take on a mistress's child.

Seeing that the train was drawing into her station, Frances stuffed the newspaper into her handbag and stood up. Usually she was so impatient to see Paul she caught the bus up to the sanatorium. Today, her thoughts much preoccupied with Kitty, she decided to stretch her legs and walk. It was uphill through the attractive village with its green and duck pond, but at the sanatorium gates it levelled out into a long drive of tall elm trees and walking became much less strenuous. Rooks, as noisily contentious as lawyers, were building their nests high in the branches, and daffodils beamed their golden light upon the drab March landscape. War or no war, and no matter what atrocities countries inflicted upon each other, nature still performed its yearly miracle of rebirth, Frances reflected, and felt comforted by the thought.

But why had Kitty denied her child, Frances puzzled. Was it the only way she could deal with her pain? To her, Kitty had always seemed the golden girl whose life was lived on sunlit slopes. Nature had bestowed on her beauty and the privileges that went with it: attention, new dresses and finally Andrew. Frances couldn't deny her own envy and yet over these past few years her sister must have gone to hell and back emotionally. She'd lost her baby to another woman and now Robert, obviously the love of her life, was dead and part of her would have died too. Frances had never imagined there'd come a time when she'd feel sorry for her sister, but she did today. Since Lincoln and her outburst, letters had more or less dried up between them, but never mind the past, what Kitty needed right now was her sympathy and compassion. Hell, they were sisters, kin, the same flesh and blood and it should mean something, particularly with Mum and Dad gone. She would write tonight and try and make her peace with Kitty, she decided, send her the cutting from the newspaper. And even though she felt strongly that it was a mistake for her sister to be marrying Andrew with such a weight of deceit between them, she would make it clear that Kitty's secret was safe with her.

The drive bore round to the right, the sanatorium came into view, and Frances remembered the defining moment when she'd turned to see Paul coughing blood. How in those first few dramatic hours when she was convinced Paul would die, the whole perspective of her life had shifted.

Andrew ceased to matter and to throw off the burden of her love for him had been the most tremendous relief.

The sanatorium was so hushed and orderly, Frances always felt she was entering a church. Even the receptionist greeted her in reverential tones. 'Good afternoon, Miss Henderson. Go through: Mr Harding's on the balcony and hasn't stopped looking at the clock for the past hour.'

Frances smiled at the girl. 'Thank you.' The balcony was long and glass-covered, like a conservatory, and looked out over a huge lawn daubed with purple, yellow and white crocuses. Paul was dressed and sitting in a chair, pen in hand and writing lyrics, Frances guessed by the total concentration he was giving to his task. She stood and watched him for a moment. He'd been incarcerated for nearly a year, so his skin still had the translucence of the sick and he was underweight, in spite of the extra rations and freshly laid eggs and milk they enjoyed here. Otherwise he was, as the doctor had promised, on the way to a full recovery and badgering the nurses constantly to be allowed to go home.

Becoming aware of her scrutiny Paul looked up and smiled, then held out his arms. 'What are you wasting time for? Come here.'

She moved forward into his embrace and they kissed. Then, noticing two elderly gentlemen observing them, Frances murmured, 'We're being watched.'

'So what, they're only jealous,' Paul answered, pulled her down on his lap and kissed her again and at some length.

Frances giggled, but she was inhibited by the other patients' interest and moved to a chair. 'I wish we could be alone sometimes,' she complained. 'For months we weren't allowed to touch or to kiss because of infection, now we can we have the whole ward gawping at us.'

'You'd understand why if you saw some of their wives. They're envious because I've got such a lovely girl to kiss. But we won't be troubled by them much longer: I've just had some brilliant news. They're letting me out in four weeks' time.'

'Is that true?'

'Absolutely. We'll have all the time in the world then, my love. The rest of our lives, in fact. I'm going to marry you as soon as we can get a licence.'

Indifferent now to the other patients' interest, Frances leaned her head on his shoulder. 'I'm so happy.'

Paul gently stroked her cheek. 'Where shall we go for our honeymoon?'

'Cornwall, I've always wanted to go there and the sea air will do you good.'

'And just thinking of all that space and freedom makes me feel better. It's been like serving a prison sentence, cooped up in here.'

Frances lifted her head. 'Go on with you. Look at the fun you had at Christmas organizing the pantomime.' Not only had Paul written the parts for the doctors and nurses, he'd composed the songs and directed it. 'And all the nurses fuss round you. I reckon a couple of them have got their eye on you.'

'Rubbish. Anyway it's you I want to be with, not nurses. But the doctors have set conditions. They've made it clear I can't go back to the old life. My lungs won't take the smoke and late nights.'

'Well I never imagined you'd want to. After all you've got your song writing and arranging and you're making a good living from that now.'

'It's your career, sweetheart, I'm thinking about.'

'Oh don't worry about me, I've got some news for you, too.' Frances had never thought she'd miss Bunty, Basil, Freddie and Susie, but she did and she realized that they'd become a surrogate family in the end. After they broke up, Susie got herself engaged to an American, while Basil, Bunty and Freddie went off to entertain the troops in Egypt. Frances, though, confined her engagements to the London area so that she could be near Paul and she'd recently been approached by an agent, a Miss Ford, and she was now on her books.

'Out with it, then,' she heard Paul say.

'Well Miss Ford reckons, with television starting up again, there's going to be heaps of opportunities for entertainers like us after the war. And guess what? She's negotiating with the BBC on my behalf at the moment.'

'I knew it was only a question of time before you were discovered.'

'Don't get too carried away, nothing's happened yet.'

'As soon as they hear your voice, they'll want to engage you and then in no time you'll be as famous as Vera Lynn or Anne Shelton.'

Frances smiled at Paul's flight of fancy, but then he'd always had faith in her, given her confidence and finally that most precious of gifts, his love.

Paul took her left hand in his. 'But I'm going to put a ring on that finger first.' He lifted her hand to his mouth and kissed it, gazing at her with such tenderness her heart filled with gratitude. Frances had often seen that same look on her father's face as he'd watched Mum going about her tasks, and again on Andrew's as he regarded Kitty. But until Paul no man had ever looked at her in quite that way and Frances had come to believe herself unlovable.

They talked themselves hoarse making plans for the future, and when a nurse came to tell Frances that her hour was up, saying goodbye to Paul didn't seem as painful as usual. She caught the bus back to the station and it trundled along stopping to pick up or drop tired, war-weary house-wives who complained to each other of the endless short-ages and queues. Frances was so in tune with life herself today, so happy to have Paul restored to health and coming home, that she wanted to share her optimism about the future with everyone. 'Don't worry, it'll be over soon,' she said to a woman sitting next to her.

The woman, her upper lip stained yellow by cigarettes, her hair under her turban screwed up in curlers, turned in her seat and stared at Frances. 'What makes you so sure, love?'

Frances smiled. 'I just feel it in my bones that life for us all is on the up and up.'

The woman prodded her in the ribs. 'I'll tell you what your problem is, duckie. I can see it yer eyes, yer in love, and that makes sensible women soft in the head.'

33

8 May 1945

Frances had come to accept that her parents' death, the smell of blood and burning flesh, would haunt her for the rest of her life. Now, as they turned into Stuart Street, an irrational fear pulsed through her and she gripped hold of Paul's hand. It looked shabby, pock-marked and down-at-heel, to be sure, but apart from missing tiles, broken guttering and bomb-blasted windows, it had escaped the worst of the bombing and an air of calm prevailed.

'What's wrong?' asked Paul, aware of the tension in her fingers.

'It was that thunderstorm last night. It woke me up and I thought the bombers had come back. Stupid, really.' Frances laughed, trying to scoff at her remembered terror.

'Well you can stop worrying about being blown to extinction. Hitler's dead and Germany's surrendered so we'll all be able to sleep soundly in our beds from now on.'

'I still can't really get it into my head that the country's at peace.'

'Well it is and that din proves it,' Paul shouted, thrusting his fingers in his ears as all around them church bells, silent since the war, started to peal victoriously.

Until today they would only have been rung if an invasion was imminent and at the unfamiliar sound, doors were flung open and people ran out into the street to listen. They stood around for a few minutes with smiles on their faces then a large woman, wanting to express her feelings, burst out with patriotic fervour, 'There'll always be an England . . .'

She had a voice like a croaking frog but no one had the nerve to tell her to put a sock in it. Instead they contented themselves with screwing up their faces in pretended agony behind her back. She finished, got her wind back and was about to continue with a second stirring number when to divert her, another woman called, 'Come on folks, let's conga.'

'Righty-o, ducks,' a man answered and grabbed her waist. In no time a line had formed behind them, and although there was little Latin grace in their movements, and a few of them didn't seem to know their left foot from their right, they conga'd off down the street, la-la-la-ing happily. The noise drew more people from their houses and, not wanting to miss out on the fun, they ran to join in. Watching them, Frances felt suddenly very emotional. These people had been through six years of hardship and danger, and yet with true cockney spirit they could always squeeze some pleasure from the hour and she felt proud to be part of such an indomitable breed.

The laughter became more hilarious and abandoned as the dancers snaked their way round the corner and disappeared. When they reappeared at the top end of the street, the line had doubled in length and had marching behind it a group of kids. Draped in Union Jacks, they banged on biscuit tins, blew on paper combs and penny whistles and with wily charm, rattled their begging bowls for any spare coppers.

Because it was VE Day everyone was inclined to indulge them and Paul threw in a two-bob piece. 'Thanks, mate,' said the young lad and whistled appreciatively through his teeth. The conga-ing line of adults were really in their stride now. The atmosphere grew warm and familiar, men whispered suggestively in women's ears and made their shoulders heave with laughter. Emboldened, the blokes squeezed waists and patted plump behinds. The women responded by arching their thick white necks, as if in some courting ritual, and for a short while everyone imagined themselves young and desirable again.

Those people who thought it beneath their dignity to go cavorting round the streets were in the meantime busy putting up decorations. Flags and bunting no one thought they'd ever have a use for again had been rescued from lofts and the dust and moths shaken out. Children were busy chalking a huge Union Jack on the side of the air raid shelter, front doors were emblazoned with Welcome Home signs for returning sons and husbands and it was a toss-up whose picture went in the window, Mr Churchill's or the Royal Family's.

'This all reminds me of the Jubilee celebrations,' said Frances wistfully. 'Almost exactly ten years ago to the day. Even the weather's the same. But we aren't the same, not the family.'

'Come on, love, try not to dwell on it,' said Paul, knowing where her thoughts were leading.

'I was such a silly young girl then. I imagined myself to be unhappy, when I had no idea of real unhappiness.' Frances wrapped her arm round Paul's waist. 'One thing's for certain, I'll never take anything or anyone for granted again, and you're to remind me if I ever forget.'

'I will, I promise.'

The kiss Paul gave Frances was interrupted by young Terry, Gloria and Walter's boy. He'd been sitting on the wall waiting for them, and he came running up waving a paper Union Jack. A little way behind waddled the elderly Tinker, a red, white and blue rosette attached to his collar and looking like a portly Tory councillor canvassing for votes.

'Hello, Terry love.' Frances bent and kissed her young cousin.

'Mum ses we're all goin' up West later on to see the King and Queen and Mr Churchill at Buckingham Palace,' the boy said, all breathy and excited, then ran back towards his house. 'I'll go and tell Mum and Dad yer coming.'

Tinker barked to remind them he was there and when Frances picked him up, he covered her face with damp doggy kisses.

Gloria was now at the gate beckoning to them. 'Come on you two lovebirds, get a move on, there's a lot of celebrating to be done before we go up West, and we're all dying for a drink. Kitty and Andrew have been here ages.'

Holding hands, Paul and Frances hurried to her bidding, following her through the hall and out into the back garden. Here, alongside deck chairs and a table laden with weak beer and British sherry, the rest of the family was gathered. Walter took a great pride in his small patch: there was not a weed to be seen and plants were forbidden to slouch. If they dared do such a thing, he would ruthlessly run a stake through them. Today the garden was bright with red and yellow tulips, which stood so stiffly to attention, Frances felt sure that Walter must come out and salute them every morning.

Frances called hello to everyone then bent and kissed her grandmother. 'How are you, Nan?'

'As well as can be expected,' she retorted. But it was obvious to Frances that the fight had gone out of her grandmother. She was battle weary. Donald had died during the war, a blessing, most people had said, but now that she had no one to look after or nag she seemed rather lost.

Paul was talking to Kitty and Andrew, so Frances helped herself to a sherry and moved over to stand beside him. 'You're a stranger,' she said, addressing her sister.

'Well that'll change in the near future, won't it Kitty?' Andrew draped an arm round her shoulder and pulled her close.

Kitty removed an insect from her sherry and nodded.

'We're planning on marrying immediately we're demobbed, so our first priority is finding somewhere to live.'

'Anywhere special?'

'It might only be a couple of furnished rooms to start

with, but Kitty fancies Woodford Green. I've got a job lined up in the City so it won't be too difficult for work.'

Frances's face registered disbelief. 'You in the City, Andrew? My, you've changed your tune.' She knew she was being tactless, but the words slipped out before she could stop them.

'Yes, you'll be voting Tory if you go on like this, Andrew,' Paul joked.

'I doubt it. Marriage is a responsibility, particularly if there are children and you want to give them a decent standard of living.' But Andrew's excuses sat uncomfortably on his shoulders and Frances could guess for whose benefit this all was. It was truly awesome, the depth of his love for Kitty. For her he was even prepared to betray the ideals he had always held so dear. Frances just hoped Kitty realized what sacrifices Andrew was making and put all her energy into making him a good wife in return.

'Well your mum will be pleased anyway. She'd always set her heart on you being a City gent,' said Frances. 'Have you met Andrew's parents yet, Kitty?'

'Yes, a couple of times,' answered Kitty, who until then hadn't said one word and looked unusually subdued.

She moved apart from Andrew and took Frances's arm. 'Come and have a natter while I change. If we're going out I'm wearing civvies. It's too hot for this outfit.'

Frances followed her sister upstairs to Gloria's spare bedroom. Sitting down in a Lloyd Loom chair she watched Kitty strip to her underwear and pull off her heavy WAAF stockings. She then unpinned her hair from its regulation length above the collar and pulled a brush through it. It was still a lovely golden colour and although her face was maturer, it had lost none of its beauty.

Kitty rolled nylons up her legs, fastened them, slipped a summer dress over her head, then stood back and surveyed herself in the mirror. 'There, I don't feel like a sack of potatoes any longer.'

'Well you'll be out of the WAAF soon and married. Is it going to be a church wedding?'

Kitty, who was fashioning her hair into a long pageboy, slammed down the hairbrush and turned round. Her expression was tense and she twisted the buttons on her dress distractedly. 'Yes, down in Chelmsford with bridesmaids, the lot. If I go through with it, that is.'

'What do you mean?'

'I mean I'm having second thoughts.'

'Don't you love Andrew, then?' Frances asked, thinking with what joy she would have once greeted such a confession.

'I'm not sure.'

'Either you love him or you don't. Is it like it was with Robert?' Frances asked quietly.

'Nothing will ever be like that. I saw him you know, just before D-Day. We spent some time together.'

'I'm glad.'

'I had every intention of breaking off the engagement with Andrew then and I don't know why I didn't. Perhaps because time's passing. The war has stolen six years of all our lives and I'm twenty-seven now. Maybe if I don't marry Andrew I'll end up on the shelf.'

'What a daft idea, of course you won't. Not with your looks. But have you told Andrew about Robert . . . about your son yet?'

A look of horror spread across Kitty's face. 'God, no.'

'Well you'll have to get it out of the way if you do decide to be his wife.'

'I'd topple from my pedestal in double quick time then.' Kitty gave a small bitter laugh.

'Maybe, but he deserves that at least from you, Kitty. Imagine if he found out later – it would destroy him. At least now he can make a choice.' How wise I sound, dispensing all this advice, thought Frances.

Kitty shrugged indifferently. 'I'm so dead inside it doesn't really matter.'

'Andrew matters, though,' Frances felt obliged to point out. 'And he's a good, honourable person.'

'Yes, you're right. But have you noticed how men get away with so much more than women? They don't carry the baggage of their past around with them, do they? They're not expected to confess to past indiscretions.'

'That's the way of the world.'

'It doesn't make it right though, does it?'

'No,' Frances conceded.

Their tête-à-tête was interrupted by heavy footsteps thumping up the stairs, then Roy came into the room, filling it with his young man's ungainliness and size. 'What are you two plotting up 'ere?'

'Women's talk, nothing suitable for your ears,' answered Kitty and busied herself swapping make-up and money from one handbag to another.

'How tall are you now, Roy?' Frances asked, thinking at the same time how much like their father Roy had grown.

'I'm six foot.'

'Tall enough for the Guards.'

'You're jokin' ain't you? It's the RAF if they still want me. And before I forget, Mr Jacobs says you're to be sure to go round and see 'im.'

'I will, I promise.' Roy had worked for Mr Jacobs since he left school. Her old employer, as defiant of Hitler as he had been of the Mantoni brothers, had stayed put in his shop right through the bombing and rationing, but he now talked of retiring to Southend and Frances wanted to see him before he left.

'I was sent to tell you to 'urry up,' said Roy. 'Auntie Gloria wants ter make a speech.'

Frances and Kitty followed their brother downstairs to the garden, where Gloria was filling everyone's glasses. She clapped her hands for their attention, paused, then said, 'This family, like many others, has suffered tragedy during these past six years and the two strongest branches of our tree are missing. But although we've lost them, my sister and Tom live on in Kitty, Frances and Roy, and through them I know the tree will put out new shoots. Edna and Tom would want us to remember them on this first day of peace, but without any sadness. They'd say that this is a day to celebrate. So I want to propose a toast. To peace and this family. Long may they both flourish.'

'To peace and the family,' they repeated solemnly, while Nan blew her nose loudly and Frances wiped away an emotional tear.

Paul had the tact to allow a brief pause before taking a small blue box from his pocket and handing it to Frances. She had no idea Paul was buying her a ring and she lifted the lid slowly. A solitaire diamond winked on a white satin cushion. 'It's lovely,' she breathed reverently, then worried that Paul might have bankrupted himself to buy it.

'Here, let me put it on.' Paul slipped the ring on Frances's finger, drew her into the circle of his arms and murmured quietly, 'It's taken a long time but I've got you at last.'

'You're a lucky man, Paul,' said Andrew, raising his glass to them.

'I know I am.'

Andrew smiled at Frances. 'Hey, do you realize something?'

'What?'

'You'll be my sister soon.' He took Kitty's hand, and threaded it through his arm. 'I wonder which of us will tie the knot first.'

Frances glanced at Kitty but she was staring at her feet, so when Gloria called into the slightly awkward silence, 'How about giving us a song, Frances,' she was grateful for the diversion.

'What would you like?'

'Can't you guess?'

'Yes, I suppose so.' Frances smiled and slipped her arm

round Paul's waist. 'All shadows fly away/when I remember yesterday/when love came to me/to you and me . . .'

It was as if Kitty was hearing the song for the first time, and the words and her sister's voice, harmonious and pure, caught at her heart. Making her decision, she pulled away from Andrew. It was no good – she could never love half-heartedly, not after what she'd had with Robert. She would go on alone. It might prove hard, but it was unlikely she would end up a lonely spinster like Miss Yeo, her old supervisor. Even if she never married, what did it matter? If women had proved themselves in war, then they could in peace and there were plenty of challenges out there. Perhaps she could go to college, even university. Maybe she'd become a scientist, a top businesswoman, a Member of Parliament. Freedom beckoned, and her head grew dizzy at the possibilities. Feeling only slightly penitent, Kitty glanced sideways at Andrew and put a bit more distance between them. Bracing her shoulders, she murmured bravely, 'To the future, kid,' tossed back her glass of sherry and slipped away into the house.

'. . . the day you left/the day you went from me . . .' Kitty didn't hesitate or look back and as Frances came to the end of the song, she glanced over at Andrew. He knew. His face was already ravaged by loss, the mouth unsteady, his eyes barely holding back tears, and his misery smote at Frances's heart. I must go to him, he needs me, she thought, but as she went to move from Paul's side she felt his grip tight on her wrist.

'No.' Paul said it very firmly. 'There is nothing you can do, Frances.'

I can, she wanted to yell, I can take that terrible pain away.

Paul gave her a small shake. 'Frances, you've got to decide. Do you truly love me?'

Frances's hesitation was as imperceptible as a breath of

wind. 'Of course I do.' To show she meant it, she turned to face him then, with the tenderest of smiles, reached up, wound her arms round Paul's neck and kissed him.